S0-BWT-382

MAD DOG MOUNTAIN

a novel by

Richard Day

MAD DOG MOUNTAIN

by
Richard Day

Library of Congress Card Catalog Number
2003113324

ISBN 0-9664659-1-1

Manufactured in the United States of America
First Printing 2004

Published by
Sutton Publishing
P.O. Box 20
Old Greenwich, CT 06870
suttonpub@sbcglobal.net

Illustrations by Miles Parnell

Mad Dog Mountain is dedicated to my sons:
Peter Briggs Day, mountain partner
and Tyler Hopkins Day, Ty-man

To the Reader:

Mad Dog Mountain follows Two Dog River in a series. While it is not essential to read Two Dog River first, some of the references in Mad Dog Mountain will not be clear unless Two Dog River is first read. When bringing-forth a story, I strive to be completely open to its creation. Therefore, what happened to the characters in Two Dog River, I admit, was a complete surprise and cannot be dismissed. Their story of spirit, character and adventure begged for continuance. Their carnality was a question waiting for an answer. I had no choice. They and the Greater Reality commissioned me to write this tale. I hope that I listened well and wrote truly.

October 2001

Addendum

Winter 2004

This author was changed by writing Mad Dog Mountain. As I changed, I noticed that our culture has been changing as well toward greater moral and sexual darkness. Given these realities, the explicit content in Two Dog River, is no longer acceptable. The work is, therefore, pulled from general distribution and being revised. Readers can contact the publisher as to the status of Two Dog River. Contact information is on the information page of this work, Mad Dog Mountain.

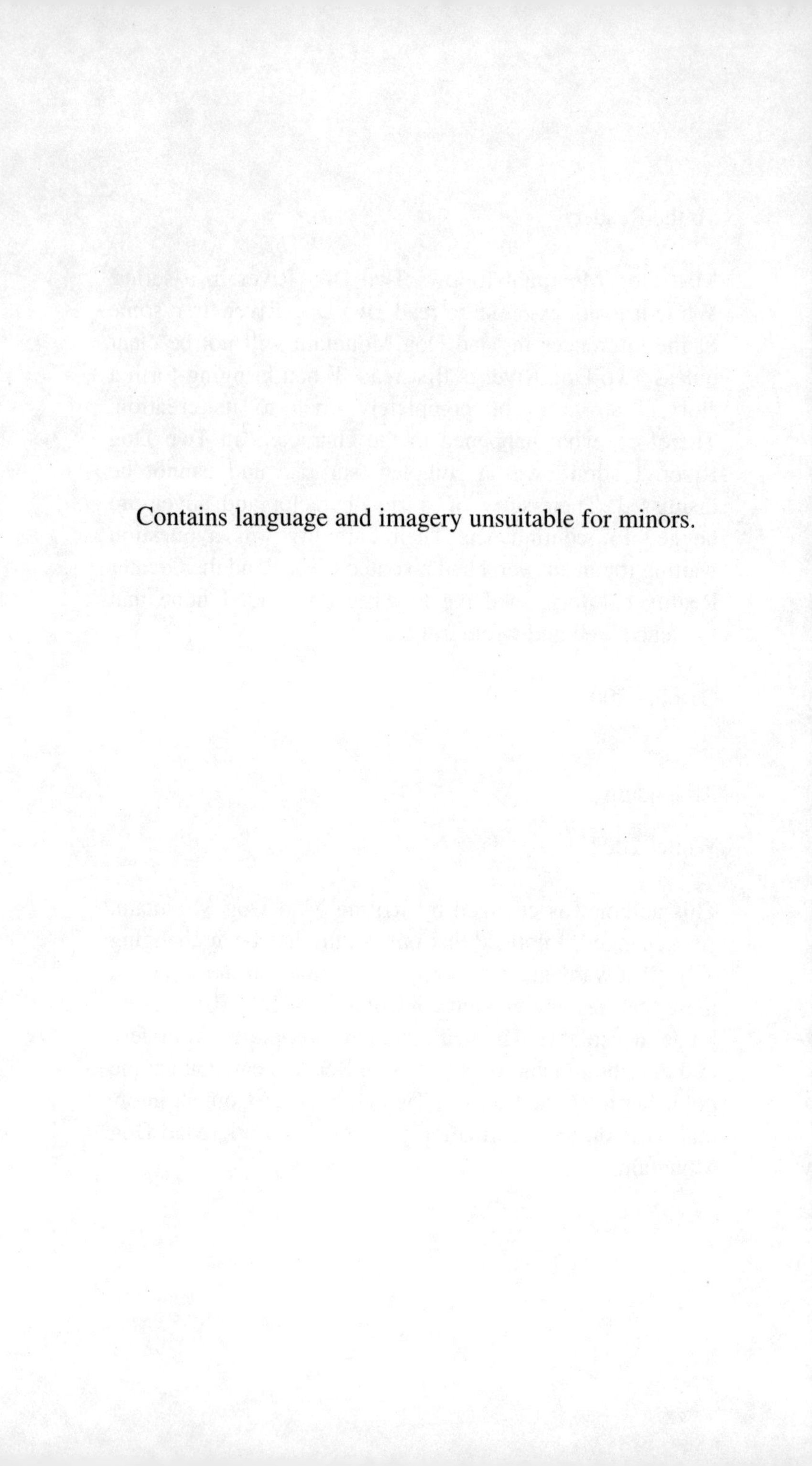

Contains language and imagery unsuitable for minors.

Contains language and imagery unsuitable for minors.

The Lord created me the beginning of his works,
before all else that he made, long ago.
Alone, I was fashioned in times long past,
at the beginning, long before earth itself.
When there was yet no ocean I was born,
no springs brimming with water.
Before the mountains were settled in their place,
long before the hills I was born,
when as yet he had made neither land nor lake
nor the first clod of earth.
When he set the heavens in their place I was there,
when he girdled the ocean with the horizon,
when he fixed the canopy of clouds overhead
and set the springs of ocean firm in their place,
when he prescribed its limits for the sea
and knit together earth's foundations.
Then I was at his side each day,
his darling and delight,
playing in his presence continually,
playing on the earth, when he had finished it,
while my delight was in mankind.

— Proverbs 8:22-31

I find more bitter than death
the woman who is a snare,
whose heart is a trap
and whose hands are chains.
The man who pleases God will escape her,
but the sinner she will ensnare.

— Ecclesiastes 7:26-27

MAD DOG MOUNTAIN

CHAPTER 1
NANCY

Nancy Ann lay in bed, closed her eyes and listened to the cottonwood trees gently fluttering. She felt the silence of her babies asleep and realized that it was nearly 9, and the sun had not baked her trailer home. Autumn in the Powder Horn Range. Just cool. Bright, deep blue outside. Nancy breathed in thankfulness. Deeply. She felt good again. As a child of winter, her body craved to forge hot passion into frozen air. Nancy is "Boomer." She explodes down mountainsides. Fast, really fast. Top women's downhiller. Untouchable. But that was then.

Nancy pulled up the sheet and the soft merino blanket, opened her eyes and stared vacantly, remembering how it all ended and where it all began — the wild river re-emerging from sacred darkness, streaming verdant life along its banks, coursing from the arid foothills into the high plains, brilliant and golden. Then swelling full and rich into irrigation canals. Overflowing. Silent, persistent and unnoticed. The River, her water, suckling the hot and blazing life of the high Powder Horn Basin — rich in potatoes, corn, wheat, barley and hops. Carbos. The staff of life.

The earth cooling; the sun growing bright and weak; The River, her body, shimmering into the sky and gathering into frozen peace; then falling, blowing, drifting and swirling in white brilliance around her very own shoulders, curving waist and bodice.

Nancy arched her back and placed the soles of her feet together. Her finger passed between the head of her thighs. Nancy sucked in through her nostrils. A line of sweat lined her spine and dampened the bottom sheet. Her eyes gazed at the pictures above her bed. Charlie, "Ace Man," her husband. Deceased. Her parents, the hippies. Deceased. Her babies, beaming with life. Those who are gone. Those who are here, and those who are coming. Creator, Preserver, Destroyer … Judge, Redeemer. The curtains danced in a rising breeze, while a metal window framed Mad Dog Mountain in a blue sky.

Nancy fell back and waited for the battle, for the dull weight to fall upon her chest and push back-and-forth with all kinds of tingles and urges. Light outside. Dark in the corners of her small bedroom. "Horny white trash," Nancy mumbled and lay with her feet and arms dropped apart. She stared at the ceiling and vacantly smoothed both hands between her soft and powerful thighs; and around her firm butt and up either side of her tapered waist and back down to her full, blonde bush. Better, she thought, at least not fat 'n horny anymore. Then she closed her eyes. Here it comes, she thought. Her blue eyes, mussed blonde hair and pretty, freckled face cringed. Nancy's chest heaved, and tears streamed out pain. "Come on," she panted, hitting the bed with both fists. Nancy rolled around on her stomach and buried her face and sobbed. "Miss you buh ... buh ... baby ... Charlie … Mom … Dad. Everybody."

The phone rang. Jessica knew to call from the East Coast. She knew the mornings were tough. Nancy reached over and pushed on the speaker. Neither girl said anything for a long time. There was no rush. Jessica was on one line. Jamie, her husband, "Moon Dog," was conferenced-in at work.

"Come on, baby, pull through," said Jessica softly. "We love you so much."

"I'm praying for you hard, Nance, right now," said Jamie. "Come on, Nancy, we're with you, hon."

"Go ahead, Nance; let it happen," Jessica said softly.

Nancy heaved into tears. Nobody said anything.

"I gotta blow my nose .. sick, depressed, trailer park trash."

Nancy got up, went to the little bathroom, came back and sat on the edge of the bed and looked at the phone.

"Jessy, I've gotta go," said Jamie with his gentle drawl. "Nancy?! Got the sitter coming right, hon? Get out and burn some road miles now. Meet up with Margaret and the girls later. Get out of there, OK? We care about you." There was no need for Nancy to reply. Jamie knew that Nancy heard him, that she was going to be OK and did not believe what she said. Been going on now for over a year since the mountain, Dhaulagiri, as everybody calls her, took out Charlie in a slide on the way to work, going over The Pass. His truck was found mangled — shaved trees and limbs entwined and impacted through every opening and then some. Chain saws, jaws of life. Avy crews. Took hours to get his body out of there. *Whew man*, Jamie exhaled to himself, feeling his eyes water as all the pain rose again. Charlie was a good friend. He pictured Nancy in the mobile home, in the trailer park, sitting there knowing that she is loved. The Powder Horns rising above. Probably some cotton from the trees blowing about. Blue and space and slightly cool. *Love it out there*, Jamie thought. *Power country. Wish I could get Nancy out of that shabby park. Offered to build her a house. Been helping Nancy with most everything. Not a problem. Such a sweet kid. Been through so much together. The River. The Cave. The babies. The whole thing. Boated with Ace for years. Got the sitter so she could get back in shape. Knew that was important. Nancy's gritty. She'll make it*. "OK, Nance, I'm with you. Gotta take a call."

Silence.

Nancy picked up the receiver.

"He's a sweet man," Nancy said, heaving a little. "You guys'll go on lovin' each other, right, Jess?"

"Course. Hey, you're not sick. Not trash. Life is good. You're going to make it, Nancy," Jessica said softly.

"Lose interest and leave. Fat 'n saggy and wrinkled. Bitchin'. End up hating each other."

"Nance … why are you thinking those thoughts?"

"I don't know, Jessie. It's like I've been there … in a future. I'm sorry. Thanks so much for calling. Can't believe you guys."

"Adisvara, sweetheart, let's breathe."

Nancy stood and pushed the bed against the far wall to make room. She rolled out her Tapas mat and stood straight and tall with her arms stretched overhead. Nancy gazed through the little window at Mad Dog

Mountain. Slashes of old snow hung on the northwest couloirs, folded between tan, precambrian gneiss. Nancy breathed deeply in and out of the bottom of her belly, firmly planted her feet and stretched upward. Tadasana, The Mountain. She knew Jessica was doing the same at home, in the ex-burbs in her tights, with her beautiful children and gorgeous home and nanny and handsome man. Jamie made money. Jessica already had it. Working in her gallery in The City when she was in the mood. Standing by her man. Nancy adored the whole connection. Nancy as Boomer the jock-chick. Jessica feeling Nancy's power. Nancy feeling Jessie's poise and breeding. The two thrived on each other. Both of them joined in Spirit.

Nancy and Jessica fell to their knees and bowed in prayer, palms together. Surrendering. Beautiful, young women. Nancy closed her eyes and pictured Him next to her. She felt Him: the Lord of all. Savior. Her chest lightened, and her eyes lifted beneath their lids. And what had been happening since The River kept right on happening — the birthing of babies; the bumper crops stuffing the valley around her feet with no one able to explain it; the mysterious healings in the trailer park; the rich and full winters. Her salvation. It all started on The River — laying at night pulsing and throbbing, feeling His life. The River. The stars at night. The earth. Endless sunshine. The cave and all the miracles … the babies. Loving everybody … the guys, the girls.

What happened on The River remains as an unfolding answer. For sure, Nancy now understood why her mother steered her away from guys by keeping her busy on girls' ski teams. "You are getting cute. Gonna get knocked up faster 'n you can say it," her mother always said. That's how Mom loved Nancy — by keeping her racing and away from the party gang in town. Nancy was just 20 on The River, that summer of her first freedom away from The Range. Usually Nancy summer-trained with The Team high on the glaciers on the volcanic peaks beyond the Powder Horns and river guided locally. But she'd won big that season, and Mom figured she was on her own. And Mom and Dad? Outdoor hippies who eventually got it together and loved her good. Permanently marginal out there, back when nobody lived in Powder Horn. From outdoor junkies to guides, to lodge managers, to expedition support, they were always nearly bust and never around. Back when, Dad dodged the draft and Nam. They both wore flowers and took drugs. Worshiped trees and rocks and something about chakras and a cosmic mind. Did yoga. Never owned much. Left a shed full of old skis. A million shreds down all the Powder Horns. Worn-out climbing gear and whitewater kayaks. Ski bibs with duct taped patches. The trailer home up on blocks with giant sunflowers at either corner. A couple of beat-up mountain bikes. Two huge photo albums. Yellowing pictures of Nancy, blonde and round-faced with sun glasses and smiling, stuffed in a kid's carry pack, holding Dad's pony tail and heading up the snow slopes of Mad Dog Mountain. Deep-red, Indian paintbrush packed against white corn — that's what Nancy chose to remember.

Mom and Dad both died in a car accident when Nancy was on The River. That was it. Nancy came back, and they were gone. A truck lost its brakes, jackknifed and hit them head-on coming down from The Area. They weren't high or anything from a mountain rush — skiing chutes, boating rivers or climbing big walls. Or any other kind of irresponsible f-up. Nancy needed to know that. She only wanted them to be her parents, starting to gray, getting tired and needing to rest and maybe even worried about her. Then there was the irony: Mom and Dad were just back from Nepal where they had been supporting an expedition on the treacherous west face of Nuptse. Mountains are dangerous and being with them is a full commitment. Nancy was alone now, a widow at age 23.

Jessica and Nancy flowed through the asanas that Nancy's mother taught her long ago, breathing and talking a little on the speaker between holds. Nancy was naked, firm, uplifted and nicely shaped. Her body had called her back after the babies — one baby after another until Charlie, Ace Man, died. Probably would have kept on having them. She discovered being a woman. Sliding into something tight of Jessie's when Charlie came home. A T-shirt tucked in with nothing underneath. Full and perky. Making him a nice dinner. Feeling him delight in her. Wanting her. Loving her. Not wearing undies. Straddling him after he ate his nice dinner and letting his hand find that out. Feeling the bulge in his work jeans. One thing leading to another. Ripping off his pants. Feeling him grow bigger and fatter inside of her. It was nice being feminine. Being a woman. Making babies. Taking his name. Him being a guy. A husband. She loved Charlie good. He didn't want anybody else. Then Charlie dying. Feeling like lead. Laying around and getting fat after her last baby. Her body longing to bike up the mountain or run on trails. Feeling heavy and hurting the first time out on her road bike after months of fat and babyin' and grief. But feeling so good, too. That's all Nancy's ever known: training, ski racing, biking and runnin' rafts. The power of her body. Finding it again was like coming home to an old friend.

Jessica and Nancy finished in Virabhadrasana, Warrior. Two beautiful bodies and souls: bold and strong, arms outstretched, front knee dipped forward, rear leg straight back. Spine erect and gaze forward. Sweat dripping. Thousands of miles apart they breathed hard back-and-forth on the speaker. Then they lay on their backs on the floor, arms to the side, palms up. Savasana, Corpse. Breathing. Opening. Accepting. A different image each time. Today Nancy calmly watched as their bodies were found in the cave. After a long silence, Nancy rolled into a fetus and opened her eyes. She sat up and reached for the phone.

"I need a man."

"Yeah?" Jessica replied sweetly. "Well doll up and get out there. You're savage, baby!"

"In Powder Horn?"

"May the Lord grant that each of you find rest in the home of another husband."

"Ruth and Naomi … It's a beautiful story."

"It is a beautiful story. Your story will be beautiful, too."

"Gonna make me cry again."

"It's hard. Wait. Be patient. Receive Him first," Jessica said softly. "Trust. Suffer in Him."

"Will you pray for me?"

"I always pray for you. You know that ... Although they go forth weeping, carrying the seed to be sown, they will come back rejoicing, carrying their sheaves."

"Thank you so much, Jessy. Do you have to go?"

"Let's talk some, then you get out. Rosa's coming today, right?"

"She'll be here soon. Love all these little guys. Kyle's running around like crazy. He's so pumped. Big grin and beaming. He's the best. I'm in love with him. I really am."

"Jpeg some new pics?"

"Tonight," replied Nancy.

"We've gotta go, sweetheart; our babies need us. I'll call after dinner."

"Call when I eat, around 8 mountain time. The babies 'ill be asleep. I love you."

"I love you," replied Jessica.

"God's peace."

"For you. I salute you, really do. The Lord be with you," Jessica replied quietly.

"Thank you so much, baby," Nancy said as her eyes welled with tears. "For everything you guys have done."

"May your suffering be a blessing."

"See you, Jess."

"Bye bye, Nance."

Nancy hung up, closed her eyes and brushed away the tears. She gave thanks for her friends and felt the Silence flood upon her. Nancy heard her lovely children stirring in the next room. The Mexican sitter quietly entered the back way. Nancy flexed and tensioned her arms and power thighs, ready. Resting pulse at 55. She stood, rolled her mat and pulled back the bed. Nancy slipped into sweats and a tee-shirt and sat back on her mattress. She exhaled the grief from her chest and shuddered. Rosa, the sitter, was weathered and short and came in holding the babies, Michael and Clay — one and two — with Kyle, the three year old, around her leg. Everybody was sucking on things and smiling.

"Hola Señora Boomer," Rosa said with a grin.

"Hola Rosa, cómo estás?"

"Muy bien Misses, you going to ride up las montañas today?"

"Sí Rosa, how do you say five, five hours?"

"Cinco horas … cinco horas de ida y vuelta!?" exclaimed Rosa.

"Sí Rosa."

"Ooh," Rosa whistled through her teeth, bending over and handing down the babies in their pajamas with their little pastel blankets. Kyle climbed in with his stuffed animals. "Strong Misses, ah que valor. What courage."

"It takes courage to live one's life."

"Sí Misses, valor del espíritu."

Nancy gathered an armful of babies around her. She bounced them up and down, feeling their weight and growth. They felt good. Michael and

Clay laughed and sucked on pacifiers. Rosa went back into the little kitchen to prepare their hot cereal. Everybody snuggled and hugged and gazed and sucked. So much gets said without words. Nancy spoke to her boy babies and the biggest, Kyle, who held five stuffed animals and put his little head on her lap. She knew he missed his daddy. Nancy reached around Michael and stroked Kyle's head and told them all about what her day would bring — biking up the mountain, what it would look like, the vistas that grab you, the cool air, the beautiful pines up high and how fast she would zoom back down and how she knows they will be big and strong and come with her soon. Come skiing too. Nancy rubbed their bellies, and they sucked and looked and laughed with their little round tongues and mouths. Nancy spoke and thought at the same time. She never felt her boys as a burden. They were so much already. Little people. Soul travelers, flesh from her flesh and a miracle from beyond, from the moment of conception. So happy to be with her. All of them together. They took her from downhilling and The Team and the life she knew. But she had no regrets. Nancy loved her boys forever and even more now that she was alone.

An hour later Nancy was at mile post 20 pumping on her rich-purple, De Bernardi ti frame. Campagnolo everything. Perfectly fit to her hem and arm length. Worth about as much as she made in six months at the convenience store. Nancy pulled up one afternoon last spring, and there it was in a delivery box on her dirt driveway. A simple note inside: Burn baby burn! Nancy cried. Jamie and Jessica had sent it, along with a new pair of shoes, a new helmet and razor shades. The little town of Powder Horn was now out of view. Nancy was biking up the west side of Dhaulagiri to The Pass at eighty-five hundred feet. Down below green potato fields patched between golden hay and hops. They disappeared as Nancy rounded a sheer bend of deep-red and orange road cut. Cottonwood and willow had sifted into green Douglas fir and alpine spruce. Almost no one passed. Quiet sun. Blue. A slight breeze. Just cool. Fresh. Nancy was in tight shorts and a sports top. A line of sweat drew down from her naked belly button. Nancy stood and pumped, and her tight bottom swayed from side-to-side. Her hair was in a French braid, and she wore a head band under her bright-red helmet. Razor shades and a fixed gaze. It was about forty-eight hundred vertical feet or "vert" to The Pass. Steep. Long. Hard. Nancy snorted out mucus, sat down and beeped her mileage and pace on the handlebar computer. Good. Very strong. Just being and letting her mind blur into the blue and pitch green. Sucking on the double hoses coming from her hydration pack — one for liquid carbos and one for water. Nice not competing, not having the goals and the pressure. It was her life now. *So let the Austrians have at it*, thought Nancy. *I'll be back for 'em. Bury their sorry asses.* "Oops, slipped," Nancy said to herself and blew out the rest of the garbage thoughts and feelings through her nose.

Mile marker 21 and thoughts became clouds. Nancy watched them drift. The way she's been feeling riding and running now was the way she used to feel only on the big win days when Nancy was at complete calm and peace, absolutely present and feeling 80 miles-per-hour. Tucked and sucked. She hardly had to breathe she was going so fast. Everyone staring with a sick lump in their throats when she blew across the finish line. Killer. In some sort of trance, she'd have trouble hearing all the endorsement people and coaches, teammates and interviewers, until some weeks later after Nancy won a string, she'd notice herself walking or driving to practice, anything. She'd suddenly snap-back and be alone and half broke as usual. Mom and Dad were off somewhere. She'd come down and have to cope with it all.

Mile marker 22, and the black skid marks passed under her thin Vittoria tires. A couple of weeks ago, she heard an engine wind up behind her. Something felt wrong about the noise. She turned and saw a dented mini pickup swerving around on the wrong side of the road. The engine screamed right behind her. Then a black Pathfinder with a mountain bike on top rounded the bend above. The two were head-on at four car lengths. Nancy gripped both brakes, popped out of her cleats and jumped for the embankment. The Pathfinder swerved left toward Nancy, and the mini truck kept screaming. The Pathfinder slammed on its breaks and lurched into a spin. Screeching smoke and dust exploded. Nancy dove down the embankment. Then silence. Nancy clambered back up with dirt melting into mud on her steaming body. The Pathfinder was turned around and facing uphill on the wrong side of the road. Nobody was in view. The mini truck's engine re-emerged up above, distant and whining. Silence and blue. Blazing sun. The acid smell of burning brake liner and rubber. Road dust in a cloud.

Nancy lay down her bike and pack and clicked over to the Pathfinder, slipping in her cleats and breathing hard. She made the passenger side and looked in. Her stomach cinched. Nobody was in the car. Weird, she thought. Nancy's fingers and arms trembled. She skidded around to the driver's side and looked in. Nothing. Dust still settling. Nancy reached for the driver's seat release, and the seat popped forward. A guy was stuffed behind. No sound. No movement. "Shoot," Nancy said to herself. "Watch for neck and spine injury." She gently pushed his head to the left and felt for a pulse. Nothing. Nancy opened the passenger side and found a wrist. Still nothing. Then she thunked two hands down — one grabbed his hair and the other his belt — and yanked him out. "Huh," Nancy grunted. She swayed and lay him down on the blacktop. A couple of cars pulled up. Two guys jumped out with a big, plastic tool box that looked like a medical kit. Nancy tilted his head back, sealed his lips with hers and gave two full puffs.

She compressed his chest, stiff armed — not really knowing if she was getting the whole thing right. Nancy turned around and blew hard once again. Then back to a compression. The grade was steep so she reached for his red fleece that was lying on the back seat and placed it under his feet, straddling him with her crotch in his face. Her French braid hung out the back of her helmet. Nancy turned quickly around. Her pretty face with her shades ripped off at some point. The mud and her naked belly and full breasts tucked into her sports top. Nancy sealed his mouth and went to blow and froze. He was staring at her. Their mouths held together. Then Nancy lifted and looked into his sweet blue and green eyes. Nancy sat up, threw a thigh and an arm over and straddled him on hands and knees. She took him in below her. She was breathing hard, and her chest rose and fell. Nancy's eyes widened. Cute guy. Slight curls where his dirty-blonde hair grew over his Native, patterned and collared, short-sleeve shirt. A smooth and slender face. Tanned. Slim but muscular. A quick glance at his ring finger. Empty. Nancy quickened a little down there. She stood and bent down for her shades. The guys with the box knelt and started asking questions. Nancy walked to her bike dusting herself off, and she knew that his eyes followed. She grabbed her pack, mounted and stood and slowly pumped away. Nancy looked behind and saw him laying there twisting around to watch her. She sensed that she already knew him from a mystifying distance of experience.

"Could have at least hung around a little, seen if he was OK, maybe asked him back for dinner. Something," Nancy said to herself as mile post 23 passed. "Lonely, really am; gonna stay that way."

Nancy pumped on and thought about the cute guy. She thought about how much cooler it was now, just a few weeks later. Nancy reached the final bend before the grade leveled at The Pass, and it was breezy and piney. She heard a car come up behind, slow and hover off of her rear wheel. "Come on," Nancy said to herself, "go ahead, take a good look. It's cute. Yeah it's tight." *Shouldn't be that way*, she thought. *Poor thing. Gonna be a guy somewhere in his forties. Wife he's having trouble recognizing. She does her thing. He does his. Never gets any*. "Go ahead check it out." Nancy stood and pumped. *Guys are easy*, she thought. *Got no patience with Margaret and the rest who have guy problems. Their own fault. Guys are sweet. A husband. You're their permanent nymphet, their mother and their best admirer. Easy: a dick, a stomach, a goal. Whatever: climb the mountain, do the girl, build the business, eat. Conquest. King David, man. Let them lead. Don't get on their nerves. And give 'em space*. "Nucky 'em good. Feed 'em. Simple," Nancy breathed to herself. *Guys can have good hearts. Treat you well. It's up to you*, Nancy thought. *'Course that was Ace Man. He was older. Have no clue about guys my age and younger*, Nancy thought again. *Seem kind of pathetic*.

The car didn't pass. Nancy felt safe most of the time. *There can be creeps out on the highway*, she thought. *I'm alone now too. There've been noises at night around the trailer*. Nancy's palms began to sweat a little. She'd heard stories of women never being seen again. *Probably should start carrying my Glock*, she thought. Nancy turned with a tight face. "Shhh," she whistled through her teeth. A woman with long, blonde hair with buzz-cut sides smiled with the corners of her mouth as if she wore a rubber mask. "Come on, leave me alone," Nancy said to herself. A small, white wagon slowly passed and pulled in front. The buzz-cut sides drove and looked at Nancy in the rear view mirror. She slowed a little, and Nancy had to back off pedaling. *OK, so what's going to happen here?* Nancy thought. Nancy raised her arm and frowned a nasty question. The blonde slowly accelerated, still watching in the rearview mirror. Nancy read the bumper stickers on her rear fender and hatch: My other car is a broom … I am Sekhmet hear me roar … … Born again pagan ... My womb, my choice … Hug a tree. Weird, liberal stuff, Nancy thought. The wagon disappeared over the rise. Nancy was a Republican. Of course, the exact opposite of Mom and Dad: she owned guns, hung the flag and believed in God, America and capitalism. It used to grieve her parents to no end.

Nancy made the plateau and kept on coasting. She always went a little further to the slide path. Raw and beautiful, the path was choked with huckleberry bushes and bright, purple larkspur. There were patches of sky-blue flax and yellow arrowroot. Stripped trees and logs stuck up from avalanche alder. Down below there was a pile of naked, white granite and tan earth. Buried underneath and below all the raspberry bushes was Charlie's mangled truck: a slowly rusting corpse. *Never did get it out of there*, Nancy thought. Nancy stopped and got off her De Bernardi. She sat on the edge of the pavement in the bright sun and could see where the avalanches coming down Mitchell Bowl behind her scraped the road. The earth below her feet had eroded up and underneath the black top. Nancy twisted and looked above. A massive ravine was headed by a breathtaking wall and bowl. A cascade of water ran down its center. *Classic trigger zone*, Nancy thought. *Loads after a storm or even with wind blown snow and then bang-crash. The spaceheads on trays drop in all the time*, she thought again. *Probably what set off the one that took out Charlie*. "Like zero regard. Lost souls," Nancy said quietly.

Up and behind her was the rounded South Ridge of Dhaulagiri, The Snow Princess or Mount Mitchell. That's where the junkies bootpack up in the winter to access all the backcountry acres. Telein', freein' the heel in deep powder. Pinning the wild snow. Across the way and in front of Nancy were all the chokes and couloirs and meadows that fill in the winter and become the bowels and chutes of the Southwest Kingdom. The whole expanse was vast and green and dashed with grasses and bright alpine flowers. It was stark and clear, and Nancy felt very alone. Her throat grew heavy, and her eyes swelled. The mountain air cooled her damp chest while the pines hushed in the breeze. Nancy pulled off her clammy top and hung free and full. Her breasts lifted and pointed to the sides slightly. Nancy folded her legs and put her hands in prayer and bowed her head. She touched the blacktop and the earth and whispered to Him, "Thank you, Lord Jesus. Look after 'im." Nancy breathed in and out. Silence. "Lord, please send your Peace." Nancy straightened her spine and lifted her head. Tears blurred all the green and colors. Nancy unwrapped her legs and stood. “Whew, come on,” she said to herself. She dropped her shorts and peed off the embankment — long and hard like a horse. Nancy pulled back on her top and slowly walked up the shoulder eating a bar and pushing her bike. At the crest Nancy hopped onto her seat and began to coast. “Come on, baby, payback time,” she said to herself.

Nancy felt gravity begin to pull her back — back to her babies, back to working part-time at the convenience store, to taking graphics classes down-valley in Dale, to church on Sundays, to charity work, to bills, to the outdoor clothing idea she and Jessica were working on and back to her whole life. Nancy tucked in low and screamed around bend number 5. It was here she had to brake and work the next couple of turns; then boom … she'd send it all the way to the valley where the warm ranch and farm air caressed her temples and scratched her nose and smelled sweet and dusty. Then Nancy would cruise the flats to home. She felt good. She felt tired but good. Nancy missed her baby boys and wanted to make them dinner and play together. And listen to Rosa's gentle Spanish. Then eat a huge bowl of pasta along with veggies, soy milk and yogurt. And talk with Jessica over dinner. Later Nancy would read the Holy Bible, then wrap in her clean sheets and pastel blanket and feel the cool, mountain air drift down from Mad Dog Mountain. Drink it in and sleep. Deeply. Peacefully.

CHAPTER 2

JIMMY

Autumn in the Powder Horns is fleeting, and it is possible in mid-October to bank turns in pitch-white thigh-deep through solid, golden aspen groves on a sunny day. Gold, white and blue are the occasional jewel set against the surrounding days of brooding clouds that swirl the peaks until the real storms of late November descend.

It was now the first week in December, and a dark, early winter day cloaked the Big Pine ski resort. There was a fine, misty white collecting in perfect stellar crystals on the back of David Winchester's or Red Bone's ski glove. David thought about that day a few weeks back in October as he rode Lift 3. He was cold and decided to get off at the halfway point and hike to the North Ridge. The lift was slow. It was old. *No one likes to ride slow lifts anymore*, David thought. *Never have gotten used to ridin' any lift*. David slid down, shaking his hands that were stuffed into a pair of worn gloves with duct tape around a couple of the fingers. David was tall, slim and powerful. His face was weathered dark and starting to round as he approached 30. There were creases now at the corners of his eyes. Silver streaks of gray highlighted his coppery brunette hair that he wore in a tight pony tail that came just out of his ski hat. At the bottom of the ramp, David dropped to both knees, placed his hands palms down on the top of his three pin bindings and popped out. He flipped his telemark skis, telies, or just "pins," onto their backs and swung off his pack. David dug inside for his climbing skins that were folded together and tore them apart from the adhesive as much as he could before he had to shake off his gloves and undo the rest. David's hands were weathered-brown, almost black. There were calluses on his finger tips and creases and healed over gashes on the backs of his knuckles from work and climbing mountains and rocks.

David moved quickly and precisely. He could do anything in the mountains blindfolded. David put his gloves back on. His fingertips and toes started to numb, and he had to stand and shake and stomp back to life all the years of frost-nipped winter climbing, guiding and backcountry teleing that have left his extremities partially dead. David bent over and laid the skins down on the face-up skis. He clipped them over the tip and smoothed them back, being careful to get a good bond. In fluid motion David flipped back the skis, stood and put on his pack while he stepped into his three-pin bindings and pressed them down with a ski pole and began to move up and across the packed slope. Midweek, early winter and nobody was at The Area. David grew instantly warm and unzipped his red patrol jacket with a white cross on the back. His radio squawked. Arctic jays flitted about over the firs lining the slope, and some remaining aspen leaves shivered in the slight breeze. David looked up and lifted his eyebrows. Nice, he let himself feel. Good to be out of the office and not worrying about everything. David had bought into the area with some other investors or, rather, he bought in with his life, and they funded everything. David managed Big Pine — for shares and living. Big Pine or Piney or just The Area has always been a small, family business set on the edge of a vast back country. Big Pine was nestled at eighty-five hundred feet and connected to the world by one road that nearly tunneled over in the winter. David lived in Big Pine with his wife Margaret and their three year old daughter, Hanna. The Area was his life now. He went from tucking everything he owned into a pickup truck to being part owner of a ski area in only three years. There was nothing at Big Pine but alpine meadows with spectacular vistas of the Powder Horn Range, including the rocky peaks and rounded ski summits and all the open, natural lines.

Thoughts of work passed in and out of David's awareness. They calmed as David was called to feel like Red Bone again. Hiking. Being free. Released for a couple of hours with the pretense of patrolling. He thought back again to that day of early pining in October when he was out in the back acres on the west slopes of Mad Dog Mountain well beyond The Area. Freein' the heal on telies and surfing skis. A ragged raven watched Red Bone from up high: all alone, drop the uphill knee, bank to the outside edge of the uphill ski, weight the little toe, then weight and carve over on the inside edge of the downhill ski. Both at the same time: big-toe-little-toe. Break and twist at the waist and face the glorious fall line, who draws like arms pulling you to her. Opposite heel comes up, uphill ski slides over and both surf to the other side: swooping, smooth, tight and rhythmical. Back-and-forth. Cold shots of paste and crystals in your face. Feeling yourself sink then rise as if to fly. Then back down. The crystals tearing evenly under your boards. The downy paste grabbing slightly as the crystals round and settle in the October sun. Nicking a few rocks and logs because there's no base. Wearing knee pads and a pair of moth-balled, rock skis with soul. A graceful carving turn in thigh deep in October with the deep blue and white and gold. The raven watched Red Bone pant at the bottom of the run. David's eyes smiled and looked up at the expanse of thirty degree slope, completely fresh and even except for his line of symmetrical turns snaking down through the aspen grove. David felt a satisfaction speak to him from Beyond.

"That's telein'," David said to himself, seeing the golden day in his mind. "Soul riding." He picked up his pace toward the North Ridge. David made the ridge and the orange and black boundary line and warning signs. He kicked up one ski at a time and tore off his skins. He was sweating and breathing hard, and he felt good.

Just above, Jim Peters stopped on the undulating, traverse path and checked his freeable bindings that held down the heel of his Rondenee boots: expensive gear that was given to him as a college graduation present. He grabbed his goggles and stretched them in-and-out from his smooth face. "Can't see," Jim said to himself, "fog, man, come on." His finger tips trembled, and his stomach had twisted into a knot. *One day off from preppin' salad*, he thought, *the first chance to get over to this side of the range, and its gotta be closed in.* "BS, man," he mumbled. *Been waiting a long time to get the Piney Chutes*, Jim thought again. Jim was a few years out of college, 24 years old, and he'd come to ski extreme shots. He'd been in the range climbing since early fall, living from his truck that his mother bought him until he'd gotten frozen out last week. Jim had never been to Big Pine. But these were the Powder Horns and this was Piney with its famous North Chutes, and he was going to ski them.

Jim pushed off and raced on until he popped out to the open boundary line, where a vacant space spewed clouds and stellars. A tinge of doubt froze Jim's movement. Jim usually hung with a group of girls and guys he'd come to Aspen Crest with on the other side of the range. Suddenly Jim felt very alone away from his group on the edge of the exposed boundary. The nervous spasm seemed to ask: *Why am I here? What am I doing? Why do I want to be in the mountains?* Jim gazed at the stellars whirling around him and pictured the first images of big wall mountaineering and extreme skiing he ever saw. At that time, something grabbed him like two strong hands. Jim could feel the fingers sink below the skin and hold his rib cage. His vapid life of school and before that the vague passage through the shadowland of formal neglect — busy parents, nannies, day care and summer camps — seemed to fall away. Jim felt a pull. A pull to find something. He kept looking until he entered the mountains with a youth challenge one summer in high school. And the two hands have never let go. They keep holding and pulling Jim to Their mysterious source—a Source and a Power that Jim cannot name but can feel growing in him after each intense ski run or rock ascent … so that he wants more and more.

Any line goes, Jim thought to himself as he tried to focus and push away the question that kept seizing his attention — *why am I here?* Jim's legs felt suddenly weak. *Come on, man. They all go. Any line,* he thought. *Yeah, they all go, and they all tell the stories. The deaths,* Jim thought and shrugged these off. He knew about the boundary too. Jim knew he could get seriously busted if caught now because there were new owners of Big Pine. He didn't care about this either. Jim cared about himself, about feeling the power suckle him. "Not a problem," he breathed, pushing aside the why questions. Jim looked up to the crest of the ridge and counted each funneling gap. He released and traveled down the line counting one .. two .. three. He wanted to drop into Chute Number 4 in one continuous movement like he was being filmed. *Run the line, look for the patrol, duck the rope and send. Sweet,* Jim thought. He felt the growing strength in his quads from climbing and early season skiing as he tightly controlled his rondenees. "OK … sendage," Jim breathed. He blew around a corner and nearly knocked David flat.

"Hey," David said, "what the fuh …"

"Whew haaa!" Jim shouted as he ducked the line in Chute Number 6 and disappeared. *No problem,* Jim thought. *Can avoid the homeboy. Unlock at the bottom and tour away from The Area. He won't be able to follow locked in alpine gear.* "Whoa," Jim gasped. His stomach collapsed, and gravity slammed him like a ton of bricks. The chute instantly dropped away to what looked like vertical, and his knees trembled. The base was bottomless. He sank to his chest, and his skis nicked rocks. Jim pummeled and dug-in too hard, slamming the granite wall. He smashed his head and the side of his face, shattering his goggles. A pulsing pain stabbed from his right shoulder. Stopped dead, Jim looked up and realized he could not climb out. It was too steep and loose. *The patrol guy was up there*, he thought. "Come on, dick," Jim spat and cursed at himself, "commit." Trembling and shaking from fingertips to toes, he dug out and lunged down, spitting and hissing a vapor cloud through his teeth. Jim clenched his pole grips and only managed to make one turn before the walls narrowed. The turn threw him forward then back on his heels. He shot out ass-first through the body-size gap at the bottom of the chute. Jim flew through the air, and he couldn't tell up from down. He straightened his skis and held his breath. He didn't have a clue as to what was below. Jim sucked up his knees and floated. "Come on, come on," he whimpered to himself. Doosh. Jim landed on his butt on a thin section, slammed his ass onto a rock band beneath a powdery layer, shot backward, smacked his head then somersaulted forward in the air to land on his butt in the deeps with his skis stuck up vertically.

Jim sat for a second not sure how he got there. Then "WHEW HA!" belted from the bottom of his gut into the indifferent, slate colored sky. He stood and brushed off his sore ass. The slope opened, and he swung turns to the bottom where he stood looking back up, shaking and panting and bending over his poles. "Sweet," Jim panted as he gazed and saw only cliffband, chutes and the drifting creamy-white of a cold December fog. "I'm oudda here," he said and kicked off. Blood dripped from a gaping wound above his right temple and plopped onto the white around his feet. His entire body trembled, and he was covered with crystals. Jim looked down and saw his red blood on white. "Damn," he said and patted the gash with his glove and kept going. "Yes!" Jim spat, "Chute Number 4. I own it. Psyched!"

Meanwhile, David watched the whole event from the top of Chute Number 5. *Tourist,* he thought. *Another wahoo. Pisses me off, 'cause I'd be the one to have to drag his sorry ass out with slides and rock fall and a family waiting for me. Chute 6 is a death slot. Plus we got sued last year when someone hopped the line and got hurt in there. Guy was lost for hours and claimed we were liable because we didn't rescue him "in a timely fashion,"* David said to himself, imitating the whiny lawyer's East Coast accent. *OK, this should be easy,* he thought.

David packed his skins and made a quick check of his gear. He clicked on his radio and called the patrol house. David closed his eyes and breathed slowly in and out, emptied his mind and relaxed. He hadn't been in Chute 5 in a year, and David tried to picture it. He remembered the rock band that comes just before exiting left. Years and years of experience melted into every fiber of his body, and David felt the years, all the experience. He wondered sometimes if there was even more time beyond these, a brilliant future already known. David stood and wondered if he'd be able to keep skiing as he had when he was younger — or would he get old and blow a chute and get hurt or die. *When would the end come?* David thought. Or was the end just a beginning at which he now stood? An endless beginning. David let these thoughts drift and began drop-kneeing easily down the forty-five degree chute, swinging from side-to-side. He felt his platform with the start of each turn; then he drifted through to the next compression. David knew it was cold and early season when the crystals tumble over themselves and can slide on depth hoar. Not much binds this time of year, or anytime, since the base is rock. David was well aware that the chute could easily release. Tighter and tighter he swung until he could almost reach out with both arms and touch the granite walls. He was in complete control. It felt good. David watched for the yellow rock band and fired left as the chute closed. His edges scraped, and sparks flew from striking the flinty gneiss that thrust into granite. Boom. David sailed, back knee tucked and front leg ready to absorb the landing. He aired and was able to watch the guy below the whole time. The guy below was unaware of David as he skied down. David adjusted his line, landed and straightened his turns to gain speed.

Jim almost jumped out of his skin when the red coat and white cross drop-kneed, blew a white cloud and suddenly ran him up the south side of the ravine wall. They both landed at the same time with David on top. David rolled onto Jim's head and planted his butt. He bounced hard up and down a couple of times as if trying to get up. He augured his ass on Jim's face. David squeezed his butt cheeks hard and tight .. ffffsssss-blahh. He jabbed his poles and slowly rose, waving his hand across his nose as the rancid stink from a healthy fart waffled in the frigid air. "Musta' been the bean burrito this morning!" David pronounced in a loud cowboy drawl. "Guess what wahoo? You're bagged." David offered Jim a hand up, and Jim looked straight ahead. Jim reached behind and pushed up with his poles.

Just then a thudding sound shook the air where they stood. David dove, knocking over Jim. The slide funneled through Chute 6 where Jim had just dropped and tore down to the dark rock on the cliffband below. The shallows triggered, and the whole mass stopped beyond where Jim had dusted off. There was a hiss of settling snow and then quiet.

"Shhhi," David whistled through his teeth. "Let's get out of here quick." David rolled onto his back against Jim and got on the radio.

From where Jim lay he could feel David's bulk and see that the slide had decimated the landing where he stood just moments ago. Jim looked down at his blood dripping onto the snow and felt nothing. Being buried and killed or alive and well felt the same. He just didn't care. Jim went along and played the game of life: having parents, kind of; growing up, sort of; having interests, kind of. Nothing else now except for the mountains and skiing. There was something flat about Jim's life—he pushed against the world and kept going. He got nothing in response. Nothing firm. Nothing back that stuck to his feelings or his guts. So being alive or not felt the same to Jim. Not a big concern either way. But Jim felt a tension—deep down and unspoken. Being in the mountains kept forcing something. Several times now Jim had been vaguely aware that he could die out here, easily. The why questions kept coming back: *Why am I here? Why am I alive? Why do I not care if I live or die? Should I care? How do I care? Does anyone care about me?*

"Can you get off?" Jim asked David almost inaudibly.

"Skeeter?" David asked as he talked into the radio, grunting to his skis. "Slide activity. 'Course I got 'im. You called the Staties? Here already? Perfect. See you at the bottom of Lift 3." David slid the radio into his parka, speaking to Jim, "Thousand dollar fine now, hombre. Take you right down and book you. Mandatory summons. No Powder Horn address, you wait in Dale under supervision. Can take weeks. Now I'm going to administer first aid; so be a good boy." Jim pushed up again. He blocked David's hand as David went to apply gauze to his face wound. Blood still dripped all over the place. David got back on the radio. "Skeet, you there? Make a record. Tried to administer first aid for a face wound; victim refused treatment. Have you refused treatment?" David asked Jim, raising his eyebrows. Jim bent down and scooped up powder. The snow would not pack into a ball; so Jim pressed the loose crystals to his face. His eyes winced, and a couple of tears forced out. There was blood on his face and broken goggles. Jim's shoulder felt like someone was pounding it with a bat, and his head and ass throbbed. "OK, let's roll 'em," said David looking up and down at Jim. He noticed his boots and skis. "Rondenee? It's a French word. Means can't tele." Jim stared ahead. He flushed with embarrassment and felt light-headed and nauseous.

David snowplowed keeping Jim right at his side as they funneled down the North Ravine. Jim looked up at David's face. Then it clicked.

"You're Red Bone."

"Was."

Jim sighed and his body felt mushy. He thought to himself, *Can't believe David Winchester bagged me. Had no idea he was workin' here. He's a legend, Red Bone. Someone I've always wanted to meet. Winchester's stuck all the hard drops in the Powder Horns. Been all over the mags.* "Hey," Jim exhaled, "can we work something out. I'm sorry."

"No you're not."

Jim turned to stop, and his legs wobbled. He bent over his poles. "Come on, man, don't turn me in."

"Keep moving."

Jim stood again and began to slide. They glided through some firs, and a pasted branch slapped him in the face. It stung. *Gotta at least try,* he thought.

"Hey, so what was the South face of Dalpo like?"

"Steep."

They made a flat and stopped. Lift 3 was visible through the spruce.

"Come on," whined Jim, knowing that he was whining and hating himself. *Cut the crap,* Jim heard himself think. *Take it. Get it over with.*

They slid to the bottom of the lift. The state police and a snow cat were below on the plowed-out road.

"You want to pay my bills?" asked David. "Hassle with all the help? Drive for hours and show up in court because some dickhead hopped the line, and it's somehow my fault? Wrestle with the paper work and enviro crap just to update lifts? Do your wahooin' somewhere else. Got no patience. I own the place now." There was a long, tense silence. David went on thinking to himself as he churned inside. *Put up with the bitching wife, worry about what you'll do if this fails. What possible living you're gonna make out here. With a family now. All you used to be, gone. Bound in. Working from predawn to after midnight every day. Stuff breaking. Impossible expenses. Worrying about attracting clientele. Babysitting 'em when they do show up. Enviro protesters in your parking lot 'cause you want to put in better lifts so you'll have half a chance of making an f'n living and a life. Someone burning down the new lodge last year. After all that half your income taxed away to the government.*

"SO WHAT IS IT GONNA BE ASSHOLE?!" David shouted and went to grab Jim but stopped himself as Jim backed off, staring at him. A hushed silence returned. Stellars fell on David's jacket arms and gloves and stayed as crystals. It was cold. Both guys wanted to move. Jim's mouth slackened. He was ashen and looked ahead. Jim turned and started sliding down to where the state police were waiting with their lights flashing. "Where are you parked?" David called after him. "They drive you down. It may take a while. We need to know your vehicle."

"Upper lot. Black Pathfinder. Bike on top."

David stepped away and got on Lift 3. Jim went to jail.

When David made the top, he was freezing. He slid over to the patrol hut, took off his skis and kicked open the door. It was warm inside. The scented pine from the wood stove smelled comforting. David sat in front of the stove on a stump and opened the little door and gazed at the full bed of coals. He closed his eyes and went through all that just happened. David glowed with the coals, and his words, feelings and actions became thin and ran from him. David thought about Margaret and Hanna and felt how much he loved them. He watched himself and realized that he didn't need to drop down the chute and risk getting hurt or even killed, and he didn't need to be a jerk to the guy — that being a jerk leads right to grabbing the guy by the throat. The guy could have been him a few years back. He only needed to wait at the bottom of Lift 3 and take him in, simple. And he didn't need to run all the lousy thoughts around about Margaret and The Area. David closed the stove door. He sat and grew warm and dry and realized that he had changed and that nothing was the same since The River. David watched himself and his life as if looking upon a stream from a bridge. And most of what he saw was empty. In this emptiness he returned again and again to what really mattered and what deeply satisfied. Folding into the cave on The River was like collapsing inside-out with all that he did — boating, climbing and teleskiing — until David wanted nothing and received everything. And he saw all of himself — the part that destroys and the part that creates goodness. David saw no limits in either realm. Day-by-day, moment-by-moment, the choice for the Light was his. David stood and tapped the stove door with his boot toe. He picked up the phone on the wall and called Margaret, who was working at the front desk.

"Hey honey. Yeah. It's OK, quiet. They took him off? Right, down to Dale." There was a long pause as Margaret spoke. David pictured her dark hair and pretty features as he felt her clear voice and wanted to be close to her at that moment. David remembered the first time they met on The River, on The Lake. He held closely to these feelings that had seized him and changed his whole life. His fate with Margaret was so unexpected. This truth held off an unspoken injury whereas David knew that at any time Margaret would simply leave, by feeling or in person, to pursue her own life. Coming from the midwest to living in the mountains where winter holds for as much as six months was hard for Margaret. David felt for her. He did not want to acknowledge that little by little her leaving might already be happening. Margaret's due empowerment could kill them. Her underlying struggle for dominance and control wore David down with a hidden anger until he exploded; then resigned into his own moments. At these times, David fell to his knees, submitting to answers beyond his ability to compose. Without this surrender David knew that his marriage would be over, and he would collapse into darkness. "Do you want me to go down-mountain and pick up Hanna?" he asked Margaret. There was another pause as Margaret spoke. "The police will bring him to Dale," David replied. Margaret spoke again, and David wanted to reach out and touch her beautiful cheek bones. David replied, "Yes, great idea. Please go ahead and call the clerk's office. He can work off his fine here with me, personally. Yeah, the clerk knows us. I'll be down. Sure, I'll get Hanna. I love you." David listened to Margaret say the same. He hung up and sat down on the stump in front of the stove. David opened the stove door and looked at the glowing coals again, while outside the quiet cold enveloped the hut. The stove purred, and his last words to his wife felt good and true … I love you. A heaviness lifted from David as Silence settled into his bones with a soothing peace. He closed his eyes and prayed for the guy riding down to Dale.

CHAPTER 3
EL VIEJO

El Viejo, The Old One, sat in the semi-darkness that was neither dawn nor night but a deep twilight. He carefully lay his bones on the pine and pebble-strewn forest floor. El Viejo — or just Viejo — adjusted the shattered femur and shin bones and as many of the little bones of his feet and ankles as he could find. He viewed his hips and spine and rib cage and finally his broken neck and crushed skull. He moved off a ways and found some of his arm and hand bones. Beside these, the dog tags with his former name and address. He placed the tags in a hand and the arm and hand bones at the sides of his chest. Viejo knew the bones were in time because they were turning white and starting to dry and become hollow and powdery. Soon they would be taken by the melting waters, raised and sprinkled over The Powder Horns as crystalline dust. He saw his first generation, Lang ski boots and the tattered remains of a pair of bellbottom ski pants. He placed the splitting and cracking boots just below the foot bones and below these he aligned his delaminating, black Head 360's with Marker cable bindings. El Viejo found one ski pole with a leather grip, cracking and separating from the aluminum shaft, and placed this alongside the bones of his right hand. He placed the pants on top of his bones, starting from the waist and smoothing out each leg with care. One leg only reached what would be his knee. He found his tattered, red wind shirt with white polka dots, but it was too decayed to place over the chest and arms. El Viejo, The Old One, carefully lay it to the side. He looked at his creation. Himself. And wept.

It grew darker as El Viejo wept, and he knew that he brought upon his own darkness. The Old One knew that if he stopped he would feel the life curving and carving and descending around him in the early winter. He knew to speak to them and to guide and care for those with a glow. In so doing the Horizon would lighten, and he would slowly continue on his way toward its comfort. Presently he stopped weeping and bid farewell again to his bones, which used to frame his young and handsome body. Viejo made his way from what he knew was the bottom of the slide track from which he arose all those years ago trying to find his limbs and skis and boots and poles. The crashing boom and swimming flight had so surprisingly shredded him. He watched in horror as his body and red and white polka dot shirt and bell bottoms tore apart and disappeared into tons of frozen concrete and ravaged pines. He watched and pummeled deeply into the world, which Viejo now knew was more miraculous and beautiful and painful than he ever imagined: that there was much more to the world than only the world. He was not El Viejo then, and he sat in frozen disbelief in the semi-darkness for so long that he realized he was no longer in time and yet no longer completely released from her sensuous pull. His arms and limbs and gear were scattered over several acres of wilderness. He knew he remained across from Mt. Mitchell in the vast backcountry of what they called then, and what is still called today, the Southwest Kingdom. El Viejo had also come to know that an infinite Horizon has been calling him, and after what must be many years, he has come to answer this calling and in so doing feel all the life of The Powder Horns. And yet El Viejo was not of this life nor had he met the Horizon.

Before he watched his body tear into pieces, he was among the first to ski the wild runs of The Powder Horns. He was a young man and newly married to his pretty wife, who carried his child. When he traveled to The Powder Horns to ski the new area of Big Pine and crossed The Pass for the first time, he was grabbed by the ache in his heart. Each translucent flake sparked a violet and red passion in an untouched blanket of white and whispering desire. Then there was the girl. Alive in body, mind and spirit he embraced her frozen charms and all her pleasures; and writhed and thrust and wrapped and sucked—the irresistible girl who put bells on her toes and danced in her bedroom. Spending and refreshing, over and over again. Deep powder. Deep pleasure. He left his former life and became Groovin' Dan the Powder Man or just Spooner and abandoned his wife and unborn son.

Viejo rose from his bones and made his way to what he knew was the top of the long ridge above the drops, which fall to the deep valley of ancient pines. He followed the glowing arch of red, violet, yellow, green and gold, which illuminated his dark nether world so that he could almost make out trees and even people again. Viejo knew that the child he had grown to care for with great feeling, as if she were his own, had come again and that he must speak to her, protect her and ride with her like the wind. He followed Nancy's glow to the ridge line.

El Viejo sat next to Nancy as she prepared to descend on her mother's telemark skis and gently spoke without words to her heart. He said that he watched her husband, Charlie, on the day of the slide and that she should not worry, that a brilliant and warm light engulfed him. He was taken gently and is not suffering as himself. Viejo spoke evenly and quietly and told Nancy that she was a wonderful child, mother and wife and that he has grown to love her very much. Nancy began to descend with unsteady turns and face-planted because she had spent her life on stiff racing skis on hardpack; she had never surfed turns on the deep and wild slopes. Viejo stayed by Nancy's side and lifted and comforted her when she fell. He could see the base and the crystalline pack in each section of smooth, undulating slope, bowl and chute. He knew that a slope is a she, and she was something alive — born anew each season … and yet always the same. She changes, moves, grows and breathes and has a personality of her own and failures in her are the same as all human weakness. One gives into her lie and slides to ruin, leaving behind a path of destruction. El Viejo, the Old One, spoke to Nancy and told her that a wild slope is a quilt-work of weaknesses and far more balanced, tenuous and dangerous than anyone would ever know. Her danger is a whisper. Her whisper is evil. Evil is a lie by which she lures one to grab, to hold and to bury and rise again. El Viejo spoke to Nancy of those beckoning curves, and how with fleeting luck one passes over her bodice. Those who hold and do not find that which gives her her charms watch themselves decay in time and time alone … of the world and in the world only

… nothing more … sooner or later, empty and dark.

El Viejo told Nancy of his bones that were becoming dust. Even though he knew it might upset her, he wanted Nancy to know of his remains so that she would understand. He wanted her to know of the Light and the Horizon; and to hold loosely to the allurements of life and not give into weakness and become as he. And even though Nancy could not see his bones buried below the December drifts, El Viejo knew that she knew — Nancy's glowing colors grew brighter each day.

Nancy continued carving down the slope, and when The Old One sensed the danger of weakness, he gently guided her by speaking again without words to her heart. He joined with her body and knew the joy of movement without desire. El Viejo felt the freedom of the heel and became expert with Nancy. He felt Nancy's strength and grace. He balanced with Nancy and flowed and carved with her body until she swooped and dove with ease and freedom. He felt as Spooner again, now with a heart. And together they rode the deep and mighty surf — The Old One buried ass to chest with his big bony soul-grin and mirror shades and Nancy panting and crystal-blasted with a rainbow plume trailing into Viejo's nether world. "Far out, man!" El Viejo hollered into his silence. And he felt that Nancy was also happy, and he was pleased. The Old One knew that in some small way he had made right the path of destruction that was his former life … and that darkness was loosening her grip.

CHAPTER 4

SKIN DANCE

It was mid December now and snowing, cold and dark. Nancy stopped at the turnout of mile marker 22, slid out and creaked open the rear hatch of Mom and Dad's beat-up Subaru. She was below the clouds and wind, and it was relatively warmer than The Pass. Nancy pulled out Mom's chocolate Tua's and smoothed on a pair of worn climbing skins. She handled the telies and remembered her mother's ecumenical proclamation: "there is one ski!" *Skis with soul*, Nancy thought to herself, Mom's spirit. She had on her mother's bibs with a strip of curling duct tape on the butt, and around her shoulders Nancy tied a wide, black shawl. She pulled a patterned headband over her ears and looked at the blacktop for the skid marks and thought about the cute guy and the accident. Nancy hopped back in and continued up the mountain. Nancy liked heading to The Pass and not to Big Pine. She felt tense going up to Piney and seeing The Team and not knowing what to say to anybody. And if The Team wasn't there, she felt lonely not being on tour with them. It was simpler to dig out Mom's tele gear from the pile of skis and bikes in the metal garage and head up to The Pass for backcountry skiing in thousands of acres of wilderness.

Nancy made The Pass and pulled into the plowed space, and there were only two other parked cars. She reached under her shawl and pullover, plugged in her avalanche beacon, and its blue light began to blink. Nancy took a deep breath, shut off the wagon, dropped the keys on the floor, jumped into the wind and cold and creaked open the rear hatch again. She swung on her pack with an avy shovel tucked in, grabbed her skis and poles and bent against the swirling wind of dusty, dendritic crystals. She closed the hatch and didn't bother locking the car. Nancy pulled over her hood and climbed up the frozen embankment and kicked into her bindings. She wanted to be moving right away. The skin track rose steadily, and she bent down and pulled on her goggles. Nancy stepped forward in little sliding motions because the grade was gentle. She watched crystals bounce and explode off of her worn glove. Nancy knew the snow was dry and perfect and dangerous. Nothing was binding. Some crystals stayed and set against her black glove and showed their little branches and leafy shapes that looked like fir trees joined in the center. As Nancy stepped and glided, large spruce trees with black reindeer lichen on their north sides opened to the exposed ridge. Nancy traversed up and into the Southwest Kingdom. Her fingers turned numb with cold and then stung with heat as the grade steepened and her blood pumped. Nancy was warm now and flipped back her hood and unzipped her parka a little below her shawl. The mountain lands were hushed and beautiful in the soft, fresh down. The wind made a hollow gusting sound as it combed through the frozen firs behind her and drifted from the southwest to the northwest. Nancy noted the wind direction and the drifting. She reached to her side and pushed down a ski pole. She had to stop and lean over to keep pushing. She finally met a slow, steady resistance when her hand and the pole grip disappeared. Nancy sensed consistency in the pack, and the world around her felt like the insides of a soft feather bed.

Nancy crested the ridge and swung off her pack. She flipped one ski behind her back and turned and unstripped the climbing skin, then did the same with the other ski: the skin dance. She folded each skin on itself and shoved them into her pack. Nancy wanted to kick off quickly and not hesitate or think or worry about anything. She drew water from a bike bottle. Then she took off the ski band and pulled on her hat. Nancy zipped up and checked her cuffs. She made sure to keep her hands out of the pole straps. The poles adjusted, and Nancy untwisted and shortened them because she thought she would dive to her arm pits. Nancy bent down and re-checked her bindings. "Lose a ski out here and you're toast," she said quietly. Nancy wiggled off a glove and reached under and flipped her avy beacon to receive and heard a faint ping like a submarine movie. There were other skiers somewhere in the near distance. She slid the switch back to transmit, adjusted her parka, then stuffed her pack and slung it onto her back. The shovel handle knocked around a little.

The light was flat, and the slope opened at her feet into vacuous space faintly lined below by dark spruce. No matter who you are, it's a hundred face plants before you learn to tele in the wild deep, and Nancy had counted about 75 of her own. It was steep, and she knew to surrender to the fall line. She squared to the pull and pointed her tips straight down. As she felt the draw, Nancy dropped her left knee and arched onto her inside edge while following in a wedge on the outside edge of her right ski. "Yes," she whispered to herself and swooped over to the right and buried to her chest. A base was forming, and Nancy could feel herself rise up again. A few weeks ago when she went down she stayed down and pummeled to her arm pits. She had to bring her skis nearly parallel between turns to rise and turn again. Any movement front or back, and she face-planted and augured-in head over heels. Nancy had trouble getting back up, and it was scary.

But now she was free. Nancy ripped down to her waist and chest. Her skis porpoised up, and she slid an easy transition across the fall line and back left and felt its pull and dove again. "Whew!" Nancy breathed feeling weightless as she surfed in a free-fall of released control in the otherworldly medium. It was cold and the crystals were perfectly dry and fast. She buried deeply and rose with less and less effort. Nancy felt her skis and her weight. She grew smoother and smoother until she flew in a downy world of hushed silence. As seen from the ridge line, Nancy's black shawl flowed behind her in a white, powdery cloud. Black and white, fire and ice, she disappeared into a line of spruce like a rhythmical wisp of prayer.

Nancy cut into the trees. The grade dropped away and her stomach fluttered. She sank down and tightened her turns without losing the fall line or her swooping and bouncing rhythm. Nancy was going fast and aiming for the open spaces, even ducking trees like gates. She sucked down a rollover and came to an abrupt stop on a billowy flat with her lead knee casually bent forward. Nancy panted and howled to herself, "ahooo, yeah!" It was completely silent, and she felt calm and happy.

Below and to the east, three dark forms plowed toward her in the waist-deep through the old pines, and Nancy knew she had found them on her transceiver. They looked like telemonks bent under their hoods and double poling a chant. Nancy could tell by their pigtails and shrinking frames that they were tele-junkies and friends of Mom and Dad: married couples who had been mainlining the Powder Horns for years. They kick-turned on their skins and skis and laboriously headed her way. When the lead recognized Nancy in her shawl and her mother's clothes and gear, she said, "How are *you*?" And broke on, dazed by endorphins. Somewhat impressed and amazed, Nancy watched them traverse away to her uphill right and then disappear into creamy white. The flakes of crystals gently whispered and circled around the spruce, and a calm overcame Nancy. She looked again at the junky's disappearing track and shook her head. "Too deep to hike, man," she said to herself.

Nancy kicked off and listened to the Silence guide her between the trees until the grade eased and Wild Creek Ravine closed on either side. There were Douglas firs as wide as she was tall, and it was growing darker. Nancy wanted to find the junky's skin track and the other run-outs so she did not become disoriented. Any kind of accident, breakdown or mixup could kill her, and Nancy knew this. The pack was deep and impossible to walk in. There was no one around, and it was cold. She blew down the frozen creek bed. Wild Ridge Slide with its dwarf firs appeared on her right and rose into oblivion. On the opposite side of the creek, entire Douglases were snapped in half. She knew that if she cut left she would make the traverse and eventually hit the bottom of The Pass on the Slippery Rock/Aspen Crest side of The Range. She also knew to get out of the ravine quickly because the whole feature was a terrain trap and funneled slides that crashed down from above. Nancy found the traverse and the junky's track. Both were rapidly disappearing into white history. She traversed east until she saw where the skin track dropped into more spruce and pushed off, cutting turns across the track so as not to lose it. She finally came to the power lines. The grade turned gentle, and Nancy cruised along, feeling the utter quiet and muffled clumps diving at her as darkness gathered.

Nancy thought about how people say that the whole Wild Creek Ravine and valley was haunted, and she believed it because she always felt an overwhelming peace. Nancy believed there were spirits, and they were friendly. And, there were all the stories her mom and dad told about a ghost helping stranded or injured skiers. Soon the highway embankment and the old road up The Pass appeared. Nancy stopped and pressed out of her telies and kicked-stepped in a boot pack across the road and up to the highway. There was no one around, and it was almost dark. Nancy stomped onto the pavement and watched a few headlights blur through the falling clumps that were now becoming a solid mass in the sky around her. The Powder Horns could receive three feet from this little dump, and Nancy wanted to get back to the wagon before it got too deep or before they closed The Pass. Nancy was wet and warm and knew she would soon be freezing; so she quickly swung her little fanny pack around with her Glock and stuck out her thumb. Nancy figured that most of the passing pickup trucks would be guys she half recognized, coming home from building condos in Slippery and Aspen Crest. *Nonetheless, I've got my babies now,* Nancy thought to herself as she adjusted the release string so she could tear out her Model 27.

A couple of cars passed, then nothing. Nancy stood collecting crystals. The junkies had quit early and now stomped onto the highway carrying their skis in either hand with cables dangling. The two guys and a woman gave Nancy the first spot and passed her with wet drooping braids and the guys with crusted beards.

"Wheehee, ain't it sweet, Nance," they whistled with a huge grin and dazed eyes. Nancy nodded.

The three gathered in a huddle behind her and jumped up and down and laughed. A brand new, six-wheel pickup pulled over to them, and the driver hopped out and, passed everyone a beer, laughed and yelled and slid their stuff in the back. They all piled into the cab and took off. "Come on," Nancy exhaled to herself, sticking out her thumb and staring into the driving flakes, "a little charity maybe?" *Faith, hope and charity*, she idly mused. Headlights passed her. Then she heard a honk that sounded like towels were wrapped around the horn. Nancy turned and ran. She reached the passenger door on the shoulder side and stopped and tingled all over, and she didn't know why. The driver reached over and shoved open the door and yelled,

"Just toss 'em in back." He nodded to Nancy's skis.

Nancy opened the rear passenger door and slid in her skis and poles. She hopped onto the front seat.

"Hi."

"Hey."

"Thanks."

"No problem atall."

Nancy picked up her shawl, shook it and wrapped it around her neck and chest. She pulled off her wet gloves, wiped water from her pretty face and shook out her French braid. Nancy swung her pack around onto her lap. She looked over and knew it was him and that she was in his black Pathfinder — the guy in the accident on The Pass. He was even more good looking than she remembered.

Jim Peters pulled out. He glanced at Nancy, and his chest tightened. Jim knew it was her. The expectation he had been feeling driving up The Pass was now flesh and bone and sitting next to him. Jim watched his fingers quiver slightly on the steering wheel. His groin grew warm and started to pulse. Jim's head was light, and he tightened all over as they drove into the crazy flakes. Nancy placed her hand on the rest next to Jim, and he was aware of her hand. Jim drove with his mouth open a little and with his manhood throbbing away. His body suddenly felt firm, and he grew hot and realized that he was a man, and she was a woman, and the volts shooting around his insides pushed him to do something about all that. Nancy grew warm and slippery in between. She felt pretty and wanted him to lift her in his arms and take her somewhere. From the quick corners of her eyes, Nancy could tell that he needed to find something in himself to do such a thing. Jim realized he was driving about 10 miles an hour and sped up. His fingers quivered. Nancy placed her hand closer on the rest, and Jim was aware she had done so. It was pleasing.

Jim knew that she wanted to place her arm up and around his shoulder and look at him and maybe curl his hair behind his neck. Jim felt beads of sweat roll down his sides. He worked his jaw and rolled his head a little. Jim felt himself slipping away from where he was neither boy nor girl. He had always been in groups, in a safe place — girls as guys, guys as girls and neither as either. Now Jim was alone with this radiant force and being told he was a man. The pressure in his gut made him speak.

"Jim. My name's Jim."

"Yeah?" Nancy said, smiling and looking up to meet his green eyes.

They both watched the wipers flap back-and-forth and sensed an unexpected comfort, like they had always been together. Jim and Nancy drove in the Silence for a long time. Jim pulled into the plowed area at the top of The Pass, and Nancy's wagon was drifted to the gunnels. Jim's chest burned. He had to say or do something, and the feeling was new and scary so he just pulled up to her car and stopped. They both sat and looked ahead. Nancy went to turn, then looked through the windshield, then up at Jim.

"So can I dig out your car?" Jim asked.

"Will you ask me to go to the movies?"

"The movies? Yeah sure, the movies!" Jim laughed and slapped his thigh, and they both burst out laughing. "Just what I was thinking."

"You don't know who I am?"

"I might know who you are." There was a long pause, and Jim let it fly. "The beautiful girl on the DeBernardi. Damn. Been meaning to find you again," Jim said and listened to himself call her beautiful. "Thanks for saving my life."

"No problem," Nancy replied, smiling at him. "No one's ever called me beautiful before."

Jim's face turned red and hot. His fingertips quivered.

"It was nice," Jim said, trying to compose himself. "I mean the mouth-to-mouth and the —" Jim stopped before he blew the whole thing.

They looked into each other's eyes and lingered and smiled and laughed. Jim kept looking at Nancy as he reached behind the seat for his avy shovel. Nancy slowly left his gaze and pulled the door handle. She stepped into the swirling madness, opened the back door and reached for her skis. Together they dug out the Subaru. Nancy loaded her stuff and got in, and Jim stood by her door.

"Can I take you to the movies then? I work up at Piney. I'll come down mountain."

"Sure," Nancy replied, smiling, and they both laughed.

"How do I find you?" Jim heard himself say, and the neutered boy within watched in amazement.

"I'm in the book. Nancy Michaels. At the bottom of The Area road in Rocky Creek Park, number 15. Tomorrow night?" Nancy asked and bit her lower lip. She all of sudden understood that Jim was probably the guy that Margaret was gushing about.

"Yeah … 7?"

"Seven. See you. Oh, better, I'll meet you there — only movie theatre in town. At 7."

"Seven," Jim replied, and he stood and held up his hand as Nancy backed out, waved and smiled. She drove off down the mountain.

Jim worked his jaw and cocked his head to the side. "Whew, OK," he said to himself and exhaled and decided to let the whole thing happen like everything else that had gone down: from getting busted by Red Bone, David Winchester and almost dying in the chute to sitting in jail and being sentenced to work off his fine at The Area under David. "Just drive," Jim said to himself as he hopped into the driver's seat and sat staring at the hole in the drift that used to cradle Nancy's wagon.

***

Nancy pulled into the trailer park and her driveway. The storm ceiling was very low, and it was still dumping like mad. David's new, oversized pickup with the Big Pine logo was parked out front, and the warm glow in Nancy's chest mingled with all the good feelings she had for her friends. The flood lights were on, and she could see that the driveway was shoveled. There were flowers lining the pile of powder all the way up and down on either side. The flowers were bright red, yellow and orange carnations, daffodils and roses. When Nancy stepped out of the wagon, there were rose petals spread at her feet and leading down the driveway. The deep-red petals set against the white snow and made Nancy's heart ache with a secret love for everyone and everything. The long pile of storm crystals with all the colorful flowers was absurd but oddly beautiful and festive. Rosa stuck out her head from the side door.

"Hola Misses, mire — las lindas flores que el señior Chaz Man sent. Insistió que las ponga por ambos lados del camino. The whole driveway."

Nancy's eyes welled with emotion. "He wanted them up and down the driveway!?"

"Sí Misses. Es un hombre apasionado que lo quiero. How do you say with . . . heart?"

"Passionate?"

"Sí, apasionado."

The flowers were gathering clumps of white, and they looked like an offering to Nancy and to the all the crystals flowing around her in the flood lights — like a Tibetan butter mandala that would soon change into decay and passing. David was shoveling her roof with a couple of the guys from The Area. He poked his head over the top.

"Nance, babe, roof's gonna cave in this year again. See what The Chaz Man sent?" he asked with a big grin.

"I say bring it on, Whinny. Can't believe Chaz sent those. Man, we need him out here! Miss him so much. Hey, get that cute butt of yours down here, and I'll give you somethin' warm."

"Yeah, how warm?" one of the other guys laughed and yelled.

"Hot."

Nancy went inside and stripped off her wet shells and locked her Model 27 and put it away. Rosa handed her Michael; and Clay staggered over with a big smile and his arms out. Kyle was bundled up outside and trying to shovel with David. David came down from the roof and picked him up. They rolled together down one of the piles, laughing. The trailer was starting to become buried. Nancy bounced Michael and Clay on her knees in her arms, and they sucked on pacifiers and grabbed at things on the table. She tore open an oversized envelope, and a deed spilled out. Nancy read Abe's letter that said he and Scott the Hammer and Chaz Man had bought her an acre of land up the valley to build a house, and they'd come frame it in the spring. Nancy streamed tears because she knew those guys didn't have much money. Nancy figured Moon Dog — Jamie — had something to do with it too. She reached around her babies and wiped her eyes and thought about how it wasn't so bad having all these guys who were convinced that Kyle was theirs — plus all they'd been through together on The River. There were more flowers on the kitchen table, and Margaret drove up with Hanna to visit. The wind gusted around, and soon everyone packed into the little trailer home, cranked tunes and played with the babies. They all drank coffee or beer and ate tortilla chips with fresh, green chili fired up in the oven.

***

Late that night when all was quiet, and the storm had retreated to the alpine, three women came and stood at the corners of the trailer in their flowing robes. Like a she-wolf, the high priestess raised her nose to the winter air and sensed that the one they called Sekhmet's child had taken a boy-man, and it was only a matter of time before her fertility flowed again and the valley and the earth returned to abundant rebirth. The three women in robes tossed pine cone seeds and corn and placed eggs in the cold crystals, while chanting in their pagan hearts to their god Sekhmet — the goddess with a woman's body and a lion's head — and to her child, asleep and dreaming about taking her boy-man and feeling him throb and swell inside her as she spread her legs and grabbed his back and moaned with fertile power.

CHAPTER 5

RED BONE AND PEPE

The storm cleared late in the night, and the next morning offered a blue and cold mountain day — the kind of day that rings with light. Punch the snow with your ski pole, cast a shadow and the light, the sky, the blue comes right through the snow, as if the mountains squeeze light outward from within. The snow squeaks underfoot, and your nose stings with the cold. Jim and David kicked steps up the South Ridge of Dhaulagiri, The Snow Princess. The court had assigned Jim to work directly under David, and Jim felt a hidden thrill. For him it was not a punishment but an honor. He peppered David with questions about all of his first ski descents — from Kazakhstan to Nepal to right here in the Powder Horns. The two were getting close: taking free runs together before Piney opened in the morning and working on projects around The Area. Jim felt the gravity of fate fall on him when he was with David — the more he talked with David, the more Jim realized how many mistakes he had made in the chute at Big Pine. When David spoke to Jim about that day, he looked at Jim deep and hard — like he cared. Jim liked this but grew uneasy. David's concern brought to the surface feelings that Jim still wished to avoid — that he was unsure how he felt about living or dying in that chute. Jim brushed aside having to choose one or the other — caring or not caring. As he climbed, he indexed what he wanted to ask David. He realized he was in the presence of a master, and this awareness made him feel good. These good feelings mingled with the craving that drove Jim deeper and deeper into mountain life.

Dhaulagiri was still, and the sun was bright and a touch warm. David led and Jim followed. They had been climbing for an hour. Jim's lungs pinched, and his chest ached. He could not believe David's power and how hard it was to match his pace. Up above, Jim could see the ridge crest and a plume of white smoke. It was windy on the exposed ridge. David kicked into the boot pack and breathed hard. "We're free today, Pepe," David said.

Jim liked it when David called him Pepe. It was great getting to be buddies. Jim felt something buried down deep. Something that he ducked but wanted nonetheless. Something strong that also made him aware of a sharp and sad feeling. He never did anything tight like this with his own father, or any other guy. Never saw much of his father or fathers. Jim's parents were divorced and remarried. "No more Red Bone?" Jim asked, panting with a grin.

"Out here maybe," David replied. He liked Jim calling him Red Bone. David never got called that anymore, and the old name felt good. It brought him back to the days when he was The Bone. Days of freedom and running balls with his buddies — Ace, Moon Dog, Chaz, Abe, Jack Hammer and the guys. David liked to keep those days alive. *The spirit lives, man* — David thought to himself. *It'll never die.* So too, David sensed that something was calling Jim — that Jim needed this kind of thing. *The guy thing*, David thought. *Just guys, alone for each other, a bro day*.

"I'm gonna grab some telies," Pepe breathed.

"Free the heel and the mind will follow … the soul too," David replied.

"Yeah?"

"Arise, my friend. Start the journey."

"OK … So you didn't use 'em on something like Dalpo?"

"No. Soon as it gets hard-packed or variable or weird or if you have to climb a couloir, they're out. Can't climb, toe folds. Goin' down, pin pivots, spin. Gone. History. You don't realize how vulnerable you are."

"Right."

But … anything where you can dig in and get down; at any angle, into the 40s and beyond, much preferred. Love the feel. The grace. The platform. Plus it's harder … Feels so good to link on steeps. It's a full-on commitment, Pepe. Other than that … lock down and rondenee. Can use crampons. Get self-arrest grips for your pole handles. Save your life. Wear a whistle so you can cry for help when you're brought to your knees … and sooner or later you will be. With pins … can drop to your knees." Both guys panted and pumped higher. "Pins are about purity. Perfect powder. Prayer," David added. "About finding what's real, down deep and secret, inside yourself … Him." Jim kicked and breathed and tried to absorb what David said.

"Him?" Jim asked. David did not reply. "Lookin' forward … to a hundred face plants," Jim panted. There was a pause as each guy exhaled hard and slowed a little to catch his breath.

"Like I say, it's not so much where you end," David breathed. "It's the journey."

"OK."

Pepe and Red Bone wore mountain packs with their skis strapped on either side and their avy shovels tucked in pockets on the back. They double-poled and gripped the shafts at midpoint. Their parkas were unzipped and open. David wore a thin headband, and each had on shades. Sweat slid down Jim's chest. His smooth face was handsome and wind tanned. The top of Jim's hair was bleached but starting to grow back as dirty blonde. He was doing away with the bleached look, and he wasn't sure why. Maybe it was because of the way David and Skeeter looked at him askance — the bleached hair and pierced earring. Jim had pulled the earring too.

"And joy, joyous movement," David added, mostly to himself.

"Joy? Not sure what you mean."

David turned, still kicking upward, and looked into Jim's eyes through his sunglasses. Jim grew uncomfortable.

"So …" Jim panted, "Put my tail 'tween my legs and show me some stuff; 'specially after f'ing up Chute 4."

"Six. I never told you it was Six?"

"Six!?"

"Not Four, bro. Four would've been safer. I climb everything before running it. First rule … For me. There's often no margin for error. It's not about what you do. It's about coming back alive and not spending the rest of your life in a wheelchair … or leaving friends and family with broken lives."

"Shhhi," Jim heaved and blew out his nose. He felt suddenly hot and embarrassed.

"Easy not to know where you are. This time of year, everything's so puffy … stay out of most chutes … Watch terrain traps." They both kicked and breathed and watched the rounded, hollow steps in front of their eyes. "Small cliffs, big boulders, terrain changes, trees and steep, really good now … More anchored … Fun, better. Later … the pack settles, then the meat. The big couloirs. Air."

"The meat, Red Bone. That's what I came out here for. Extreme."

David did not reply right away. He sensed that Pepe needed to say that — that it was good for him, and he wouldn't be this way forever — that he was on his way and looking for Something. And Something was calling for him. David let it be and softly stated, "You can do it, man." The crest was approaching, and the two climbed in silence. David felt each step and breath. He listened to himself talk but what really mattered was the feeling lifting his heart — just being there and alive. David had walked away from his own death in the mountains at least twice. The final time, when he crawled out of the cave after The River, was like being on some kind of psychedelic. David looked at his hands in amazement and felt every breath. Being alive and with his friends was almost overwhelming. He recovered back with his folks and lay in bed streaming tears with his whole being shouting Thank You. David looked at his parents and for the first time felt truly sorry for them. They were broken and sick and alcoholic, and he didn't care about himself anymore. He wanted them to feel what he felt. David knelt face down to the floor, squeezing tears and asked Him for that. David and his folks talk now; they visit as grandparents and have gone into rehab. David's Dad helps around The Area. All these feelings — his deaths and his parents changing — come back to David all the time. David does not need anything anymore — hard chutes, peaks, rock solos, intense whitewater, first descents, endless powder runs, sponsorships, even The Area. He only wanted the One who leads him without effort into the heart of each moment, until David welcomes seeing snow crystals round and change and eventually run as water, or flowers radiate with bloom, then wilt and die. Both are a feeling and a sign of Forever. And Forever is right now, and it's light and good and lifts him up The Snow Princess and through each day. Pepe and Red Bone's last words drifted into the silent blue and white. After a long while David asked Jim, "What is it that you really want?"

"Not sure what you mean," Jim said, and he almost made a crack like, "Some bad ass skiing." But he didn't because he couldn't honestly answer the question, and it made him uncomfortable. Jim listened though. He did not want to admit how much he admired David. He felt there was a lot happening since he came to the Powder Horns that he did not expect or understand. He could feel himself changing—things happening to him. So Red Bone asking something a little odd was OK. *Just shut up and listen,* Jim thought. After a long silence, Jim changed the topic, "Tell me about the Great White Way."

"The Way. It's out there. Epic. Absolutely mind blowing runs. Deep in."

"How many yurts are there now?"

"Two. Both semi-legit. Should all be stocked. Packed into Rattling Brook and left some food and gathered wood … Last summer."

"Other than that I heard you use the old service cabins."

"The Great White Way. Can surf the whole range. String 'em. Gets dicey in the middle. Lots of steeps you have to commit to. Hard to find the shelters. Easy to get lost. Food gets low. Weather. Gettin' tired. Cold. Avies."

"It's cool out there, eh?"

"Not many people know about it … Or choose to know about it."

"You've got info? I got some topos and hand-drawn maps. The older guys with the braids gave me some beta."

"Jill and Doug had detailed maps, Boomer's parents. I'll dig those out from her if you're serious."

"They did the whole Way?"

"The Great White Way never ends."

Jim listened to David's reply. He changed the topic again.

"Who's Boomer?" Jim asked.

"Nancy Ann."

"Nancy," Jim said, and his entire body pulsed, which bugged him a little.

"Yeah."

"The girl with pins," Jim said but wanted to say she was the really cute blonde with the killer chest. Jim listened to himself recall Nancy's chest. It felt funny but good too. He had never thought of girls as girls or at least as much of a girl as Nancy seemed to be. "I know her. Met her." He wanted to say something else, like she was out there or kind of different but sensed David stiffen.

David reached a shallow, level area in some dwarf pines and stopped climbing. He turned, breathing hard, and looked into Pepe's sunglasses again and squinted. David studied Jim and realized that he was getting old or something. He could see young people coming along and being him a few years back. Making the same mistakes. Doing the same things. The world repeating itself. Around and around. A lonely dog chasing its lonely tail. And for a twist, this group was different and hard to understand, which made him feel even older. David looked at Jim and thought to himself how girls and guys dress the same, talk the same, look the same. Run in close packs. Need each other. As if they raise each other. *They hold off a loneliness, a sharp and deep one,* David mused. *And girls are everywhere only guys used to be. Better. Stronger than the guys. What the hell happened to boys growing up?* David asked himself. *Like somebody nuked boyhood. Manhood. Different world out there. Something like me and Pepe, two bros putting it out alone, was rare,* David thought again. *A lot of the guys don't put it out period. Keep it safe and predictable. Either park 'n play boating, or bolt guns on rock ascents. Nothing unknown. Nothing uncontrolled. Nothing like what happened on The River.* "No way," David breathed to himself. *And when the guys do put out, there's no regard for their lives.* David remembered the kid who hucked himself off the sheer Northwest face of Mad Dog last year on rondenees and miraculously lived, only to be written up all over the ski and climbing mags with glossy photos. Even picked up a clothing sponsorship. He has a talent agent now.

"Shhhit," David whistled to himself. *Was it self-destructive or brilliant or dumb or a little of both?* David wondered. *You're getting ornery, man,* he thought to himself, *really are. There have been a lot of deaths in the mountains over the past few years,* David thought again. *Rivers, rocks, back countryin'. Much, much more. These kids have no limits, no rules, nothing black and white; right and wrong,* David mused, and realized he had called them kids. *That's why they bug from work at any hassle. Impossible to keep 'em around. They've come into an endless universe where one point is no better or bigger than any other ... with them placed square in the middle. No hard times. Everything given to 'em. Everybody bending over backwards to hire 'em 'cause there's nobody else to hire. The world at their service. I sound like an old fart. They can be pretty bold though. Some brilliant stuff has been done, 'specially on the rocks. Shadows and light. Whatever happens now with these guys — and between girls and guys — is a mystery. Whatever will become of their lives is unclear, especially the guys. What does someone like Jim want? I have no idea. For me at Jim's age, life seemed less complicated. It was hard ... but simple. Work. Get out from under the old man and the humdrum, blue collar life that would have beaten me into death. Blow my mind on rivers and mountains. More and harder. Hang tight with your buddies. Bang some hot pussy, or try to, anyway. And just freakin' dive into the unknown. And wanna come back in one piece ... OK ... Get high, too ... Something I'm not proud of ... that and the fornicating. Been clean for years. Committed to marriage. But Jim? Just dunno,* David mused. *Makes me feel far from these kids and old. But I like Pepe. Feel a lot of potential in him. He needs me. Should be there for 'im.*

David also knew that he cared deeply about Nancy. A whole range of mixed feelings volted around David's chest, and he held his tongue as best he could. "Pepe," David said and paused and penetrated Jim. Jim's mouth felt suddenly dry. He leaned on his poles and looked back. "Treat her well. Nance is special … to all of us."

Jim didn't know what to say, but there were a lot of new feelings rattling around inside of him, and he assumed that Red Bone was telepathic and could read his mind. He blushed.

"Definitely … I mean I like her."

"Been going through a bunch. Lost Ace Man her husband. Recognize her from the Winter Games and downhillin'?"

"That's Nancy Sweeny?"

"Boomer."

"I asked her to the movies tonight," Jim said, and he felt good about the "I asked" part.

"Really?" David replied and again he held back a whole lot he could have said. He continued, "We'd like to raise a fund. Get her back racing. Not sure what to do. Nancy's got certain responsibilities now," David said, but he really knew that he had feelings for Nancy as a sister and in the past even as a lover. Nancy probably had his son, and he was with her through something that cannot be explained or forgotten. David let his feelings about The River and what happened out there with the girls rise to his awareness. There was a whole gang of them, girls and guys. Wild. Nobody was sure whose baby ended up being whose. Nor was anybody sure how to feel about what happened. *Was it bad? Or a step in the journey?* David asked himself. *Was there a rule book we should have followed? The Bible with virgins to wives, and Paul who says, 'do not fornicate' — back to slaying Canaanites. Manhood. Dicks. Swords. Courage. Heart for the Lord. Leadership. Obedience and power, male power bestowed from Him. Humility. A man must be a man,* David mused. *What now?* David asked, looking up. *What kind of sexual guidance should I offer my own daughter? Would I have her do as I did? No. We were pagans taken by Your love from day one. You knew what was going to happen. Took hold of us ... right to the end — to the cave and all the agony, dying and bursting in us — busting us out of there. That's it; isn't it?* David asked, lifting his eyes. *I understand. In bondage, every step I took was separate from You. Hurting You. In Freedom, every step I take now is toward You. Delighting You. I want to please you, Lord. I love them ... Would lay down my life for any one of those girls ... Or guys. The River gang, we're tight forever ... In You.*

"Whew, really are," David exhaled to himself, caught by a sudden wave of feeling that spoke back to him, welling into his eyes as tears. His chest burned. "Thank you, Holy Spirit," David whispered. *The first man was made from the dust of the earth,* he thought, *and the second man from Heaven. Corinthians taken by Your furious love. Ephesians hold hands and leave Artemis behind ... that's us ... Sinners turn and confess: believe, ask, receive. Rabbi, Teacher, teach me.*

"What did you say?" Jim asked.

"Nothing, man, just thinking. Nancy and I did this trip together ... this river trip. It got pretty epic," David replied and started kicking steps again.

"Cool. So what does Nancy like? I mean other than the movies and all the vast entertainment in Powder Horn," Jim laughed.

David laughed a little and smiled. He zipped up and pulled on his gloves as he climbed, to get ready for the ridge line pummeling. David paused and didn't think or say anything. He looked around at Jim and somehow the threat of something intimate happening between Jim and

Nancy did not seem pressing, but he heard himself say, “Go easy, man. She went through a lot fast, too fast. Just slow and nice. Maybe find flowers somewhere. Give her flowers, roses … that’s what a man does, Jim. That’s what she’d like,” David added and realized that his advice might sound strange to Jim and unwelcome. There was a long, awkward pause, and the two looked at each other. “Better yet, just hold her hand, Pepe. She’d like that,” David said, lowering his voice. “It’s something she missed growing up. Call it dating and courtship,” David said and laughed to himself. Jim looked at David with his mouth open. The two turned and climbed in silence for a long while.

At length Jim asked, “So … how did her husband die?”

“Slide took ‘im out,” David replied, nodding over his right shoulder. “Just around the corner: down the Southeast headwall of The Snow Princess. Boom. Ran across the road. Driving home from work. Being the proper guy. Supporting his family. Was a builder. Bang, man. She took ‘im. Gone. Good man. Life is fragile and sacred. Hard not having ‘im. Ace and I boated together.” There was a long silence, and David let feelings for Ace rise to the surface. He closed his eyes and sent a silent prayer.

“I’m sorry about that.” There was another long silence.

The two approached the rounded crest of the ridge and a sudden gust blasted frozen crystals onto their cheeks, and the crystals melted as soon as they hit. David replied at length, “You gotta realize, Pepe, that any of these slopes can slide at any time. Check into the white room.”

“Quick test?” Jim asked. They stopped and pulled up their beacons. Jim switched to receive, and his beacon beeped loud and fast. David did the same.

“Rock ‘n’ roll,” Jim said and zipped up everything. Jim and David started climbing again. “So you boated with her husband.”

“The Ace ran rubber. We boated … Rafted ‘n kayaked … Long and hard … Body and soul,” David breathed. “Came pretty close to dying together out there.”

“Done some playboating. Side of the road and flat-spin … mostly … fun … not much river running,” Jim replied, stopping himself from saying more. He had a sense that anything he had kayaked was nothing compared to where David had been. The slope angle rolled to level and a gust of wind blasted the two again.

"We're up. Lock in. We'll duck down the northwest side," David yelled.

The wind was blowing from the west, and the two quickly pulled out their skis and stepped into their bindings. David was off in one seamless motion. Jim watched him through his goggles disappear into the white smoke. They blew off the ridge and immediately opened to a vast expanse of slopes and bowls and ridge lines. The wind abruptly stopped, and it was still and even warm. Jim's stomach fluttered as Red Bone dropped out of sight. "Whoa," Jim said to himself as he slid to the edge and watched David parallel bounce his telies in the fresh thigh deep. Impressive." He waited until David was down to a broad gully; then traversed over to a clean expanse and pushed off. "Whew yeah!" Jim yelled and relaxed and settled into a nice rhythm. His rondenees made close turns, and the snow pack was light. Jim felt his heels slide in effortless movement.

"It's new, David said as Jim arched a final turn next to him and stopped. "All kinds of wind loading. Gotta watch that. Things feel good though. Gettin' a nice base. Have you done this line?"

"Never been up here."

"Follow me. We'll ease down and cut north and finish in the trees."

David pushed off and dropped into a smooth, easy tele turn. The angle had slackened, and they could ski together and cross tracks. David cut north and made a long turn and looked down as he did so. A wide bowl opened, and the edge fell off so Jim could not see the slope. David disappeared, and Jim followed. Jim's stomach squeezed to his throat, and he tensed and didn't want to fall or screw up. Jim breathed hard and relaxed and made wide turns that he was able to tighten. His thighs burned, and he had to stop. Red Bone waited below. Jim kicked off again.

"Nice. Look good," David said as he turned to Jim when Jim came to his side. "Don't fight the fall line. Go with her, relax. Yield. Give yourself. Surrender. Gentle but firm. OK, this gets real. Commit."

Alpine spruce cut across a horizon line. David pointed straight down, and Jim watched his pack and avy shovel drop over a sheer edge. "Shhhii," Jim whistled through his teeth. "What the hell'd he go over?" Jim gripped and ungripped his poles and felt the straps on the outside of his wrists. He wasn't sure he could follow David. Jim pushed off, and his legs felt heavy with fear. He hit the edge and lifted his skis. "Whoa," he breathed to himself as he saw the tops of pines below him. Doosh. Jim landed on his heels and immersed to his chest in downy, north-side crystals and rose and turned. His mind shut up, and his body turned on. Jim's thighs pumped, and he screamed in silence … HEEEE HAAAAA! He dove onto a buried form and launched again into the air over a massive, granite boulder. He landed in the spruce boughs and thickening trees. Jim heard Red Bone yell, and he followed the call. Jim plunged into the tight, empty spaces between the rich, green timber; faster and faster, he reacted and turned and ducked boughs and tree trunks, cracking dead branches. The two met and high ten'd and howled and panted. The horizon dropped off again, and the trees were now very close.

"Love trees, Pepe. Lead on, bro. Take us down to Panhandle Crick," Red Bone panted.

Jim pushed off and something changed. He felt more relaxed. He swayed his rondenees in tight turns and wove a sweet course through the spruce. The open spaces closed, and Jim had to place his hands in front to push away branches. He felt the powder gently tug at his skis and thighs as he floated turns. The branches sprayed crystals all over him. Jim was covered in white. David followed. The two swooped into the creek bed, which was buried, and blew down the steep banks until a skier's track was reached. They bobsledded all the way to the plowed lot and the highway on the Powder Horn side of the range. With pasted grins they high five'd and panted and laughed.

"Damn," Jim exclaimed. "Have to admit. Didn't think I could do that."

"Did good, Pepe," David panted. "That's mad dog skiing."

"Mad Dog Mountain."

"Whew yeah."

"Another?"

"Fer sure."

As they spoke their cries echoed distantly into El Viejo's nether world as rainbow colors. Viejo lifted his head as he stood close by on his ghostly skis. He listened with his heart to Jim and felt compelled to find and know him.

***

Later that evening a silver crescent moon set in a cobalt sky packed with brilliant, mountain stars.

"Every movie makes me cry," Nancy said, and she laughed a little and wiped the corner of her eye.

Nancy and Jim walked north down Main Street Powder Horn. Powder Horn was the Star Movie Theatre, which was still letting out a few people, the restaurant with a huge buffalo head mounted on the roof, a drug store, two lines of gray nondescript shops, a couple of mainstream outfitters, a funky gear shop, something new age, a cowboy bar, then a Texaco station, the supermarket and finally the Agway. Light-tan farming dust settled over everything.

"It's cool here. I mean it's real," Jim said as they walked on the frozen sidewalk.

"Yeah?" Nancy smiled up at Jim.

They reached the Texaco station, and there was nowhere else to walk to in Powder Horn. Jim could see the open road beyond the station. He touched Nancy's arm lightly, and she let him guide her across the street. They slowly walked back toward the theatre and the main intersection. Nancy had her hands in her ski parka, and Jim's were tucked into his jeans. It was cold and dry. The air was scented with pine smoke. Jim looked down at Nancy, and he was impressed. Jim could tell she was tight, and her thighs defined through her designer jeans that nicely rounded her bottom. Jim wondered what kind of destruction Nancy could bring to a downhill course and how she got her name, Boomer. At the same time, he could see Nancy modeling her cashmere sweater that defined her full and lifted chest. The combination quickened Jim's pulse, and he throbbed warm between his legs. Nancy knew Jim's eyes were all over her in Jessica's jeans and sweater, and she liked it. She felt soft and pretty and looked up to meet his eyes. They met and lingered, and it was OK. Nancy felt comfortable and did not need to say anything. She moved close to Jim and could feel his jacket and sense his breath. Nancy liked that he guided her across the street, and he was checking her out. He was coming along. She knew he could be a man or at least she wanted him as one. Jim took his hands out of his pockets and brushed against Nancy's hand in her jacket. She took her hand out of her pocket, and Jim held it. Nancy stopped, and she was pretty in the soft light from a closed shop. She looked at their hands. Two, thin tears fell down her cheeks.

"You're holding my hand."

Jim stood taller and almost said that David told him to.

"Sorry," Nancy said, wiping her cheeks with her sleeve. "It's nice. Just nice. Really nice." Nancy smiled and laughed, and they walked hand-in-hand. She looked at their hands and up to Jim. Nancy felt Jim take her hand a little more firmly but softly, and it felt good. Nancy walked and watched Jim, and Jim liked Nancy looking at him.

"Cold. Can I hold your arm?" Nancy asked quietly.

They moved closer, and Jim put his hand back in his pocket as Nancy put her arm through his and tucked her hand into his pants pocket and held his hand there. She grew warm and moist and wantedto take her other hand and softly caress him because she felt him getting large, and it was nice and comfortable. But she held his hand palms together and looked up and into his sweet blue and green eyes. They found each other in a place without words. The urges that pushed her to wrap his leg with hers and maybe kiss him and bury her tongue rose to seeing Jim as he was, and a good feeling melted with all the body tingles and everything rushed together so that the two stopped and stared into each other and did not know what to do or make of it. A distant understanding from an impossible distance quickened.

"May God bless you," Nancy said softly as she slid her hands into prayer and bowed.

"Yeah?" Jim replied and smiled and reached out and gently stroked his fingers around her ear and down Nancy's cheek until he cupped her chin as if she were a child. He wasn't sure who he was, but it felt right. The two walked a little further and reached her mom and dad's beat-up Subaru. "See you, eh?"

"Are we going to tour together?"

"You have to teach me to tele."

"Or you me," Nancy replied, looking at Jim as she yanked open the door and sat into the cold wagon. "Can I cook you a nice dinner sometime?" Nancy asked, almost in a whisper.

"I'd like that."

Jim stepped back as the engine ground over, and Nancy bit her lower lip and creaked the door shut and waved a little as she swung around and drove off. Jim stood in the cold. He watched the Subaru disappear into the open night. He got into his truck and stared and turned the ignition key and realized that his hands were numb.

CHAPTER 6

SIGNS AND WONDERS

Two weeks later Jim grunted as he knelt and banged in a set of studs in the corner of Nancy's kitchen. He sat back and puffed his cheeks, realizing that their contact with the support across the ceiling was wrong and would pop out again. "Come on," he hissed to himself. Jim's face felt hot with embarrassment because he knew he was going to look helpless. There was water dripping into buckets, and the roof was bowing and collapsing. Jim knew he had to shovel off the roof more and let it dry; then spread roofing tar on the rivets, as David instructed. The situation looked serious to Jim. *About to lose the whole roof,* he thought, *then what? Snows so freakin' hard the roof caved in.* "Gotta love that," Jim said to himself. He glanced to the kitchen clock where a small American flag was tacked underneath. Jim looked blankly at the flag and felt no emotion. He wondered why anyone would hang the flag anywhere, let alone in their kitchen. Jim squatted and rapped at the studs again. Nancy was outside walking her babies around the buried trailer park. Jim wasn't sure how he felt about Nancy having kids.

Kyle crept up to Jim, cocked his lever-action, thirty-ought-six, toy Winchester and placed the muzzle at the back of Jim's head and took aim. He was dressed in full cammo. Kyle stood about three-feet tall, so when Jim turned the muzzle was square in his eyes. "Whoa, don't shoot, little man!" Jim said. Kyle giggled.

"Wow, where'd you get that weapon … and the cammo?"

"Uncle Whinny gave them to me."

"OK."

"Men fight in battles. Not girls."

"That right," Jim replied absently, studying the two-by-fours across the ceiling.

"Uncle Whinny says for me to grow up and protect America. Keep us free. That's what men do … Die for freedom."

"Sure."

"Fight evil."

"Got it."

Kyle re-aimed and sighted through the rear sight. "Are you gonna be my new daddy?"

Jim collapsed onto his haunches and looked up at the ceiling and down at the water all over floor and back to the gun muzzle in his eyes. Jim thought about how he was late with school loan payments that his mother was making him repay. He thought about how much was left of his fine. Jim was totally broke. And he knew he could not call home for more money. His mother would brow-beat him all the way back and for what? He looked around at all the kid and baby stuff. Jim pictured Nancy working in the convenience store for minimum wage. He had never known anyone who worked in a convenience store. Jim gazed at the bowing roof and felt exposed as if there wasn't much between him and the cold and snow that was about to cave into the kitchen. Jim wasn't used to all the limits. All this reality. At that moment Jim thought about packing it in and heading back East to his mother and stepfather's. Jim's real dad was down South and that was out of the question. *Flat and hot,* Jim thought to himself. *Sucks.* But what he really felt was that he'd never see his father anyway. Thinking about his father and his separated parents and leaving Powder Horn was like staring into a void. Jim felt empty, and his guts tensed. *What's there for me in either place?* he thought. He pictured his two sets of parents dressed in business casual and talking on cell phones, endlessly. Him watching daytime TV or going to work in a cubicle somewhere; then maybe a different cubicle and a different job.

For a reason he did not understand, Jim thought back to earlier in the day when he toured on the gentle, south slopes of Mad Dog Mountain to work on his tele turns in the uncut. It was beautiful out there on the open expanse of white and blue. The rock peaks of the Powder Horns rose as snowy and golden-brown in the distance. No one was around. Nothing moved. Not a breath of wind. Silence. A line of rich, green spruce waited below. "Freein' the heal is something you work-out on your own," David told him. "Go ahead, take the morning off. Find the fall line and give your vows. Pay some dues." Jim pictured David saying this as Jim, David and Skeeter heaved on a cat-track in the shop. Skeeter shook his head and smiled with a cigarette between his teeth as if David was getting ethereal again. Jim took the opportunity and bolted out alone. Without realizing it, Jim was getting more accustomed to being by himself and listening to the voiceless voice within.

"Come on, man," Jim breathed to himself out there on Mad Dog as he gazed at the pure, white blanket dropping below his skis — skis, boots and gear, for which he still felt awkward about asking his mother to buy. "Need to make your own way," the intuition told him. "Now let yourself do it. Release. Go deep. Give over. Commit. Come on home, man." Jim pushed off and wobbled and abruptly face-planted into the cold crystals. Too much freedom. When his heels released, Jim kept on going — head over heels. Jim dug-out and sensed someone standing to the side—a red and white polka dot shirt caught his eye. Jim looked but saw no one.

"Can't follow through the line and link 'em. Why?" Jim asked himself as he sat on his haunches in Nancy's kitchen and gazed at the linoleum floor and asked why again and dropped his wrists. Jim glanced up at the gun muzzle that was still in his face. He stared at the ceiling and realized how to set the support. "Yes," he said to the beam. "I own you." Jim looked into Kyle's hazel eyes and said, "Was a time all I wanted to do was climb and ski chutes 'n powder. Big runs," Jim said more to himself than to Kyle. Kyle lowered the gun, and Jim reached over and tickled him. Little Kyle exploded into giggles. He stepped back and repositioned his rifle.

"We go to church on Sundays."

"OK," Jim pronounced and realized he had been in a church only once in his life at his cousin's wedding. His parents never talked about anything like that. Jim asked a few questions one time. His mother just smiled as if he'd brought up a quaint notion.

"Aunt Margaret and Uncle David come by and honk the horn 'cause Mommy says we gotta go 'cause we didn't create ourselfs and God believes in us."

There was a long pause as Jim cocked his head, repeating with his lips what Kyle said.

"Kyle, dude, now that is profound. You're awesome, man," Jim said, and he grabbed Kyle and the rifle and hugged him and slung Kyle over his back, surprised to feel what he felt for Kyle. Kyle erupted into laughter, dropping his gun. Jim set him down, and Kyle picked up his rifle and pointed it at Jim's head once more.

"Mommy cried again last night."

"Really?" Jim asked as feelings jolted his insides.

"You can't come here anymore."

"I can't!" Jim laughed, but he flashed hot and a little tense.

"Mommy told Aunt Margaret you've gotta go away. She's gonna have another f'n baby. Can't stop it."

"Hey, don't use those words, remember. And don't point guns at anybody. Not polite."

Jim patted Kyle on the shoulder, realizing he had spoken a little harshly, and Kyle dropped the gun. They pretended to box. Kyle laughed. Jim stood and positioned a stepladder. As he did so, he found himself remembering an old man he passed on the cat-track on the way up Mad Dog Mountain. It was easy to dismiss at the time — just an old timer from the area, all wrinkly and bent over on his touring gear: barely sliding one ski ahead of the other. Jim came up on him, and the two stopped and looked into each other. Jim could not continue. Neither spoke. The man peered deep into Jim's eyes as if looking into himself and into the past …with a wonder, a curiosity, even a sadness, but with kindness too. Jim nodded and worked to pull his eyes away from the old man. Jim continued skinning upward on his telies. The old man stood motionless, and Jim knew that the old man waited and watched him become smaller and finally disappear over the crest of a rise.

"Those ladies are back," said Kyle as he looked out the little window onto the driveway.

"What's that?" Jim asked, snapping to attention. He held the stepladder and pushed away the odd feeling the old man had given him.

"Mommy says they're creepy. Leave these at the driveway," Kyle said and picked up a statuette. Jim stepped over and looked out the window. There was a small, white wagon with rows of telemark skis on the roof rack and bumper stickers on the back. A blonde woman got out and left something on the snow bank. "I'll get it!" shouted Kyle. He ran out the door into the cold sunshine before Jim could grab him.

"What's up?" Jim asked the woman as he reached Kyle.

The woman wore a fleece top, and her hair was long and cut short on the sides. Her eyes widened as she took in Jim from head to toe and back up. She bowed and backed away and got in her wagon and drove off. Kyle climbed onto the snow bank and grabbed a statuette of a woman's lower body and a lion's head.

"Cool," said Kyle.

Jim took the statuette from Kyle and turned it around with his fingers and walked back holding Kyle's hand. He made a vague connection with the woman and the Tyvek-sided, pagoda temple in the weed lot behind the Agway. Jim had heard talk of an uneasy acceptance forced upon the town by this odd and private sect. Nobody was quite sure what went on in there. They called themselves The Temple of Female Empowerment. Jim was also aware of the controversy surrounding them having something to do with the woman who killed her babies out in Redmond. Her boy babies. Jim noticed Kyle's little hand holding his. Kyle worked his fingers and squeezed Jim's hand. He looked up and smiled.

"I like you, Jim," Kyle said quietly, and he put his head against Jim's thigh. Jim knelt on one knee and thought maybe he should hug Kyle.

"You're a good little guy, Kyle," Jim said softly. "I like you too, man."

***

Later that night when the children were in bed and R.E.M. played softly in the kitchen ... *this could be the saddest dusk turned to a miracle*, Nancy sat on Jim's lap and straddled his legs. Jim caressed his hands up and down Nancy's spine. "That's nice," Nancy said and played with Jim's curls on his neck. "I like you touching me like that," she added softly. "It's good." Jim combed his finger around Nancy's ear, and Nancy liked that too. She sensed it was good for Jim. To be a man for a woman. To want her. Nancy felt a healing in Jim. She had reached out her hand to him from the other side of the kitchen table. Nancy had come over, and Jim guided her onto his lap. Nancy knew Jim would not have initiated — that he avoided being assertive. But Nancy spoke gently to Jim's manhood, which she sensed was scared and hiding. Maybe wounded. She moved closer to Jim's face and lips and released her thoughts. Nancy felt warm and tingly. Her undies were wet, and she throbbed for him. Nancy gently stroked her hands across Jim's pectorals. "There's somethin' about me maybe you should know … That I really don't understand."

"Kyle told me."

"What!?"

"Hey, he's the dude. Put a gun right to my head and basically said, 'Hands off the mommy.'"

"Come on!" Nancy laughed but felt what Kyle was asking: "Who are you anyway? Do it with my mom, and she's gonna get pregnant and don't think about runnin' off 'cause everything is seen … Our actions and our choices follow us into Eternity, and oh, by the way, I happen to have feelings for you, so don't you leave me too."

"He's a sharp, little guy. There's no putting anything by him."

"You either."

"I guess."

"Kyle is fighting for a good life — to know what's right, what's true."

"Yeah?" Jim asked. He looked at Nancy's lips and noticed their pretty curve that pouted in the middle.

"So how do you feel about what he said?" Nancy asked, and she bit her lower lip.

"Hey," Jim said, looking down. "I mean … I like you. Really like you. It's OK this way … I fixed the roof."

Nancy laughed and her eyes teared a little. "You're sweet. Proud of you for doing that. Gettin' to be the man around here."

"First thing I ever fixed in my life."

"So what are we gonna do together?"

"Go into The Great White Way?"

"The Way?"

"How about a couple of days? Part of The White Way. Been dying to get out there. Something I wanna do. Say I did it. You know, feel good about it. Feel good about myself."

"Who are you?" Nancy asked before she could stop herself.

"What?"

"Nothing." There was a moment of uncomfortable silence. "I've got other things to fix that'll make you feel good. Safer."

"We'll keep out of trouble."

"Things can happen, Jimmy. I have children now. 'Sides, that's what my mom and dad did. Gone for weeks. Me alone. Don't want to raise my kids like that and become my parents all over again. An outdoor junkie. What about your parents?"

"Parents?" Jim asked flatly, lowering his head and looking at Nancy as if straining to understand her.

"Yeah, parents. I mean do you have them?"

"Kind of."

"See what I mean? Oh forget it. Maybe you don't want to hang out with me. I have a lot of baggage now. Not so free and easy."

"I want to be with you. Least I think I want to."

"Think?"

"Yeah I do. You guys are good for me, somehow. David and you both. How about one week max. It'll be good to get out of here."

"Long as you can have it both ways."

"Whaddya mean by that?"

Have me. Feel good. No responsibilities. No consequences. Leave any time. No commitment, Nancy thought to herself, but said, "Nothing I guess."

"So one week, it'll be fun. How about it?" Jim asked.

"Last one week pleasure cruise I came back five months later: pregnant, sick, married and even resurrected. How about that!?" Nancy laughed.

"Bit much," Jim replied, suddenly feeling an uncomfortable tension as he avoided Nancy's eyes. From nowhere he heard himself say, "I would like to have been there with you. Sounds beautiful. The River. Maybe just you and me."

"Really?" Nancy asked as a whole ball of feelings birthed inside of her. "That's sweet," she said as her eyes welled with tears. "Will you kiss me," she asked in a whisper.

Their lips met for the first time, and Nancy buried her tongue and squeezed Jim's waist with her thighs, and Jim throbbed, and he couldn't breathe. He felt Nancy grow hot and sweaty, and he wanted her like nothing else he had ever wanted. Jim felt himself growing into a new shell that would house an unfolding power. A power that was buried and calling to burst forth. A power that could hold Nancy's hand. Fix her roof. Care for her. Take her in his arms and drive his passion into her until she moaned in hoarse ecstasy. A power of deep calm with Nancy — to lead a household. To be righteous.

"Wow."

"Do you like kissing me?"

"Not at all."

"Stop it," Nancy laughed, and she pulled Jim's face to her chest and held his head. Jim felt her soft sweater and full chest. She smelled like baby powder; it was nice. "You need to know … nothing works, Jimmy. Tried every type of birth control. Nothing. It's not meant to work or something. I mean, except abstinence and morals and all. So if maybe it should happen, it all happens. Need you to know that," Nancy said, and her throat thickened because she felt like Jim was going to get scared and leave and never come back. A desperate, hollow feeling overcame Nancy because all of the guys she met now were babies and selfish. She was going to be alone and old and ugly and poor with wild and crazy, spoiled boys with no father and —

"All right, Nance, I'm getting there … sort of," Jim said, lowering his eyes. Nancy smiled and tried to push aside the empty feeling. She liked Jim nestled against her. It had been a long time since she held a man close to her chest. Nancy felt warm and feminine and relaxed with Jim. Holding and kissing him felt easy. A familiarity came upon Nancy as if a rush of stars and wind had blown them together from a future moment of timelessness. Nancy's heart secretly throbbed.

"Is that what those women are about?" Jim asked, growing hot and flush.

"They keep coming to the driveway," Nancy replied, and she didn't know how to tell Jim about everything else, all the wonderful feelings and occurrences: the woman next door whose emphysema suddenly cleared after Nancy placed her hand on her head. The alcoholic husband on the other side who stopped beating his wife because Nancy heard them one night and prayed for him. The creek behind the trailer park that sparkles clear and full even during the deepest drought. All the wild flowers that pack Nancy's yard alone. The whispers in the trailer park and in town about Nancy. The people who walk their babies by. And the blonde woman and her entourage, who bring barren women up to her mobile home, who are then able to become pregnant with twins and triplets. "There are lot of things I don't understand," Nancy added. *All the signs and wonders,* she thought to herself and felt the hidden thrill and warmth rush upon her.

"Understand beautiful, uncut bowls deep in backcountry with the days getting longer and the crystals light and downy with nobody out there but us?"

"That I understand. I mean it's not like I don't want to go. Should we go?"

"We should do it."

"You're being called from the world."

"What's that?"

"Oh, never mind, how long do you want to tour?"

"Figure on a couple of days. See how we feel. The weather."

"OK," Nancy sighed. "We've got the roof, my babies, gear, food and maps. I mean I've never been in that far."

"I've talked with David. Got your parent's stuff. I feel pretty good. Have an avy course now."

"We'll follow Mom and Dad's spirit."

"Their spirit?"

"Yeah, their spirit."

"OK," Jim said uncomfortably and quickly added, "wished I'd met your dad. David told me a lot about him."

"He'd give you a hard time … Naw I know you guys would hit it off. You want to be good in the mountains, don't you, Jimmy?"

"Tryin'."

"Daddy would know that. He'd like it. Probably never see you two again."

"So how many more face plants do I have to do learnin' to tele?"

"Ninety-eight, 99 … 100, done … When are we shooting for?"

"End of the week."

"This is good for you. I like the passion," Nancy said, brushing Jim's hair to the side.

"It has been good out here. Hey, gotta go. Up early tomorrow greasin' cats. David already gave me the time off."

"So you had it planned anyway? Typical guy. But that's good, actually. Do I have to be a guy now?"

"No, definitely not. I like you as a woman. Just this way."

"Will you kiss me again?" Nancy asked softly, and she put her hands on his chest. "You're a nice kisser."

"Well, sure, I mean …" Nancy leaned forward to let Jim take her closer. He gently pulled her near, and they kissed deeply then looked into each other's eyes for a long time. Jim stood, and Nancy stayed wrapped around his waist with her thighs and legs; and her arms around his shoulders. Jim put his face in the nape of her neck.

"Bye."

"Bye."

"You gotta let go now."

"I don't want to let go."

Nancy slowly slid off. They held hands and separated.

"I'll come by after work tomorrow."

"Bye," Nancy whispered.

"See you later," Jim said softly.

He lifted his hand, and Nancy tilted her face to invite Jim's touch. Jim brushed the back of his finger tips gently down Nancy's cheek, and it felt good — Nancy made him feel good. Jim felt a new beginning: a force charged by Nancy's admiration, eager to climb mountains, to ski powder shots and to take Nancy in his arms. Jim sensed himself changing and journeying into a new land where familiar rules and boundaries were vanishing.

CHAPTER 7

2 BRICK AND SHAG CARPET

On the other side of the Powder Horn range, it was down to Butch, Jonesy, Bird Man and Deek.

"SKI TRIP, SKI TRIP, SKI TRIP," the guys chanted as Butch snapped on gum and the plane banked for its descent into Aspen Crest. The plane landed, and the guys reached over their seats and slapped each other on their balding heads. "WHEW HA COWBOY!" The other discrete passengers were wrinkled men with second and third wives their daughter's age. Their young wives were dressed in fur coats, hiking boots and tight jeans. They all tried to ignore Butch and the guys, who gawked and ribbed each other. When the plane stopped, the guys stood in the aisle in their T-shirts and parkas and resumed chanting as they stepped out of the hatch. "SKI TRIP, SKI TRIP, SKI TRIP."

"Guess you boys're gonna have a good time," the captain said and winked.

It was bright and blue. The January air stung Butch's eyes as he stepped down the ramp. They walked into the Aspen Crest terminal, which was lined with boutiques and Native rugs and paintings on the walls. Aspen Crest was not Powder Horn and not even Aspen Crest but Slippery Rock. Corporate marketing at the Aspen Crest Resort didn't like the name Slippery Rock, so they formed and named their own town. Aspen Crest — the ski area — has always been there, over The Pass, on the opposite side of Powder Horn and was one of the hottest areas anywhere, just impossible to get to until recently. Now because of the new airport, the area exploded with condos, conference centers, bulldozed and manicured slopes, high speed capacity quads and live jazz bands at midway lodges that served French chardonnays and poached salmon. But Butch and the guys knew Aspen Crest as just "The Crest" and have come out on the annual ski trip since their single days. Back then they had to fly to the state capital then drive for hours. But it was worth it. The Crest was always empty. It offered — and still does — some of the steepest, most challenging terrain in the world. And the guys hit it hard — a big pack of them. For Butch, The Crest goes back even further: his mother brought him here to learn to ski when he was a child. Butch knew it had something to do with his deceased father. Now the guys were down to four. Except for Butch they were overweight with layers of gray and wheezing through the terminal. Deek and Bird turned in circles and dropped their jaws as they passed firm and ski-tanned girls in ghetto jeans, hanging from their shapely behinds.

"Oh yeah," said Butch to the guys, "I love my wife. I love my wife. I'm happy I have kids. Keep saying it. Helps."

"I love my wife. I love my wife," they all moaned as they piled into each other and stared at one girl talking on a pay phone with long, blonde hair and a tee-shirt with nothing on underneath. Pierced everything. Butch watched her firm nipples slide under her T-shirt.

"Whooom," Butch whimpered in a high pitch as he flexed his muscular arms and chest. Unlike the other guys he was rock-hard, loved skiing, took it seriously and trained year round. Butch went for hair implants and wore them long in the back and cut short on the sides without a trace of gray. They were all from the Midwest, and Butch and Deek were managers in a meat packing plant.

"SKI TRIP, SKI TRIP, SKI TRIP," they continued chanting on the way to baggage claim. They stopped at the carousel and dropped their mouths again and stared at another girl. Her boyfriend gave them a blank look.

"When was the last time you got it?" Jonesy asked the guys.

"I don't know what it is anymore."

"Um, um — that sweet thang. F'n guy does not, and I mean does not know what he's f'n got there. Kids these days don't see women from men."

"Right here, square on," said Butch, and he leaned back and held up his arms like he was carefully placing something down on his face and wiggled his tongue from side to side. The other guys laughed.

"Hey, man, it is bruuuuu …tal, really."

"Maybe we're gonna have to stop coming out here."

"Why stop now? I'll forget forever," said Butch and everyone laughed.

"You callin' Lynn?" Jonesy asked Butch.

"Yeah, yeah, she's not at all happy with this one," replied Butch.

"Got the whole treatment right? Holds out."

"Butchy boy, you're meat now my friend, none for months."

"Sex as a weapon."

"None of 'em are happy," said Deek.

Everyone laughed except Butch because it was true. The last ski trip argument with his wife made him shake, and Butch felt like he was fighting for something that was slipping away for good. "Goin!" he blurted at her. "Ski trip. Known about it for a year." That night he found pictures of them skiing together back when, and Butch got a pit in his stomach as he traced her curved figure with his thick finger. He felt like some cosmic betrayal had trapped him in her strident heft that had nothing in common with how she was back then. And all he could see now was his wife becoming her mother. "Nightmare," Butch said to himself. He pushed away all the painful images and feelings that burned like a smoldering fire.

"Gotta hold out," said Butch to the guys, and he put his arms around them. "It's down to us now. The bitter end is near." They held each other like a line of dancers and chanted.

"SKI TRIP, SKI TRIP, SKI TRIP," and stopped and stared at another girl walk by.

"What if we never came back," said Deek.

"Very simple."

"Just never go back."

After the guys got all their skis and luggage they stood out front and waited for their ride.

"PUUUSSAY!" shouted Jonesy over the whine of jet engines. Everybody laughed and howled into the parking lot.

"Man, you got it bad."

A van pulled over and a girl hopped out.

"Spread Eagle Condos?"

The guys stopped talking and laughing and opened their mouths and leaned back.

"Wow," said Butch.

"And you're gonna drive us there!?"

"Yeah guys, come on!" she laughed. "I mean Golden Eagle Condos."

She was young and tight with a vivacious smile and straight brunette hair. Her eyes flashed a hazel green, and she even had little freckles on her cheeks from skiing in the sun. Her face could highlight anything from evening wear to the jeans and designer flannel shirt she wore. Her hand-sized breasts bounced a little and rose.

"Let's party," Butch said to her.

"OK," she replied and flashed Butch a smile.

The other guys raised their eyebrows.

They loaded their bags and piled into the van and sat with their mouths gaping. Butch got in the front seat and felt suddenly hot.

"So I'm Butch. What's ya name?"

"*I'm* the Snow Princess," she replied emphasizing I'm as if there might be some confusion.

"The Snow Princess," Butch repeated looking back and dropping his jaw with his mouth closed. The other guys laughed a little. "You have some girl friends?" Butch asked. "Maybe you all can come by for a little fun tonight."

Jonesy crossed his hands back-and-forth. The other guys smiled and laughed.

"He's kidding," said Deek.

"Cool, that's what everyone's saying again, I'll come by," she replied enthusiastically and bounced up.

"Well, we'd just love to have you," said Butch, turning and winking to the guys.

When they reached the ski area and the condos, Butch reached into his back pocket and pulled out his wallet to write the condo number on a card.

"I don't need that," she said, turning and looking Butch over with her eyes. "I'll find you. Let's party!"

The other guys watched and raised their eyebrows again.

"You're on, Butch, man," laughed Bird. "Can't let the Snow Princess down."

"Yeah, you can't let me down," she said and bounced around beaming and laughing a little.

"Come on guys, let's hustle," groaned Jonesy as he pulled his graying bulk out of the van. "We've got all day; that's two runs for me then the bar."

"See you later, Butch," she said as the guys finished piling their stuff onto the sidewalk that was brushed spotless.

"OK," said Butch, and he gave her a wink and grin, "later." She drove around the complex circle and smiled and waved on the other side.

"Butcher Man, why do I get this feeling she likes you. Maybe you haven't lost it after all. Think you can still fire up the ole boy?" Deek asked and everyone laughed and slapped each other on the back and started lugging dunnage and ski bags into the condo.

* * *

An hour later they were at 10,450 feet on the top of The Crest and stepping into breezy sunshine from the tramway house. Butch wiped his red Herman Munster ski boots on the astro turf that was swept clean by an attendant and felt the warmth from a roaring fire in an architecturally perfect hearth. "BS, man," he said to himself looking at the hearth and the fire and the green turf. Another attendant offered him a tissue from a box. He ignored the kid and leaned forward over his poles, snapped his goggles in-and-out and felt the synthetic curls of hair on his neck. He looked at himself suited up in a tan one-piece and ready for action. He was the Butcher Man again. Skier. Nothing else mattered. There was no other life. Butch watched the guys stuffed in their pants and parkas and felt uneasy. How long would it be before he was the same as them or old and shriveled and far from the Butcher Man? *You're dead a long time,* Butch thought. *Get it now while you can.* He grabbed his skis from another attendant and lay them down and clicked in his toe and heel. Butch pushed off with a gaggle of women and children in helmets on the groomed surface and slid easy turns. Except for Black Forest and North Peak, every slope at The Crest had a groomed side now. "Not skiing," Butch said to himself as he watched little kids slide down what used to be a decent bump run. Butch passed it off and figured on a couple of top-to-bottom cruisers with the guys, then dropping into the lower flanks of North Peak. He knew the guys wouldn't ski what they used to and would end up in the bar watching a game. The guys stopped on a cat track, heaved over their poles and panted.

"What's it gonna be this year, Butcher Man?" asked Deek.

"Only one left's the big one," said Bird.

"Yeah … maybe," Butch replied as he looked up at the rock spires of North Peak and the sets of out-of-bound couloirs streaming down in steep arrays.

"Cochran's, man," said Bird. "She's waitin' for The Butcher."

"Go right ahead, my friend. Got a wife and family now. That's my excuse. I'll watch from below," said Jonesy.

Butch kicked off, and the guys followed in a stiff, thigh burning, chest heaving bunch. Butch felt good. *Cardio and weights always pay off,* he thought. *Power squats. Protein shakes and vitamins. Who says you can't roll back the years?* He had new boards, and they felt sweet. Butch turned it on and dropped into some powdery bumps and spanked them from crest to crest. The refracted crystals exploded in his face. "Get it on, man," Butch said to himself. After a couple more runs of mixing it up from steep to bumps to cruisin', the afternoon light grew rich, then a pink alpine glow spread from the western horizon and radiated around North Peak. Butch shouldered his skis at the top of the last tram, ducked behind the summit house and started kicking steps up North Peak. It felt good, like being home again. *Real skiing,* Butch thought. *Get me some.*

"Bar," Deek yelled as Butch appeared over the summit house and gave the thumbs up. The guys knew Butch was going to scout or fire off a balls run. They liked that.

Butch ducked the orange rope and ignored the boundary, warning signs. "Screw it," Butch said to himself. "Place used to be open and free." He made the rock-exposed ridge and stepped carefully to the edge. A funnel peeled away below his toes and little balls of snow rolled down and collected upon themselves and disappeared. "Nice," Butch said and gazed at the untracked couloir, which dropped into pink and cream-colored light. Butch carefully lay down his skis and turned and faced the slope. He gingerly kicked in and down. It felt good. A soft but firm base. Butch kicked-up and lay his skis side to side and clicked into his bindings. He closed his eyes and rolled his shoulders and squatted up and down and breathed and rolled his neck. He thought to himself how he's done Jimmy's Couloir before. But it was the first day, and he hadn't been skiing all winter. He liked that no one had been down there. Jimmy's was special and for him alone. Butch felt the drop calling him. He side-stepped to the edge and dropped in. *Easy, easy, relax, man,* he thought to himself, *you still got the charm.* Butch fully committed to the drop. There was no coming off the fall line. He hopped tight turns, and the pack was soft and only shin deep. Butch felt good, and he closed his turns and sucked up and aired down a vertical section and whooped and shouted and landed and reached over with his downhill pole and kicked around. The funnel opened and eased. Butch reflexed left, popped over a cliff band, landed in the bowl below and made fast wide turns on his shaped skis. He ducked the boundary line at the bottom and didn't turn back. *Patrol catches you now and the trip's over,* Butch thought and looked from side to side for red coats. *Nothing. Oh yeah, the kid's still hot.*

At the bottom the guys weren't in the bar, so Butch stomped back to the condo. When he rounded into the complex, he could hear music thumping from the unit. *Sounds like they found some fluff,* Butch thought. He left his skis and poles by the lockers, then opened the door and got knocked over by a wall of perfumy, sweaty tequila smell. Ancient disco music blasted on Deek's boom box. Jonesy was on all fours in nothing but his drooping underwear with the girl in the van straddled on top of him in her jeans and bra and swinging her shirt.

"BUTCHERMANNNNNN!!!!!" Deek blurted, and his face was red and swollen, and he was absolutely blasted. "TEEEEQUUUUILLL-LA!!! WHEEEEW HAAAA!!!

"No, it goes like this," the girl shouted and got off Jonsey, and her shiny hair flung around, and her nice chest pointed. She grabbed Butch's hand and flung it up and didn't seem the least intoxicated. She took Bird Man and Deek and Jonesy by the hand, and they all got in a line. "The hustle!" she laughed and doubled over. The other guys were holding shot glasses and bottles of tequila and beer and bellowed.

"Whooooooo!" They raised one arm with her and swerved to the side and back. The music throbbed. "YOU SHOULD BE DANCIN', YEAH."

There was a pounding at the door that no one heard or cared about. The cheap flooring creaked, and a cracked, hollow space opened where one of the guys had fallen against the wall. An overstuffed chair was on its back and popcorn was burning in the kitchenette.

"Whoooooooo! Come on, Butchy boy, we're partyin' down with the Snow Princess."

Someone shoved Butch a shot and a Bud. He stood in his one-piece and stared at the girl's body, and his throat tightened. Butch fired back the shot and pounded the beer. He stepped over and put his hands on her bottom and started dancing. "Yeah!" she yelled and swung her wild hair from side to side, and Butch stared down at her and felt his hands run up her curved sides. She unzipped his suit and pulled it off. It fell to the floor and wrapped around his ski boots. Butch danced in his long underwear and boots. She kept dancing and bent down and undid his boots, and Butch stepped out of everything. Then she slid off his top and lightly ran her hands around his chest. Butch felt a surge, and he pulled her toward his groin. Her hazel eyes widened, and she smiled. She swayed her hips and bent over and pulled down his long underwear, and Butch danced in his jockeys. Deek yelled, "Shots!" And passed everyone a glass.

"YOU SHOULD BE DANCIN', YEAH" pounded out, and Deek took off his shirt and his sweaty gut hung down. He stood cross-eyed and slurred to the Snow Princess, "Topless, every … one's got … be taaahhp… less."

"Whew yeah!" she yelled with her vivacious laugh and reached behind and undid her bra and bounced free, and the guys bellowed,

"Whooooooo haaaa!" as their pasty-white guts glistened with sweat.

Butch looked down at her chest, and he pulsed huge in his jockeys as she danced closer and cocked her hand and lightly ran it up Butch's shaft and opened her eyes and smiled. Butch cupped her breasts which were uplifted and jiggling, and she raised her arms and swayed close to his crotch. Butch was busting out down there, and he blushed when her hand passed by again. He stepped into his bedroom to pull on a pair of jeans. Butch breathed hard through his nostrils a mixture of stomped-down emotions. A tear squeezed from the corner of his eye, and he quickly wiped it away. He'd been having trouble with erections with his wife … with their forced interest in each other. *No problem now,* Butch thought. *At all.*

"Come on, dance with me," the girl shouted, following Butch into the bedroom. She took Butch's hand. She let go and smoothed her hands up and down his broad pectorals, and her eyes opened wide again, and she swayed her hips. Butch could feel her firm nipples on his bare chest as she drew close. Two of the guys fell and crashed onto a standing light that went out. Deek stood up and swayed and puffed out his cheeks and a guttural sound exploded.

"Whoa …. alllIffffff," as he heaved, and a wave of vomit splashed against the light, rose-colored wall.

"WHEWWWWWWW!!!" shouted the Snow Princess, and she reached up and swayed her arms and looked down.

"YOU SHOULD BE DANCIN', YEAH."

"Hey, come on this is gonna get ugly," Butch shouted to her. "Let's get out of here."

"Yeah? Already?" she pouted.

Butch pulled on a fleece top and a pair of jeans. He went out and found her bra and shirt. They both swerved through the guys, and she danced as Butch shouted to them, "yeah right" and smirked with disgust. He knew they would be even more useless for skiing tomorrow, and an empty feeling threatened to grow in his core, a feeling that kept returning again and again. Butch and the girl pulled on their jackets and boots.

"Whew, they're too much," she exhaled and laughed as the two stepped into the cold, evening air. "Come to my place. I have a hot tub." They walked out of the complex and down the service road to a line of original ski houses at The Crest.

"Right, good luck getting any vert out of 'em tomorrow. So what's your real name?" Butch asked as the girl bounced along beside him.

"Um, I'll be … Tami Barkley … just because it's so … doable."

"Doable, yeah," Butch smiled. "Dan or Butch. Butcher Man. The guys call me that."

"Nice," Tami said smiling, passing her eyes over Butch from head to crotch. "Here's my pad, or maybe that's not the word anymore," she said and laughed. They stepped up to an old A-frame structure, and it was dark and mildewy inside. Butch wasn't sure what he was looking at. There was a pile of Hart and Scott skis in a corner that looked like leftovers from a garage sale. A yellowing poster curled off a wall and showed a guy skiing in a cowboy hat and was titled "Billy the Kid." A lava lamp slowly boiled up and down and some kind of crusty pot with a sterno can underneath sat against a wall. "Oh, fondu. Think that's long out," Tami said as she followed Butch's eyes. "Here, throw your coat anywhere." They both peeled out of their jackets. Butch kicked off his boots, and the deep, rust colored, shag carpet felt soft and oily on his socks. The layout was open and swept to a kitchen with Z brick lining the walls. There was a large, pine dining table where a pair of ski boots, that also looked like they were from a lawn sale, lay on their sides. Crumpled on the floor was the polka dot mat of a Twister game. "Hey, music!" exclaimed Tami as she bent down to a long row of dusty, vinyl records and pushed up the lid on a nicked stereo cabinet. The record crackled a muffled chorus singing, "up up and away ... for we can fly." Butch stood there. He realized that he had not been alone with another woman since before he met his wife. Butch looked at Tami's shape and back and hair, and his chest grew heavy.

"My kids would like that," Butch said.

"Ah-uh."

"It's Twister, right? Haven't seen that in years."

"You don't have to talk about it."

"Wife and kids. We could all play together."

"You don't have to talk about it," Tami said again cheerfully but firmly.

"Hey, maybe I shouldn't be here."

"But she's not me now."

"What?"

"I'll make pasta. I have champagne."

"Yeah?"

"Here, you open this." Tami handed Butch a bottle of champagne, and he started untwisting the cork. Tami watched him as she filled a pot with water and got cheese and things from the frig. "You have a nice body you know," she said softly and gave Butch a coy smile.

"I didn't know that."

"Yes you did silly. There's still a lot in you. Saw you on North Slide today."

"Really?" Butch pronounced and smiled. He liked that she saw him. Butch knew that he skied well. He wanted to keep skiing hard and well.

Skiing was what he lived for.

Butch found two champagne flutes in a cupboard that he didn't want to spend much time looking through. There was some kind of gray film on the shelf, and he picked the two cleanest glasses he could find. Butch poured the champagne. Tami came over and stood close to him.

"Hey, cheers," she said softly.

"Sure, cheers."

"How long do champagne bubbles last?" she asked. Butch didn't know what to say. "Come on, hot tub!"

"Cool."

"No, hot, hot." Tami went into a bedroom and came back wrapped in a towel. "This is yours," she said and handed Butch a towel.

"Perfect."

Butch stepped into the bedroom and changed and came out with the towel around his waist. Tami forced open a sliding door that was frozen in place and went out and pulled off the lid on a cedar tub that steamed. She slid off her towel, and Butch caught a clear view of her curved and perky body and a tight, full bush. His pulse quickened again.

"Hey, come on," Tami said and waved.

Butch filled both glasses once more and carried the glasses and the bottle to the porch and set them in the crusty pile of snow behind the tub. He slid off his towel and climbed in.

"So how old are you anyway?" Butch asked as he melted into the tub with a groan.

"Hey … I have no age really."

Later when a single candle lit Tami's bedroom, she straddled him on top and whimpered as she felt him between. Butch ran his hands up and down her curved sides and almost cried.

"Look ... at my belly button," Tami said, and Butch leaned up and gazed at the pierced ring and kept passing his hands all around her nakedness and underneath where she was wet and warm. "That's what's in now. Fuh huh, huh un." Butch pulled her to his face, and he felt dizzy in the musty air. Tami turned and took him, and Butch's eyes bulged. Tami slid onto her back and pulled him on top of her. Butch looked at himself and knew he could still be big and throbbing and want someone. And someone could still want him.

“Come inside me ... deep,” she breathed

“No, should, shouldn’t, gotta, uh, uh, guh ... ho,” Butch groaned, and his face was hot.

“Ooo Butchy, can’t go now. Don’t leave,” she exhaled and worked her heels up and down and held him with her hips and thighs. Her young face glowed beautifully in the candle light. And she lay back and closed her eyes and yearned for her man — with a desire that has no beginning and no end — while Butch pulled on his clothes and pushed aside the fringes where the bed sheets smelled like rotting fish and where old condoms floated in the hot tub, collecting pubic hairs and semen and boiled in a broth of churning mortality. And where cobwebs and dust gathered on the rafters and where the windows grew oily and old beer spills and shots and popcorn and cheese mulched into the shag carpet and where the Z brick lifted from the walls in the corners where no one wanted to look.

CHAPTER 8
PAGAN SON

El Viejo, The Old One, rose because the Fire burned in his chest. As the Fire stoked, the Horizon grew into translucent blue, white and yellow brilliance. The Light filtered into the surrounding darkness, and Viejo looked up and squinted. His heart lifted as he placed his face to the dirt and became thankful. Viejo placed his palms together and gazed at the ragged skeleton by his side and felt no likeness with its fallen existence. El Viejo knew he was being called. But he chose to turn into the darkness to find Nancy and to follow another stirring in his heart of which he was uncertain, but of which he knew the Horizon spoke. El Viejo slipped into his boots and skis, relaxed the cables on his bindings and drifted north with joyful, ghostly strides. The Fire burned on while the Horizon stayed close, and El Viejo knew that he was saved.

As Viejo made his phantom tour in their direction, Jim helped Nancy heave on her pack. He huffed on his, and they both kicked off. They toured along Tin Cup Creek and passed the north couloirs of Mad Dog Mountain. They were headed deep into the backcountry to the Blue Hotel, the first yurt on a string of shelters that linked The Great White Way from south to north. In a few hours, Jim and Nancy were well behind Big Pine. Back at the trailhead the white wagon with all the bumper stickers pulled up, and Princess Ra, Golden Lady and Moon Shadow donned their robes and spread flowers and sunflower seeds around Nancy's rusted-out Subaru. Princess Ra — the woman with the long, blonde hair and short sides — and the others shed their robes, shouldered their packs and started in behind Jim and Nancy.

At the same time, Butch opened his eyes to the bright sunlight streaming into the condo. He groaned as every joint in his body swelled with pain. His lower back was frozen from banging bumps, and his knees felt like they were about to explode. Butch's shoulders were stiff, and he had a dull headache. Butch exhaled loudly, rubbed his stubble and stopped when he smelled the first two fingers on his right hand. *Nice,* he thought. Butch draped his arm over and lay his fingers under Deek's nose.

"Um," Deek grunted as he lay on his back with his hands on his hairy belly and his eyes closed, "that sweet thang."

"Isn't that the best smell in the world, Deek Man? Nectar of the gods."

"Um," Deek grunted again and rolled on his side, breathing stale booze on Butch. Butch's eyes watered, and he waved his hand. "You bury the hatchet?" Deek asked, smacking his lips and keeping his eyes closed.

"No ... Eatin' ain't cheatin'."

"Yes it is. I'm calling Lynn," mumbled Deek as he rolled over and put the pillow on his head.

Butch lay back, and he thought about Tami and regretted not going all the way with her. *Probably never see her again. Never get another chance.* Butch felt his balls that were swollen and probably blue, and he wanted her full lips and mouth all over him down there again. Butch started to pulse hard thinking about her.

"Really sweet thing," Butch said to Deek. "Doesn't get any better."

"Um … you know, probably not."

"I'm up, man. Gonna stick it today. The big one, Cochran's."

"If it feels good do it."

"Only one life to live."

"One life, Butcher Man, go for the gusto."

Butch sat up and dropped his legs to the floor. He swung his knees from side to side, clenched his teeth with pain and watched all the loose play in his knee joints. Butch stood and denied the knots and aches and the feeling that his head was packed in styrofoam. He walked through the carnage of the living room and stepped into the shower, then dried, brushed and shaved. He did fifty pushups, rolled his neck, stretched to the sides, grabbed some toast and downed four ibuprofen.

"I be profen. I be skiin'," Butch said to himself as he sat on his bed and slid on one knee brace and decided to pull on the other one as well. Both his knees were shot. Butch thought about how the doctors told him that he shouldn't ski, let alone bang bumps and chutes. Butch quickly passed this off and stood and flexed his Ski to Die tattoo on his bicep in the mirror: the burning heart crossed by skis and poles. "F it," Butch declared. He dressed in his ski gear and stepped into the cold sunshine. *All right, come on, psyched. I feel good? Yeah, I feel good. Great day at The Crest. Some hot pussy last night. Just like the old days. Little warm up and then scout the big meat and send it. More hot pussy. Find her again. Finish the job.* Butch walked into a dumpster because his head was foggy, and he was looking at his boots. His groin throbbed thinking about Tami. "Come on, man, get with it," he said out loud.

Butch cruised a couple of groomers by a midway lodge where Reggae music pounded first thing in the morning and gave him a headache. After another run Butch started to feel better and went into the lodge and slid out of his one-piece suit. He completely stretched and did more pushups, ate hot oatmeal and started visualizing Cochran's Couloir and all the magazine articles and pictures. Butch thought about how David Winchester had never sent Cochran's, and he rolled his head and brushed this off. *Everybody hits a limit sometime, even Winchester.*

"All right, let's go," Butch said to himself. Spasms of adrenaline shot around his stomach. He pulled out his wallet and took a long look at a small picture of his wife and two boys. Butch's knees trembled, and he dropped to the floor shaking. "Ho," he blurted as his eyes welled with tears. He lifted himself up and knelt and shuffled another picture into view: his father, whom he never met, dressed in 1960's ski gear — a red wind shirt with white polka dots — standing on The Pass in brilliant sunshine. The big thumbs up. Butch found the picture in his mother's dresser when he was a kid. He'd kept it close ever since. Butch stood, zipped his wallet back in his suit, gathered his things and left.

Butch rode the West Lift so he could look up at Cochran's, which he did through a small pair of field glasses, while children and business men in helmets on the quad stopped talking and watched him. Butch knew about Winchester's rule of climbing big drops first, and the thought kicked around his chest. The question was airing and clearing the long rock band that was pasted with white and mostly hidden. *Doesn't matter. Don't do it this year, never gonna, 'cause this is it.* He tried to push away the sad feeling, which sat as a lump in his throat and would not go away. The feeling threatened to spread and paralyze his arms and legs. Butch tucked the field glasses into an inside pocket and exited the lift. He side-stepped up to the cat-track. Butch wanted to get moving and be warm and feel the couloir call him. He wanted to be in touch with Cochran's. "Come on, baby," he spat and said to North Peak and to Cochran's. When he made the track, Butch pulled out the glasses and took another long look. He closed his eyes and visualized the run again. Then Butch skated to the summit chair and got on with a kid holding a paper cup of coffee with a hole punched in the lid. The kid had on a pair of old Rossies and tele boots and bindings. There was a wrap of duct tape around the band of his goggles. Butch took him for a local. The kid blew his nose over the side, looked ahead, then at Butch. His eyes lingered. It bothered Butch, who stared at Cochran's. The kid took a sip of coffee through the hole in the lid.

"Guy in the tan one-piece. Didn't I see you drop down Jimmy's yesterday afternoon?"

"Not me," Butch answered, and he listened to his own voice. It was annoying to be distracted by the kid.

"That's out-of-bounds."

"Really."

"Serious if you get bagged now, dude."

"Don't get bagged."

"Guy lost it jumpin' the band in there last week on a board."

"Figures. Was his name Dude, too?"

The kid ignored Butch's question and took another sip of coffee.

"Got pretty hurt. Screwed it up."

"Don't screw up's the lesson I guess," Butch replied, and he didn't want to say anything more to the kid. Butch figured the kid wasn't even born the first season he stuck Jimmy's.

The summit house was busy, and Butch had to wait for the kid and everyone else to clear, which he did, then ducked behind and quickly kicked up and disappeared over the shoulder. No one saw him. "Free," Butch said, and he reshouldered his skis and slowed his breath and kept climbing. It would be a long climb. When Butch reached the top of North Peak, he was well beyond the mood of any ski area. The exposed, alpine rock was painted with yellow and orange lichen. The wind bit his face, but the sun was warm when he turned to the side. A blue-black sky squeezed all around him. Butch zipped up and swung his arms and squatted up and down. He had to click-in by standing his skis on exposed rock. "Don't even think about walking back down that ridge," he said to himself as he peered over the edge; then back down the way he had climbed. Butch inched his skis closer to the edge and stood tall. He looked straight out over Cochran's and took a few deep breaths, spread his arms and jumped.

Butch was surprised at how beautiful the pack felt and how easy it was to turn. The couloir was wide and pitched over 50 degrees. When Butch dug a platform, he simply aired into the next turn, weightless. Butch knew if he lost it, there would be no stopping. He would tumble forever. He squared to the fall line and hop-turned in perfect symmetry. The mountain was powerful, and Butch felt the rush of gravity and all the space and distance around him. The pitch fell off, and Butch released. The top layer slid into a slough, and Butch knew he was surfing the big one now. *Great if someone was runnin' film. Getting' pics.* Everything began to slide and hiss around him. Butch felt looser and looser on his skis. But he breathed and let the slough pass and cascade over the horizon that was a void drawing closer. The edge dropped away, and Butch felt his skis grind over rock. Butch kicked up and looked down. His stomach turned inside-out.

Butch panicked. He felt sweat trickle down his back along his thermal underwear. Butch flayed his arms and legs as he saw up-close the sheer magnitude of the rock spanning endlessly below. He realized what he had done. "Shit, shit, shit," he sputtered and watched with perfect clarity as he hit the rock … hard. Butch smashed flat on his back and head with an agonizing grunt that collapsed his chest. He couldn't breathe. His skis blew off with the impact as his legs and feet buckled. He somersaulted forward into the air as his arms swung helplessly. Butch felt sick and stupid as he crashed again onto his back. He saw solid blue, the summit of North Peak, Jimmy's shoulder, the upper lift and again — blue, summit, Jimmy's, the lift and again — blue, summit, Jimmy's, the lift … Butch somersaulted into nausea and vomited. The sky and Jimmy's spun together, and puke stung his nose. Butch was in the air for a long time. Then it all stopped. Butch wasn't sure if he was up or down. He quickly patted himself and grabbed his head to make sure it was still there.

OK, OK, fine. Made it. Made it, Butch thought. *Don't get up yet. Wait.* He lay there, and all he saw was white. Butch put his gloves to his eyes and rubbed, but nothing changed. There was a loud ringing, and his whole body pulsed like he was being zapped by a ray gun. *Alright get up now, man*, Butch thought to himself. He knelt and could hear voices. Butch stood, and blue mixed with white, then shapes of people appeared. Butch's head floated back-and-forth, and he shot out one bent, remaining ski pole to keep balance. Butch fought the urge to cry out for his mother. He clenched the pole grip and opened and shut his eyes; and shook his head and worked his jaw. Suddenly everything came into focus. Butch looked down at his ski boots and started walking away toward the cat-track. *Just walk it off*, he thought. *Don't look back.* He stumbled ahead, then turned and witnessed the scene behind: a group of ski patrol and skiers had gathered around a mangled body in the snow. *Keep walking*, Butch thought.

Everything was clear. The sun was white, then it turned solid-yellow and glowed into a deeper and deeper blue background. Rainbow colors hazed upward and fired around Butch's peripheral vision. The colors turned dark, and the sun changed to a warm, white light, and Butch felt like he was walking into a tunnel toward the light. "NO … COME ON … NO!" Butch hollered and hissed saliva through his clenched teeth and squeezed the pole grip, blinking and forcing back tears. "Nothing happened," he shouted. "Fine, gonna be fine." The warm light departed, and the surroundings returned. Butch felt clear again as he walked with his bent pole and heard a yell.

"Hey, Butcher Man!"

"Yo!" Butch yelled as Deek mule-kicked over Slippery Slide; and it was the old Deek, and he was young and tough and spanked from crest to crest.

"He ha Butch!" And the young and slim Jonesy and Bird Man blew by with Donny and Stinger, who followed in tight clothes and long, slim boards.

Butch smiled and waved and shook his head and kept walking. *Just the guys*, he thought — *back then now*. Butch did not want to think about how it didn't make sense. He wanted to speak to himself, to make sure he was OK and still there. *Just walk to the top of Grizzly. Tell the lift guy you lost your skis and ride down*, Butch thought. "Easy," he heard himself say and was relieved and looked up at Cochran's and exhaled, "Whew, awesome. Did it. Skied the big one. Too bad no one was there to get pics." When Butch reached the bottom of the mountain, he slid off the lift and stepped through the ropes. Tami Barkley ran over carrying a snowboard.

"Hey Butch, you skied it!" she said, lowering her voice a little and turning so the attendants wouldn't hear. "Look, it's sooo cool, boarding. Everyone's doing it now." Tami held up a black snowboard with a white graphic of an Eastern figure with a shapely waist and legs; four arms and an orange ring of fire surrounding it all. Aum was written up the deck. Tami wore baggy, off-color clothes and a black ski band. Her shiny hair hung down to her shoulders. "Check this out." Tami stuck out her tongue wide and showed Butch a tongue stud. "Yoahh honna luh thah," she said with her tongue still out. "So-oh cool. Everyone's doing it, and like I wanna tattoo, and my body feels so good because it's young again, and hey you got my blood goin' last night you know. Still want you, big guy. Oh, and come with me," She grabbed Butch by the arm, and Butch felt good about Cochran's and Tami finding him. He felt himself stir down there and was glad they were heading in the direction of her A-frame and bedroom. "We're goin' backcountryin'. Got everything ready. Was up early. It's fun. Ever been telein' and sleeping out in the yurts. Totally cool. Hey, you're carrying The Captain Morgan's!"

They walked all the way to Tami's A-frame with her chatting the whole time. When they stepped inside past the rotting fondue pot, dusty skis and Billy the Kid poster, Tami slipped off her coat, and Butch watched her tight, shapely body and upturned breasts rise from her baggy pants that hung down below her curved waist. Butch unbuckled his boots, kicked them off and took her in his arms and ran his hands around her waist and picked her up and kissed her hard and deep with his tongue.

Butch carried Tami to her bedroom, and they peeled out of their ski clothes as they wrapped tongues. When they were naked, they knelt and faced each other on the bed and Tami got really close and held Butch with her hand cocked. Butch could feel her firm nipples on his chest and smell her sweet scent. Tami took him with the tongue stud, and he snorted through his nose and thrust his pelvis. Tami came back up and worked her way onto Butch, and he felt himself slip inside, and his eyes opened and filled with tears.

"Slow-oh-dow-n, um, feel-eels-so-oh good," Tami breathed as she rode him. She worked her pelvis and waved her arms over her head and closed her eyes. "So, huh, huh big," Tami breathed and fell back. Butch banged his head against her headboard until Tami's chest heaved, and she panted in raspy spasms. They both collapsed onto each other in a tight wrap of skin upon skin.

***

Later that afternoon a thin layer of clouds fingered toward North Peak and the surrounding Powder Horns and gradually thickened. It was showering crystals now in lazy, dry clumps. Butch watched them drift through a background of shifting purple and yellow. His head felt light, and he wondered why he didn't care about not having his toothbrush or even his own clothes. He didn't know where he was or where he and Tami were going. Butch felt himself radiate in and out of his body. He was curious that he just left and didn't bother to say anything to Deek and the guys.

"Do the boots fit OK?" Tami asked as she toured ahead of Butch, gently gliding along and lifting her heel — one then the other — in her plastic telemark boots. Butch looked up then quick-stepped forward. His heels rose, and he fell flat on his face. The oversized mountain pack crashed down on top. He lay pinned and wondered why the snow didn't feel very cold. They were following a parallel ski track along a narrow trail in a silent world of Douglas firs and deep white. Butch crawled on all fours. Tami kept moving, unaware that he had fallen. From behind she was a red, mountain pack and two arms and legs with skis down below. Tami stopped and turned, and Butch caught the profile of her shapely bottom in black shell pants as he grunted onto his telemark skis. Tami's hair was in pigtails, and she wore a thin, patterned headband. "He was about your size — the last boy fr — oh never mind as long as it all works. Hope I packed everything right for you. I mean guys aren't that particular — thermals, top and bottom, extra set of gloves — you one-piece works OK? Hot? Ski band, hat, shades, lip balm, extra socks, all the food, avy shovels, beacons, skins, sleeping bags, pads, a stove, gas … matches! Hope I got everything. Gear is so cool. Are you having a good time? Awesome isn't it?" Butch groaned under the crushing weight of the pack as he rose to his feet. Then he realized his thighs had stopped burning, and the pack was now weightless. The skis and especially the boots were strangely loose. Butch watched a trace shadow of his body peel out and back.

"What's important?" Butch asked and followed his voice as it spiraled in hazy, blue waves into the surrounding white, yellow and purple. Then he answered his own question and laughed, "Will the Captain's hold out!?"

Tami laughed, "Hey, with the Snow Princess nothing lasts, and nothing passes either because everything is always the same, because it's always changing, passing and returning."

"Whoa."

"And you're left with nothing but yourself!" Tami exclaimed enthusiastically. "What could be better? Hey, come here and kiss me again. Exciting," she said lowering her voice and leaning over with her wet hair and sweaty face. "Ravaged me today you know. Get to that love yurt and rock 'n' ro —" Tami stopped as Butch leaned over and kissed her, burying his tongue. But he kept going and for about the tenth time his heels came up, and he fell on his face. The load returned so he couldn't move. "Silly, come on. It's going to be great up there at the Blue Hotel, man."

Tami slid off leaving Butch to heave up onto all fours and finally to his feet. After some indefinite time of Butch sliding along and staring at the drifting flakes and the back of Tami's pack, dusk began to close, and they reached an abrupt slope. "Skin time, Butch the man," Tami said energetically. "Kick and glide is not gonna make it now." Butch stared, then shook his head and pinched his eyes. He patted his hands around himself to make sure his body was still there. Meanwhile, the lazy flakes spiraled and tumbled in red trace lines. Tami waved her hand in front of Butch's face. "Hey, you're not tired out are you? Drop your pack and pop out of your skis." Butch did as he was told and watched like a child as Tami spread on his climbing skins and hers. Together they left the packed trail and dug up to their thighs against the slope in the powder. They switched back and forth until a pine-covered ridge crest was made.

Tami went forward for about 20 feet on the flats, then back and forward again in a grid. All the while she peered at her boots in the gathering darkness. Her pole pinged on something metal. "Ah, found it," Tami said. "Buried." Her voice startled Butch who stared into the descending flakes that looked like drunk fireflies. Tami bent down and brushed off a metal cap and carefully backed up and dropped her pack. She took out her avalanche shovel and started to dig. "Hey, come on, big guy, you've gotta help."

"What's there?" Butch asked and listened to his voice depart into the fading purple and yellow. He wondered why he didn't care about not knowing where he was or what he was doing there.

"It's the yurt, silly. Buried. Awesome."

They dug until a wooden door was excavated out of nowhere. When they had cleared a pit, the plastic sheets of a structure also appeared, and Tami yanked open the door. They stumbled into a black, cold space. Butch pulled in their packs, and Tami dug around for a flashlight. When she snapped it on, the interior of a circular, Mongolian tent appeared. The structure was draped over accordion, wooden sides and pine-pole rafters. There were bunks with foam, a plank floor, counters with some dried goods; and a wood stove in the middle with its pipe shoved through a collar in the ceiling. There were pans and big dented pots under the counters on the floor. It looked like the impacted dirt and grime had been swept clean by the last denizens. Butch looked around. He wanted to speak and hear his voice.

"Where am I?"

"The Blue Hotel," Tami answered. "A yurt. This one's kind of secret. No one's been up here in a while. Cool, eh? Here, you dig around the edge. There's a wood pile somewhere. May have to go down pretty deep. But we've gotta have a nice, hot fire, Butcher Man. Dry out. Get good and warm."

After a while Butch stumbled in covered with snow and carrying an armful of white encrusted wood. The yurt glowed in soft candle light, and Tami was boiling water on a little mountain stove that sounded like a blowtorch. Butch watched the water start to steam. He carefully placed the wood in the stove and opened the damper. Butch watched each of his movements. He found himself staring at the stove door. Butch wasn't sure if he stared for a minute or an hour. He shook his head and shoved in yellowing pieces of the *Aspen Crest Gazette* and lit them with a safety match from a box on the floor. The fire roared to life, and the stove creaked. The yurt swelled with heat, and Butch told himself everything was all right and that he should feel good.

"Hey Tami, come here, baby," Butch heard himself say as he knelt by the stove and felt a slight delay between his lips moving and his voice sounding. "What about a cocktail, you sweet thing?"

"Oooh, like it when you talk to me like that," Tami said and came over and dropped a knee by Butch. They stared into the flames then knelt together and kissed. "Yeah, heat this place right up ... You having fun yet? Isn't this great!? Love being young. Nothin' better than yurtin'. So in now, although I must say I didn't have a big problem with fondue, Twister and central heating. I mean anything that's in is in when you're young. Oh, never mind. Hey, I brought you something." Tami stood and opened the wooden door and reached outside into the frozen wall of snow. She pulled out a pint and opened it at the counter. "Beer, micro brew. Very cool. Made right at The Crest. Now that's *in. Very in*," Tami said, thrusting out her hand.

"Beer," Butch grunted.

"Yeah beer. Guys love beer. Fire that down and get ready for Powder Horn Mud Slides! And bean burritos. I'm cookin', man!"

Butch slid out of his shell boots and his one-piece and sat on a bunk in his thermals and drank the beer. At first he felt and tasted nothing and thought it was frozen until he watched a brown stream run down his chest. He held up the bottle and stared at it for some time. Then Butch took another sip and tasted beer. It tasted good. Butch drank and looked down, and he could see the beer flowing into his stomach like an X-ray picture. He watched the beer with curiosity drain into his gut.

"Mud slides, yeah, let's do 'em!" Butch heard himself say as he looked at his navel and fuzzed in and out of his body.

Tami went outside and packed tin cups with snow and mixed in powder from a packet. She shot each cup full of rum from a tall plastic bottle and stirred it all together.

"Heeeha," Tami said and handed one to Butch. "I got mine." They raised their cups and toasted. "To the world!" Tami shouted. They both drank, and Tami worked her way onto Butch's lap and straddled him in her tight long underwear. When she spread her legs, she drifted a musty odor, and her armpits smelled pungent. The yurt was warm from the stoking fire, and Tami took off her top, and her perky breasts pointed in Butch's face. "Hey," she said softly, "you can drink and suck at the same time. I'd like that."

Tami stroked Butch's hair implants, and her nipples swelled with pleasure from his tongue until she moaned, and the air grew sweet and musty and mingled with spicy arm pits. Butch felt her grow lathery on his thigh. Then he felt nothing, then everything. Butch throbbed and wanted to bury his shaft into Tami and feel skin against skin. Then he blurred away from his body and watched himself with her. Finally Butch slipped away altogether and dreamed wild dreams that were not dreams at all …

***

Later that night Princess Ra and her entourage found the yurt with headlights and by smelling the smoke from the wood stove. After a while they settled into Tami's mud slides and disappeared together into the darkness in a pile of sleeping bags. The tangle migrated until Butch was surrounded in seething, fermented nakedness with one over his face and the other glancing up and down his swollen shaft as they wrapped tongues and growled with pleasure into each other. A third caressed Tami and wrapped with her while Tami watched her own wonder as the lioness-women idols were inserted as sensual objects, then adorned as glistening observers around the periphery. Incense and cannabis rose in a burnt offering until one of Sekhmet's servants, Golden Lady, took Butch's shaft in both palms and worshiped its rootedness in the continual finality of corporal life. She turned, and Butch saw her blonde, short-cropped hair. He watched the aging wrinkles on her back rise and fall and her pelvis work in sweating passion. She raised her arms in strange ritual and groaned with hoarse pleasure when his seed erupted into her barren womb. Meanwhile, the other two, Princess Ra and Moonshadow, circled and chanted his name … Pagan Son … Pagan Son.

CHAPTER 9

SPACE AND TIME

The next morning was blue and creamy as remnant moisture blended into sunshine. The pines stood wrapped in a fresh, dusty cover and nothing stirred. Jim perched with Nancy at the top of a boweled slope well to the north and east of Mad Dog Mountain. A wisp of crystalline dust fell from a branch and drifted their way only to disappear. The wide vista opened to piney ski peaks and distant rock spires. Jim pushed off and shot his lead ski ahead in a casual surf and dug low and square to the fall line. He pictured Red Bone on the same shot. "Come on, man," he said to himself, "hush the mind. Let it all happen." Nancy watched and smiled. She loved Jim's unfolding style that started cautiously then surfed boldly as he twisted and held the line, only to hesitate before flowing back into confidence. Nancy sensed Jim's secret places in his movement. Nancy watched and imagined Jim taking her in his arms as she melted under his driving passion. Jim was coming along, or so Nancy hoped.

For his part, Jim saw the smooth cream open and beckon before him. The blanket twinkled a billion sparkles. Jim felt his shoulders rise as gravity pulled him forward. His feet and skis passed without flaw through the puffy slope. He worked the base up to his thighs and recoiled exploded turns while tightening some and surfing others in a wide arch. His body had stopped aching in frozen sweat, and the sun warmed his back a touch. Every time Jim crossed the fall line, his stomach swooped to his throat, and he nearly closed his eyes to avoid coming off the line and blowing the turn into a tangled digger. But he stayed. He could feel it now. Being right in center. The rhythm. "Yes," he breathed to himself. When Jim spooned at the bottom behind their mountain packs, he lost his balance and fell forward then backward then forward again onto his face. Jim pushed up, dusted himself off and waved to Nancy. He pulled away a shell glove and rubbed his cheek to make sure he was still alive and not transfigured into the powdery blue that glowed all around him. Nancy dropped in, and Jim followed her tight, powerful turns and squared racing discipline as she loosened into a relaxed rhythm with the wild powder. Jim was relieved to feel warm. After spending the night forced into a snow cave — buried in a womb of frozen water — he and Nancy emerged to a brilliant morning: freezing cold and wet, but released into pure, back-country freedom.

"Man, you're getting good," Nancy panted as she skied into Jim and wrapped a pole and arm around his shoulder and smiled. "Been sneaking' out and practicing? Hey, not mad at me for last night are you … Pepe?" Nancy asked, smiling. Nothing entered Jim's mind as the glow in his chest for Nancy spoke to his hands that lifted her shades then his. He gazed into her blue eyes and smiled. Nancy smiled back. Jim took Nancy in his arms and lips and kissed her, bending Nancy back until they both fell into the cold crystals and melted downward as they kissed and laughed into each other. Jim closed his eyes and felt like he was swooping downhill with Nancy, across the fall line and into a strange new region. "Whoa," Nancy said, searching Jim's handsome, green and blue eyes and tracing a gloved finger around his lips, "we're not talking the L-word, are we?"

"Don't know about that," Jim said as he lay on Nancy and looked into her eyes and felt the cold crystals on his thighs and arms. "Not sure what it is."

"Are you?" Nancy asked.

"What?"

"Sore about last night?" Nancy asked, scrunching her pretty face to show concern.

"Was great," Jim said, forcing his enthusiasm.

Jim pictured the night before, where he stood anxiously in the closing darkness and drifting snow as Nancy's face became drawn. She refused to go to the Blue Hotel for some unnamed feeling. With no other option, they dug into the snow and hollowed-out a cave. Nancy said that her father had taught her how to make a snow cave. Jim could not believe they were going to sleep in the snow, but after serious digging they curled up in their bags while a warm candle glowed on the snug walls. Jim's mountain stove purred with a pot of ramen noodles. They were wet but warm. The tiny space cradled them into each other's smiles. They fell asleep laying together side by side in the tight space.

"You don't mean it," Nancy replied.

"Tryin' to," Jim said with a smile.

"Are we gonna get sick of each other?"

Jim didn't answer because he had no idea what to say. But he did feel something inevitable overcoming him. Little by little he was accepting and absorbing Nancy. Beyond thinking and even feeling, something in Jim knew that he and Nancy could go on and on together. But this didn't help the uneasy feeling in Jim's gut when Nancy pressed him with her questions.

"So where are we going, Nance?" Jim asked, ignoring her question.

"Really are getting too hot to handle out there, Jimmy," Nancy said as they pulled each other up and brushed off. Jim unzipped the top flap of his pack and pulled out a laminated map. He traced his finger along the Great White Way as he and Nancy looked at all the handwritten notes left by her parents. "You call it," she said.

"I'd say Rattling Brook … and Peak 21."

"Rattling is OK. I mean it's deep in. I've never been there. Was Mom and Dad's favorite."

"That's on The Way. Would really like to do the whole thing … sometime. Peak 21 … I've heard all the stories … from David. Everything feel OK, Nance?"

"Everything feels fine, more than fine, Jimmy," Nancy said lowering her voice and laughing softly as she slid close. "I'll follow you to Rattling Brook yurt. I'll follow you anywhere." Jim felt his knees grow weak as Nancy traced her finger from one cheek to the other. His face flashed hot. They kissed and then touched foreheads. "Not bitchin' at each other yet," Nancy said softly.

They separated, and Jim grunted up Nancy's pack. Nancy bent down and helped Jim shoulder his. With Jim in the lead they toured north and east into the fresh blanket along the rolling terrain. They crossed the beaver pond that fed Tin Cup Creek and gradually started ascending through an ancient grove of aspen. When they reached the ridge crest, Jim and Nancy dropped their packs and took powder shots, then climbed back to the ridge. They eventually crested above the Rattling Brook drainage in a pale sunset. Nancy and Jim descended in deep powder in the semidark to the yurt that was nestled among the giant Douglases. They were far into the wild backcountry where no other tracks appeared, and Silence pressed all around.

***

Meanwhile, back at the Blue Hotel, Butch sat on his bunk in the stale dark and rubbed his chin. He didn't feel any stubble and wondered why. He watched a guy with long, blonde hair and buzz-cut sides making pancakes on a mountain stove. The door opened spilling in glaring light, and Butch squinted. He realized the guy was a girl, and there were two others by her side. Tami came in carrying a plastic tub packed with snow. She dumped it into a big pot on the wood stove.

"There, melt water," she said, panting and flinching as she straightened and braced her back with her hands. "Whew," she exhaled, looking at Princess Ra. "That's a party last night … I guess. Different anyway. Always something new." Butch listened to Tami's voice and thought it was someone else. It was deep and raspy.

"It's our lifestyle," Princess Ra said matter-of-factly as she snapped back her coarse, blonde hair and slid pancakes onto plastic plates. Her features were hard and angular.

"Lifestyle … right," Tami replied. "Kind of like anything goes."

"Anything does go," Golden Lady replied and smiled dryly, turning and revealing her short hair.

"So I mean just out of curiosity, what are you guys into?" Tami asked.

"We're pagans," Moonshadow answered, looking at Tami. Tami looked back at her crew-cut head.

"Pagans, OK … got it; always something," Tami said and went on to herself, "Hippies, yippies, rednecks, disco, fixed heel, free heel, snowboard, noboard, fondue, microbrew … back to pagans!" … She watched Butch.

Butch stood and creaked his way with bent knees in his long underwear and bare feet to the door. He stepped out and squinted; then realized he viewed the world through a tunnel as darkness closed his periphery. He looked down at his feet on the snow with his narrow vision but felt nothing. He did not have to pee and this puzzled him. When Butch stepped back inside, he looked at Tami in the light from the open door and noticed that her face was rounder and creased. Her hair was duller and her figure seemed swollen.

"Hey, Butch the man," Tami rasped. "How's it goin'? You ready for some serious tele fun today? Whew, need to sit down," Tami said, and she sat on the bunk with her elbows on her thighs and her mouth open.

Butch creased his brow and tried to focus on her face. He felt scared and hollow like he couldn't talk. He worked his jaw in circles.

"Hell yeah, show me to her, Tami babe," Butch heard himself say.

"That's the spirit," Tami blurted with effort and groaned as she bent down to get a zip bag of oatmeal from his pack.

"So are you guys staying here tonight?" Moonshadow asked flatly, barely animating her somber, chiseled face.

"Maybe," Tami rasped. "I mean are you guys … girls leaving? Maybe we're a little more mellow," she laughed. "Could move on."

"Yeah, where too?" Princess Ra asked.

"Just on," scratched Tami's voice. "We don't like to be tied down … Do we Butcher Man? We freedom ride," Tami laughed, rasping and coughing as Butch stared through his gathering darkness at her. The entourage regarded Butch from the corners of their eyes.

Butch sat down on a bunk. His hand felt his wallet in his ski suit, and he took it out and shuffled through the pictures found in the fold. His wife and children. His lost father. Butch's chest ached. He pictured himself as a little kid with his dad, locked in a snowplow, held in his dad's arms and being taught to ski — something Butch never got to do. Butch had named his first son after his father and after himself. All three share the name, Dan, Dan Michel. Butch wanted his dad to know that he was a skier too … like him. Butch knew what his mother would never say — that his father got whomped out here in the Powder Horns by an avalanche, skiing the wild snow. Butch got this much out of his uncle years ago, man to man at Butch's stag party. "Dad was a skier, a good skier, wasn't he?" Butch had asked his uncle. "What happened to him? I need to know." Butch stuffed the pictures back into his wallet and shuddered heaviness as he breathed in. Darkness slowly but steadily closed around him.

***

That evening the Rattling Brook yurt glowed warmly in the soft light of a kerosene lamp. A woodstove hummed radiant heat, while outside, the Mongolian structure was buried among the massive firs. Up above stars flowed like pulsing jewels in the cold, black sky. It was absolutely still. Jim lit a candle in an Italian wine bottle coated with wax and blew out the lamp. Unsure of what to do, he came over to where Nancy sat on a bunk waiting for him.

"You can take me in your arms, Jimmy," Nancy whispered.

Nancy rolled onto her back to accept Jim, who sat down next to her. Nancy reached up and touched Jim's cheek. He collapsed over her onto his elbow. Nancy slid off her thermal top. Her large breasts spilled out, and she lifted her back to offer herself to Jim. She gave up fighting all the "don'ts" and "can'ts" and "shouldn'ts" and "what if's" that bound her body and mind, and she didn't know why. Nancy inhaled and raised her chest even higher as Jim took one throbbing nipple then the other with his mouth and tongue. Nancy swelled and ached and slid closer to Jim so as to submit to him. Jim watched himself take Nancy. He felt a surge of power emerge from a hidden recess, called forth by her. Jim pulled off his top and held her as they nestled into their billowing sleeping bags. Nancy titled her head and opened her mouth to accept Jim's advance. She lightly pulled him close to her and let Jim hold her tightly around her shoulders and back with his arms and hands. Jim held Nancy and kissed her. Their tongues entwined in sensuous communion. The smell of spicy dried sweat mingled with a musty aura and filled their senses. "Is this OK?" Jim whispered as they peeled into nakedness. Nancy answered by kissing Jim again lightly on the cheek and lips. She slowly parted from him and lifted her breasts to his mouth again.

"Cuh .. onsequences, Jimmy," Nancy exhaled as she lightly guided

Jim's fingers between her open thighs. Nancy pulled the soles of her feet together and lifted her pelvis, inhaling through her nostrils and whimpering with pleasure. Nancy did not want to think. She wanted everything to be alright and to move toward the union with Jim in body and soul she felt was possible. Nancy pushed aside the unspoken doubts and tensions that kept churning to the surface.

"Maybe I'll be OK with it," Jim whispered, and his slithery fingers gently found her again.

A blend of feelings trembled Jim's body. He felt the solitude with Nancy in this far off place and secret darkness. At her mercy, a new and tender manhood blossomed under Nancy's gentle care— as if two Jims lived in his body. Nancy and Jim kissed again with their tongues, and Jim lost his breath. He felt like he was cast into a free fall as Nancy grabbed onto his buttocks, and her whole body trembled under him.

When Jim entered Nancy, her eyes opened wider then closed. She moaned as she drew him in deeper with her heels. Jim ran his fingers through Nancy's hair as he propped onto his elbows. Nancy carefully lifted Jim's head to find his eyes again. She smiled and lost her breath in a sweet moan. Jim kissed her hesitantly, and Nancy lifted her shoulders and breathed into Jim's ear. She closed her eyes, cringing with pleasure as she spread her knees and grabbed Jim's buttocks and panted, "Huh, huh" and arched forward in the grip of deep pleasure. "Cuh, cuh, um, inside, dee he per, buh, buh, baby," Nancy panted as they rocked together, and she opened and closed her eyes.

Jim kissed Nancy on her full lips and raised and looked into her. His chest felt like hands were pulling him to a place above his throbbing shaft, which squeezed within Nancy's hot, wet potency with exploding feeling. He felt overwhelmed by her passion and the sweet, musty smell dizzying his head. Their eyes met and fixed, and Jim felt the other Jim's heart begin to throb with feeling for Nancy. The burning wet intimacy of skin upon skin became the feeling in their hearts. Each cared only for the other. Jim watched as their bodies became a warm light that lifted away from their skin and bones to a place where they entwined in pure affection for each other. Jim held on, and the two rocked together and rose into this great Beyond. But the further and deeper they went, the more Jim folded away into his own numbness. The other Jim, the one who was taking Nancy and feeling for her, receded. He sat with his arms across his knees and put his head down. A heavy feeling overcame Jim. He returned to his skin and to Nancy but felt nothing. He turned his head away from Nancy's eyes. Jim watched himself as he erupted into her. Nancy's salty tears streamed down her cheeks as their sweat and semen and mucus dampened their backs and sleeping bags.

***

At that moment El Viejo glided along toward a column torching into his darkness like a rainbow colored bonfire. He knew this light was Nancy and Jim because he could feel them. Viejo also felt others moving behind, as dark holes in the darkness. The Old One strode toward the column and felt the same agony of guilt and dread that gripped him in hopelessness all those years ago when he first entered his nether world … when he realized what had happened — that he had departed from his wife and unborn child. El Viejo knew that in his past life he was completely free — free to choose and to live with those choices. Yet what and where was he now? Into what had he passed? Such mystery had opened Viejo's eyes. El Viejo, The Old One, knew now that he was created — created and given a fate, a beautiful fate. But he ignored this fate by collapsing into weakness — weakness that rose as a lie to destroy his life. El Viejo had come to see that his freedom was only in relation to his own destruction — that all along he was created and called to a greater freedom. Yet he turned from this calling. Viejo also knew now that every man was in time and had no choice but to witness his material fall away and that Viejo's past life was an act of desperation. The Old One glided along and felt these things. He remembered sitting in his darkness when the first Light of the Horizon appeared, and a gentle arm was placed around his shoulder. As Viejo suffered, he understood more and more about his shy Visitor — his Creator, his Redeemer, his Father. Viejo had come to realize that he cannot escape His love — that such care was in and of and all around Viejo and spoke to him without ceasing. Yet to listen … to accept Him was also a choice — and when reduced to the core, a man was a soul and a choice.

As Viejo glided on his skis — lifting one heel then the other — and realizing all that he realized, he glowed and could see his old skis and boots. His wiry body appeared in his ragged clothes, and he touched himself. He was almost solid again and could nearly smell the cold, mountain air. He began to drift on the snow and to light the surrounding trees with rainbow colors. El Viejo moved with blissful, phantom strides toward what he sensed was a rendezvous with all of his choices.

***

Nancy held Jim for a long time and listened to the silence. The candle glowed into the darkness. She let out a long sigh. "Umm, that was nice, Jimmy; you're wonderful. Leaking all over the place." Nancy rolled over and dug out a small towel from her pack and shoved it between her warm legs. Jim lay curled with his eyes closed. "Hey," Nancy said, laying back down and passing her fingers around his face, "you OK with everything?"

"Not sure what's happening to me."

"Everything's alright. Was incredible," Nancy said, looking up hopefully. She kissed Jim on the cheek. They both closed their eyes and drifted into a drowsy sleep. After a long while, Nancy woke and spoke softly. "What are we gonna do about what's gonna happen, Jimmy?"

"Huh?" Jim grunted. "Have to talk about it now?"

"Have to talk about it sometime."

"Maybe not now."

"Sometime?"

"Sometime. How do you know what's going to happen is gonna happen?" Jim asked, keeping his eyes closed.

"Always does."

"When will you know if it's happened?"

"Soon."

"Can you tell if it's a boy or girl?"

"Yes."

"Not easy to understand."

"Jimmy, you're not gonna leave me are you?"

"Shhh," Jim said, feeling a sudden apprehension in his stomach. He closed his eyes and rolled over on his side away from Nancy.

"Don't turn away, Jimmy," Nancy whispered. Jim rolled back. "Will you hold me?"

Jim opened his bag, and Nancy slid into his arms and pulled her sleeping bag over both of them.

Just then the door kicked open, and Jim jolted to all fours above Nancy. "Jeez, what the … who's there?" Jim asked the darkness as he tensed and looked and lowered while keeping Nancy under him. The candle was just about out, and Jim watched a large figure in a ski suit stare at them. The door banged again and another figure stumbled in. Jim felt the rush of cold air.

"Got company, sorry … we're the pagans! Or at least they are. Three more coming," said Tami as she dropped her pack and stomped snow all over the floor. The water droplets hit the stove and hissed. "You guys 'r cozy in here." Tami paused and lifted her nose. "Wow, reeks of sex," she rasped. "Come on, Butcher Man. That means none for us with all this company, unless we go pagan style. He ha, get everybody in the act … Butcher, settle in. We need mud slides fast. Really spooky, we followed this light the whole way here after it got dark. Took us right to the yurt. The pagan chicks are freaking out, right. Guess they don't like that kind of thing. They're coming. One of 'em had to stop. Get ready for some alternative partying … whoa. They're f'n wild, man … swingers," Tami laughed and coughed and sat down on a stump. "This trip is too much. Butcher Man! Come on, babe; we rule! Break out the Captain's. Hope you guys weren't planning on an intimate affair out here."

Three more bodies with packs stomped inside, and the yurt was stuffed. Princess Ra and the entourage raised their noses and froze. They circled around in feline curiosity until they got close enough to see Nancy. They looked at each other and stood in front of her.

"Yeah?" Jim asked. Nancy lifted her head and right away recognized the entourage by their short hair.

"Who are you?" Nancy asked with a sleepy groan. "Why do you come to my trailer?"

"We're followers of Sekhmet — want you to know you have special powers from her," Princess Ra replied. "Fertility powers."

"Now this is getting interesting," Tami said, digging stuff out of her pack.

Butch sat down slowly on a bunk. His darkness was nearly complete, and he was too afraid to speak. He lay back and closed his eyes and left his body again. It kept happening all day. Each time he fell, he lay and drifted off to look at his body. Butch now found himself outside of the yurt on the ground. The snow was gone. He sat against a tree on the dirt with his head wrapped in his arms and wept.

"Let's not get into it," said Nancy. Jim felt her tighten. "Some vague, new age thing," she added, rolling over into a ball.

"Guess we've got an open mind," Golden Lady said under her breath, and she raised her fingers at Nancy like claws and hissed. Her stringy, blonde hair was trimmed below a sweat-soaked headband. The candlelight revealed traces of creases and wrinkles on her face and brow.

"Stop it," Princess Ra shot at Golden Lady and looked at Nancy with concern. They all moved away to their packs and started to unload stuff onto the floor and bunks.

"Perfect, a cat fight," Tami said, breaking an uneasy silence. "Just what we need, eh Butch? Hey, what I really need is a drink and then something to eat. Let's party. Peace and love everybody." Tami went outside with mugs ringed through her fingers. She came back with snow packed in each. Tami mixed up mud slides for the gang. Then she and Moonshadow got water boiling for dinner. "Mac 'n cheese, something easy," Tami said hoarsely to Moonshadow, coughing and hacking. Tami groaned and rubbed her back. "Whew man, long day. Feelin' it now."

"Is he alright?" Jim asked Princess Ra, nodding over to Butch, who lay stiffly with his eyes open wide. Princess Ra looked at Tami.

"Sure," rasped Tami. "Just tired out. He's an old fart too. Hey, you're cute. May have to trade in Butcher Man for a new model." Tami laughed and coughed. She passed around the remaining mugs. "Here's to Sekhmet."She laughed again and raised her mug high.

After a while, everyone finally went to sleep, and the yurt was quiet with breathing bodies all over the floor and bunks. Jim unwrapped from Nancy and crawled out of bed. He pulled on his thermals, slid into his down jacket and slipped on his boot liners. Jim stepped over the bodies cocooned in bags and made his way through all the hanging shells, undies and socks to go out and pee. Outside, the wind combed in rushes through the firs, and it was snowing … hard. Jim felt small and exposed as the cold clamped his body. He wondered how long he would last without the yurt and his gear.

***

The next morning Jim lay on his back in his sleeping bag with his mummy hood snugged. It was completely dark in the yurt except for Nancy's headlight. She wore her ski hat and fiber-filled jacket and was reading a notebook. Jim watched his breath rise in a vertical column from the small opening around his face. He was warm and did not want to get up or move. A squeaking, creaking sound blended with hoarse grunting and shook the bunk frame.

"He, he, he. Huh, huh."

Jim closed one eye and turned to look, trying to be discreet. He saw a mound of sleeping bag thrusting in and out. The bunk shook harder and a rough female voice moaned.

"Ho, ho, huh, duh, duh … stahh, ha, ha, puh, Buh, Buh, chy."

"Come on," Jim said to himself. Nancy bit her lower lip and a tear fell from the corner of her eye as she read. The whole bunk started to shake, and Jim had to unzip and free a hand to hold onto a pine post. A splitting sound mixed with moaning and heavy breathing, and the frame collapsed. Jim fell on the floor on top of a body with Nancy on top of him. The moaning bodies piled on top of other cocooned, sleeping bags. "What's goin' on!?" Jim shouted.

Jim swung Nancy's headlight around and flashed at Tami and Butch, who were naked. Jim saw Tami's butt droop in saddles. Her dull matted hair was streaked with gray and covered her face. Her shriveled breasts sagged. Hair puffed from under her armpits. And she stank like crusty fish and pungent body odor.

"Whew, fertility power," Tami whispered and wheezed and laughed. "Butcher, bringin' down the house, baby."

"Come on, this sucks," Jim said to himself. He and Nancy squeezed out of their bags as the entourage rolled onto their sides and sat up. Jim yanked at the bed frame. "Shove a stump under, will you Nance. Pain 'n the ass man."

Nancy and Jim propped the bunk and slipped back into their bags. Jim's head throbbed, and he trembled with cold. One of the entourage sat up and dug in the woodstove to start the fire.

"Jimmy, look at what I found," Nancy said quietly.

"Yeah?" Jim asked pretending he was interested as he slid into his bag and leaned over, trying to ignore the burning pressure in his bladder.

"A hut journal."

Jim looked at the opened page and read the top entry on the curled paper. *March 10, new snow last night with sloughing on the north-side cliffs. Rutschblock test failed again at mid-level on Peak 21's south facing track. Toured low today. Some fun shots through the trees. D.S.*

"Not the most exciting reading," Jim said, pulling his drawstring tighter. Nancy smoothed the page back and lightly ran her finger around the small entry.

"That was my dad."

Jim picked himself up and saw for the first time that Nancy had been crying.

"Nance, what's up?"

"Miss 'em," Nancy replied, folding over the page.

Jim took the beaten-up notebook in his icy fingers and read. *March 12, beautiful snow-showers drifting in early spring light. Sun. Dark squalls ... back to blue skies. Dusty, fresh waist deep. Not a sound. Everyone's gone laughing on shrooms, and my heart aches. Came back early. Miss my baby so much. Wondering how Nancy is doin' racin' in Europe. Can I get a second chance to be her mother? Jill Sweeny ... Mountain Song.*

Jim set down the notebook, and there was a long silence in the stale, cold air. Jim was not sure what to say.

"Mom, eh?"

"I need go back, Jimmy. I'm sorry. My babies," Nancy replied as Jim reached up and wiped her tears. He hugged her and felt icy nylon. The idea of returning early grated Jim's mood. Nancy began pulling on her thermals. "Gotta pee bad. Can you help me find my stuff?"

Jim felt like he was about to burst himself but wanted to avoid having to get out of his warm bag again. The fire in the woodstove started to creak and heat mixed with cold drafts in the porous yurt. Jim forced himself up and took Nancy's shells down from a nail. He stepped between the bodies on the floor in only his briefs and pulled open the door. A solid wall of white packed what used to be the opening and offered a dull light.

"Wow, look at that; gotta suit up, Nance," Jim said as he turned and watched his breath drift into vapor. He struck a safety match on the counter and lit a kerosene lamp. The door stayed open, and Jim heard a muffled wind roaring down from the high alpine. *Stormed in,* Jim thought, *big time.* Jim pulled on his long underwear and zipped into his shells. He balanced and slid into his boot liners and dug out of the yurt. Jim tunneled toward daylight. When he broke through, it was hammering outside. Jim had never seen anything like it. *Jeeze*, he thought to himself, *this is serious*. He waded into a drift and peed and felt his body heat drain into the cold. Jim slid back in, shut the door and grabbed a flashlight. He shot the beam around the roof. *Not good,* Jim thought. The hodgepodge of two-bys and pine poles were bowing, and the plastic material between sagged and ripped. One corner had collapsed. "Gonna loose the whole shebang," Jim said to the room. "Let's go, better get up and shovel, or we're screwed."

"Is that an order?" Moonshadow asked as she propped on her elbow in her bag on the floor and pulled a ski hat onto her dark, shorn hair with flecks of gray.

Jim felt stunned by shame; then angry at his own feeling. He kept his back turned to Moonshadow. The yurt was tight, and only two or three people could stand at a time. Nancy swerved through the bodies and climbed out of the entrance.

"OK, we're gonna have to work out the space thing," Jim said to Princess Ra, still ignoring Moonshadow. "Oh, Jim … my name's Jim."

"Pleased to meet you, Jim, Princess Ra."

"Princess what? What the heck kind of name is that?"

"Whoa, tiger," said Golden Lady to Jim, combing out her knotted blonde hair with her fingers. She pulled her hair back and snapped the short, dry strands into an elastic.

"Stop it," Princess Ra hissed.

"Watch out, I'm a certified man hater," Golden Lady said to Jim. "Chicks with dicks."

"He's being masculine. Let him take charge," said Moonshadow with baby tones as she took in Jim, and her eyes widened.

"Then we'll F his brains out," said Golden Lady.

"Get nice girl babies, Sekhmet's daughters," said Moonshadow.

"Birth of the universal consciousness. Our salvation," said Golden Lady.

Jim jerked back his head, avoiding Golden Lady's eyes. The yurt felt suddenly cramped.

"Praise the lord," said Moonshadow.

"Our redeemer, the living goddess," said Golden Lady.

"Stop," Princess Ra hissed and cast a worried look at Nancy, who climbed out the entrance.

"Ho," groaned Tami from a dark corner.

She stood in her long underwear. Jim watched her sagging breasts and gray streaked hair as she creaked on bare feet across the dirty, floor boards. She reached the door, yanked it open, turned and dropped her underwear and peed in a long, steaming column that dripped onto her leg as she stood. Jim watched with his mouth in an o.

"Hey, what the fuh … going on?"

"Incontinent, cutie. Be tolerant of the old. Be there soon enough. Hey, pagans, sleep well? Sorry 'bout all the commotion. He ha, morning madness; get it when you can," Tami wheezed. She hopped to her bunk and to her lifeless hulk of a companion. Tami leaned over and dug around her pack for a bag of granola; then lay back eating one pinch at a time.

"Wow," Jim said to himself shaking his head with a sick look. He grabbed an avy shovel and scooped the frozen, yellow pile, yanked open the door and flung it out the entry tunnel. "Not a barn."

Nancy slid back into the yurt, took off her shell jacket and nested onto the bunk. Jim shed his wet gear, stepped between the bodies and sat on the foam mattress next to Nancy, who was sitting upright with her eyes closed and her hands in prayer. Jim sat and ate a Pop Tart and vacantly watched Golden Lady prime a stove to boil water. The cold, dark space wafted a stench of body odor, morning breath and dank women.

"Jimmy, can I know where we stand?" Nancy asked quietly as she opened her eyes.

"Alright, Nance, does it have to be now?" Jim whined, as he lowered his voice and noticed that the entourage was stuffing bags and dressing but listening to them and watching Nancy. Nancy bit her lower lip and her eyes welled with tears.

"Alright, alright, hate it when you get like that," Jim whined again, trying to whisper. His eyes were scratchy, and his head pounded with a dull pain. "What do you want from me?"

"Some sign that you're there for me … for us … A commitment," Nancy said and immediately regretted saying it.

She bit her lower lip again and thought to herself that she was pushing Jim and that her own force would crush a new part of him that was blossoming in fits and starts — that she was blowing the whole thing. But something felt wrong. Something that might never change. Nancy groped for the truth, and the truth always came to her, no matter how difficult and no matter how much time it took. Nancy's hands grew clammy with nervousness. The others kept moving about pretending not to listen. Nancy wiped her wet cheeks with the palms of her hands.

"Commitment? What's the problem?" Jim whispered.

"I shouldn't have done what we did. Was stupid. Was wrong."

"So what happened, happened. I'm easygoing about it."

"I answer for everything I say and do. I'll get pregnant; I know it," Nancy whispered, trying not to be heard by the entourage.

"Answer to what, to whom? I don't understand. What am I supposed to do about that?" Jim whined.

There was a long uncomfortable silence where Nancy thought to herself … *maybe make a promise, with feeling, to me, to both of us.*

"Just —"

"I don't get what you want," Jim interrupted, speaking louder and looking ahead.

"Be a man," Nancy said almost inaudibly, and her head felt hot and dizzy. She wasn't sure from where her words arose.

"Man?" Jim pronounced and cocked his head back, dropping his chin and turning to face Nancy. "What the hell is that?" Jim snapped. "I'm fine. Don't like being told what to do. Who to be. What do you really want?"

"Nothing I guess," Nancy whispered mostly to herself. "I guess nothing. Shouldn't 've brought it up. I'm sorry."

"Maybe there's nothing to want," Jim said under his breath.

"What did you say?" Nancy blurted through teary eyes.

"Maybe I can't be this thing you want. Don't even know what it is," Jim said. Nancy tried not to show a growing feeling of hopelessness, even pity as she looked at Jim. "OK, let's forget it," he said, avoiding Nancy's eyes. "We're here to tour and tele ski. That's all. Nothing else too complicated. I need to get out of here for a while," Jim said and did a double take as he realized that Butch was standing next to him in his underwear and one-piece suit, unzipped to his navel. Jim noticed a nasty gash on the top of Butch's head where caked blood coated his oily hair. Butch held out a piece of folded paper. "Dude, what's up? Can you talk? What's going on here? Getting to be a freak show." Jim looked at the folded paper and noticed the scrawled handwriting ... *for my wife, Lynne Michel ... 18 Dearborn Lane, Akron, Ohio 44301.* "Wife?" Jim muttered to himself.

Butch gazed through a long, dark tunnel where at the end he sensed more of a light and energy than a person. He could hear Jim's voice, distantly. Butch knew there was a guy, another guy — that's all he knew as his darkness closed even further.

"Are you two spousal equivalents?" Moonshadow asked Jim bluntly.

"Eh?" Jim grunted absently taking the paper and shoving it into his bib pocket, while nodding a condolence to Butch to get rid of him.

"Coupled?" Moonshadow asked again.

"No, no," Jim replied.

"We're all married," Golden Lady chimed in. "An alternative family."

"That's good," Jim replied, bending and reaching for his tele boots.

"Why should a family be only a husband and wife — man and woman?"

"No reason," Jim replied absently as he suited-up.

"We're going to marry that beautiful, Douglas fir out front too, Ariadne," said Golden Lady. "Today at noon when the vibrations are right, when the sun peaks on its meridian. When we can channel our goddess — her living presence. Come to our wedding."

"Nance, I'm sorry. I'm oudda here. Goin' on a short tour," Jim said, ignoring Golden Lady.

"Isn't that a nice little, male privilege," Golden Lady said to Jim, who tried to ignore her in the close space. "Do what you want, whenever you want."

Nancy sat wrapped in her bag. She read another entry by her mother. She felt a sick, empty feeling in the pit of her stomach as if something dreadful were about to happen ... or had already happened ... as if a great loss was upon her.

March 18, Here is my world cast free yet enslaved by my own boundaries, my own needs and wants and pleasures. My loneliness. A slide out of nowhere today down the Butter Bowl on Peak 21. Terrifying. Trees stripped raw of their bark. Near miss. No one buried. Why do I live? I hold a picture of my baby girl, Nancy Ann. I love you sweetheart. Will you ever know that? Jill Sweeny ... Mountain Song.

"Stop it," laughed Tami, coughing. "Hear that, Butchy? They're going to marry a tree. Heck yeah, we'll come to your wedding. Go ahead, marry a tree. Marry a rock, another woman, your f'n pet goldfish, two other women. Whatever, man. Anything goes! We'll be there. We'll bring the Captain's!"

"Nance, Nancy," Jim said. "I'm gone." Jim was fully dressed with his hat and gloves and hood pulled over. His goggles were perched over his hat. Nancy looked up with her face blurred with tears.

"'K," she croaked. "Careful."

"Hey, come on. What's up already?" Jim asked, trying to sound like he cared. He stood over Nancy and absently pulled her to his chest as she sobbed. Princess Ra looked over and frowned. Jim felt helpless and annoyed. He was feeling that things were going too far with Nancy, and he wasn't ready for all this and wanted his own life back. Jim released Nancy and turned and burrowed out of the yurt. Butch followed him like a shadow.

Nancy watched Jim crouch and disappear out the door. A dead weight fell upon her: the weight of a last moment in a finite world. Nancy's limbs felt suddenly heavy and rubbery. She worked her jaw trying to call for Jim … knowing what her feeling portended yet helpless when witness to her prophesy … and to the other secrets within her, which overwhelmed Nancy with hidden awe.

Outside, Jim glanced at Butch, and he saw a pale, middle-aged guy looking off into the distance. Jim followed Butch's gaze but saw nothing. "Dude, kind of want some solitude," Jim said to him. "Couple of sweet, powder shots by myself."

"Where're you tele-studs goin' without the Snow Princess?" Tami rasped, poking her head out of the tunnel. She was dressed and ready to go.

"Nasty," Jim whispered to himself, looking at the aging creases on her face. "Freakin' circus. I just wanna tele, that's all I ever wanted to do," he said slapping his thighs with his gloved-hands. *Not all this other crap,* he thought. *Never wanted all the baggage. Just free 'n easy, man. Do not lean on me.*

"Get shovels. Guys have beacons?" Jim asked Tami. Tami slid back into the yurt, then re-emerged with their daypacks and shovels. Jim stabbed at the powder on the roof with his pole. He took a step closer and sank to his chin and thought about digging out the yurt. Jim clawed back up. "Screw it," he hissed to himself. "Let them figure it out." Jim slung on his pack, dug out his telies and smoothed his climbing skins along each ski bottom. He mounted his skis and started wading through the storm crystals, lifting and double-poling so as to move forward. *Touch moist,* Jim thought as he scooped up rimed, star-shaped crystals at his waist. He lifted his goggles and looked closely at the handful of snow with a pretense of knowing what he was seeing. Jim dug in again. It was snowing so hard that he lost sight of the yurt at 20 paces. Jim kicked-turned around and passed Butch and Tami. "Can't see; never find our way back," Jim shouted at them from beneath his hood, figuring they wouldn't understand anyway.

Jim returned to the yurt and started climbing toward what he thought was true north and Peak 21. Jim dug through the spaces of aspen and fir. Butch kicked forward, bolt upright, and Tami trailed. The trees opened, and Jim sensed a slope. He did not know what was above or below or where the wind had dumped snow. Jim felt uneasy. He pushed through the navel deep snow that was puffy like a planetary medium. Then a soft slab grabbed at his digging ascent. *Variable wind loading,* Jim thought. *Not good. Couple of fun shots, keep to low angle, get out of that stinkin' yurt.* He felt like touring away into his own day, into his own world and his own mountain range of perfect powder runs. "Getting weird," Jim said to himself. *Don't know about this whole thing with Nancy. Maybe she's confused or something.* Jim missed being back with his group of friends — the girls and guys without any demands on him, *just cruisin' around, skiing and climbing*, Jim thought. Thinking about this retreat eased the anxious pit in his stomach. The slope rose to a skiable grade. "Long traverses, easy, safe, gentle slope," Jim breathed to himself. *That's what I'm going to do, head back over to The Crest when I finish my fine at Piney.*

El Viejo stepped lightly behind Jim, and he could almost taste the crisp mountain air. Viejo's deep bliss rose and fell in his chest. El Viejo followed Jim and felt him — he felt compelled to speak to Jim's heart. "At the end of the day, Jimmy, what is it that you're gonna get?"

Jim felt a sudden flaming tightness overwhelm him. He shook his head and tried to ignore the feelings melting his muscles and bones. The night before with Nancy flooded into his mind's eye, like a powerful and distant memory that he was now compelled to re-live over and over again. A desperately lonely feeling rose in Jim. He pictured Nancy's smiling eyes and missed her terribly, as if he might never see her again. The feeling in his chest fused the two of them together. Jim slowed and stared into the maelstrom of crystals swirling around him. Jim's knees collapsed. His muscles spoke to him, saying to choose what has happened or turn. Jim stopped and hung over his poles. "What's goin' on?" he said to himself. He twisted around, and Butch was staring at him. Jim nodded, and Butch made no motion. Tami lumbered behind as a dark lump.

"From where do you come and where are you going, Jimmy? Who are you? Why are you here? Why do you live?" Viejo asked gently but earnestly.

"Hey, young studs, slow down for the Snow Princess," Tami screeched, and her voice sent shivers up and down Jim's spine. Jim turned under his hood and kept digging. "Not tryin' to dust me are you, Butchy? Tired of me now, aren't you?" she asked wistfully. Jim stopped and waited for her pathetic figure. "You don't know who I am," she said absently as she reached the two guys. Jim moved slowly away, and Butch followed. "Don't leave me here. I'll come for you again, Butchy. You'll find me. I'm always your craving — all of mankind. The dawn of man's desire. I'll be back. I always come again. Over and over. Come again. With a nice, young body. Can suck on me again, Butchy. Feel so good. I'm old now. Got old," she continued in a strained, crackling voice. "Come again, Butchy. All over me, Butchy … Don't leave me here. I got old. So old." Her voice trailed off to nothing, and Jim turned to see a haggard woman stooped in a clawed, dark ball in the opaque light of the storm. She could have been mistaken for a crumbling stump.

Jim stood, and Butch stepped closer. Jim stared into his vacant eyes and felt icy and empty. Jim met Butch's gaze and looked behind at the collapsing woman and pushed away a tense feeling. His mouth turned dry. Jim wanted to tour away, but he could not, because he witnessed himself in Tami and Butch. Sadness. Tension. Fear. Jim gripped and ungripped his pole handles, lowered his head and worked his jaw as hazy visions rose from the impossible expanse of his future. With his eyes locked onto Butch's empty pupils, Jim pulled off his glove with his teeth, zipped down his bib pocket and unfolded Butch's note. Jim removed his eyes from Butch and read the contents.

Ski trip ... day two. Lynne, I'm sorry, baby. Sorry for the kids, the boys. For you. Do the best for them. For yourself. Sorry for goin' out like this. Cochran's is callin', baby. The big one this year. The last run. Butcher Man ... skier.

"Turn back, Jimmy. Turn," El Viejo whispered to Jim's heart. "She's gonna rip, Jimmy."

Jim felt a heavy, sick feeling overcome him. He gazed at Butch's hollow eyes, and his guts tensed again. Jim looked at the note collecting crystals; then shoved it back into his pocket and pretended that he did not understand the scene before him and the feelings roiling from deep within his guts.

As Jim zipped his shell pocket closed, he realized that he was moving downward. "Things goin!" Jim shouted in his mind. The snow sheered below his boots into powdery blocks, and Jim spun and kicked and lunged back down the slope toward a line of trees. Then he spun in slow circles. He pivoted on his three pins and could not move forward or anywhere at all. Jim sensed Butch's stiff figure fall and disappear into the white void behind him. The air rumbled. Jim balanced to stay upright and rotated with spread legs and arms into a stand of aspen. He held out his hands and felt stupid and powerless as he face-planted into the moving snow. Cold crystals packed into Jim's mouth and nostrils. The flowing mass gained momentum and wrapped him onto an aspen trunk. Jim's upper body flowed around the trunk and stretched down hill, belly first, while his skis hung up and augured in. One ski twisted left and deep, and the other rotated the opposite way around the trunk. A thudding crash sounded below. Jim turned awkwardly to his side. His legs, feet and skis twisted and buried around the tree while his head pulled downhill. Snow flowed around and forced his body away from his legs. He could not move. Pressure built on his skis and shins as the snowy plasma thickened and grew heavy. "Haaaaa," Jim exploded as his tibia bowed and burst through his skin. "Ahhh," Jim screamed and frantically gripped his leg and flailed his arms, trying to push up as more flowing mass buried and forced him downhill. Jim was sweating and shaking. The pouring snow stretched him downward as if he were on a rack. "Ha, ah, ah," Jim moaned and panted as he cried and flailed. The piercing pain shot up his right leg and seized his entire body.

The snow stopped moving. Jim quickly dug away his face and torso. He lay back and grit his teeth in pain. Jim fuzzed in and out of consciousness and felt like he was about to heave. "Nance, come on, Nancy. Find me," Jim panted and opened and shut his eyes as he wrestled with pain and nausea. He felt the cold press around him. The descending crystals were a solid wall, which blurred black then white. Jim knew it was snowing so hard that his tracks would soon be covered. "Never find me," he breathed. Jim shook and moaned while cold, clammy sweat covered his skin. "Not good, not good," Jim spat in panicky spasms. His face grew hot with humiliation. Jim knew he could slip into hypothermia and shock and that he was within 400 feet of the yurt. Jim clenched his jaw and lay back helplessly. His body began to feel numb. He knew he could freeze to death. Jim blinked and hissed saliva through his teeth. "Come on; fight for it. Fight," he screamed. Jim lunged for his useless legs and twisted to rise. The pain floored him backwards like a lead pipe slamming onto his ribs. He felt the upper part of his shin loosely work one way as if separating from the fixed lower section. "Oh jeeze, jeeze, what's going on?" Jim panted, then blurred into blackness and puffed his cheeks, trying to stay conscious. He vomited and blacked-out. Jim lay unconscious while the descending sky buried his pinned body.

Jim came to after some time and forced his abdominals to an awkward sit up. He was partially buried in solidified and fresh snow. There was frozen puke all around him that still smelled pungent. Jim hugged himself and shook. The slightest movement shot an excruciating pain up his legs and into his spine. Jim was scared and cold, and his lips trembled. Jim focused his eyes over his pit and uphill at a descending object. Through the cloudy-white, a gorilla-like figure rose then fell and disappeared. Then rose again with a lead ski surfing across the slope. Dust billowed behind in the hush. The figure carved downhill and abruptly stopped on a drop knee. A guy with pigtails and a snow-crusted beard dug-out of his last turn. He stood and squinted down at Jim.

"Brighter than f'n blazes, man," the guy said squeezing his eyes as if straining to see.

Jim stared back and tried to speak as his lips trembled. Tears had frozen onto his cheeks.

"Help me," Jim stammered. "Legs are pinned … ahhh," Jim moaned and shivered.

"How inconvenient," the guy said, looking down at Jim, then up and into nowhere. Sure, I'll help you. Do what I can … I'm supposed to talk to you about marriage," the guy mumbled. "Shhhit." There was a long pause. Jim squinted and stared at the guy trying to make sense of what he just said. "How did I know that?" The guy asked at length to anyone and no one. "How did I even get here? Where am I going?" He continued, trailing off and staring into the crystals and blinking. "Lost soul. Really am. Marriage? Marriage is like a dirt road. Dirt road with deep ruts. Who do you blame? The road for being dirt? The cars for having to travel on it? Or the maker of it all? Shhhit," he whistled again and squinted and sat down with his telies collapsed in front of him. "Or yourself?" he added. He flopped his poles to the side and gazed downward. "F, man." There was a long pause. Jim stared at the guy and grit his teeth in pain and trembled with cold. The guy spoke again in quiet tones. "So I'll tell you then … A speck of dust gazing at itself. Snow is water and water reflects. A frozen speck of dust gathers water around itself in an icy crystal. A speck. A tiny speck that only sees itself in its own crystalline reflection. Falling and falling without end. Every movement, every turn: run, word, touch, kiss, step … every plan — moment by moment ... My whole life, my whole world was nothing but a reflection of myself. Nothing else, man," the guy said gazing ahead. He turned and revealed a turquoise earring stud on his right ear lobe. "That makes me a little snowflake." There was a long pause, and Jim swallowed hard and felt a lump in his throat. Jim did not know what to say or do. He could only lay there and listen. "So naturally nothing else existed," the guy continued, "except that which existed in the tiny reflection of myself as I fell and fell. Anything that wasn't me wasn't seen. Or discarded. So when she started to look like a man, lost interest in me and dried up, she was no longer me — my reflection." Jim gazed at his blue, squinting eyes, pigtails and creased face. The guy got up and stomped and flung his braids behind, and Jim could see strands of silver-gray in his dirty-blond hair. "So I took myself — my anger, my resentment — and hung it on a nail. Drove the f'n nail right through her forehead, man. Rode her like a mule," the guy pronounced and smacked himself on the forehead with the heel of his hand. Tears flooded his eyes.

The guy wiped his eyes with his arm and squatted back down and sat on his haunches in silence for a long time. He stared into the void of descending crystals, straining as if looking for something. After a long pause, he spoke again and said that his waking moments with his wife became a like a machine, like a cranky, old car turning over purpose and purpose only on a rutted road — and that a man and a women at some unspoken level grow to resent each other … maybe even hate each other. "Burrow deep into each other's nerves and f'n twist there," he said quietly. He paused again for a long while, so that Jim could absorb his words. Then he spoke about how in a way that he could not understand, he also felt deeply for his wife, Song of the Mountain, as he always called her. "I called Jill that from when we first met, when she was young and tight and fresh and wanted me all the time. Hell, two, three times a day. Whew," he exhaled and gazed off into the aspens, shaking his head as tears fell down his cheeks. "Those were the days. Those really were the days." He went on and spoke softly about how he was always loyal to her and to their life together — that at the bottom of the ruts were deep unspoken feelings for each other, lost in the day-to-day grind of purpose. The guy with the turquoise earring stud and pony tails went on to say that all of their time together, a lifetime, came back to him now — all that it means — that blood and bones; nerves and neurons live much more than can ever be told. "And that my friend is a true miracle — that a thing such as us — dust of the earth — makes sense of the world … that we can see and feel: the good, the bad, the ugly, the beautiful, the sad, the happy, the lonely," he said and his voice trailed-off, and tears welled in his eyes again. He paused for a long time and let the crystals collect on his face and eyelids as if contemplating their perfect, ephemeral being. "But mostly the good," he added thoughtfully. The guy went on to say that he knew not where he fell, a falling that he bore alone that never seems to end. "I miss my Song of the Mountain; really do," he said and hung his head. "This is all I know for now," he added lowering his voice. "This is all I can say — that I failed to see something in marriage … in life. I missed something Larger that called me all along to my wife and that still yearns for me as I fall without end. I ask a lot of questions now. I really do," he said and sought Jim's eyes. "Ones that I should have asked a long time ago. I have come to believe." He paused again for a long time and looked up to sky. "And then there's my little girl, my daughter," he said suddenly exploding into tears and sputtering like a pressure valve had let loose. "She's my little baby. Miss her. Don't be me again. Find the better way." The guy sucked up a big breath but could not stop himself and wept in bursts. His face was tortured, and he turned away. Jim felt an urge to reach up and touch him. "I miss her, man. Really do. Can feel her a lot. My little girl, Nancy Ann. Treat her well, Jimmy, right? Jim's your name?" he asked, looking down and into Jim's eyes. Jim met his eyes and nodded.

The guy's voice grew quiet and stopped. He stood and looked down at Jim. "Nuff of my BS. Now blow your whistle, Jimmy, hard. I felt Whinny with you. Bet Red Bone gave you a whistle," he said nodding at Jim's chest and zipper pocket. "David gives everybody one. After I found and pulled him out of a crevasse on Denali, Red Bone swore he or anybody he was with in the mountains would always have a whistle. I love that guy. Really do. Can feel him a lot. You must know Red Bone … David Winchester, right? Blow on it, Jimmy. Blow your heart out, man. Blow for salvation. Cry for help." Jim nodded. The guy pushed off, sank a tele turn, stopped and shouted back, "D.S.'s muh name, Singer." Singer looked down and then up to Jim. He side-stepped back up, wheezing and puffing and digging to where Jim lay burying again in white dust. Singer bent over and looked into Jim, and Jim stared back at his seeking, blue eyes for so long that Jim no longer saw eyes but a bundle of human passion following his own questions into oblivion. "What I'm trying to say," Singer whispered earnestly, "is selfless devotion, man. I expect nothing but selfless devotion for my little girl, Nancy. I love her with all my heart." Singer nodded and turned away. He buried a tele turn and carved into the endless, white and gray of the winter storm, whose shadow-like aspens cried Heavenward with knotty branches.

Abruptly alone again in his pit, Jim tried to understand what just happened and what he heard. He took off a glove and looked at his fingers. The tips were starting to turn black. Jim pictured his fingers freezing and falling off one at a time — then his feet and his legs and arms. Jim absently patted his chest. A trembling, gloved-finger caught an orange emergency whistle on his pocket zipper. Jim remembered David making him wear it.

Jim closed his eyes and saw himself standing on a dividing line between darkness and light. He slipped into the cool shadows of deadly relief, and it felt good. *Easy,* Jim thought. *Just let go and be done with it. What difference would it make if I die?* So, too, Jim found himself bending forward and biting the whistle with his lips. He blew hard, over and over again, as seething currents of care and indifference churned to the surface. The shrill cry pierced his heart. After some indefinite time a voice startled him to attention.

"Jim … Jimmy … Pepe, man!" El Viejo, The Old One, yelled. "Can stop … I hear you. I've come for your salvation!"

"Huh," Jim grunted and looked around, straining to see.

He was in a world of white. Jim frantically dug away a foot of snow and frozen puke from his face and torso. His lower body stayed buried.

"Got a match in your pack, Pepe?" Viejo asked softly.

Jim turned his head and squinted. He saw a wind-tanned old guy with a shrunk-wrapped head. He was dressed in a ragged polka dot shirt and torn pants. The old guy was dug in and sitting next to him against an aspen. He reached over and under and gently pulled away Jim's pack from his back.

"Hel … help me," Jim croaked. "Get me oudda here."

"Easy, Jimmy. Dan, Dan the Spooner's my name," Viejo said as he untwisted Jim's waterproof match container, struck a wooden safety match on the bottom scratch pad and cupped the match around a Camel nonfilter with his bare hands. A huge cloud of bluish smoke billowed into the descending sky. Viejo inhaled deeply. "Um man … now that, that Jimmy is truly a temporal pleasure," he exclaimed sitting back against the aspen and looking over at Jim with kindly warm eyes. Jim stared at him. "Wow, Jimmy, am I happy. Deeply happy. What a beautiful day. What a beautiful storm … creation," Viejo pronounced, looking up and smiling into the wall of rimed crystals and blinking as they hit his eyes. "God's creation, Jimmy. Now what can I do you for?"

"Help me … please," Jim blurted and cried and twisted to reach for his leg. "Hurts."

"Um man … just one more drag. Always just one more, isn't it, Jimmy? One more run. One more woman. One more beer. One more road trip. Another hit. More and more. Never enough. That was me. Broken mess. Didn't know it till it was too late. But that's not quite you is it, Jimmy? No, that's not totally it." Viejo mused to himself. There was a long silence, and Jim looked into Viejo's twinkling eyes as Viejo looked back into Jim's soul. Jim calmed. "Shoot man," Dan, El Viejo, suddenly declared, jolting up as he sat. "You're lost, Jimmy. Abandoned in a sea of neglect and castration. Where are your feelings? Where is your heart? Your manhood? You call for no one? Mother? Father? What about your father, Jimmy? Is anyone out there for you? Do you care? Has anyone ever truly cared about you, Jimmy? Now's your time. Gotta break free, man. From the tapestry of your life. From your place in this picture that's telling you who you are, how you should feel and see and know. It's killing you, Jimmy. Now's your chance. Break free and commit. Commit, Jimmy. Find your soul!" Dan, El Viejo whispered emphatically, leaning closer and squeezing his eyes as if suffering from dire happiness. He closed his eyes and leaned back and smiled with his entire face and inhaled deeply through his nose. Jim swallowed hard. His mouth felt like cotton. He started to cry uncontrollably, and tears gushed down his freezing cheeks, welling from a deep pain he did not know he possessed. Viejo, Dan the Spooner, flicked away the cigarette. He turned and brushed the snow off of Jim and carefully nudged his arms under his back and shoulders. Dan knelt and held Jim closely in his arms like a child. After a long while Jim gazed into The Old One's beaming eyes and calmed. "Dig deep, Jimmy. Real deep," Viejo whispered. "That's what it's all about." El Viejo paused, placing his head on Jim's chest. Jim looked into the snowy sky and poured tears. "Who is it that made you?" The Old One asked gently, holding Jim. "Who is it that saves you? Who really cares about you? Why do you live, Jimmy!? Feel it, man. Feel it in your heart, Jimmy. Why do you live? Who are you, really?" Dan whispered ardently. "Where are you going?" Jim listened like a child and felt the back of Viejo's fingers brush away his tears as he held him in his arms. "Know Him in the center of your belly. Give yourself, Jimmy. He'll be there," Dan the Spooner whispered and hugged Jim. "I love you, man. He loves you."

Dan rose and spread his arm down Jim's leg. He placed his hand on Jim's forehead and closed his eyes tightly so that creases formed in their corners. Jim watched his mouth move but could not hear his words. Dan opened his eyes, and Jim could see that they were watery. The Old One stretched down to the tree, dug away the snow, pulled back Jim's pant leg and gently rubbed his wounded shin. Dan slowly took one boot and ski and then the other and freed them from around the aspen. He lifted Jim and placed his pack under his back. Then Dan rose and bowed his head with his hands together. "Lookie there," he whistled to himself in awe, gazing at Jim's healed tibia. "Halleluiah, brother. I'm oudda here. The last run, Jimmy!" El Viejo, The Old One, exclaimed and stood and slid on a pair of mirror shades that balanced on his shrunken face. "Get on back to Nancy now, Jimmy. She loves you, man. Really loves you. You guys are good together. Stay together. Commit, Jimmy. Commit. A man and a women. Married in Spirit — let no man put asunder!"

Viejo reached down, and Jim watched him slip into a pair of antique skis and bindings. El Viejo, The Old One, looked down at Jim and smiled, and Jim forced back a smile. Viejo kick-stepped around and poled downhill. Jim turned and watched his wiry frame rise and fall as his ragged clothes flapped in the peaceful, chest deep snow. Dan The Spooner, The Old One, disappeared into ghostly white and muted tans, while the aspens watched in frozen peace.

Jim closed his eyes and took a deep breath. His thoughts had stopped. Jim heard only his breath and felt a core of heat in his chest. He sucked up his abdomen and heaved his legs and skis to the side and up and over downhill. Jim reached behind with his poles and pushed up. He was standing. "Oh man," Jim panted and shook. He bowed his head in the direction Viejo disappeared and almost said, "Thank you." Jim reached down and pulled up his bib and examined his leg. It was swollen in a bloody lump. Jim took a few tentative steps forward and felt sore but OK. As he dug back toward the yurt, he realized that the others had been buried in the slide. He pushed this awareness away, whimpering a little and gingerly plowing downhill with his climbing skins still attached.

After a hundred yards an unnamed tension forced Jim to unzip his parka. He turned his transceiver to receive at eighty meters and heard a faint ping. Jim kick-turned and dug down and toward the direction of the slide. He watched the lead-lights pop to life, one after the other, as the ping amplified.

When the terrain leveled, Jim smelled burning garbage as if a massive dump fire was billowing out-of-control. He lost the leads and ping and tried to care. Jim wondered about the burning smell. The world around him was white and swirling and apparently on fire. Jim was not sure where he was. A vague obligation plowed him in one direction; then the other until the ping resumed. Jim unzipped and flipped up his avalanche beacon. The ping grew louder and became rapid beeping. The lead lights flashed again as Jim moved down and northeast. The valley tightened, and Jim reached a point where he sensed two sides of a ravine joining. He began to descend through tight stands of aspen and subalpine spruce. Jim adjusted his beacon to receive at 35 meters, then 15 and finally eight — all the time moving down and listening and glancing at the leads flashing — until he realized he was standing on a pile of concrete snow. Uphill, aspens were bent and freshly stripped. Jim looked at their green undersides of exposed bark and bony core. A plowed swath of snow lay beneath a new layer. The beeping kept sounding strong and steady. He zipped apart his shell and unsnapped his beacon. Jim clicked to two meters, bent over and held the beacon in his hand and swayed one way, then the other.

Jim looked up at the stripped trees and suddenly realized how tight the Rattling Brook area was and how much vertical was loaded above. Jim wondered if the yurt itself was safe from slides and if the bowls and chutes of Peak 21 would crash down at any minute. Jim wanted to leave. Then he wanted to stay and be taken away forever by waves of slides. As Jim was pulled back and forth with these feelings, he wondered about Nancy and a dull ache gripped his body and feelings. Jim wondered too about the smoke, which wafted around with the occasional gust of wind, suggesting a passionate fire burned without reserve. Jim realized he was staring vacantly into the white void and abruptly set his beacon to receive at zero meters. He bent over and marked the outer boundaries where the beacon faded with each pass. Right, left, up and down. Jim marked the middle with an X in the snow, set his beacon to the side, pulled his avy shovel from his pack and started to dig. The snow was compacted hard. Jim reached for his beacon and swayed back and forth close to the surface. The ping sounded frantically and all the lead lights flashed. Jim was sweating and shaking, and his legs trembled as he labored to exhume whatever was entombed below and pulsing upward. Jim fell to his knees and chopped and dug until the blade bounced off something hard.

Jim bent down and carefully chipped and flung away blocks, which had nothing in common with the downy world surrounding him. A brown plastic boot appeared. Nothing else. Jim dug down the leg and brushed and scraped away the periphery until a rump emerged. She was upside-down. "Jeeze," Jim whistled to himself as he saw that the other leg was twisted and mangled over her head. Jim realized it could have easily been him. He lay on his stomach and dug until a large pit opened, and the body flopped free. Jim grabbed both boots and yanked Tami to the surface. An ice shield covered her worn face like a frozen mummy, and her eyes stared ahead from behind her matted hair. Jim lay the body to the side in the fetal position, tore off his glove and placed two fingers on Tami's aorta. Nothing. He carefully cleared the ice from her face, brushed aside streaks of gray and black hair; and placed his cheek to her mouth. Still nothing. Jim did not know what to think or do. His beacon sounded away. Jim unzipped her shell and turned off her transceiver. Silence. He was breathing hard and sweating.

Jim sat down and stared at Tami. She stared back at him with icy eyes and with her mouth turned up in a zany smile. Jim felt sick. He realized she had once been very pretty, and he felt badly. He never felt badly in such a way, and he wasn't sure what to do about it. Jim stared into the endless crystals and became dizzy as if he were falling into some infinite space and time. Utterly alone. Meanwhile, he could not push away the picture of Tami shriveling and curling into rotting flesh and decaying plastic shells until her bones whitened and collapsed, and she lay among the summer debris of raw granite and avalanche alders. All around, an indifferent universe offered its frightening existence. Loneliness seized Jim like a vise. He placed his fingers on Tami's eyelids and closed them. They popped open. Jim did a double take.

"You dig my sorry ass out of the white room?" rasped Tami.

"You're alive!?" Jim stammered, startled to hear his own voice.

"Hell yeah, think you could do away with me that easy? Where's Butcher? Need to find him. Can't believe that thing slid. Barely skiable. Wow," Tami exhaled brushing herself off. Jim stared at her with his mouth agape. "Find Butcher, will you? Can't be far."

Jim nodded as if in a trance and stepped off the pile and turned his transceiver back to receive at eighty meters. Jim plunged up to his neck in the fresh snow and wallowed for a step or two. Nothing. "No, there it is," Jim said to himself. He swam through the powder to the east, adjusting his beacon as the leads flashed hot. Finally there was a frenzied beeping. Jim set the beacon to zero and placed it to the snow surface and scanned. He dug down with his glove and immediately fingered something fleshy. It was Butch. Jim carefully chipped away the snow from around Butch's body. Jim cleared his face, gently slapped Butch and yelled, "Hey!" Butch moaned, sat up, opened his eyes and stared through Jim. Jim fell back on his haunches, floored.

The deathly, white world around Jim fuzzed in and out of blackness, and he grabbed at his legs in panic. Jim awoke and found himself shaking uncontrollably with cold, laying in his pit and free of the aspen. He was alone. Jim felt nothing from the waist down. A slur of confused questions swirled around his head. *Who came? The others? Where am I? What's happening now? Fingers, toes OK? No one here? No one for me? Does anyone care about me?* Jim flopped his head and arms from side to side. He was covered with snow, and he pushed away the powder so he would not be buried alive or dead — Jim was not sure.

CHAPTER 10

SNOW ANGELS

After Jim left, Nancy wrote him a note and placed it on his sleeping bag. She looked at the empty bag laying open and felt a lump in her throat.

"Will you see that the guy I was with gets this note … Jim?" Nancy quietly asked Princess Ra. "I'm going back."

"You're going out alone?" Princess Ra asked.

"Hey," Golden Lady purred, stopping what she was doing and stepping closer to Nancy, who was sitting on the edge of her bunk, "leaving Sugar Burger here with us?"

Moonshadow slid behind Nancy. The two worked as a shadow and in one invisible motion lifted Nancy's top and sports bra. Moonshadow straddled Nancy from behind with her legs, opened her hands around Nancy's chest and lifted and inhaled deeply. Moonshadow released long enough to rip off her own top. She quickly nestled back.

"Mmmm, Sekhmet's child," Moonshadow moaned and ran her tongue by Nancy's ear as Golden Lady pulled off her own top and knelt on the other side of Moonshadow with Nancy pinned between. The two entwined their tongues. Nancy blushed and rolled away. Golden Lady and Moonshadow fell over and slithered into each other on the bunk, peeling off long underwear into nakedness and enwrapping and writhing.

"Mmmm, pow, puh, puh, pow ... er to Lord Sekhmet," they breathed into each other. "Her child fills us with her puh ... ow ... er." They moaned, burying into each other like cats preening.

Nancy stood shaking her wrists and trembling. "What's going on!?" She quickly pulled her bra and top back on and started packing her things.

Golden Lady rolled over. "What's the matter, your narrow world enslaved you in its white-male God of bondage — of right and wrong? Or do you want your one-way, one-truth Nazis to marginalize us — a perverted sideshow to humankind? HUMANKIND!!" She screeched. "Womin as subservient to your man Deity? Think we're perverts?!" She screamed again. There was a stunned silence. Nancy stood shaking.

"Right on," chimed in Moonshadow. "I am Sekhmet; hear me roar. Sekhmet lives. Sekhmet will come again. Sekhmet will claim her daughters. Or burn in hell with your man-idol slave master."

"Wow," Nancy said, jerking back her head. "Where did that come from? Do you mean mankind?"

"What did you say you little, right-wing bitch?" asked Golden Lady, rolling over onto all fours.

"Quit it Golden," Princess Ra blurted. "She's special. You're hurting her feelings."

"Not," shot back Golden Lady. "Sick of your crap about her. Been through this for months now. She's a patriarchal sympathizer. A miserable little fundy like the rest of 'em, who'd just as soon disband and throw us out of town. They worship the evil man-god of capitalism. They've raped Sekhmet's body, deprived us in marginalized bondage under the grip of male-power, developed our lord's sacred regions. Her endangered mountain cats. Cut her trees. Next year instead of burning we level the whole ski area."

"Shhh stop it!" Princess Ra shouted to Golden Lady, thrusting down her fist. "Damn it." All three realized that Nancy was staring at Golden Lady.

Nancy flexed her hands in and out and forced herself not to speak. Her stomach cinched into a knot. She felt uneasy about being the topic of their conversations. And Nancy could not believe what she thought she heard. Last year the new lodge at Piney was burned right to the ground — the same day the courts approved construction for the new quad. Everybody figured it was the greenies. An investigation turned up nothing. The damage just about killed Big Pine and Margaret and David's chances of making it up there. Nancy stood and closed her eyes. She focused on her breathing and calmed her pulse and whispered to herself, "Rescue me oh Lord from evil men; keep me safe from violent men, whose heads are full of wicked schemes. Their tongues are sharp as serpents' fangs, on their lips is spiders' poison."

Princess Ra's eyebrows creased in worry as she considered Nancy. She tossed a sleeping bag over the two heated females and looked at Nancy as if to apologize. She bowed her head to Nancy. Golden Lady watched with her mouth in an big O.

"Please forgive them," Princess Ra said quietly.

"Oh come on," whined Golden Lady. "You're pushing things, Princess, really are."

Nancy regarded Princess Ra, who stood before her in the semi-dark of the yurt. Hanging shells, undies and crusty socks hung from nylon cord and surrounded the two.

"Will you see that he gets my note?" Nancy asked again as her eyes filled with tears. "It'll be on his bag."

"I will," Princess Ra replied softly, bowing her head to Nancy.

"What is that all about?" spat Golden Lady. "Bowing to her!?" Princess Ra ignored Golden Lady and started getting a daypack together.

Nancy finished packing and suited up. She stuffed an energy bar into her mouth and squeezed out of the yurt, hauling her pack behind. Princess Ra dressed and sat on a bunk with her head down. Outside, Nancy greeted the freezing cold and chaotic storm by pulling over her hood. Then she dug out her skis, slid on her climbing skins, kicked into her bindings and heaved on her pack. She took a deep breath and looked down and then up. Nancy unclipped her waist band, dropped her pack and popped out of her bindings. She yanked an avy shovel out of the snow by the yurt door and wallowed into the powder and started shoveling off the edges of the shelter. It was hard work and sweat trickled down her sides and legs. When the edges and as far back as she could reach were clear, Nancy slid back inside. The three women watched her in silence. Nancy pushed up the roofing material in the corner where Butch and Tami's gear lay soaking in leaking snow-melt. She spread out their sleeping bags to dry, then rearranged the support beams so the leak funneled down the side. She made sure Jim's clothes and bag were dry and rechecked to make certain he would see her note. Nancy took one last look around at the squalid and dark space where her parents had passed and saw the world collapsed on itself as the two women encircled each other again with legs spread and mouths between in self-referencing desire. Nancy crawled back outside, kicked into her bindings and plowed through the waist-deep powder up the tight valley. She absently shuffled through the downy-deep with her poles dangling and her arms outstretched with palms face up. Princess Ra waited a few minutes; then crawled outside to follow Nancy.

Nancy dug slowly between the monolithic pines without thinking and without any particular plan. The pack was heavy, and it was nearly impossible to move in the deep snow. She bent over and felt disappointment sap her muscles. *What am I going to go back to?* Nancy thought to herself without deliberate thought. *Will I always live alone? What kind of life will my boys have? Will I ever find a man, a father for them? What has happened to men? Are they all gone? Is there any hope for Jim? Who is he, truly? Is there hope for the two of us? Should we have done what we did? What will become of the person now in my womb, an illegitimate child? Am I a depraved fornicator? Shacking up. Will I grow old and ugly and lonely?* Around and around spun feelings and thoughts until Nancy collapsed into the snow and lay staring at the descending turmoil. Most of all she tried to deny the sinking feeling that Jim was gone. It was times like these when Nancy knew she had to place everything at His feet. She pictured herself curled there. The discipline was in surrendering, in letting all the thoughts and feelings go, in opening and falling at His feet. *Father, forgive my sin,* Nancy prayed. She pushed up and knelt over her skis in her pit. Nancy dropped her pack, shook her poles from her wrists and held her hands in prayer. She bowed her head and squeezed her eyes, crying for help. Pure white crystals and Silence softly covered Nancy. Her thoughts stopped, and Nancy's eyes lifted inside their closed lids. She felt light and airy and remembered this was how she felt the first time she ever prayed for anyone — the first time after the cave when she asked for help and for healing, for David. He bawled out Margaret one night. Margaret came to Nancy in the morning in tears. And Nancy prayed for David, for both of them.

Nancy straightened her back and closed her eyes. She held out her arms palms up. Nancy knelt for so long that she grew cold and stiff and several inches of powder collected on her outstretched arms and hands. But inside she glowed warmly. Nancy sang quietly to herself … "Purify my heart .. let me be as gold and precious silver. Purify my heart .. let me be as gold, pure gold. Refiner's fire .. my heart's one desire .. is to be holy .. set apart for you Lord. I choose to be holy .. set apart for you my Master .. ready to do Your will."

The Old One softly approached Nancy from behind. "Nance, Nancy," El Viejo whispered, "Need to go back. Jimmy needs you. Needs you bad. He's in trouble. Crying to be saved."

Nancy opened her eyes as spasms of nerves shot through her peace. The uneasy feeling about Jim rushed to the surface. She had to find him. Nancy went to rise and sensed someone standing behind her. She turned slightly to see Princess Ra watching. Nancy closed her eyes and held out her arm as if to feel her visitor. A rush and glow filled her being — the same feeling Nancy had when she placed her hands on the woman with emphysema in the trailer park.

"Your real name is Catherine," Nancy said softly and smiling … with her back still turned to Princess Ra. "You are a seeker. I can tell."

"That is my name," Catherine said quietly. "How did you know? Tell me about all the babies born in the valley. How our barren women can give birth. About the woman in the park, about your life and what you have found. I want to understand."

"You have been in pain," Nancy said softly, turning to face Catherine and holding out a hand to her. "I am sorry." Catherine's eyes filled with tears. "I sense that you have been through a lot. The pain from him? What he did to you and didn't do. Your father? For all the secret places. Offer them."

The two held gloved hands and looked into each other's eyes. Catherine started to cry, and her chiseled features softened in the wintry light.

"For what I have become?" Catherine asked. "Nothing satisfies. I'm desperate. Nobody knows."

"He will forgive you, Catherine. He will fill you," Nancy replied and stepped over and hugged Catherine as she sobbed.

"For all that I have done? I am empty," sobbed Catherine with secret tears as she went limp in Nancy's arms.

Nancy released and placed her hand on Catherine's head and goggled ski hat and whispered a prayer from memory … "O Blessed Redeemer, everliving God, Maker of mankind, we beseech thee, by thy indwelling power, the distress of this thy servant; release her from sin, and drive away all pain of soul and body, that being restored to soundness of health, she may offer thee praise and thanksgiving; who livest and reignest with the Father and the Holy Ghost, one God, world without end. Amen."

Silence came upon the two. "World without end?" Catherine asked. "I want to understand. Thank you," she whispered, taking off a glove and wiping her eyes. "Need to go back. It's not safe to try 'n go out. I was worried about you."

"Thank you. That's sweet. I know. I need to find my man," Nancy said, still speaking in nearly a whisper. "A woman needs a man. A man must be a man. I have an uneasy feeling that something may have happened."

Behind them Dan, El Viejo, lay in snow with his skis to the side and spread his arms and legs in-and-out, with a huge grin and beaming eyes. When he rose, a snow angel glowed purple. Purple on white. One after another all the way back to the yurt. Nancy slung on her pack. She followed Catherine and witnessed the angels in quiet awe.

***

Meanwhile, Jim blew on his whistle as the storm fully buried him. The world silenced into darkness. He felt the gentle weight of gathering crystals press down on his chest. Each was an eternally fresh and perfect seraph. They gathered as messengers from Beyond and tenderly insulated his body from the dropping temperature as dusk began to gather. And one came to Jim. He opened his eyes, and she was beautiful and kissed him on the cheek and lips, and he wanted to be carried away in her arms to warmth and to safety.

***

When Nancy and Catherine slid into the clammy yurt, it was pungent and steaming. Two stubby candles offered a feeble glow. Moonshadow and Golden Lady were in heated discussion and ignored Nancy and Catherine.

"Why are we even talking about this again?" asked Golden Lady.

"Because it's after six weeks now," replied Moonshadow anxiously.

"But so what. Six weeks, six hours, six days, six months. It doesn't matter. It's your choice. Your body. Your right."

"You wouldn't do it part way out," said Moonshadow

"We birth only her sacred womin. Sacrifice the evil seed until her daughters greet her return."

"Make it up as you go," Moonshadow said under her breath.

"What did you say?" Golden Lady asked, stepping closer to where Moonshadow retracted on a bunk. "You've stalled again. Did this last time."

"Didn't answer my question," said Moonshadow, looking down.

"About what?"

"About partial-birth, OK?"

"No, I wouldn't, OK."

"No, it's not OK. Why not?" asked Moonshadow.

"I don't know," replied Golden Lady.

"What do you mean you don't know? How can you be so sure about everything and not that?"

"Because it's a baby then."

"Not a few weeks before?"

"Don't give up your right."

"What's the right?" asked Moonshadow.

"To choose."

"What? Finish the sentence," said Moonshadow.

"Ra, she's doing that thing again. Really pisses me off. Talk to her," Golden Lady said turning to Catherine.

"Let's not discuss it now. Not in this company," Catherine said softly, wiping an eye.

"What happened to you? What's wrong?" asked Golden Lady.

"Nothing."

"So if part way out is wrong, then why isn't it wrong a few weeks earlier?" Moonshadow asked Golden Lady again.

"Because part way out's a baby, all right. It's a baby," Golden Lady said slapping her thighs with her hands. "Does that make you happy?"

"So I feel that now it's a baby," said Moonshadow. "At six weeks. Sweet little, boy baby. I want to keep it."

"It?"

"Yeah it."

"If it's a baby now, then what was it two weeks ago?" asked Golden Lady. "Why does that make any difference?"

"Cells."

"Cells."

"Yes, just cells."

"Some sort of science project? Not life?" asked Golden Lady.

"Yeah."

"And four weeks later it's something else? You don't make any sense."

"No, you don't make sense. You just said it's a baby part way out. It's a baby then. It's a baby at four weeks. And I'm wrong. It's a baby at two. A baby at one. A baby at conception."

"You're babbling. Your body is your life. Your right. All life — make it, give it, take it."

"What is life?" Moonshadow asked without looking up.

"What is life!?"

"What I feel," Moonshadow said quietly, turning away, "from somewhere deep inside of me."

"Our goddess —"

"I don't want to do it again," Moonshadow interrupted, wiping a tear away from her eye and hugging herself and rocking back-and-forth. "Not now, not earlier, not any time. Never. It's wrong."

"What!? Give me a break. It's your body. Your choice. Our choice. Our religion. Our life together. You're always doing these selfish things that really piss me off!" Golden Lady screamed and leaned over Moonshadow.

"Finish the sentence," replied Moonshadow, hugging her knees and rocking back and forth and avoiding Golden Lady's searching eyes.

"No, you finish the sentence," Golden Lady yelled and thumped Moonshadow on the chest shoving her backwards.

"Whoa," said Nancy, "can we calm down? I need your help to tour-out and find my friend."

"No, this's none of your self-righteous business."

"Finish the sentence," Moonshadow said cowering behind the stove on a bunk. "I just want you to hear what I'm suppose to do again."

"Your choice," shouted Golden Lady.

"To what!?" shouted back Moonshadow.

"To kill a baby, OK? Does that make you happy? To kill a baby. A boy baby."

There was a stunned silence. Moonshadow reclined further on the bunk behind the stove and hung her head.

"I'm not even sure who the father is," she said quietly. "'Sides, why do you care so much about bioregions, supposedly endangered lynx; and rocks and trees and not my boy baby. You don't kill those things. Don't want anyone even near 'em. Just can't do it again. Done it so many times." Moonshadow wiped her eyes with both grimy hands. "Just bitter and jealous 'cause you can't have 'em yourself."

"What did you say?" asked Golden Lady bending over the bunk toward Moonshadow as she slid further back.

"Never mind."

"You'll do it if I say you'll do it."

"What!?"

"Because I'm the man."

"Oh get ou —"

Golden Lady lunged and grabbed Moonshadow, who curled into a ball. Golden Lady slipped and crashed against the wood stove. There was a singe of melting plastic and burning flesh. The pungent odor knocked Nancy and Catherine backward.

"Shoot, I'm gonna throw up," Nancy said, coughing and waving her hand across her nose as she stripped gear from her pack, then ducked out of the yurt to go and find Jim. Catherine followed. When Nancy stood outside, she had no idea what to do. Her hands trembled with concern as she pushed into her three pins. Nancy pulled her hood over and closed her eyes and started to plow down valley. Catherine followed right behind.

"Alternate setting our beacons to receive from send," Catherine said, and her voice startled Nancy.

The two dug onward, and Nancy felt hungry, dehydrated and weak. Fear gripped her in a clammy sweat, and her head swam. She had lost track of time and noticed that the light was fading into the storm. Nancy pushed through the waist-deep snow and closed her eyes. She fell over and passed out. Nancy did not know if she was awake or dreaming when she saw a vision: three dark forms appeared before her. They pushed uphill from the opposite direction. Nancy heard, "Hey Nance! Here! Nance, I was missing you so much. Worried you were worried." Jim lunged through the waist deep and wrapped his arms around Nancy, who bent back a little shocked. Jim kissed Nancy on her cheeks and lips. "You are beautiful," he said, gazing at Nancy. "Strong and beautiful woman. Man am I lucky to have you. Can't believe what happened. Thing slid. Barely over 25 degrees. Got pinned around an aspen. This old guy helped me. His name is Dan … Dan Spooner. He's probably back at the yurt by now. Cool old dude. Can't believe the gear he's turning. Then I found and dug out these guys. Did it all by myself. An avy rescue! They're alive! What was the fire I smelled burning? Everything OK at Rattling Brook?" Jim asked in one excited breath.

"OK," Nancy said, a little stunned.

"Nance, I saw your father today."

"What?" Nancy asked as she watched Butch and Tami approach stiffly. "What are you trying to say, Jim?"

"Singer. He's cool. Put it right to me. What I needed to hear. 'Preciate that. He does not f' around," Jim said thrusting down his hand.

"Jimmy, you OK?" Nancy asked, and she remembered with affection her father's rye and blunt style. "Let's get back now. It's getting dark."

Tami and Butch trudged up to Jim and Nancy. Butch pushed along bolt-upright with his hands out like Frankenstein. Both had lost their poles.

"Wow," exclaimed Tami, "now that was a ride. He ha! Whew, my back hurts," Tami groaned, bending over and rubbing her lower back. "Joints all ache. Come on, Butcher, I need a drink. Better yet, I need a drink and a pagan. How about two pagans. Two drinks. Two more pagans, one at each end." She laughed, and her rough voice faded as she passed Nancy and Jim. Tami and Butch blended into the frozen dusk.

"It is beautiful," Jim said emphatically, opening his arms and slowly twisting around, fixing on the pummeling crystals and trying to catch some with his tongue. His eyes appeared to be glazed. "Come on, Nance, let's go back. I'll make you dinner and give you a nice backrub. A full-body, love rub. You know what you asked me and all this morning? Well, I feel really good about us being together. I'm gonna be asking you something big soon. The right time and place. Learned a lot out here today. Want to change my life. Want to commit. Realize life is passing away before my eyes — that life, life in the body is beautiful and fleeting, and I want to spend mine with you — that there's more to everything than what we see. Found a hidden part of myself I want to give to you, forever." Nancy watched Jim and raised her eyebrows and dropped her head.

Wow, Nancy thought to herself. *Some changes, I guess.* "I like it," she said under her breath and turned and followed Jim back to the yurt. Her heart secretly fluttered under her shell jacket as she let herself nearly melt with warm and hopeful feelings for Jim and for both of them together.

Nancy found herself in the rank and crowded yurt. Everyone was standing up and moving around and bumping into each other. Nancy fuzzed in and out of awareness as voices became loud then soft.

"Sugar Burger, you're back," said Golden Lady to Jim. "We were so worried. Have a fun playtime? Sweet lit'le thang." She pouted and gave Jim a kiss in the air. Jim nodded and smiled to Golden Lady and slid off his daypack.

"Nance, let me clear a space for our wet stuff," Jim said with a deep voice. "I'll hang it all up. Then you settle in for a full body rub." Just then the roof collapsed above the kitchen area, and a pile of snow thudded onto the counter.

"Lot of weight on that roof," said Jim. "Here, let me get it. I'll prop up the beams and then go out and clear." Golden Lady lunged onto the counter at the same time that Jim reached up for the beams, and their torsos competed for the tight space. Golden Lady got knocked to the side. "Better to let me do it, little sister. I'm the man. Taller," Jim nodded and smiled to her. He pulled over a crate and stood facing Golden Lady, ready to step up again.

"What!?" shouted Golden Lady, and she swung her arm back and whomped her clawed-hand onto Jim's balls. "What are you now, John Wayne!?" There was a dull thud, and Jim doubled over with his mouth opened in a silent scream. Everyone froze. Golden Lady locked her grip. Then a terrifying howl pierced the squalor of the dark yurt.

"HAAAAAAAAAAAAAAAAAAAAAAAAAAAAAA!!!!"

Tears squeezed from the corners of Jim's bulging eyes. Nancy couldn't believe what was happening. Golden Lady let go, and Jim hobbled over with his eyes popped and saliva spewing from his puffed cheeks and mouth. He sat down on a bunk, trembling and steadying himself with one arm. There was a tense silence as everyone started to move again.

"Drink!" Tami exclaimed. Nancy focused on Tami as everyone else seemed to disappear. "The great cure-all," Tami continued. "Whenever I have any questions about the meaning of life, caved in roofs and the like, I avoid 'em and go teleing … or better yet, have a drink! Butch? you feel the same, don't you, baby? 'Course you do. Here, come to The Snow Princess, Butchy. I'll suck on you. Make you feel good. Feelin' good is what life is all about. So everybody get along and have a good time, right? Have a good time. Feel good. Very simple." Nobody replied.

"Apologize for being male-dominant," Golden Lady said to Jim, who was doubled over and whimpering.

"Now that's not keeping it simple, is it?" Tami asked.

"Shut up, you washed-up old bitch," spat Golden Lady.

"Whoa," said Tami, and she dropped her eyes and lay back on her bunk.

"Leave him alone," Catherine said forcefully to Golden Lady.

"What are you gonna do about it, Ra? I have principles. We have principles. At least we used to. Don't trust you anymore. Fought long and hard for our rights."

"You're getting old. Old and vicious, really are," Catherine said to Golden Lady. "It's been there all along; now it's swallowing you up."

"And you're any better or different?" asked Golden Lady

"I liked him trying to be a man," said Moonshadow. "It was quaint."

"Quaint and dead. OK?" asked Golden Lady stepping closer to Jim, who looked up, hesitantly. "Now apologize for being a male-dominant, sexist, chauvinist, misogynic pig," Golden Lady said sternly to Jim as she shook her finger at him.

"I'm sorry," Jim stammered, choking back tears. "It slipped. Won't ever happen again. I promise. I know better."

"Fine," said Golden Lady, "apology accepted. Next time I want it in writing."

Nancy heard Golden Lady's reprimand and sat with her mouth in a big O, stunned. She pictured thousands of these hideous women and their notions in every nook and cranny of life and school and institution. Their insidious destruction exacted its toll through each gender sensitivity class to coed team to female empowerment day to fabricated harassment to the death of the simple stay-at-home mom. And Nancy wondered if this explained Jim. The rest of Jim was like herself, Nancy thought — a refugee of parents absorbed by themselves. "Lord help us all," Nancy pleaded.

Tami made her way over to Nancy. "Here sister, have a drink," Tami said to Nancy. "Looks like you need one. Maybe Sugar Burger needs one too." Tami handed a mug full of mudslide to Nancy.

"Thanks," Nancy croaked, taking the mug and placing it on the floor. Tami came in and out of Nancy's focus. "Sorry about the nasty comments they made. Who are you anyway?" Nancy heard herself ask.

"The Snow Princess," Tami said wistfully. "The woman on the beast. The great prostitute who sits on many waters. What else do you want to know? Over and over again. Nothing more; nothing less. World as world. I rule it," she said with a shrug and sat down. "Some have called me evil," she added, flashing a coy smile up to Nancy. "Am I evil? … Well, maybe a little. All are intoxicated with my adulteries. Come and devour me."

Jim wiped his eyes and curled up in a ball behind Nancy.

"What you just did was morally wrong," Catherine said to Golden Lady.

"Get over it Ra. You've gone spongy. Siding with the oppressor."

"I've repented," said Catherine softy, lowering her eyes.

"You've what!?" shouted Moonshadow and Golden Lady together.

"I want to live in the glory of God. I want to follow Jesus."

"That's bizarre, Catherine. You've gotten strange. Really. And you're done. I'm taking your place as Princess Ra," said Golden Lady. "That's it. Had it."

"I'm goin' straight."

"Straight?!"

"Dancing!" Tami shouted, suddenly jumping up. "Watch me do my dance, pagan witches; watch my dance and know your master."

Everyone in the yurt fixed on Tami. She slid bell rings onto her toes and fingers and stripped off her top and long underwear bottom so she stood only in her panties in wrinkled nakedness. Tami lifted one leg and placed her arms just so. A strange, sing-song tune emitted from deep within her abdomen, and she closed her eyes and hopped and danced, and the bells rang. As she danced, the skin around her belly and breasts, legs and arms tightened and lifted. Her waist grew shapely, and her hair began to shine its copper-brunette again. The corners of her mouth rose in a sensuous smile, and her hand passed between her legs and ready lips. Tami became young and radiant. Her bare breasts lifted to the sides slightly. Nancy and the entourage stared, transfixed. As they gazed, Golden Lady and Moonshadow felt their joints freeze. Their hair grew coarse and white and matted. Golden Lady held out her hands and watched them crease and shrivel. The two women shrank in their thermals until they fell below a nasty dowager's hump. Meanwhile, Tami smiled with her eyes closed. She smoothed her hands around her curved waist and bodice, inhaled deeply through her nostrils and yearned for a new man.

"Stop her!" screeched Moonshadow. "She's killing us."

Golden Lady lunged for Tami, who stepped lightly to the side. Golden Lady crashed into the woodstove. The stove slammed onto its side, and the top banged off. Burning embers spewed onto the damp floor and hissed while a flaming log instantly ignited the nylon shell of a sleeping bag draped onto the floor. The plastic cover on the bag exploded into flames. Choking black smoke filled the yurt. The fumes knocked Nancy to her knees, and she stared wide-eyed at the instantly unfolding disaster. Catherine covered her face and stomped on the flaming bag. As she did so, flames peeled away as if they were liquid and ignited someone's down parka. Thick, plastic smoke stuffed the yurt like it was a toxic steam room. Nancy dropped to the floor frantically trembling and grabbed at gear and sleeping bags.

"Get out," shouted Catherine. "Everybody out."

There was coughing and screaming. Outside, Nancy watched the yurt erupt into a column of yellow and orange flames, which illuminated a billowing, black cloud. The fired danced upon her watery pupils as a dream.

***

The surroundings grew darker and darker. Nancy jerked her head, startled by a voice.

"Nancy! Wake up. Come to. What happened? You OK?" Asked Catherine.

Nancy lay in the snow, dazed and confused. Her muscles felt rubbery and limp with fear. The sky fell in slow motion, and she began to breathe fast and hard.

"What? What happened? Jimmy?" Nancy asked looking up at Catherine. "The yurt's on fire."

"Nancy, you blacked out. Fell over," said Catherine, kneeling down beside her. "Here, let me help you up. Have some water. Something to eat."

Nancy stood. "Come on, don't lose it now; don't get helpless," she panted to herself and shook her head, falling over her poles. Catherine lunged to hold her. Nancy closed her eyes and visualized her father and the stories he told her about rescues and accidents in the mountains. "Come on, Daddy," Nancy whispered to herself as she watched her legs start to move. *What should I do? I know you love me,* she thought to herself.

"Catherine," Nancy said, turning on her poles. "I'm scared. Haven't eaten much today. I'm getting loopy. Just lost it. Thought I saw Jimmy again. The yurt was burning down."

"We need to go back up," Catherine said, handing Nancy a water bottle, as Nancy unwrapped an energy bar and bit off a frozen chunk. "Jim and the others are not down here," Catherine continued earnestly. "They can't be left out all night. Something bad has happened."

Nancy took the bottle and drank and gnawed off another big hunk of frozen bar. With one hand, Nancy unzipped her coat, reached in and turned her beacon back to receive at eighty meters. She picked up Catherine's beacon, and the beeping stunned her to attention. Nancy tried to place everything as real — that it was growing dark, and Jim was still missing. Her head felt light and swum from side-to-side. Nancy passed the water bottle back to Catherine. They kick-turned and headed back up the tight valley.

"Switch your beacon to receive," Nancy said with a mouthful of bar, turning to Catherine, who was right behind her. The two plowed ahead in the snowy silence.

"Let's traverse behind the yurt now," Catherine said. "I'm not going to give up."

Nancy closed her eyes and kick-stepped around to start a switchback. When she opened her eyes, a faint purple glow shone on the smooth blanket ahead of her. Nancy pointed her pole to the glowing snow angel. But Catherine did not see the form. Nancy fought every impulse to keep heading down to scan for tracks and beacon signals below the south-facing drops of Peak 21. Static sounded on each beacon. When they were about 200 feet above the yurt, a barely perceptible ping rose through the background blur.

"Listen, listen," Nancy said. Both girls stopped and slowed their breathing. "Keep moving forward."

The ping grew steadily louder and each adjusted her lead accordingly. As the lead lights and beeping went crazy, Nancy's heart leapt to her throat. She could not comprehend what they were going to find. The aspens were spaced comfortably, and the grade was gentle. The snow drifting all around was peaceful in the closing dusk.

At eight meters the lights all flashed, and the grade had steepened to about 27 degrees. The aspen stand was tighter. But the scene made no sense to Nancy. At five meters, the two girls stood among thin aspens. There were no ski tracks. Only a beautifully, creamy-smooth slope fell away into the winter night.

"I don't get it. Dig, dig. He's here. I don't get it. I don't get it," Nancy said over and over as she slung off her pack, ripped out her shovel and started to dig into the darkness. Her arm muscles trembled, and she fought against turning limp with fear.

Catherine adjusted her beacon to zero and scanned close to the surface. "More this way," she said, as she scanned up, then down and left and right. "Right below here." After a couple of big shovelfuls, Nancy's plastic blade ran along material and something dense.

"Oh man, oh my," Nancy panted. Both beacons went nuts, beeping and flashing.

"He's just laying there."

"What in the world happened? Where are the others?" Nancy breathed. Adrenaline volted around her limbs. They frantically brushed away the snow from Jim's face where an ice mask was forming around his mouth and nose. A whistle protruded through the frozen and fleshy crust. "Pulse," Nancy said. She tore off her glove and gently pulled the whistle out of Jim's mouth with trembling fingers. Nancy put her cheek to his blue lips as she felt for his aorta on his neck. "Oh good, oh thank goodness. Breath and pulse."

"Here, shovel the snow back. Can we bring him to?" Catherine asked.

Nancy unzipped Jim's jacket shell and turned off his beacon. An abrupt silence magnified the darkness. Nancy felt herself ease for the first time. She sensed her father as she recalled his voice and remembered his mountain stories. "Never panic," he had always said, as if he knew Nancy would some day follow him into the mountains. "Work methodically but quickly. When a victim comes-to, be positive. Be calm." Nancy nodded her head as if her dad sat next to her and spoke. "Don't let things escalate. Don't add to escalation by panicking and blundering. Don't add trauma to trauma. Be cool. Calmly re-establish control. Work through checklists. Start an action plan. Be very calm and deliberate. That's what happened on Denali. Just got out of control, man. Fear and panic are your enemy. They kill in the mountains."

"Warmth, hot fluids, check his extremities," Nancy said clearly to Catherine, who dug out and stomped down a platform next to Jim. Nancy pulled a headlight from her pack. She cleared Jim's legs of snow and winced when she felt his left shin. "Dig down, carefully," Nancy continued. They both picked away the snow until Jim was clear. Catherine pulled out a sleeping bag and ensolite pad from Nancy's pack. They popped Jim's bindings and gently freed his legs. Nancy carefully unbuckled his boots, while Catherine examined his fingers. Nancy gingerly pulled Jim's foot from his tele boot and peeled off his sock. She flashed the light on his toes. Black seeped into frozen white. Nancy pulled up his shell leg on the shin that she had felt. The light showed a fist-size lump. "What's this all about, Catherine? What am I looking at?" Nancy asked. She felt herself shake and start to breathe in spasms and cry.

"Slow down. Easy, easy, Nancy," Catherine said as she looked at Jim's leg and feet. "That's healed, partially," Catherine said as she bent closer; lifted his long underwear and ran her finger carefully over the lump. There's scar tissue," she said to herself. "Did he have an old injury there?"

"No, nothing, never. What is this, Catherine. I'm scared."

"Here, quick, forget it; get both boots off. Lift away his pack. We'll roll him into the bag. Need to heat 'im up. Core heat. Get in there with him, fast." Nancy sat on her haunches with her mouth open and seemed unable to move. "Let me, let me," Catherine whispered.

Catherine removed Jim's other boot and pulled him onto the pad. She took off Jim's jacket shell and her own. Catherine dropped her shell pants, pulled off her top, then Jim's and lay down next to him. Nancy tucked the bag over them both. Then Catherine slowly pulled Jim on top of her and hugged him, skin to skin and core to core. Nancy shook her head and fought against a heavy sensation that seized and immobilized her body. She retucked the bag around the two and pulled out her down coat and draped it over their heads. Catherine held Jim in her arms and placed his head in the nape of her neck. She rubbed her hands up and down his back and sides and contracted and released every muscle in her body in rapid motion. She began to break a sweat as she and the fiber-filled sleeping bag heated. Catherine breathed hard and snorted through her nostrils. After a long while, Jim's icy body began to warm, and his mass felt softer on top of her. It was even colder now and pitch-dark. They were all burying again in a fresh dumping of crystals.

"What's going to happen, Catherine?" Nancy asked anxiously.

"Let's try — n wake him up. Cold puts you into deep sleep. Semi-unconscious," she replied. "Jim, Jimmy!" Hey!" Catherine shouted and shook Jim's shoulders. Both girls heard a groan.

"Oh good, good," said Nancy as she watched on hands and knees. "Come on, baby. Wake up to me," Nancy pleaded to Jim. She lay down and got under the bag and jacket and stroked Jim's face and ski hat with her hand. "Come on, sweetheart." She kissed him on the cheek. "What happened to you out here, Jimmy?" Jim groaned again and moved.

"Good," Catherine said. "Poor baby's just cold. Guess I can still make a guy hot," she said and both girls laughed a little. Pressure released like a hydraulic valve let loose. Jim opened his eyes.

"Hey, hey, Jimmy," Nancy said loudly into the snowy stillness. Jim turned his head one way, then the other, unable to focus. His eyes found Nancy's face, and they wandered listlessly. Nancy kissed him lightly on his cold lips and all over his face. "I love you, Jimmy. Gonna make it. Get you back now."

"Have to keep those feet and hands wrapped well," Catherine said as she hugged Jim. "Don't bang or rub. Skin 'ill fall right off. I don't understand the shin."

Catherine slid out from under, and Jim groaned again. The two zipped him into the bag, closing it around his head with the drawstring.

"Good thing I thought to keep that bag and pad in my pack," Nancy said.

"Alright, not perfect. Gonna have to haul him out of here. Luckily it's downhill. Never be able to move otherwise," Catherine said.

"What about the other two. Were they with you? Did you know them?" Nancy asked.

"No, met them at the Blue Hotel. Turn on your beacon."

Nancy turned her beacon to 80 meters and heard only static. She stepped beyond Jim and submersed to her chest and scanned with her beacon. Catherine dug out a small flashlight and twisted it on. Nancy carefully swept away a foot or two of dust. "Look," Nancy breathed. "Shine here. A slide layer. It slid. Soft slab. This slid. That's what happened. Oh man, the others must be buried. Catherine, what are we gonna do? It's dark. We've got Jim to deal with."

"Nothing," replied Catherine standing and pointing the tiny beam of her flashlight into the darkness. "The girls can go when we get back."

The two stuffed everything into their packs, including Jim's boots. Nancy slid Jim's skis down the side pockets of her pack. The tall skis knocked around awkwardly. Both girls got on either side of Jim, grabbed the material around the face hole of the sleeping bag and pulled. Snow covered his face, and they stopped to protect the opening with one of Catherine's pullovers. The load was heavy, and they wallowed through the deep snow on their skis. But the nylon bag slid along as each crystal received its precious burden and submitted to gravity.

Meanwhile, below, Butch sat outside the yurt on the piney ground in darkness. He could faintly hear the others. Butch looked at himself and perceived the outline of his body. He passed his hand through his chest and wept without control and clenched his teeth in silence. Tears streamed in ghostly saltiness. Butch's only desire was to find his remains and hold onto his flesh and bones.

El Viejo, Dan the Spooner, circled around and around Butch, wringing his hands. He could not see Butch. But Dan could feel him. Feel his agony. Feel painfully what Butch was going through. Dan had never known anyone to enter his nether world. Dan reached out to touch what he felt with his heart. But he could not touch Butch. As Dan paced around Butch, the day that Dan pummeled into darkness came back to him with the clarity of a movie reel playing over and over: huddled around the silver spoon, everyone's nostrils flaring, ripped on cocaine, higher than a kite. "WHEW!" Dan bellowed. "Powder, man!"

Everybody laughed into the wild, blue sky, including the flashing girl who put bells on her toes and tore off his clothes at every chance. Powering along the Southwest Kingdom like an invincible freight train. Feeling the snowpack whomp, settle and crack; and ignoring all of the screaming intuitions rising up in him and saying, "Turn back!" Even Dan's friends shouted at him to stop. Dan could still hear their voices as he waved them onto the bowl. The entire slope collapsed under his Head 360's like sugar cake; he slammed into the first tree and knew that his head had been severed from his body. Then Dan sat in darkness, stunned and scared. He gushed forth a montage of shame, guilt and sadness, even embarrassment. Streaming tears onto the ground, Dan heard the flashing girl, Satan himself, laugh and dance and fade into the distance.

CHAPTER 5

THE SPEED OF LIFE

David Winchester lay awake in a cold sweat. It was predawn. Something was wrong. Terribly wrong. He was absolutely certain. *What was it?* he asked himself. David felt his wife Margaret breathing softly next to him — the quiet breath of life that arises from mystery and returns. David swung out of bed and leaned over Hanna's little bed. In the glow from a night light, David gazed upon his daughter's precious face and watched her chest rise and fall. *Fine. Everything's fine here,* David thought. He stretched out his arms between Hanna and Margaret and bowed his head as if to cherish and sustain them … to give thanks. Moon Dog, Jamie Lynch, was visiting. David lowered his arms and watched the light squeeze under the door from the adjoining guest room. Moon Dog was on East Coast time. David knew he would be up running numbers for The Area. David lay back in bed and listened and felt the storm finally clearing. He sensed an opening sky and wind-blown stars because a cold draft squeezed through the sliding windows that overlooked Big Pine. A snow machine whined up the mountain. It was Skeeter, David thought, doing powder shots with his buddies from town. Probably wearing headlights. The sound was comforting but did not ease his nerves. David pictured Skeeter and the guys on top of the snow-covered mountain, dropping into dusty waist-deep with big grins and pasted beards. Soon Skeeter and the crew would fire-up the cats and groom the entire area so that the tourists wouldn't get hurt in the uncut. David slipped back in bed and pulled up the quilt — a beautiful hand-stitched Amish quilt given as a wedding gift by Moon Dog and Jessica. His finger tips quivered. "What's goin' on?" he asked the darkness. He jerked up and slid into his thermal top and bottoms.

"Moon," David whispered as he opened the guest room door.

Jamie sat at a small desk, enveloped by a folding light. David gripped with feelings for Moon Dog as he realized that he looked older, hunched over the laptop with his bifocals. Jamie was a friend and a father to him. They were both from the East and had boated together for years, including The River.

"David old buddy," Moon whispered, "do you know how to say condominium? Do you know how to live and breathe real-estate development?"

"Shhhit," David laughed, "don't look too hard at those numbers."

"'Cause if you don't, my friend, if you don't start developing real estate and other capacity, this enterprise is toast. Period. Do you hear me?" Jamie asked directly, lowering his head and looking at David over his glasses. "These numbers are scary. Not gonna be able to service your debt. About to get eaten. How anybody makes money runnin' a ski area is beyond me."

"I hear ya, Jamie. Various problems with more condos. Septic. Regs. Enviros. Never mind. Something's wrong."

"I'll say. Grow a thicker skin, David. That's called business overhead. Hire lawyers, get a PR firm, grease a politician, rack it up and pass on the expenses. Do or die, my friend. Build sympathy with the town, with the zoning boards, with the state, with the whole country. Tell a story. Be distinctive. Offer deep value. Get on the map, Red. Don't just survive — flourish. Grow or die. You're not going to squeeze enough money out of vendor leases and lift tickets. No way."

"I know. I want all those things. Need you out here full-time, man."

"You guys can do it … I'm sending out my marketing and branding guy, Michael Thornburgh, this summer.

"Moon, you're right. We need help, fast. Need capital, too. I'm all ears. I want to work hard and succeed."

"Once I see marketing, I'll pull financing together."

"Great, I really, really appreciate your help, Jamie man. You're the best," David said and patted Moon on the shoulder. "Something's got me on edge. I think it's Nancy."

"Should be on edge, buddy. David, we're talking imminent bankruptcy. Do you hear me? Only a true friend can hit you with it right between the eyes. Now look, you've got potential. Lots of it. Beautiful location. Fun for families. Conferences. Retreats. Summer events. Need a golf course. Whatever else. Think big. Don't blow this. Got a good thing. Business is hard. Have to be tough, persistent," Moon said making a fist.

"I've got you," David replied. "I don't expect sunshine pumped up my ass."

David pulled a chair next to Moon and put his hands behind his head.

"I know you're workin' hard. Work smart, that's all," Moon said lowering his voice, realizing he may have come on a little strong. "Aw," Moon exhaled, picking up a pencil and tossing it back down. "Submit," Moon added, looking up at David and thinking about what he said because it was meant more for him. The two regarded each other in comfort. "Hold tight. Let go. Want and don't want … all at once. That's the hardest part," Moon Dog said quietly in his soft drawl. "Take life seriously; don't take it seriously at all."

"Seek first … what is in us … beyond us … who we are," David replied. "We know where we're headed … ultimately."

"The Kingdom of God," Moon said, exhaling and shaking his head, suddenly overcome with a feeling and vision he could never explain. There was a long silence. "And now?" Moon asked. "You've got a wife and child to support. What are you gonna do if this fails?"

"Pray," David blurted, feeling heat surge into his chest and limbs, "to Jesus Christ the living God, maker of all, who is with us right now at this moment, who never lets us down … The Kingdom begins now … I'm grateful for our friendship, Moon," David said quietly, meeting Jamie's eyes. There was a long, comfortable silence, as the two guys looked into each other and honored the living reality to which David pointed.

"Um," Moon grunted thoughtfully, "you're right, man."

"Look, I hear you, Moon," David said at length, leaning back in his chair. "I know the picture. I'm totally in. Set it aside for now. Something's going on with Nancy."

"Are they late returning?"

"Not exactly."

"We need the Chaz Man," Moon said, laughing quietly.

"Jamie, I'm serious. I've got a definite, bad feeling."

"I remember the last time you got a bad feeling, a definite, bad feeling," Moon Dog replied, smiling.

"Knew something big was coming on The River."

"Should have listened to you, right?" Moon asked.

"Should've. Could've. Would've. Were busy saving your old lady."

"We go back, eh Red?"

The two gripped hands in the soul-man shake. David's throat choked with emotion.

"Too far, Moon Dog."

"Getting to be old bros," Moon replied. "What's the guy like she's with?"

"Good question. Young, inexperienced. Seems like an OK guy. Has potential. I like him."

"Solid?"

"I have no idea. Just don't understand these dudes comin' along, Jamie. I really don't. Can't say what he'd do or not do."

"Does he know who he is; who he really is?"

"You mean is he saved?"

"Sure."

"No. Not at all. I've prayed for Pepe. A lot. He's touch 'n go. I dragged him out of the chutes in December at the bottom of what could be called a suicide run. I don't think he cared if he lived or died. Another disposable kid."

"Um," Moon grunted in thought. "All right, tell me about the next Red Bone adventure, 'cause I can see you've got that look."

"We need to snow machine into the back country. I really think Nancy's in trouble."

"Snow machine across dumped-on slopes. Bone man, we just got about five feet of new snow."

"Stay low."

"Where to?"

"Don't know yet."

"You have feelings for her don't you?"

"We all do."

"You do in particular. Alright, let me call down to Jessy in the trailer. Let her know. How many days?"

"Two or three. May have cell contact. I'll figure out where we're going and brief Skeets. Let's get the gear together … fast, Moon. This is a bad feeling, Jamie. Really bad. The worst I've had in a long time."

Moon stared at David, and the two guys locked eyes again as a soft pink began to spread over the top of Big Pine and filter through the guest room window. Moon Dog turned and phoned down to Jessica, who was staying with Rosa and Kyle and the babies. David pulled out his shells from the guest room closet and suited up. Margaret stirred.

***

Two hours later Moon Dog and Red Bone were screaming through a sea of deep powder behind Big Pine with the north couloirs of Mad Dog Mountain hanging ominously overhead. They were following Tin Cup Creek and headed to Rattling Brook Ravine. David gunned the throttle, and the snow machine lunged and sank. David and Jamie had already stopped twice to dig out the machine. They were pulling a covered skid trailer with their packs and skis. Jamie wrapped David's waist with his arm and checked his global positioning unit with his free hand. Snow blasted over the windshield in a tunnel. The machine swooped down a dip and thudded headlong into a powdery drift. The engine spun to a high pitch then gurgled to a stop. Silence.

"Come on," spat David.

"Maxed," said Moon. "Too deep. I'm lovin' that. Aren't we supposed to be having a fun powder day?"

"Right, fun is forever. Forget digging out again; we'll tour from here," David said.

"Tour. You make it sound so genteel. Why Rattling anyway?"

"Just a feeling," David replied as he swung off the machine and sank to his chest.

"Whinny," Moon said as he took in the depth of the fresh pack. His glacier shades accentuated his round face, which was starting to crease with age. "This is serious." David hauled out their packs. When Jamie heaved on his, he puffed out his cheeks. "Getting too old for this stuff, man. Are you sure?"

"Nance and I have a special relationship. I can feel her. Really can. Know she needs me."

"We all have a special relationship with Nancy. All right Red Bone, let's slog."

"Wait, we're half cocked," David said and turned. He put his hand on Jamie's shoulder. David closed his eyes, bowed his head and placed his other arm out to receive the Spirit. David squeezed his eyes hard, and Moon Dog lowered his head. "Father … living Father … Lord Jesus … protect us. Guide us by your Holy Spirit; be with us. Amen."

"Amen brother," Jamie whispered and patted David's shoulder.

Red Bone and Moon Dog started digging forward, and it was sobering. Both grew instantly hot and pumped sweat. They dug ahead one slow step at a time. Snow squalls opened and closed a blue sky, bringing snowy darkness, then creamy light. Both David and Jamie imagined burying graceful turns down a thirty degree slope with the sun on their backs. But neither guy questioned what they were doing.

As Moon Dog pushed behind David, he lifted his eyes to the world around him. The beauty gripped his chest — the peaks, the pines, the crystals fluffing through his fingers like cotton. So too, Moon felt the deep comfort of being with David again, his buddy … in the mountains, in the power country. Whether on rivers or back slopes, the two were tight. Moon Dog always felt a quiet awe for David's intuitions, his natural abilities, his uncanny means to perceive and flow through the most intense moments. Moon knew that without any fanfare David was tapped into the one Supreme reality that surged with his every choice, his every motion and breath. On telies, rivers or rock, David possessed a grace … an inner peace that welled from the higher Source.

Moon breathed hard and thought about David. Moon felt his thighs burn. He sensed all the years as a satisfying fatigue. Moon Dog knew that the long goodbye had started. As he grew older, Moon eased into more and more limits as to what he was willing or able to do out here. Yet, Moon Dog felt his surroundings more intensely than ever … until he stood transfixed by a single crystal shimmering purple, blue and crimson in the brilliant, milky sunlight and pointing to Beyond.

"Moon? You OK, buddy?" David breathed, stopping when he realized that Moon Dog stood motionless behind him.

"Um good … it's all so good … so beautiful."

David turned, lifting both poles and dug ahead, honoring Jamie's repose. David knew that Moon was changing — that he did less but looked around and appreciated more. David let it be and toured onward. Moon Dog stepped forward again and soon matched David's pace, heel for heel.

***

At dawn the same day, Nancy sat up in her sleeping bag in the stale darkness of the abandoned Forest Service cache. The ten-by-ten, plywood space was buried and packed with bodies lined in a row. The walls and ceiling bowed and leaked snow melt. Nancy remembered the night before. When she and Catherine had progressed a few hundred yards dragging Jim, the haunting light from a blazing bonfire danced through the snow and trees. Nancy could not believe her eyes, and her gut cinched with apprehension. When the two girls reached the burning yurt, Nancy stared in wonder at the fire sizzling into an ugly pit and shooting flames into falling crystals. The smoke billowed a horrible black and smelled like burning plastic and garbage. No one was there. Catherine held out her arm and bowed her head. "It's my sin. Churn it up and burn it away. Please burn it away," she begged and fell to her knees. Both girls turned numb with confusion and fear. Jim lay at their feet as if wrapped in a body bag. Then a light floated toward them through the darkness. They watched the light come closer and become a body. Moonshadow trembled and fell to her knees, stammering. In fits and starts, she blurted what happened. There had been an argument — an accident where the woodstove knocked over. She and Golden Lady scrambled outside. Golden Lady dove back in to get everyone's gear. Moonshadow followed. They held their breath and were singed by the fire. The smoke stung their eyes as they blindly grabbed dunnage and shoved it out the door. Golden Lady passed out from smoke inhalation. The yurt exploded into flames. They had to escape, fast. Moonshadow yanked out Golden Lady. She pushed away the remaining gear and was repelled by the flames, which roared with burning plastic. Moonshadow revived

Golden Lady, and she remembered the cache from hiking in the summer.

"I'm worried he's going into deeper shock," Nancy whispered to Catherine, pushing away the images of the previous night.

Nancy pictured Butch and Tami's gear piled outside, unclaimed in a frozen heap. The reality of their presumed deaths fell as a dead weight upon her. Nancy sat up in her bag and placed the back of her hand on Jim's cheek and patted carefully down his chest. His skin still felt cold and clammy. She and Catherine had been up all night checking on Jim and wrapping naked with him with sleeping bags piled high. Nancy felt tired and punchy. Her eyes were swollen with fatigue. They revived Jim twice, but he kept falling back into a shock-stupor.

Catherine squeezed out of her bag and flashed a headlight onto Jim. She loosened the drawstring around the hood of his sleeping bag, and put her cheek close to his mouth. She unzipped the bag and placed her fingers tips carefully on Jim's aorta. Catherine then placed her hands under her armpits to warm them, touched Jim's core against his skin and felt up and down his body. She pulled out her hand and shook a limp wrist.

"Good sign," she said. "Peed on himself."

"Is that good?" asked Nancy. Catherine leaned over and unzipped Jim's bag to check him further. A putrid stench wafted outward. "He's lost his bowels. That can't be good," Nancy said with worry and fatigue in her voice.

"We'll wash him out," replied Catherine, trying to comfort Nancy.

"I'll help wash him," Moonshadow said. "I feel really badly about all that has happened. We should search and try 'n find the others — their bodies I guess." Moonshadow twisted on a small flashlight and slid into her shells and boots. She kicked a piece of plywood to the side and crawled out and up the snow tunnel. She immediately slid back in feet first. "Storm's passed. I can see stars. There may even be sun today."

"Thank goodness," said Catherine. "Very shallow breathing and pulse," she continued. Catherine flashed the light onto Jim's face and lifted his eyelids. Jim's pupils stayed half dilated. "Gotta be making some heat now. He needs more hot fluids even if we have to pour them down his throat," Catherine said quietly. "Some kind of liquid carbos too."

"This is iffy, Catherine. I'm scared," Nancy said, and her lower jaw trembled.

Catherine leaned over and put her arm around Nancy's shoulder. Moonshadow exhaled tensely and rubbed her hand up and down Nancy's back and frowned with concern.

"Look," said Golden Lady, as she watched the three girls, lying on her side and peering out the face-hole in her bag. Steam rose in little waves from her nose and mouth, "I realize you're upset, but we didn't get him into that slide. We're on our own backcountry trip. We're not respons—"

"We'll do everything we can to save him, Sherry," Catherine said to Golden Lady. "You've done plenty so far."

"Why are you using that name?" asked Golden Lady.

"Because it's your real name. Your baptized name."

"What has gotten into you?" snapped Golden Lady. "And what do you mean, 'done plenty?' Accidents happen — his, ours, the others."

"It's not just the yurt," said Catherine.

"I don't save men."

"What do you do then?" asked Nancy.

"Get payback for thousands of years of oppression."

"I don't buy any of that," Nancy said.

Golden Lady sat up and glared at Nancy.

"Is that a judgment?" Golden Lady snapped. "You and your kind have done a lot of damage. Patriarchal sympathizers and Bible toters. Intolerant," she said under her breath.

"No, what I'm saying is that I don't have to swallow it."

"You're a bigot."

"We are all broken," Nancy replied softly lowering her head. "Broken and depraved. I'll pray for your soul … and mine."

"I don't need anyone praying for me. Keep your patristic, Bible garbage to yourself."

Catherine hugged her knees and placed her head down. Golden Lady's words stabbed into her because they could have been hers not long ago. Catherine felt feelings — feelings for Nancy, feelings for Jim, feelings for herself, feelings for Sherry, Golden Lady. A yearning kindled into flame, and the flame ached for something — something just out of reach but present. Catherine felt herself breaking apart as she became the burning feeling erupting in her heart and lighting the dark fringes. Truth was bursting forth from mire to become a radiant blossom. "No, it's our turn now," Catherine blurted as tears streamed down her cheeks. "To make right. He's our doing. I've watched him. The burned-out shell of our war: weak and ineffectual; gender eradicated; unable to be strong, to make vows, to have deep and true feelings, to lead. We killed him … killed men. I must save him. I want to repent. I'm tired of being mad and lonely; tired of the endless battles; tired of what I've become, of what I've done; tired of being ugly and angry," Catherine sobbed. Golden Lady jerked, opened her mouth and dropped her head. She stared at Catherine.

"What?" Golden Lady asked slowly and sternly, "you need therapy or something Cat, really. And you're banished. Out, O U f'n T," Golden Lady spelled. "And don't ever call me by that name. Not who I am anymore." There was a long, tense silence, and all three listened to Catherine sobbing in spasms. "Fine, have it your way," Golden Lady continued. "I'm gone. I'll ski back and alert somebody. Don't expect anything more. Good luck."

"Can you live without your anger?" Nancy asked Golden Lady softly, searching for her eyes in the dark space.

Golden Lady avoided Nancy's eyes. Nancy's words entered Golden Lady and stuck as a burning lump in the pit of her stomach. Golden Lady zipped out of her bag. Her hands trembled as she stuffed things into her backpack.

"Can you live without being dependent on men?" Golden Lady snapped tersely, not looking at Nancy. "Under their rule."

"A woman needs a man," Nancy replied quietly as Catherine and Moonshadow watched her, "must yield to man. Let a man be a man. Let her be a woman. Let him love and please her and her him. Be happy together, for a lifetime and beyond. Let him lead," Nancy said almost in a whisper.

"Excuse me?" Golden Lady blurted, dropping her head and lifting her eyebrows. "If men are men at all, they're useless, irrelevant and potentially dangerous. Case in point," she finished, nodding at Jim's motionless hulk.

"Woman was made from man," Nancy said, almost inaudibly. "A man is a women's all. I very much love and admire all the men in my life."

"Am I hearing you?" Golden Lady asked, and Nancy fought away the feeling of fingers scratching down a blackboard. "Exactly what planet have you been on? Women have power and control now 'case you haven't noticed. In command of their own lives. The man-woman thing is a tool of oppression. It's history. Gone. Biological differences are meaningless. Crawl back into your cave ... with your caveman for that matter. Let him drag you around by the hair," Golden Lady snorted.

Nancy did not reply but put her hands in prayer and nodded her head toward Golden Lady. Everyone watched her lips move. Nancy turned and placed a hand on Jim's forehead. She bowed her head, and Catherine watched and did the same, hesitantly. "Oh Lord, holy Father," Nancy whispered, "by whose loving kindness our souls and bodies are renewed, mercifully look upon this thy servant, that every cause of sickness and weakness be removed, and Jim may be restored to soundness of health in body, mind and soul. We pray tha —"

"Stop it!" Golden Lady exploded, wiping a tear from her eye. "Imposing your bigoted religion on us. You're destroying me. Everything was fine before you came along. My own happiness. My lifestyle. My girls. We have our own god, and she's just fine thank you. Our Savior is leading us to cosmic consciousness that JESUS DOESN'T OWN! We have our political causes. Our purpose. What's good. You're taking it all away. STOP IT!" Golden Lady screamed. "And you two keep away from her. She's subversive. GET OUT OF HERE! GET OUT OF OUR LIFE!" Golden Lady continued screaming at Nancy and slamming her fists down on the dirty plywood floor. Jim's head banged up and down. He opened his eyes and groaned.

"Oh, um … where am I? … Nance? … Nancy?"

"Jimmy, thank goodness," Nancy said sweetly. "It's me, baby. Everything's all right. Gonna get you out."

"Give him fluids, quick," said Catherine, rising and ignoring Golden Lady. She propped up Jim's head, and Nancy placed a water bottle to his lips. Jim drank, and water trickled down either side of his mouth. He lay back down and shut his eyes. "He's finally warming up," said Catherine. "Let's get moving. We need to keep the shock from deepening."

"We should try some more hot tea," Moonshadow said gently to Nancy. "We have to eat something too. Going to be hard; can't see how we're going to get him up the ridge." Moonshadow paused, and there was a long silence. She looked over to Nancy and found her eyes. "I'm sorry for what happened, Nancy. For everything. What I said. Please forgive me too."

"Thanks," said Nancy, "I do."

"OK, gone," said Golden Lady. "When both of you are through inserting your heads up your asses, look me up at the Temple."

"Fine, go ahead," said Catherine, as her head swayed from side to side with weariness. "Thanks a lot. Could show a little empathy. That leaves three of us to pull. Can't carry him. It's going to be tough going. Really tough."

***

When Jim awoke, it was daylight. He was no longer buried. He squinted into an opaque light that revealed an open slope of fresh down. Jim was draped around the massive shoulders and back of a man with a short, blonde ponytail. Jim could see deep-purple tattoos emanating from secret places below and reaching a peaked crescendo around his thick neck. The man wore only a blue thermal top that was soaked with sweat. He breathed evenly and rose with powerful kicks up the steep slope. The man showed no sign of stopping or even slowing. Jim was strapped in between the man's back and an empty mountain pack. Climbing webbing was slung around Jim's butt and thighs and wrapped around the man's waist. Jim's feet and tele boots dangled loosely, and Jim sensed that his buckles were undone. Jim could not feel his fingers. His hands were stuffed into oversize mittens that were not his. His skis and Life Link poles rested in the side pockets of the pack and swung back and forth with each step forward. Jim lay his head down sideways between the man's neck and shoulder and held onto his wide muscular chest. Jim felt light-headed. He had no idea who the man was or where they were going, and he was too weak to protest or even speak. It was utterly still on the mountain. Jim felt himself rock forward on the man's back with each step, as if he rode a mule. The man sensed that Jim was awake and twisted around awkwardly. There were pockmark scars on his face that looked like healed-over punctures and slashes, and his eyes were fierce, yet glowed with a kindness as he nodded to Jim and climbed higher. The alpine sun warmed Jim's back. He closed his eyes and fell asleep.

After some time, Jim opened and rubbed his eyes. He lay on a bunk under a wool blanket and colorful hand-stitched quilt. Jim looked out a framed window in a small, one room hut. A woodstove offered a scented radiance as it snapped and purred. As the view came into focus, Jim realized that he was high on the Southeast shoulder of Peak 21. He had memorized all of David's pictures of the peak. From where he lay, Jim could see the distinctive, scooped summit, reached by a technical climb up the exposed East Ridge. From the summit it was possible to launch into the scoop that opens to an expansive south-facing slope, dropping 3,000 vertical feet back into the lower reaches of Rattling Brook Ravine. Straight, steep line. No obstructions. An epic ski. Rarely done because of the remote location and constant avy danger. Cheerful sunlight packed through the windows and spilled onto a varnished knotty-pine floor. Jim looked out another window and saw that the hut was nestled among dwarf spruce just inside treeline. He could see cables attached to the structure and secured to the side of the mountain. Jim looked around at the neat shelves and light-pine wall boards. He could see that the walls were thick and insulated. Jim was dressed only in his thermals. Wrapped in the blankets, he felt warm and comfortable. The hulk of a man sat on a stool by his side and carefully swung Jim's feet off the bed. Jim realized for the first time that his hands were soaking in pans of tepid water. The man pushed Jim's thermals up above his knee caps and slid his feet into a wide bucket where a thermometer floated. Jim squeezed to a sit-up to see his feet. The man placed his thick arm lightly around Jim's shoulders to help him see. Jim looked at the man, now dressed in bibs and a T-shirt, and tried to comprehend the endless ripples of lean muscle packed one on top of the other as his chest and back flared to a defined V. There were blazing tattoos on the outsides of his biceps. His forearms were thick, and his large hands showed a dark, weathered top and smooth inside callus. The man stood and reached for another bucket of water, and Jim could see that his bibs hung loosely over his left buttock as if half his butt cheek was simply gone. The man sat down and held up Jim's feet. He ran his fingers in a line above the section of Jim's toes that were frozen in blackness. Jim swallowed hard as he assessed the damage. He could see that he may loose each big toe — if not all of his toes. Jim lifted his hands out of the pans and examined his finger tips, which were also black. Jim did not know what to think or do. He lay back and looked up at the pine-board ceiling and watched a single cobweb wave in the rising heat from the woodstove.

Jim felt the man's palm run across the wound on the leg that had bowed around the aspen and El Viejo had healed. A large first aid box lay open at the man's feet. The man bent over and looked at the healed wound closely and with wonder. He creased his eyes then lightly ran his fingers over the lump again. He placed Jim's feet back in the bucket and propped some worn pillows behind his head and back. The man did not speak and worked with the utmost care as he shook a thermometer and placed it under Jim's tongue. The man lightly touched Jim's forehead and brushed his oily hair to the side. He rose and went to a sink by a kitchen area. The man returned with a steaming washcloth lightly dabbed with soap and swabbed Jim's forehead and face. It felt good, and Jim lifted to meet his comforting touch. The man pulled a clean towel from a nail and patted Jim dry. The big man bent over and took out the thermometer, held it up and read the figure. He touched Jim's forehead again and wrapped the blankets tighter. The light outside on the mountain began to glow into a textured yellow, and Jim knew it was late afternoon. Jim watched the man pump a gas stove, then pull floured tortillas and hunks of cheese and dried beef from an ice chest sunk into the counter. He popped the lid off a tin can and took out a bag of dried black beans. The man lit the stove, which then hummed softly. He stepped over and opened the door, reached around the corner and packed a chuckroast coffee pot with snow. The man closed the door tightly and placed the overflowing pot on the waiting stove.

Jim realized that he was famished. His stomach began to roll and gurgle as he anticipated smelling dried beans soaking in steaming water. The water on the stove began to boil and steam onto a window above the stove. The man poured boiling water into a mug in which he placed a tea ball, retrieved from another tin on a shelf above the sink. The smell of cinnamon and roasted chicory root mingled with pine smoke. The spicy aura filled the snug space, and Jim melted into his blankets. The big man came over with the steaming mug and held Jim's head as he gingerly guided the mug to his lips. Jim could feel his wide fingers cradling the back of his neck and head. The tea instantly warmed Jim's core. He closed his eyes and fell asleep again. When Jim awoke, the man was propping him up with more pillows. He bent down and lifted Jim's feet and poured into the bucket a small amount of hot water from a kettle that had been slowly churning on the woodstove. He poured hot water into the finger pans as well. Jim felt a slight warmth this time as the man mixed the water with his hand. He then checked the thermometer in the bucket and placed the thermometer in one of the pans. The man retrieved a tin plate from the top of the woodstove with two bean and beef burritos and knelt down to Jim. Jim raised his dripping hands and nodded thank you, then realized he could not hold the plate because of his frostbitten fingers. Jim's hands trembled, and he started to tear and tried to force himself to stop crying. He could not, and the man got up and placed the plate back on the stove. He came over and held Jim as he sobbed. The big man looked up and beyond the ceiling. After some time, Jim calmed. The man gently slid away and rested Jim back onto the pillows and nodded that it was OK. He retrieved the plate of food and sat on the edge of the bunk next to Jim and put his arm around his shoulder so as to hold him up. With his other hand he held the burrito in three fingers to Jim's mouth as Jim balanced the tin plate with the top side of his bandaged fist. With his teeth, Jim tore off large hunks of burrito that slid down the sides of his mouth and onto the plate. The man wiped Jim's mouth with a clean dishrag that smelled like fresh soap. Jim grunted and breathed through his nostrils and looked up to the man and into his encouraging eyes.

When Jim finished, the man set the plate on the floor. He held Jim in his powerful arm and pulled the blankets up and onto his legs so that Jim would be warm. The light on the mountain turned white, then glowed pink. The man held a tin cup of cool mountain water, and Jim drank deeply. He relaxed back and closed his eyes and swallowed. The pink light turned silver, then darkened to indigo-blue until Jim could see stars in the mountain sky, framed by the window just above his bunk. The big man lit a single candle. At length a half-moon rose and spread a soft light around the peaks. A mysterious light from Beyond — from the same light and the same Person that could make a man or a baby, a marriage or a mountain, a cosmos or any number of worlds. Easily. The man rose and lit several more candles. He stuffed chunks of wood into the stove, pulled on his thermals and shells, buckled into his plastic tele boots and stepped out the door sideways. Jim heard shoveling; then the man returned.

The big man held his hands over the woodstove to warm. He stood for a long time, and Jim warmed and tried to fathom the constant effort that was being expended for him. This awareness made his body feel heavy, and Jim's eyes nodded shut. The man went back outside, and Jim faintly heard shoveling, then chopping as he fell asleep.

***

Meanwhile, back in Rattling Brook Ravine and worlds away, Nancy and Catherine bent over Jim, who was stuffed in his sleeping bag as a makeshift litter. “Is that deeper shock?” Nancy asked Catherine as Jim moaned and thrashed from side to side.

They had slit holes into the sides of the bag and passed through their poles, handles first. When Nancy, Catherine and Moonshadow pulled, Jim’s limp body crumpled and buried in the loose snow. It was two steps and heave. In one hour they had progressed only a hundred yards up the slope from the cache and burned-out yurt.

“Nance, I’m sorry, honey, this doesn’t look good,” Catherine replied. “Maybe Moonshadow and I should sprint out. This may be getting critical.”

Nancy listened to Catherine as her voice drifted in a snow squall. Abruptly, the sky lifted, and they were bathed in sunlight and fresh, dusty crystals.

“We’re not going to make it up the ridge are we?” Nancy asked as she listened to her own voice and felt detached from its source.

“Let alone any further,” replied Moonshadow.

“Should two stay or two go? asked Catherine. “Or do we all wait for the help that Sherry’ll get?”

“A helicopter?” asked Nancy.

“It’ll take her all day to get out. Help will be alerted in the late … late afternoon,” said Moonshadow as she pulled off her headband and shook snow out of her short hair.

“Won’t fly in the mountains at night … in the dark,” Nancy said to herself. “That’s tomorrow morning. We’ve got another night out.” Nancy pictured the former yurt with its warm, dry woodstove and fought back a sick, hollow feeling that Jim could very well die because they burned it down. She struggled to contain a bundle of aches and spasms — from anger to despair to fear. “Turn around then,” Nancy said to Catherine and Moonshadow. “We’ll wait. We have to wait. He could go into cardiac arrest … Right? We should all be here.”

The girls looked down at their skis and over at Jim. Catherine knelt and placed her finger on Jim’s aorta.

“Shallow,” she said softly. “Alright, we’ll wait. Let’s haul him back. Try ‘n make more room in there.”

Catherine attempted to sound hopeful, but she was tired from being up all night and felt uneasy about having to trust Golden Lady to seek help for Jim.

***

About five miles away as the crow flies, Moon Dog and David were starting to gain elevation as they plowed through the thigh-deep snow. Moon pushed behind David, and the straps of his pack dug into his shoulders. They were both dripping with sweat. David looked up to the ridge lines through the big, alpine spruce. He moved and plotted the safest course up, across and down the folding terrain. The backcountry kept disappearing into white and reappearing as remnant snow squalls closed and opened. David knew the area well but felt a tinge of nerves every time the landscape whitened into blindness.

"Having fun yet?" David breathed to Moon without turning. "Could be at the gym."

"Did … get in shape for this trip," Moon panted as he held David's cell phone and twisted his torso one way, then the other to pick up a signal. "Got a bar, Red Bone old buddy."

"Good, mark the last spot 'cause we're gonna lose it once we cross over and into the Rattling drainage. Peak 21 blocks everything."

"Peak 21 is everything."

"The mystical mountain."

"On the White Way."

"The endless way," David breathed.

"Epic shot, eh Bone?" Moon asked, snorting and blowing out mucus through his nose. "Peak 21 … when was the last time you sent her?"

"Long, long ago … dropped in … with Scott the Hammer. Freaky up there. Felt like I was never coming back. The thing whomped and settled the second I touched down. I stopped and looked up at Hammer. He hesitated. I knew what he was thinking. Not a cloud in the sky. Solid blue. Silence. He aired off the summit cornice. Drop-kneed. Floated forever. When Hammer landed, I felt the pack collapse under my skis. Shhh," David exhaled hard. "Scared the heck out of us. Buried and surfin' 'em ass-deep, Hammer and I dove and floated side by side. Bliss. But scared.

My knees shook I was so scared. Just figur'd send it down the throat .... this may be the last run." David laughed. "Vast snow slope."

"Um, um man."

"But she held. Must have been unstable at altitude only. I don't think we stopped till the aspens right above Rattling. Seemed to go on forever and ever. A dream run. Back at the yurt, we sat and stared. Didn't speak for an hour."

"Good snow?" asked Moon, nodding and working his jaw as if he were chewing gum.

"Downy ... waist deep up high ... heavy and settled down lower ... waited till late season. Think twice about doin' that kind of thing now."

"Ask twice."

"It's possible to stick it just right."

"Roll the dice," breathed Moon.

"Yeah? Nothing is a roll of the dice. All is His."

"You're right."

"The real story on Peak 21 is the back side, the North Slope. Never been skied. Extreme. Long, long ... beautiful steep bowels, over cliff band, into slots, back into bowels, more cliff, then a final slot. I'm sure it can be done. Total commitment. Don't blink. Don't even think about coming off line."

"Shhh," whistled Moon. "Been there, man, on rivers."

Moon bumped up against David's pack as David stopped.

"Finish the run; shed your skis; grab a boat; drop right into the upper section of Wolf Creek. Another first descent. Raw and beautiful, steep, continuous whitewater. Far out," David said as he looked to the ridge line. "Something I've always dreamed of doing. Mountain dreams."

"What's up Red?" Moon asked as he noticed David gaze to the ridge.

"Somebody's on top; check it out."

Moon stepped to David's side and pulled a palm-size pair of field glasses from his shell.

"Let's take a look see."

"Moon, you have more freakin' gadgets than —"

"Single person, big multiday pack. He's dropping down now, slowly ... ooh, face plant. This may take a while."

"Here, come to the base of the ridge," said David. "We'll wait for 'im.

See if I'm going crazy. If I'm full of it, maybe we'll cave-in here for the night and give Nancy and Pepe some privacy … if they're even there. Plus we could yo-yo this drainage. Get some sweet payback."

David and Moon slug off their packs and after 20 minutes of waiting grew cold and restless. Soon a figure made wide arching tele-curves through the spruce above them.

"Hey!" David yelled.

The figured descended gradually, ducking from behind the firs and finally coming to a stop by David and Moon. It was Golden Lady. She regarded the two with a stony silence as she brushed herself off and took a haul from her hydration tube.

"Where'd you come from?" asked David, smiling and nodding. "Rattling?"

"Might have," replied Golden Lady.

"Sorry, I don't get you," said David. "Did you see a guy and a girl?"

"Look, the backcountry is f'n ruined, OK?" snapped Golden Lady. "There are more people back here than I can count. Incompetent and dangerous wahoos." She bent her knees and hopped her pack higher onto her hips. "Have a good one," she said and turned and kicked-off onto David and Moon's track.

"Yeah, so," laughed Moon. "That was helpful. You've always had a special way with women, David."

"That was a woman?" asked David. "Now what?"

"Why are you asking me?" Moon laughed. "Easy. I'm cold. Let's go. Need a yurt, a fire and a beer. Not a wet, freezing snow cave. I'm old now, Bone baby. Too old for all this." Moon laughed and then grunted as he heaved on his pack. The two guys started snaking their way up the tracks that Golden Lady had just cut.

David twisted to look after Golden Lady. He squinted in thought. She was gone as if she never appeared … like a demon. David bent his head and concentrated on his breathing and feelings. He knew in his gut that something was wrong and what just happened only tweaked him more.

***

When Jim awoke, the big man placed Jim's hands into the pans of water. He checked and reset Jim's feet in the bucket. The man then regarded the water in the pans for a long time and dipped his fingers and sprinkled a few drops on Jim's forehead as if performing a baptism. He looked up and closed his eyes. The man looked back down at Jim and smiled and reached for a towel to pat Jim's forehead. Jim could feel a tingling sensation again in his fingers, and this was consoling. He strained to hold up his heavy eyelids and watched the man sit on the stool at his feet and read a small leather-bound book with a golden cross on the cover. Jim faintly heard a mumble of prayer emit from his flared chest. Soon Jim fell into a deep sleep. Several times during the night he awoke and was aware of being lifted and jostled. Jim sensed that the man attended to him nearly constantly. When Jim opened his eyes the next day or the day after — he was not sure — the sun was setting as crimson-red through his window. There was no one in the little hut. The stove warmly hissed a large kettle in a slow, rolling boil, and two candle lanterns offered a soothing, votive glow. Jim listened to the Silence and lay snugly wrapped in his blankets. His hands were lightly coiled in gauze.

Jim heard the slap of skis. The door knocked open, and the big man stepped in with a case of Heinekens on his shoulder. He silently nodded a kindly hello to Jim. Jim nodded back. Behind him a girl stepped into the hut, exhaled, smiled at Jim and brushed snow off of her shells. She brought a glow with her into the snug cabin. Jim could not help lifting his eyes to her as a feeling electrified his chest. The big man set down the case of beer. He opened the box and pulled out a green bottle, which nearly disappeared behind his hand. He popped the cap with the back edge of a kitchen knife and handed the beer to Jim. Jim sat up and took a big slug, holding the ice-cold bottle between his palms. The frosty beer washed around Jim's mouth and ran down his throat. Jim heaved a sigh, lay back and closed his eyes. The big man caught Jim's attention when Jim opened his eyes. He lifted his eyebrows and nodded sideways in the direction of the girl, who was taking off and hanging up her shells. The man rose, took a bowl and stepped outside. The big man returned with the bowl stuffed with snow and opened and packed in several bottles of beer. He zipped up his shells and nodded again to Jim and left, closing the door snugly behind him.

Jim lay back and sipped his beer, holding the bottle for a long time to his lips. He finished one, bent over and grabbed another with his two palms as if bowing. Jim became aware that he had not spoken and wanted to say something to the girl but could not find what to say. The girl pulled off her top and her breasts bounced out and lifted. Jim looked at her breasts and curved waist. She was strong and toned. He could not take his eyes from her. She had rich, brunette hair, which fell from a part, and she smiled over to Jim. She stood in her bare feet and thermal bottoms, climbed up a mounted ladder on the wall behind the woodstove and pulled down a large, shallow bucket. She placed the bucket on the floor and poured in hot water from the kettle on the stove. Then she primed a pump next to the kitchen sink and pumped water into a plastic pitcher and dumped this into the steaming bucket. She repeated each step several times, touching the water in the bucket and frowning until the temperature was just right. Then she slipped into nakedness, and Jim watched her perfect, heart-shaped bottom as she stepped into the bucket with a washcloth and a small bottle of organic peppermint soap. The glowing space instantly billowed with a scented, minty steam. The girl ran the washcloth around her curves and did not leave Jim's eyes. Jim's throat cinched with her beauty.

"I know," she said, and her voice rang beautifully. "You're looking at me like that because you respect my mind and want to get to know me as a person." She laughed tenderly, and Jim blushed. Jim felt his entire body melt as his groin grew warm and pulsed.

Who are you? Jim asked without speaking as a feeling stirred in his chest.

"The Tele Goddess," she said affectionately, laughing a little and smiling at Jim, knowing his thoughts. "I am a child of God now," she added, smiling warmly. She stepped out of the bucket and wrapped in a towel. "I made you that nice quilt." Jim regarded the quilt bundled around him. Steam rose from her skin. She dipped a bowl into the minty water and stepped lightly to Jim. She bent over and lifted away Jim's blankets and placed his shell jacket under him so as not to wet the bunk. She pulled off Jim's top and bottoms. She dipped the washcloth and swabbed Jims legs and up his sides, under his spicy armpits and around his chest and face. She took the towel and slowly dried him, being sure not to touch his feet and hands.

"I know you, Jim," she said softly, almost in a whisper and wrapped the towel around herself again and lay down next to Jim. "I care about you," she said, looking up for Jim's eyes. His face was scrunched, and his chin trembled. Tears squeezed from the corner of his closed eyes. "I know about it," she whispered. "I know all of your secrets. This and everything. Where you have been. Where you are going. Your wounds." Jim closed his eyes but could not avoid remembering, as if the pretty girl gently massaged his past to the present. His chest burned with pain. Over and over again, he is 11, 12 and 13 years old — on his own: lips, a tongue, a mouth on his erect sliver. Girl-children. His tongue between their bald, pubescent lips. Different gum chewing preteens in designer T-shirts with fingernail polish and pierced ears. Many. Twirling heads and bodies in a titillating frenzy. Groups of boys and girls. Children as no longer children. Condemned as bodies only. Haunted by shame. Severed from feeling. Material. Jim heaved tears, and the girl lay next to him and pulled over the soft wool blanket. She stroked his face and wiped his tears away and nestled her head onto Jim's chest. He grew quiet. "You don't have to live with it forever," she whispered and looked up to find Jim's eyes. "You don't have to live with anything painful forever." Jim stared at the ceiling, which blurred with tears. Jim erupted again, and she sat up and held him in her arms and rocked his soul-wound and whispered that she loved him. Jim fell asleep, and the pretty girl rose and pulled on a fleece top and thermal bottom and pair of thick rag socks. She made a dinner of pasta with fresh pesto that made the hut smell sweetly of olive oil and basil. She woke Jim in her arms and fed him fork-fulls of pasta with sips of beer.

Thank you, Jim whispered, again without words, and looked into her eyes and away. He lay back and closed his eyes. Jim reached up and stroked her neck and shoulders. Jim parted her hair and ran the back of his hand down her cheek. She was pleased and lightly kissed Jim on the cheek.

"That's nice," she said gently. "Deeply like me, Jim. Fall into fondness with me. I do like you so much." Jim grew calm and warm. A longing, a sadly exciting yearning kindled deep within Jim — a new feeling, something unexpected where somehow the pretty girl and feeling were close. Jim could no longer hold open his eyes. He fell asleep, while the sweet-smelling and pretty girl and the mountain peace settled into his bones … and the feeling faintly glowed.

***

When David and Moon reached Rattling Brook, it was growing dark. They were both wet, and the temperature was dropping fast. David felt his shells freeze and grow brittle, and he knew he had to change into dry layers fast. He was a few glides ahead of Jamie and slid silently into the clearing between the giant Douglases where he knew the yurt waited. First David became aware of all the tracks and drag marks in the snow. His stomach tightened. He knew the tracks told a story. But right now they made no sense to him. David seized his pole handles as he stepped to where the yurt once stood and looked into the empty pit. Black soot and lumps of melted plastic stuck through a layer of fresh white snow.

"What the hell's going on?" asked Moon coming up behind David. His voice shattered the silence and jolted David.

"Something happened."

"Something happened. The yurt burned down."

David flung off his pack and with quivering hands, bent down and popped out of his three pins. He tore his avy shovel from its shove-it and jumped into the pit. David picked and shoveled through the charred debris.

"David, Whinny," said Moon Dog "you're not thinkin' that are you?"

David stopped. His chest heaved up and down. He pictured finding Nancy's blackened bones and gouged flesh. Feelings for her flashed through his entire body. He panted harder and frantically flung away pieces of molten roofing and half-burned lodge poles. Tears erupted from his eyes.

Moon turned to the north as a tired voice rang out.

"Hey … hey who is it? Jamie? Jamie man!? Oh, baby, what are you doin' here? Can't believe it."

Nancy bit her lower lip and lunged her thighs toward Moon.

"Child!? That you!?"

David froze and looked up over the edge of the pit, shifting his head back and forth like a dog. He held the shovel and tore up the bank, shaking and streaming tears. David lunged and dug toward Nancy.

"Damn man, damn man, scared me, really did," he sputtered to himself and met Nancy by taking her in his arms and kissing her all over her face and bending her backward.

Nancy hugged David back and tried to calm him.

"OK, ho-k, ho," Nancy breathed. Her eyes glowed into David's.

"I love you, baby," David said, burying his face in Nancy's neck and holding her tight with his arms. "Scared me."

Nancy held David and reached out for Moon. "Come here, baby. Oh," Nancy exclaimed and held both her men closely, shutting her eyes tightly to feel them.

"Child! What happened?" asked Moon, smiling warmly into Nancy's drawn eyes and pulling her over to kiss her on the forehead.

David wiped both his cheeks and stood bolt upright, trying to quickly regain his composure. Nancy found his eyes.

"That's the way you feel about me?" she asked David softly.

"That's the way I feel," David replied, looking away slightly.

"I love you guys; come here," Nancy said as the corners of her mouth trembled with emotion.

Nancy pulled David and Moon close. They put their arms around each other and rubbed their heads with gloved hands. The three burned in a tight circle of feeling as everything flooded back: the river, the cave, the babies; Painted Man and the miracles.

"OK, what happened?" asked Moon. "What's going on out here? Who was the woman that blew out in a huff? Who's hurt? How did this hap —"

"Jimmy's hypothermic and frostbit, bad, really bad. Touch and guh … huh, huh," Nancy stammered as she stood with her eyes closed and started to cry in heaves.

"OK, Nancy, alright. Where is he?" Moon asked. He leaned over and held Nancy, gently tucking her head with his hand onto his broad shoulder.

"Everything alright at home? My babies?" Nancy asked as she pointed a limp arm in the direction of the cache. "Came to see what was left in the fire."

David quickly slung on his pack with a grunt and clipped into his skis. He bound off following Nancy's tracks.

"Everything's fine, sweetheart," Moon said gently, holding Nancy. "Jessica's at home with Kyle and the boys. They're OK. Everything's fine."

The sky closed in, and a snow squall wrapped Moon Dog and Nancy as Moon held and rocked Nancy in his arms. Darkness fell, and the sweat on the back of Moon's neck-hairs froze stiff.

***

Jim opened his eyes and bright, cheerful sunshine streamed into the hut. Brewed coffee filled every nook and cranny with a rich smell. The stove glowed warmly, and the room was scented with pine smoke. Jim had lost all sense of time as the repetition of sunrise into sunset into starry mountain night flowed endlessly through the surrounding quiet. How he had gotten here, how long he would stay and what would become of him held little meaning in the morning sun. Jim felt warm wrapped in his blankets and quilt. He inhaled through his nose, and the light and the smell of coffee filled him. Jim lay and noticed that he rushed with feeling: a feeling he had never felt before. Starting from the base of his spine, the feeling tingled around his groin and up and down his vertebrae and glowed in his chest and radiated throughout his entire body with lightness. Jim lay and felt the rushes of tingles settle into a yearning — a powerful yearning for something: the pretty girl, who she was and where she was from, for something, something more … Jim could not tell. He pulled the covers around and looked out the window with his eyes wide and longing, almost painfully longing, unable to comprehend the simple helplessness of the moment. The feeling was not of his making. It came from somewhere else — from Whom or from where Jim did not know. But the girl — the beautiful and sweet smelling girl — and even the man — the tattooed and powerful man — were a living touch of this feeling. Little by little Jim opened to their care and to their increasing quietude. Jim lay still. He did not want anything to move or change. He wanted to feel like this forever, and yet the feeling stirred Jim to follow and to find. Excitement mixed inside of Jim: excitement, longing, glowing, aching.

The Feeling nearly lifted Jim. He gazed out of his window into the dark mountain blue until his bladder burned and his stomach groaned with hunger, and even these sensations brought a lightness to Jim. He carefully crawled out of bed and lowered onto the floor on his elbows and knees. Jim kept his hands and feet in the air and crawled outside. The mountain air was cold and fresh as he knelt and peed and with effort propped himself on the beam to relieve his bowels. Jim grunted and breathed with satisfaction as he lifted his eyes to the rarified light. Jim felt strong. He crawled back inside and found a plate of cheese and crackers with slices of apple and a tin cup of steaming coffee waiting for him. Jim sat on his bed and ate in solitude and Silence. Jim thought about the powerful man and the sweet smelling girl, and he wondered where they were. He noticed that the hut was kept clean and his blankets and clothes were aired and washed. Food and meals were always provided; his waste was eliminated; and Jim noticed that upon rising on some mornings his skin smelled fresh and clean of peppermint. Balm had been applied to his damaged skin. Jim could see that the man and the pretty girl provided for him constantly in the secret depths of his sleep as if they did not want to disturb what was acting upon him.

Jim chewed the apples and cheese and sipped coffee, and it was good. He placed the plate and tin cup on a stump and propped himself on pillows against the pine wall. He sat and looked out the window to the dense, green firs and onto the dazzling snow slope extending beyond his view. Jim glowed and thought about the man and the pretty girl. He held up his hands. Jim looked at his fingers and palms … sensing that he occupied a body, and the person was more than the body … and more than both person and body — more that wanted to live, that wanted to climb mountains and to ski down them with heels free … free to feel, free to pummel in dusty-down, free to rise and to fly with arms spread. Jim realized that he had always felt this longing, and the longing was his calling … calling him to something Greater. The calling, the girl, the man, the time, the place. A whirlwind of kaleidoscope crystals. Feelings of gliding and soaring — of hushed pines and open white — of Nancy's smiles and touches: her hand on his shoulder, looking up to him … calling him out … to Beyond. The mountains calling to him. What had been lived, lived without notice, flooded into Jim — as the person, the body, the soul, the inmost heart, opened to the Light … and Jim realized that he was on a journey.

***

Below Jim and beyond Rattling Brook, Butch came to see that the darkness was not complete but rather a deep twilight. He perceived his immaterial form and desired his bones and body and his life back. A faint light showed at some distance. Butch moved in its direction for no other reason than fear and weeping had exhausted him. As Butch moved on his phantom telies, the presence of trees and rocks was faintly recognized, although voices had long since departed. Butch felt his wife and two boys somewhere off in the dark twilight, out of reach. Bird Man and Deek and Jonesy too. They were not gone, nor were they near. So too, Butch sensed his own wreckage. The devastation he wrought stood before him as a presence in the silent darkness.

Viejo, Dan, toured along in his decayed gear and clothing and felt Butch. He did not want to admit why he had found this lost soul. But Viejo knew. Heaviness and spasms of nerves tormented his cavernous insides, telling the story — the story that he struggled to accept. El Viejo worked his jaw with an inner pain. Guilt and dread cloaked The Old One as darkness once again descended around him like a lead curtain. He was falling back, back into despair. Yet Viejo, Dan, toured with his arms out and palms up as if holding a bowl — a bowl hollowed by pain and repentance … and thankfully filled with salvation. Viejo toured and bowed his head to the Greater Will that he knew was close at hand.

***

At Rattling Brook Ravine the strength in Moon Dog's quiet voice soothed everyone. They were all packed together in the box. "Treat it as shock," Moon said as he held Nancy and stroked her head. She lay bundled in her sleeping bag with her head in his lap. "But I don't believe he's in shock," he added. Catherine, Moonshadow and David huddled around Jim. "His temperature is now 98.6 on the dot," continued Moon. "You guys did everything right. Warmed his core right up." Moon reached around Nancy and placed the thermometer back into David's expedition first aid kit that was packed in a zip suitcase.

"Well what's going on with him?" asked Catherine, showing a hint of fatigue and irritation in her voice. "What's the deal with his shin?"

"Go ahead," continued Moon, "this is the twenty-first century, and we're all rational, scientific, red-blooded Americans. Hell, me included. He's not in shock … He's in a trance … His wound? Healed miraculously."

Moon spoke in his gentle Southern drawl. The others listened with their mouths open and stared. There was a long silence as everyone tried to digest Moon's words.

"Oh come on," blurted Moonshadow curling back up onto her pad and bag in a dark corner, "I'm sorry; that's too much for me to believe. Let's just chopper him out in the morning so I can go on with my little life and made-up religion. I like it that way." She laughed. "Nice and comfortable."

Nancy looked up and smiled and reached out her hand to her. Moonshadow reached and took it.

"Thanks so much for your help," Nancy said to Moonshadow. "You two have done way more than you needed to."

"Please," said Moonshadow, "we're the ones that wrecked the yurt. Always alone out here anyway. I hope someone would do the same for me if I got messed —"

"Belief?" interrupted Moon, looking up and raising the question to no one in particular. He looked around at the four walls. Everyone watched him. "This box is like a catacomb, a tomb."

"Yeah, Jamie?" asked David.

"The tomb is empty," Moon stated thoughtfully, looking up at the ceiling. "The tomb is empty." There was a long pause and everyone looked at Moon Dog and waited for what he was going to say next. "Jesus rose and returned in the flesh — solid flesh and bone — open wounds and all to His mother and to His friends, for many to see … Easter is just around the corner, my friends."

"Whew … amen," David exhaled, shaking his head trying to comprehend the incomprehensible.

"If the tomb is empty and if it did happen, if Jesus rose from the dead and if He returned in the flesh and if He lives now, right here and now, with us and in us, in the Spirit, what does that mean for our lives?" asked Moon. Catherine lifted her eyes and sat up closer to Moon's feet. "By Whom are we made? Where do we return? What is life? What reality surrounds us all the time — of which we are often not aware? Who can we become?" Moon asked, and his questions soaked into everyone in the tight space. There was a long silence, and Nancy reached over and gently checked Jim's pulse. "Who heals us? … So too, what keeps us from believing, from knowing, from experiencing that the tomb is empty, that He has risen, that He, creator God of the universe, actually walked in the flesh with us … in life and back from death, from the greater reality, the Kingdom." Moon bowed his head and worked his jaw. "When I was young, heck, younger," Moon corrected, and David laughed a little, "all I was was a dick, skin and bones, muscle, testosterone and adrenaline: a boat, a paddle, a pair of tele skis. Whitewater kayaking. Freein' the heel. Crystals into flowing water. Me and mine. More and harder. Jamie Lynch. Nothing else. Master of my own universe. My own god." David and Nancy laughed softly and smiled at Moon. "What happened to us all on The River? What do we know now? Who are we since? … Something greater, far greater … way beyond our comprehension … everything by comparison, insignificant. Sure, we'll treat Jim for hypothermia. We'll keep him warm and care as best we can for him and his feet and hands and watch … watch him constantly until help arrives. Our technology will cradle Jim in logic and reason and whisk him away in a helicopter to medical care. Tubes, meters and medicines. Absolutely the right thing to do, of course. But that is not what's really happening to this boy … this boy becoming a man. This man finding his soul. This soul coming home. There's a miracle happening right before our eyes. A transformation … Go ahead, call it shock if you want. Even call it an accident. But he's in a trance. He's been taken into the great Beyond. Hallelujah," Moon whispered and let his words fall into pregnant Silence. He stopped talking for a long time. Everyone lay still.

"I believe," Moon continued at length, "that Jim will soon pass." Moon looked down and worked his jaw. "One way or the other, he will die and change. That's the call. That's the cost." No one spoke. A long silence passed. "He will be even more himself: beautiful and new … of His handiwork … for you Nancy," Moon added quietly and held Nancy to his chest. "Don't ask me how I know, but I can see this: the Holy Spirit is counseling." Moon Dog placed a hand on Jim's shoulder, bowed his head and closed his eyes hard. Nancy sat up with tears streaming down her cheeks. David did the same, and he and Moon Dog placed their hands on Jim's shoulders. "Father, Lord Jesus, Creator God and Ruler of all the universe, heaven and earth," whispered Moon, pausing for a long moment, "You are here with us right now. I know You are with us. I can feel You in our moment, our beautiful moment that You give … that You have created … with my friends, whom I love so much, and with our new friends. Come to Jim wherever You have taken him. Lord Father, Daddy, minister to Jim, whom You care about so deeply, who You spoke into being. We pray to You, Lord Jesus, that Jim will know You, know

Your living and loving Presence — and in this knowing, know who he truly is … Your child, Your son." Moon kept his eyes closed, and Nancy and David bent their heads in extreme concentration. Both whispered. "Yes … yes Lord we pray." Nancy reached back with her arm and pulled in Catherine, whose eyes poured tears. Catherine reached for Moonshadow and hugged her close. A candle glowed in the corner and cast huddled shadows along the plywood wall. There was a long Silence, and Catherine heaved sobs into Nancy's lap. Everyone listened to her cry.

"I burned down your lodge," she said, turning to face David. "I've seen you before, at The Area, at Big Pine. I know you work there. We did it. I want to say I'm sorry. I want to pay for —" and she started crying so hard that she choked on her words.

Nancy sat up and dug out a wad of toilet paper for Catherine and wiped her eyes. David tensed with shock and anger. He lowered his head and worked his jaw. His limbs turned warm, and David felt pity for Catherine. He placed a hand on her shoulder and bowed his head.

"Alright," Moon said softly, finding Catherine's eyes, "you are forgiven. You can be changed. You can be saved. Ask. Just ask. Repent."

"I want to pay," said Catherine. "I will turn myself in … when we get out."

Moonshadow sat in the corner with her mouth slack and listened to Catherine.

Moon Dog found Catherine's eyes again. "Catherine, what's more important? … Here is your choice — black and white, no shades of gray — you are either saved or not saved. In Light or in darkness. Let the Lord bring it all to the surface — selfish, shallow, weakness, hatred, pain, anger, hard-heartedness, pride, arrogance, delusion, fear, ignorance, ambivalence, attachment, false teachings, idols … sexual immorality, all the evils … all the sin … to be burned in His loving fire. A personal relationship with the loving God." Catherine quieted. Moon continued, "And, what about Jim? What is his journey? Why has he been taken like this?"

"Because I scared him off," rasped Nancy.

"Out of his body?!" exclaimed David and everyone laughed a little, breaking the tension in the small space.

"What happened?" asked Moon.

"I wanted too hard."

There was a long silence as Moon and David collected their thoughts.

"What has to change in Jim for him to want back?" Asked Moon. "Can you give him that? Can you do it for him? Can he do it himself? See what I mean, Nancy?"

"I understand. Not easy for me, that's all."

"What if he's never known anything like you?" asked David. "You've got a lot of feeling, Nance. A lot of heart." David placed his hand on Nancy's back. "I think you're a strong woman … have received a lot of power. Gifts."

No one spoke.

"You have feelings for him?" Moon Dog gently asked Nancy at length. "Strong feelings?"

"Yes, I care for him," Nancy whispered. "I love him. I don't understand why. I can feel we're supposed to be together … could be … have been … will be — something bigger's going on."

There was a long silence as Moon Dog considered Nancy's words and feelings and revered the Spirit. "What are his secrets?" Moon asked Nancy gently. "Can you speak for them? Can anybody? Who can know his secrets and change Jim, change any of us? What has been his journey? And what can a woman do for a boy — a boy that needs to become a man? What if he never becomes a man? Stays a boy forever. Abandons his destiny — who he is intended to be … with you, perhaps. Becomes lost and broken. Your feelings and needs are natural needs of a woman. But only men can seek the Spirit in other men — go beyond world into deep brotherhood. Jim is our responsibility, ours as guided by the Lord. Surrender for your answer, Nancy. Be patient," Moon said and pushed up against the wall and closed his eyes and inhaled deeply through his nose. "I love you child," Jamie said and leaned forward and took Nancy in his arms as silent tears fell down her cheeks.

"I have touched Jimmy," Nancy whispered almost to herself. Her voice sounded raspy with fatigue. "I know that deep inside he is very beautiful. David may be right … both of you. It scared me. Angered me. Frustrated me. I wanted too badly. Are they all like him now? Will I be alone forever? What about my boys? They need a father. Boys have to have a man, a father."

"Wait Nancy, wait," said Moon Dog softly. "You will never be abandoned. Nor will we. Surrender to His will. Be patient. Wait on the Lord."

Moonshadow shifted uneasily in her corner, and Catherine lay on her back with her head propped on Nancy's legs. She closed her eyes and listened. The space was dank but warmed by body heat. A single candle glowed peacefully.

***

For Jim on Peak 21, the brilliant morning sun once again streamed into the hut, and he opened his eyes. Jim wanted to push away the dream that kept returning during the night. "Jimmy," little Kyle had said in the dream as he reached up and took Jim's hand, "I miss you a lot." Jim sat on the worn easy chair in Nancy's kitchen. Kyle climbed onto his lap and put his head on Jim's chest. Jim had no choice but to feel … to wrap his arms around Kyle, hesitantly, and to hug him. "When are you coming back, Jimmy?" Kyle asked. "Will you take me skiing, Jim? At Big Pine?"

Jim lay awake in the morning light and shoved away the dream and his feelings for Kyle, which stuck in his throat. Jim's feet had begun to itch. He flung back the covers and examined his toes. A thin layer of pale, dead skin flaked off while underneath their color was a healthy pink. Jim carefully swung his legs over the side of the bunk and placed some weight on the soles of his feet. Weight, gravity and movement. It all felt good. Jim stood. He sensed no pain. Jim raised his hands. His fingertips were also flaking slightly, but there was feeling in all of his extremities. He had grown new skin. He was healed. Jim carefully stepped across the pine floor. He gingerly toed around in a circle, feeling the cool boards and looking at himself. Jim wondered how he had gotten a body and from where he came. This awareness tightened his stomach, and Jim pushed aside the feeling. He wanted to keep things simple, not deep. Jim whistled while he lit the gas stove, boiled water, then made a bowl of oatmeal from dried oats found in a tin box. Jim ate spoonfuls of oatmeal and sipped a mug of herb tea and looked out the window. The tingles and rushes came upon him again. Jim's muscles twitched, and he put the mug down and paced around the small floor. Jim opened the door and stuck out his head, stretched and pulled up on the door jam. *Beautiful out here,* Jim thought. He saw his skis and poles and avy shovel. Jim's insides rolled with spasms of nerves. "I'm oudda here," Jim said to himself. *Just head on down,* he thought. *Been real, I guess. Been nice, anyway. I'm gone, man. Back to my truck, to my life … whatever it was. Back to the Crest. Blow off that stupid fine. Do some skiing. Maybe smoke a blunt. Have a beer—hell, a couple. Some backside runs off the Crest. Powder days. Get my salad-prepping job back. Find the group. We'll hang together. It'll be sweet. No problems. No worries. No Big Pine. Nothing too involved. No pressures. Just chill, man. Easy.*

"OK, so here I go," Jim said, aware of his own words as he slapped his hands on his thighs.

Jim pulled on his socks, thermals and shells. He carefully slid into his boots and stepped outside. He squatted up and down. *Feels fine.* He stood and jumped up lightly on the healed leg. The cool mountain air stung his cheeks. Jim toed into his bindings, closed the trap with his pole tip and shoved his avy shovel into the pack left by the man. He stepped onto a double track leading to the open slope. *Just send it, man — all the way to Rattling. Pick up my stuff and head out. I suppose I'll call those guys, tell 'em what happened. Very easy.* Jim cleared the spruce and pitch-black immediately rose in front of him. The rushes and tingles abruptly stopped. But the longing deep within would not leave. Jim gripped and ungripped his poles in confusion as a clammy sweat oozed down his chest and sides. Jim cocked his head to the side trying to ignore the preternatural dread that curtained his descent. He pushed off into darkness. Jim dug down into a tele turn. He stopped as panic clamped his guts. Jim placed a hand to his nose and pulled it back. He saw nothing. Jim stood and panted. He clenched his jaw and denied the darkness as he hopped around and dove into several more turns. Jim felt gravity lift him downward as he buried to his butt in the soft, unseen medium. Jim's legs wobbled as fear held him. He tumbled head-over-heals in the cool crystals, which melted onto his warm skin. Jim sat for a long time and did not know what to do. Finally he sensed a faint glow. He spread out his arms and felt the slope and realized that the glow was coming from uphill, from where he had started. Jim took off the pack and dug inside. He felt a pair of climbing skins folded onto themselves. Jim stomped a platform, felt for his bindings and popped out of his skis. He spread the skins on the bottoms as if he were a blind man feeling each movement. Jim mounted his skis and started traversing upward toward the light, which grew stronger the higher he ascended. At length he was squinting in blinding sunlight on the dividing line between darkness and light by the alpine spruce and the ski track that lead back to the hut.

Jim stood for a long time at this threshold. His thighs and chest burned with feelings of helplessness, which he denied by shrugging his shoulders and gliding back to the hut. When he stepped inside, it was warm and light. Someone had stoked the fire and brewed coffee. The rich smell filled the cozy space. Jim stripped out of his shells and threw them in a pile onto the floor. He sat on his bunk and clenched his jaw. Jim hopped back on the bed and looked out the window. A heaviness bore down on his chest and became anger that shot through his limbs. Jim heard the slap of skis outside the door. The door opened, and the pretty girl stepped in. Her dark, tanned face beamed, and her hair was braided in pigtails. She brushed snow from her toned thighs and shapely bottom.

"Whew, it's so good. North facing shots … um, um. Warm sun, cool shadows. Goodness overflowing with goodness. Hey Jim, feeling better aren't you," she stated sweetly, bending over and picking up his shells. She shook the melted snow off of them.

"I wanna go," Jim said. His own voice sounded strange to hear. Jim folded his arms. "What's happened to me? Where am I?" Jim asked as he shook his arms away and tears flooded his eyes.

The girl found Jim's eyes and smiled. "Well … today's a special day," she replied.

She carefully laid his shells on the end of the bunk and smoothed out each arm and leg. She went outside and brought in his skis and poles. She set his skis against the wall, side by side and examined his bindings and edges. She placed his adjustable poles next to his skis. The girl did all this methodically as if preparing Jim for battle. When she finished, she came over to Jim and stood before him and took off her shell jacket. She smiled and held out her hand for Jim. Jim pushed away on the bunk and dropped his chin. The girl sat on the edge of the mattress, still holding out her hand. Jim took it and turned away. Finally he turned back. Her hazel eyes and dark skin were robust and compelled Jim to gaze upon her healthy features. She rubbed the back of his hand with her thumb.

"That's it, Jim," she said softly. "Do not be afraid. I will be praying for you. I care for you very much." The pretty girl, the Tele Goddess, sat before Jim, and he reached for her other hand and pulled her hesitantly to him. "I like that, Jim," she whispered. "I know you feel for me." Jim kissed her soft lips, and she closed her eyes. She reclined next to Jim and gently ran her hand around his chest and legs and brushed where he pulsed. "Good, big and strong; there you are, good, Jim," she said and nestled her head onto Jim's shoulder and looked up to his eyes. "Never be ashamed. Do not be afraid. You will be a man, Jim. Soon, truly." Jim exhaled and pulled her onto himself, looking up at the ceiling and feeling her strength and glow. "Feel for me, Jim. Be strong. Take courage. You will go now … deep and far, but we are close. You will be my harvest." The Tele Goddess slid off the bunk massaging her hands down Jim's chest as she slid away. She stood and pulled on her jacket and stepped out the door, turning to smile warmly at Jim. The door stayed open, and Jim felt suddenly alone. A tension overcame him. Jim tried to ignore that he understood all that he just heard. He hopped off the bunk, pulled up his thermals and stepped to the door, but she was gone.

As Jim looked, the big man came ducking through the spruce bows up above on his telies. He lightly aired and landed on a drop-knee by the door. The man nodded and smiled to Jim, raising his eyebrows with great enthusiasm. He was wearing an old and worn mountain pack.

"It's your big day, Jim," he said directly, slinging off the pack and smiling with his eyes. His deep voice startled Jim.

"Whattaya mean? What's going on here? Who are you two? What is she talking about? I wanna go back," Jim said loudly and slammed the door against the side of the hut with his heel. The big man opened his eyes wide with surprise and stepped past Jim into the hut. Jim followed him inside. "What's happening to me?" Jim yelled. "I didn't die or something, did I? Is that what this's all about?" The man did not answer but checked to see if Jim's clothing and gear were ready. "Hey, answer me," Jim shouted again and picked up the stool and flung it at the man, who ducked. The stool bounced off the back wall and smashed onto the kitchen counter breaking plates and mugs and sending the stove and silverware flying. The big man sat down away from Jim on the edge of the bunk and lowered his head patiently. "I wanna go … my own way. I don't need all this bullshit, man. I NEVER WANTED ANY OF THIS … WITH YOU, HER, EVEN NANCY. LEAVE ME ALONE. EVERYBODY JUST LEAVE ME ALONE!" Jim hollered and ripped the covers off of the bunk. He whipped them around and knocked the stove pipe apart sending smoke billowing into the small space. "Hear me!? Then talk," Jim demanded and slapped the guy on the backside of the head and quickly stepped away. The powerful man sat patiently. He thumbed through the small, leather-bound book. "SAY SOMETHING. I WANT WHAT'S MINE! MY LIFE BACK! WHY CAN'T I GO!? WHAT'S GOING ON!?" Jim screamed and cried and grabbed the stool. From somewhere deep-down Jim watched himself. From this place Jim knew that his words were small ripples on a deeper current of fate, which pushed him onward. "Face it; face it," Jim's inner voice said to him from deep within. "Come out and see. Come out from hiding." His cheeks turned beet-red, and Jim fell to his knees snorting through his nose and smashing the stool on the floor again and again. He flung it away, and the stool broke through the window above the bunk. Cold air poured inside. Jim stood and beat the wall with his fists. He turned and kicked over the stove. Coals and fire spewed onto the floor. The man stepped to the side as flames and smoke began to fill the inside of the hut that was now in shatters. The big man held his leather-bound book in one hand, grabbed Jim and Jim's boots, shells, hat, gloves and gear and carried them all out the door. The hut was on fire, and black smoke squeezed through the door behind them. Jim knelt on all fours in his long underwear on the snow, coughing and heaving gulps of air. They both had to back away and hold up their arms as the walls ignited into roaring flames and heat exploded outward. The man stood and did nothing as the hut burned. Jim sat on his haunches and pounded the snow until he was exhausted, and the heat forced the two even further back. The man watched Jim. After some time the roof caved in, and the once cheerful structure was reduced to a smoldering, black heap. As the fire calmed, Jim felt the cold. He sniffed and pulled on his shells and boots that lay scattered on the snow around him. He sat back, put his head on his knees and wrapped his arms around his head. "Say something to me," Jim asked the man without looking up. The man stood silently holding the small book.

"The Lord created Me, the beginning of His works —" the man read with passionate interest. Jim lifted his head — "before all else that He made, long ago." The man paused and bent down and buckled Jim's tele boots, still holding the small, worn, leather-bound Bible. He zipped Jim's shells and wiped the tears from Jim's cheeks with the back of his large hand — "Alone, I was fashioned in times long past, at the beginning, long before earth itself." The man read and paused again, nodding to Jim to grab his skis and hat and gloves. He waited and handed Jim his poles, then gently pushed a pair of sunglass onto Jim's nose — "When there was yet no ocean I was born, no springs brimming with water." The big man nodded at Jim and took Jim's skis one at a time and smoothed on a pair of climbing skins. He continued reading — "Before the mountains were settled in their place, long before the hills I was born, when as yet He had made neither land nor lake nor the first clod of earth." The man took his own skis and spread on his worn climbing skins — "When He set the heavens in their place I was there, when He girdled the ocean with the horizon, when He fixed the canopy of clouds overhead —" The powerful man stopped reading and shouldered his pack. He bent down and pressed into his bindings. He nodded for Jim to do the same. Jim sniffled and looked at the burning hut. He bent over and stepped into his bindings. The man turned and slid forward and resumed reading. Jim followed him — "and set the springs of ocean firm in their place, when He prescribed its limits for the sea and knit together earth's foundations. Then I was at His side each day, His darling and delight, playing in His presence continually, playing on the earth, when He had finished it, while My delight was in mankind." The man finished and closed The Book and placed it carefully into his parka.

Jim sniffed and looked up and squinted with a recognition as the words both soaked in and bubbled from where he already understood … hidden and deep and calling him once more. Calling and calling … without ceasing. Jim closed his eyes and shyly met the longing. Another feeling arose, which Jim named with tears brimming in his eyes and gratefulness aching in his chest … the feeling of knowing that he had always been called, always protected and guided … in David, in Nancy and even in little Kyle. And in his mom and dad and in the mountains. He knew that his life was shallow and starved compared to this powerful Fullness glowing and rising within him — that all of his rebellion was thinning into nothing, and yet for now Jim did not know who he was or where he was going. He looked up to the big man.

The big man abruptly kicked uphill away from the darkness below them. Jim followed, and the darkness closed at his heels, and Jim knew that his past life was in the darkness somewhere and gone for good. After weaving through the dwarf spruce, they eventually gained an open, alpine ridge. Jim steadied himself as the exposed drop on either side flooded into his senses. He fell to his knees. The man continued carefully sliding one ski ahead, then the other on the soft snow along the edge of the spiny ridge. He turned again, and Jim gazed upon his face. Jim stared at the man, at his eyebrows, for a long time … which were now pure white.

***

"Nancy, Nance, wake up," Catherine whispered tensely, shaking Nancy, who was curled in her bag on the hard floor of the cache.

"Um, what's that?" asked Nancy rubbing her eyes, looking into Catherine's flashlight.

"He's convulsing," Catherine said loudly so as to wake the others.

Moonshadow stirred, but David and Jamie remained motionless. Nancy leaned over and saw Jim's body twitching violently in his sleeping bag. He was sweating and grunting. Drool fell from the corners of his mouth, and his eyes rolled back beneath their lids.

"Oh man, this's scary," Nancy said as she shook Moon Dog.

Catherine leaned over and unzipped Jim's bag and checked his pulse.

"Racing and shallow," Catherine said with a tinge of panic in her voice. "Think he might be going into arrest. Get ready for CPR. Wake up those two. I couldn't. This is serious," Catherine mumbled to herself. Her hands quaked as she felt again for Jim's aorta. She placed her ear on Jim's chest to listen to his heart. "Kate — Moonshadow — what time is it?"

"Four."

"Chopper better be here first thing, first light, or this guy may be finished."

"These two are out. I can't wake them. Here shine a light," Nancy said. "Hey Moon! Whinny. Hey you guys f'ing wake up, will you. Shine the light."

Catherine swung over her headlight and flashed the beam onto Moon Dog and David. They both lay on their backs with their bags unzipped and held each other's hand. Their eyes were wide open.

"What's going on here?" asked Catherine. "Strange."

"Moon, hey, Jamie! Red, David wake up! Jimmy's going into arrest," Nancy shouted, but neither guy moved or even blinked.

***

"I need your help," Jim said to the big man, sucking back a nervous tension. "I don't understand where I am going." Jim's head felt dizzy as he adjusted to the exposure, which deepened below his skis with each step forward. Immediately behind, the darkness closed like a tide creeping upward. The big man placed his hand on Jim's shoulder and nodded kindly. He turned and looked ahead and upward. Jim looked and saw the ridge expose into bare, golden rock. The man turned and resumed climbing. After several more balancing kicks the man hesitated and carefully bent down. Jim came up behind and straddled the snow crusted ridge. He looked up. A series of sheer to overhung faces shot above them. The big man slung off his pack and pulled out a rope and climbing harness. He spread the harness in front of Jim on the snow and nodded for him to step into the leg loops. "Can't I just go back?" Jim pleaded, but he already sensed the answer, that was immense yet beckoning. He looked up and for the first time faced the unknown.

Jim went to turn, and the way behind was still cloaked in darkness. The sun shone brilliantly overhead through an indigo blue. The two were perched at a dramatic height. Jim tossed the harness back to the man. The man paused and found Jim's eyes. He squinted with concern. "I don't want any of this," Jim mouthed as he listened to his own words, which had nothing to do with his heart now — a heart pounding to climb. The big man looked at Jim and then up at the ridge with a worried expression. He carefully balanced down and undid Jim's bindings. He slid Jim's telies through the side straps on his mountain pack and did the same with Jim's poles. He guided Jim to a crouching position, held up the pack with the skis and guided Jim's arms through the shoulder straps. Jim abruptly leaned backwards and found that he was standing on toe holds on naked and golden granite. Darkness lay to the south while several thousand feet of air led to snow slopes on the north side. Unsure of how he got there, Jim found himself up on the rock face. He breathed in panicky spasms. The big guy lunged upward, holding the end of the climbing rope for Jim to tie onto. Jim hesitated, and it was too late. The man fell away below, and Jim clung onto small finger holds with his gloves. Jim looked down, and the big man looked up still holding the end of the rope. Jim's legs trembled. It was awkward clinging to the small, frozen holds in telemark boots and gloves with the skis throwing his balance from side to side. The big man dropped his arms and lowered his gaze. He fell to his knees with his hands in prayer. Jim's forearms started to swell with pain. He could not climb down and jumping off would risk breaking a leg or missing altogether and pummeling off either side of the ridge. He was committed to going up.

Jim felt sweat soaking his skin from his head to the bottoms of his feet. He turned a foot to the outside to gain a better edge and released one hand. He pulled off a glove with his teeth and shoved it inside his parka. Jim did the same with the other glove. The rock felt cold and gritty on his sensitive fingers. "Alright, come on, move," Jim said to himself. He puffed out some good hard breaths and eyed the next set of holds. He looked down, and the man nodded for Jim to continue. Jim extended forward but the holds were out of reach. "Come on, do it," Jim said to himself. He felt the tingles and rushes return and mingle with a powerful surge of calm and control. Jim stood on his toes and extended in a glide upward. Quivering, his fingers strained to reach, and he bore down on the next granite chip. There were no footholds. Jim kicked and scraped the snow off of his boots and pulled into the airy space until his right foot met his right fingers. Jim released his hand to make room for his toe, gasping and puffing. The toe folded awkwardly, and Jim began to shake uncontrollably. "Come on. Come on, man, don't pop off. Stand it up." Jim breathed. "Help me," Jim secretly pleaded. "Help me." He pushed up on his right foot and extended his right hand to a flake. The stance was solid, and Jim stood and panted, shoving his hand deep into the flake protruding out from the wall. He could feel his fingers peel from its smooth, cold insides. His fingers slid, and Jim knew that he was about to fly off. "Why was I made?" Jim let himself ask as he slapped into flake, closing his eyes and cringing; puffing his cheeks and shaking. The angle had folded over vertical, and it pulled on Jim's arm that was burning with pain and sliding out again. Jim slapped into the flake again with his open hand. He looked down, and the man stood watching in silence. Jim looked up and tried not to absorb what appeared to be an endless distance to where the face met open space. Jim's legs and torso began to shake violently. He breathed and quieted his mind and slapped deeper into the flake once more. Holds and features emerged from the textured, granite face. Jim stepped a leg back and lunged for a hold with his free hand. Immediately the shaking stopped. From hold to hold Jim began to breathe and move. "That's it; stand it up," Jim whispered to himself. Higher and higher he climbed, feeling the rushes of power and energy descend upon him from the longing in and of and surrounding him and everything. The angle leaned over even more. Each movement demanded complete devotion. Any hesitation, and Jim would miss the holds. Each focused lunge was a pull for life as his feet kicked free. "Why was I made?" Jim breathed and climbed. "You know," the Whisper replied, entering his thoughts. "Now you will know."

Jim's chest heaved, and he realized that he cared — that he could not let go. His forearms burned, and the pack with his skis and poles was heavy and awkward. He dropped an arm and shook it limply and thrust upward again and again. Finally he worked his way to the right and north and threw one final move with his heel and crested on the summit ridge. He lay heaving on the edge and looked down. The big man was now small. The man thrust up his fist with a bent arm and hollered, "YEAH!" A smile burst onto Jim's face, and tears welled from his eyes and fell into the cold space. Jim felt the big man feeling for him, and it was good. Jim carefully pulled onto the ridge that was pasted with snow and partially melted hoarfrost that looked like beautiful, white feathers. Jim climbed and crouched with his left hand holding the frosty spine. He looked down one last time, and the big man waved him onward. Jim waved back. When he reached the summit, Jim could see that the angle was less severe on the opposite, west side. Snow packed to just below the summit crest, which was bare and strewn with shale. Jim stood and felt his chest breathe in and out in big gulps. The sun pressed through his shades and into his shrunken pupils, while the sky blued into a deeper black.

Jim knelt on the summit. He did not know how long he stayed, for time ceased to have meaning for him. It was utterly silent. Jim felt calm.

All the whining and complaining leached out of his soul and into the deep sky and awesome surroundings. The mountains seemed to extend forever in all directions. Jim did not recognize the peaks and felt that he was in a removed land. The darkness below sat like a cloud layer, threatening to move upward and swallow him. Jim stood and looked down to the west. As Jim's eyes focused, movement emerged from the field of white. Jim lifted and strained his head from side to side and squinted. Two figures slowly kicked their way up the ridge toward him. Jim turned and side-stepped down in their direction. As they drew closer to each other on the steep, snow covered arm, Jim recognized a familiar kick-style in the lead figure. Emotion leapt to his throat. "Dave, Red Bone, hey!" Jim shouted. The figures stopped and looked at each other. One put a hand on the other's shoulder. Jim plunged down to them until he stood panting in front of Moon Dog and David, who stared at Jim with their mouths half open. David said nothing but kept staring at Jim as he reached out and touched Jim's arm with his forefinger. "Hey guys, dudes, I mean hi," Jim said. The bizarre events, including standing before these guys, stood in witness to the deeper feeling of excitement welling up in Jim with an ever more powerful elation. Moon and David turned in a slow circle, trying to comprehend their surroundings.

"Whoa," said David, gazing all around. "Rad, man."

"This's heavy," said Moon, shaking his head.

"How do you figure we get back?" asked David.

"Wake up," replied Moon.

"Or fall back asleep? Into life or back into death?"

"To shadowlands."

"Really is no ending."

"Jim is it?" asked Moon, looking up to Jim and lifting his chin.

"Pepe," corrected David.

"Good to meet you, man. We're a little on autopilot here, buddy," Moon said and stepped up and touched Jim as if he too were surprised to feel flesh and bone.

"Check out the light," David said still looking around in amazement. "The sky is so dark."

"You must be Moon Dog," Jim said hesitantly.

"In person … I think."

"Jimmy, you alright?" asked David.

"I think so."

David gathered himself and resumed kicking ahead to gain the summit.

"You're on today, Pepe."

"Guys, I mean, I'm not sure what's happening," Jim said, listening to himself.

"Neither are we!" laughed Moon.

"That's the north side of Peak 21," said David, stopping and nodding to his left, "and you're on to lead us down the first descent."

"I am."

"You are."

"What about the big guy? The guy with the pony tail?"

"What?" asked David.

"The guy with all the tattoos. The pumped dude."

Moon and David turned and stared at each other. David's chest fluttered with emotion.

"Whattaya mean, Jim?" asked David.

"What did he look like?" asked Moon. "Tell me something about him."

"He had tattoos all over his body. Flaming boats and paddles on his arms."

"Wow," exclaimed David. His jaw dropped, and his eyes were wide.

"What else?" asked Moon. "Anything else distinctive?"

"Half his ass was gone."

Moon and David both turned pale and caught eyes again.

"The Painted Man," David said under his breath.

"He brought me a case of Heinekens."

"A case of beer?" asked David.

"And a girl."

"A girl?" asked Moon.

"He hasn't changed!" David laughed. "Dude, was she cute!?"

He and Moon exploded with laughter and shook their heads.

"Well, yeah. I mean beautiful actually … She cares for me," Jim added, looking down shyly.

"Really," Moon Dog exhaled with his mouth slack as he stared around in wonder. Tears streamed down his cheeks. "I believe it. Wayne, The Painted Man … lives … I love that guy. Wayne died years ago on the North Branch, back East. He saved our lives on Two Dog River."

"Did you touch him?" asked David.

"He touched me. Cared for me. In the cabin. With the pretty girl. Healed my frostbite. He's right down below the ridge. I soloed up here. On rock. I was just with him," Jim declared and peeled off his gloves and held up his hands to show David and Moon his healed fingers.

"Praise the Lord, Jim. That's all I can say," breathed Moon. "We can believe. Wayne, The Painted Man lives … wow. Puncture wounds all over his face?"

"Yeah, lots of scars. Whattaya mean died? Where am I? What happened to me?" Jim asked, and his questions rose like bright balloons into an endless future.

"Pepe," said Moon, "I'll hit you with it straight, bro — just hear it and have faith because it looks like you're gonna need it. I have little or no idea what's going on … OK? The Holy Spirit is guiding us. I trust a calling happening here — God is. You were created by Him. We were all created. Everything was created," Moon declared and raised his arms and slowly turned in a wide circle, smiling skyward — "in deep mystery. This is life after death … There is no death. Only Life. The Lord Jesus is sovereign. Our Creator, Redeemer, Guide. The Giver of life. Our Judge. I pray that you will accept His loving grace, Jimmy. Whew man … too much," Moon exhaled and lowered his head, overcome with emotion. He found Jim's eyes and kicked by, looking around in awe.

David shook his head with his mouth agape and continued upward as well. Jim followed the two. The three climbed in silence until they stood on the summit. Jim's single line of footprints disappeared down the East Ridge. David and Moon witnessed Jim's tracks and dropped their packs and pulled out their telies.

"Go ahead and put on your skis, Jim," David said, nodding to Jim's pack.

Jim slowly dropped his pack and pulled out his skis, shifting his eyes between David and Moon. He bent over and pressed into his three pins, still watching the two, unsure of what to say or ask or even think. David side-slipped down and tried to peer over the edge of the north side.

"What's down there?" Jim asked as he squeezed and released his pole grips.

"The meat," replied David straining to look over and down. "Long, really long. A series of bowls, then cliff band threaded by slots, more slope, even steeper, more cliff that has to be aired … big air, a wide couloir, then a final slot. Don't come off line. Commit to airing the bands; you won't make it otherwise. We'll follow your lead, Pepe," David said and spat to the side. "Stay on route. She goes down the throat from here, from the peak. Be firm. Be relaxed. Keep breathing."

"I mean — I dunno," Jim said, but the Feeling within — the deep and ever present Feeling — lifted Jim's eyes and thrilled his legs to step forward. Jim looked down and breathed and met the swelling Feeling. He gripped and ungripped his pole handles and breathed hard. Sweat trickled around the corners of his eyes.

"And no giving up — not caring if you live or die," David added. "Live your way down this run, Pepe. Live big." David nodded to Jim. "You're being called, man."

Moon stepped close to Jim, and Jim watched Moon Dog's movements separate from his voice. Moon locked eyes onto Jim and told him that he could do it — that he had to do it … that he had much more inside than he chose to realize and that if Red Bone felt the North Side was a solid line — not a suicide run — but a solid, respectable line, then ski it they would … he would, more importantly. Moon spoke directly to Jim, and Jim lowered his head and leaned over his poles as he listened to Moon Dog. Moon's strong, soothing voice entered Jim, and he felt Moon Dog inside his muscles and heart and guts. Moon continued and told Jim that it appeared that Jim's life as he knew it was over and that if he did not commit to his destiny as graced by God, then his existence would be a tragic failure, and neither he nor David wanted that because they liked him. "We love you, Pepe," Moon Dog said directly. "You're a good bro, and we care about you, and Nancy cares about you too — a lot," Moon added and fused onto Jim's eyes. "She loves you, Pepe … After a certain point," Moon continued firmly, not letting Jim turn away, "you're going to have to make your own decision: to come out, to commit, to fall onto your knees, place your face to the dirt and surrender to Him — to the real and only Power. Hallelujah, Jimmy. I pray that you will make that choice. The Power. The Glory. It's here, Jimmy. But we can only take you so far. The rest is up to you."

"It's already happening," Jim whispered, looking down. His knees wobbled.

Moon listened and absorbed what Jim said. Jim looked up and watched as Moon pulled a large Buck knife from his parka without taking his eyes from Jim. He opened the blade. "Pepe," Moon said directly, "this's gonna hurt me as much as you."

Jim pulled back his head. He was dripping sweat and felt light-headed. But Jim lifted his chest as Moon took him gently but firmly by the collar, unzipped his shell with the knife-hand and in one motion sliced across Jim's chest and through his thermal top. Blood erupted from the gash. Jim gazed upon the bloody slash. The world slowed to a stop in the strange reality. Moon shook the blade down, and thick red blood dripped onto the white snow. Moon wiped the blade on his pant leg, folded it and patted Jim on the back and gripped his shoulder. He locked onto Jim's eyes with a steady kindness. David came over and hugged Jim and patted him on the back. Then Moon and David nodded downhill. David gave Jim a gentle shove. Jim stepped down a ways, catching his balance and looking at the two guys. He took his eyes away and gazed at the dark blood seeping down his chest and pooling around his waist. The wound burned, and warm blood seeped into Jim's crotch and ran down his thighs. Jim looked at the blood, then up to David and Moon.

"Send it, Jimmy," David said firmly but softly with love for Jim. Jim felt David, and emotion choked him with tears. "Pick a good line, man. We're right behind you, Pepe," David added, kicking around and landing at Jim's side.

He gave Jim another nudge, and for a reason that erupted from the hidden Presence — the Presence Jim thrilled to know — he turned, pointed his telies down the throat and abandoned himself to the blind roll-over. Bleeding and trembling, Jim snapped to attention, and his legs firmed. Every muscle in his body riveted to attention as Jim buried on one knee, squared to the fall-line then aired into the next turn. Jim heard David and Moon Dog bellow behind him; and their cheers of approval flooded his being with Power — Power and Glory. Jim held the line as he felt himself air into weightlessness. He buried to his chest in powder crystals that blasted across the top of his shoulders, across his blood and sweat, by sinew and bone and body and mind … until everything became soul. Jim breathed through his clenched jaw and gripped his pole handles. "I want," Jim whispered, naming his secret. "I do want. Lord God, help me. I want You."

***

At Rattling Brook in the cache, Nancy half-awoke from a dream. In the dream she heard voices in the box — David and Moon's. Still dreaming she rose and felt around in the pitch black for her shells and boots and hat and gloves. Nancy dressed by feel, crawled to the outside and braced in the frigid, mountain air. The Milky Way glowed above and dusted over the horizon. Nancy felt the universe in the crystals and trees; and up to the peaks and beyond to the stars and around again in an endless river of pulsing eternity. She found her skis in the pale starlight, brushed off her climbing skins pasted to the bottoms, pushed into her bindings and followed the skin-track just set by Moon and David. The track took a direct line up Peak 21. When she passed the spot where they had found Jim, the trees opened to a slope. Moon and David's tracks disappeared into its endless expanse. Nancy stood and stared at the untouched blanket beyond their last kick. She awoke to Catherine's voice and the brown light of a fading headlight.

"Pulse's going out — like a wick. Get ready — CPR," Catherine spat.

Nancy struggled to wake up and to make sense of what she was hearing. Moonshadow kept her ear on Jim's bare chest over his heart and appeared to be asleep. Catherine had one finger on Jim's aorta and her cheek to his mouth. Nancy lifted herself. She slapped and yelled at Moon Dog and David. Both stared, still holding hands. Neither moved.

"Past first light … way past," said Nancy as her voice cracked with fatigue and nerves. "Thought a chopper'd be here. Easy trip … from Dale. Ten minutes. Fifteen. She hadn't said anything to Moon and David. She didn't — she's not gonna call in a rescue. She won't do it."

Catherine and Moonshadow looked at Nancy and swallowed hard, realizing the same truth. Moonshadow rolled away, curled into a ball and started to cry. No one spoke.

"What's going on with those two?" Catherine asked frowning.

"Guys," whispered Nancy to herself, "have their own world. For each other. They've gone for Jim. To save him. To try."

"What!?" Catherine exclaimed, straining to hear Nancy. Her fingers trembled. She looked down at Jim, and her eyes grew wide. Suddenly she snapped-to, spread her quivering fingers all around Jim's neck and squeezed her head onto his chest.

"Out … Nah, Nan … cy. He's out. I got nothing now. Quick," Catherine stammered.

Nancy lunged over and sealed her mouth around Jim's, tilted his head back and blew hard twice. Catherine felt for Jim's sternum, measured up, wrapped her fingers, placed the heal of her right hand down and stiff-armed a compression with a grunt. Her coarse hair fell forward.

"Oh man, oh man. Why is this happening?" Nancy pleaded. "Lord, stop it. Please. Stop it. Bring him back. Bring Jimmy back to me. Come on, Jimmy; hang in there, sweetheart. You're too young to die."

***

As Jim carved and aired, the grade fell away, and he had difficulty touching down. Jim watched the horizon draw closer as his stomach squeezed into his throat. He leaned into the fall line and dug into the slope, pant-ing and holding on as he continued to slide down slowly on his side. He twisted and shoved his elbows out as a self-arrest and came to a stop. Jim looked up. David appeared to hover above as he drop-kneed, compressed and aired, keeping square to Jim's position. David's final turn sent him over Jim. He landed below and arrested with his elbows as well. Jim looked up again and saw Moon Dog's small figure saluting them on.

"Moon Dog isn't coming?" Jim shouted down to David, listening to his own voice as if watching sound waves vibrate into space.

"Says he's old," returned David. "That he's already proven himself to be brave, truthful and unselfish. Been through many battles. He says he'll be with you, Pepe, forever — that he'll find you beyond. Be prayin' for you. Moon Dog says you're a man now, Jimmy, that you're doin' great, that you're finding your soul, who you're really meant to be." Jim lay panting and looked at David. "A lot of speed down here, Pepe," David continued, turning to look down. "I recall a slot over this band. A short band. Trust me. Send it," David panted and yelled. "Cry to the Lord for strength."

Jim worked his way up and touched the grade in front of his face. Steep, he thought. Steeper than anything he had ever skied before. Jim looked up and around and felt the sheer immensity and the power of the slope. He wondered if at any moment it would release and send them both into oblivion. Jim's legs began to quiver. He hopped around fighting fear that seized him like a clamp. "Come on, come on … can do it," Jim breathed to himself as he drop-kneed then stood to a parallel position to gain speed. The void and the lip met Jim as he awkwardly resisted tumbling forward out of his heels and collapsing with fear. Jim felt a scrape under foot, then he was weightless. Jim tucked. He instinctively threw himself forward and prepared to land with a drop-knee. Jim watched his arms extend outward and his chest rise, held by the greater Spirit. Air. The mountain with all of its compelling space surged into Jim.

"Jimmy," David's voice and feeling whispered throughout every fiber of Jim's being, "I'm with you, man. You're skiing well. Excellent. Land square. Let it tumble. Dig in fast. Gain control." Jim watched the dark cliff band fly below him. A silky expanse of white opened where rock met snow. Jim felt his right knee rise as he landed and tumbled into the air and landed again on his butt. He bounced into the air and this time turned sideways and landed in a tele-turn and kept snaking downward.

"Yeah, Jimmy! Hot. Beautiful recovery. You're on, bro!" David exploded through Jim's neurons and blood as the slope funneled into a couloir. Jim aired over the lip with his legs tucked. The walls tightened on either side. Jim landed, dug-in and stopped but kept sliding because it was so steep. He kicked around and threw himself onward: pummeling between turns in a tight coil. The couloir funneled out of sight as it turned left. Jim made the corner and could reach out and touch the walls.

"Nice, Pepe, excellent control in here. Go with it," David continued to whisper to Jim's being. The couloir slotted Jim onto a desperately steep slope — one that Jim would have difficulty even climbing. Jim reached down with his lead pole and aired around — turn for turn in a twisting rhythm, barely touching the now grainy crystals. The horizon dropped off, and Jim felt nauseous.

"The last band, Jimmy. This's the big one. Commit. Turn and get speed … now!"

Jim felt himself turn and fall forward directly down the throat of the fall line. He waved his arms and once again launched into blue space. The band was overhung, and Jim saw nothing below his feet until he cleared the lip. His stomach stuffed to his throat. He felt the rush of air straighten his fall as he held out his arms and gripped his poles. Flying. Still flying. Jim wondered how long he would hang in the air. He watched the slope below meet his face. Jim smashed down and somersaulted around and realized he was in trouble. "Dig deep, Pepe," David whispered. "Deep inside yourself. Cry out to receive Him, Jimmy."

Jim felt himself breathe and relax as the greater Presence calmed him with power and confidence. Jim watched as he rotated and flew into another funnel. He landed on his back in the fluid snow and tucked around face-first, awkwardly tumbling again and again. "Be it, Jimmy. Relax. Don't fight her. Let the movement happen. Relax and firm at once. Don't splay out. Gain control little by little." Jim watched as he rotated once more and tucked his skis. They collapsed under him, dug in and held, only to spit him out like a spring. Jim could see the couloir funneling into a narrow slot. "Use your arms now, Pepe," David whispered again. Jim fought a sickening feeling as he realized he was tumbling out of control down a 55 degree slot with a blind exit rapidly approaching. He was falling down a mountain — down the north side of Peak 21. "Now, Jim!" David yelled inside of him — deep inside Jim's core.

Jim came around again and dug in his elbows and scraped the sugary granules with his pole grips. He slowed to a slide and lay panting with his face and head buried in the cold snow as he slid downward. "Recover, man. Slow the slide. Rest a second," David said, still speaking without words to Jim's being. Jim's chest heaved with pants. He started to cry and vomited into the snow. The wound across his chest stung and burned. Blood soaked the inside of his shell and spilled out, leaving a wide swath of bright red as Jim slid and eventually stopped moving. He tasted iron as he put his face to the bloody snow. Jim lay gasping for air with his chest and heart bleeding feelings. He looked up at the long slash of red blood.

"Combat, Pepe. This is the final slot. Excellent arrest … wow. Stand it up now, man," David said earnestly. "Finish her off. Brilliant run. You saved yourself. Your life, Jimmy. A life worth living. You want to live. Feel that? Feel the love for life? That's His life loving you back, Pepe ... that's God. Send it now, man. Get as close to Him as you can. Find yourself in Him. Here it is, man!"

Jim gripped the grains of snow in the shady couloir with his gloved fingers and ignited with feelings — feelings for Nancy. Intense feelings that made his heart ache with regret. *It's too late,* Jim thought to himself. *It's too late.* He clawed his way up the bloody slope as if trying to climb back to Nancy — back to her pretty face looking up at him, back to the life they could have had together.

"Stand, Pepe," David said, and Jim stood. His head cleared to a focus as each detail of his surroundings — the rock, the snow and the sky sharpened to stark clarity. His legs trembled, but the Power coursed into him. "Come on, Pepe. You're on, bro. Home free now. Feel the Glory," David pronounced. Jim sensed his legs grow firm. He closed his eyes, took a deep breath and kicked around. "Yeah!" David yelled through Jim's insides. Jim compressed down the couloir. The walls closed, and Jim had to straighten his skis. He tucked his arms together and shot through the narrow exit gap. Jim landed on a gentle 30 degree slope of pasty, navel-deep powder. His entire body released as his telies floated between turns, and Jim felt the soft pull of crystals across his bindings. He sank to his thighs and rose again as if being rocked by gently caring arms. Jim watched the valley and a ravine lined by pitch-green spruce pull closer. He stopped, and his chest heaved for air. It was absolutely still and warm. Jim dripped with sweat. He could hear the blood rushing by his inner ear. He looked back up at the impossible heights and tears of couloirs. Jim stood and turned and floated downward.

As he lost elevation, the crystals began to round into a thick paste and grab at the bottom of his telies. Jim's skis scraped onto bare granite. The rush of water wafted in and out of his consciousness. Jim was hot and soaked with sweat and blood. The cover thinned and slushed between turns. Jim ground to the lip of a roll-over and rushing water filled his senses. The rounded crystals below Jim's skis released back into their primal form — water from the first moment of creation. Jim slid over the lip as snow became flowing water and carried him downward toward the ravine, scraping and sliding over granite slab, glistening brilliantly with water and sunlight. Below, a raging torrent wedged between the two slopes of naked earth and polished granite. Jim spun in circles and fell onto his back. He slid without control down a domed waterfall. Jim was soaking wet in the freezing snowmelt. He twisted onto his stomach to stop and was shot into the air. Jim landed on a mushy pile of old snow in the ravine and slid into the water … into the exploding creek — the headwaters of the Wolf River. The icy water squeezed away his breath. Jim's skis and poles were gone, and he did not know how.

"Jimmy!" David shouted to Jim's heart over the roar of whitewater. "Don't panic. Feel me. Do as I feel." Jim felt himself buoyed. He looked around and was sealed into a rockered cylinder and holding a double-bladed paddle. "Stroke, Pepe … with me," David commanded emphatically. "The perfect run, man … from high elevation powder on 21 right into the Wolf at early flow. Been a dream of mine for years. Never been run. Let's live it together, Pepe. Don't ever lose your dreams, Jimmy … with the mountains … with your soul ... with God. We'll all stay close to you. Be praying for you … Now paddle, Jimmy; stroke for broke!"

Jim felt himself thrust forward and get shot to the side as if body-blocked. Two light-brown waves converged from above and buried Jim in icy water. Suddenly the bottom fell away, and Jim was airborne in all the roaring water, which exploded into pitch white in every direction. Jim looked up as Peak 21 disappeared behind the ravine walls. Water erupted everywhere, and Jim felt David pumping through his arms, swinging the paddle back and forth and shouting, "Heehaw!" The horizon dropped away between enormous and rounded boulders. Jim felt the boat snugged to his hips. "That's it, Pepe. Wear your boat. Now roll with this corner. Throw a brace. Easy. Stroke and kick-back." Boom. Jim cleared the top of a massive boulder, which exploded a pounding hydraulic on the downward side. "Nice, Pepe! Keep sending it. Relax and breathe!" Douglas firs, naked rock and tan earth flew by as Jim careened into blasting white. Jim swayed and carved and paddled. He got hammered upside-down and felt David set the stroke and roll him up as water stung his nose, and he burst back into brilliant sunlight and roaring whitewater.

The gradient finally eased into swift current, and the Wolf became dark and deep. Jim swept around corners into alpine meadows radiant with flowers of crimson, yellow and powder-blue. Purple larkspur and saxifrage burst with color. The mountain flowers and tufts of fresh, green grass packed between drifts of old snow. The grade leveled further, and the mountain finally released Jim. He felt the two powerful Hands let go of his chest. Jim lay back on the deck trembling and stared up at Peak 21's massif, whose final couloirs pointed beyond to the impossible heights. A single cirrus cloud brushed the summit. The receding roar of the Wolf and a hushed whisper of wind in the firs absorbed Jim. Quiet. Jim's fingers quivered, and his entire body throbbed with power. He drifted into pastel-green meadows where white, red and yellow rose in the light with startling vibrancy. Jim washed onto a small gravel beach on the opposite shore from Peak 21. He had crossed over. Speckled granite, raw earth and deep-green firs mixed with all the colors and snow-covered peaks. Screaming beauty. Jim pulled out of the cockpit, dripping with holy water and gazed at the stunning universe around him. He stood shaking with his mouth agape, with his eyes smiling, with his heart and soul and courage and wound and with his brilliant first descent down Peak 21. As Jim stood, he looked to the summit, and his heart ached for Nancy … who was on the other side. He stepped onto the meadow and watched as darkness curled over the mountain like a wave cresting, then breaking and rushing upon a shore. Sweating and breathing through his nostrils, Jim fell to his knees and faced the oncoming darkness by squeezing his hands into fists and bowing his head.

***

"Oh, I'm getting tired," Nancy pleaded as she shoved down on Jim's chest with stiff arms in the cache. "Shake those guys again. Got to bring them to."

"Hey, hey you guys! Get up damn it. We're in arrest here. Serious," Moonshadow yelled.

"Get David's cell phone. Sprint up the ridge. Try a call again, quick," said Nancy.

Catherine bent over, sealed onto Jim's mouth and blew hard, deep into his lungs until his chest rose. Her other hand remained pressed on Jim's neck. She lifted her head.

"The breath of life," Catherine mused to no one, "can I give it to him?

A body now, but where is the life? What is it? Where did it come from and where did it go? Who is Jim? Where is he now?" Catherine asked. Her face was drawn with fatigue, and her hands curled with fear as she recognized her own mortality.

David and Moon blinked their eyes at the same time and stared at each other in the semi-dark.

"Nance?" Moon asked, rubbing his eyes.

"Moon, Whinny, quick, Jimmy went into arrest."

David and Moon Dog tore out of their bags. David placed his head on Jim's chest as Nancy frantically pumped.

"Stop Nance, stop a second," David whispered tensely as he pressed his ear to Jim's bare chest. "Nothing." David's mouth went slack. Everybody was shaking and talking and bumping each other at once. "Moon, the cell. Get out; try an' call again," he sputtered.

"What happened to the chopper?"

"What time is —"

"She didn —"

"Compress —"

"Keep —"

"How long have you been —"

"Compressing."

Everybody suddenly stopped as Moon flashed a light onto Jim's pallid face.

"Come on; get with it!" Nancy shouted. "Don't give up on Jim. Please."

***

The light pulsed brighter, and Butch found himself in a ravine. He sensed huge fir trees surrounding him and snapped in half. Their perished trunks pointed downhill as if swept to humility by a Sovereign hand. The glow focused on the ground where Butch witnessed powdery bones strewn among the remains of torn clothing. The shifting snow had elongated a skeletal form. Butch knelt and arranged the bones, starting with the shattered femur and shin bones and as many of the little bones of the feet as he could find. Butch placed the head and neck vertebrae together. His throat choked with emotion when he found the red and white polka dot wind shirt. Butch reached inside his suit for his wallet and found the pictures … of his wife and boys … and of his father. He held out the picture of his father next to the bones. Butch sat back and fingered something metal on the ground. He bent over in the soft glow and read the imprinted dog tags: Dan R. Michel: DOB 1935 … Skier.

"Son," El Viejo said, kneeling down to Butch and putting his arm around his shoulder and letting what he knew gush forth. Butch could not hear or see Dan, his father. The corner of Dan's mouth trembled with emotion. "My son. This is my son," Dan repeated over and over again, sobbing. Dan lifted his eyes higher, and his hands trembled. The Horizon lit into a translucent blue, white and yellow brilliance. Dan, Viejo, The Old One, closed his eyes. He felt the presence of the Lord Jesus Christ placing an arm around his shoulder. Peace filled Dan. "I will never leave his side," Dan whispered to the Savior. "We will look upon our true faces. Together as father and son … my son."

Butch collapsed into darkness once more. Dan, The Old One, knelt and scooped Butch, Dan Michel Jr., into his arms … scooped his lost and broken soul into his arms and carried him to a place where wild, mountain ferns grew sweetly and where the fresh snowy peaks shown above through giant Douglas firs and where the Light from the horizon would surely brush upon him … when he was ready … and when Dan whispered to his son without ceasing … "I will never leave your side."

***

The roar of helicopter blades finally broke the mountain silence as Nancy and everyone waited and worked on Jim in a clearing just beyond the burned out yurt at Rattling Brook. Nancy spoke later about cramming into the BellJet medivac with Jimmy in a swirl of noise and freezing snow dust. She spoke about all of the medical machines and readouts and beeps and flashes and voices — about the defibrillators greased onto Jim's fleshy chest and heaving Jimmy into the air like a slab of cold meat. She shook and cried with every jolt.

The pulse-ox and EKG machines immediately burst into a piercing whine. The readouts froze on a straight line. Voices over the headsets grew frantic. Nancy sat up straight and closed her eyes. An overwhelming Peace flooded into her every cell and fiber and deep into her soul.

Nancy placed a hand on Jim's forehead and stroked him with her gentle fingers. Knowing far more than the machines and biomechanics, Nancy whispered her intercession with closed eyes, then calmly brought her hands together into perfect prayer. It was a 10 minute ride to the medical center in Dale — up and over Peak 21, past Mad Dog Mountain and Big Pine, into the high basin and done … 10 minutes. That was it. Ten minutes, 10 seconds, 10 hours, 10 years, 10 thousand years or a lifetime … For Nancy time was no longer time. They landed at the medical center into a crowd of lights, ambulances and personnel. Off to the side, the coroner waited to begin his exam.

CHAPTER 12
EL VIEJO'S RAPTURE

The darkness rushed over Jim on the meadow next to the river and brushed back his hair like a sudden gust of wind. Jim rocked backwards with the abrupt force. He clenched his teeth and closed his eyes. The darkness rushed by as if bent on damning someone else and became a receding storm line. Jim blinked as the soft, clear light returned. Silence. Jim's chest swelled with feelings. The corner of his mouth trembled, and his face crumbled. Hidden tears flowed from his eyes. Jim cried for his mother. He knelt on the soft alpine grass and reached for her — to be grounded in the world again. Jim felt for his father too. He allowed all the feelings to erupt. Anger, grief and mercy melded until mercy dominated, and Jim felt pity for his mother and father. For their shallowness. For their nearly perfect failure as parents … and he sensed a perfection waiting for them. Jim's chest heaved, and he let himself feel the Fire within, Who burned with a loving craze: calling, wanting, seeking. Jim gripped and ungripped his fists and worked his jaw and faced the Fire … with his wound and courage with Moon Dog and David's spirit and with Nancy's prayers. Jim knelt exposed in the sharp mountain light. He lifted his face and shut his eyes to the sun — a sun with warm texture that touched deep inside of him. Mountain wrens called back and forth in the quiet. Jim collapsed to all fours and watched his tears pour onto the tufted grass and earth as Nancy's face welled from his emotions. He felt her beaming eyes and clear skin. Her strong shoulders and happy smile. Her soft, blonde hair. Her laugh. Her voice. Her touch. Her special look for him alone. Her gaze deep inside. Her radiant soul-health. His mountain lady. Jim ached for Nancy. It was unbearable, and he panted and heaved with feelings. Jim squeezed his eyes shut and yearned to go back — to find Nancy again. To touch and give her all of his feelings. Jim fell onto his side. His mouth gaped as his tears gushed onto the earth. Jim looked at his hand and gripped his chest and his heart and the core of his feelings for Nancy and for everything and everyone. His chest glowed, and Jim held onto his heart with both hands and rocked on the ground on the flowers.

"Help," the Jim of the world stammered. "I need help," the Jim of the world cried while the deeper Jim felt himself break apart and burn in the loving fire of the One watching.

"Jimmy!?" El Viejo, The Old One, called as he stepped across the wild flowers on the meadow in his tattered ski pants and polka dot shirt. Dan stretched out his arms wide with a big smile and his mirror shades. He was carrying a large mountain pack. "I'm here for you, man."

The sun and clouds and sky suspended while the river folded and eddied along the shore. The mountains stood behind.

"Dan?" Jim croaked, rolling over and looking up. "I'm dead. I died, Dan."

Easy, Jimmy," Dan said gently. He pulled off his shades and looked thoughtfully down at Jim. "Gee, I'm happy to see you, Pepe. You made it! Made it to the other side. Can't forget about you. Got two sons now!" Dan exclaimed and stepped over to where Jim lay. Dan bent under the pack which had another strapped on back. Dan leaned and dropped the enormous load with a grunt. He knelt and lifted and pulled Jim to himself and hugged him with quivering arms. Jim's mouth trembled, and he started to cry again. "Wow, look at you," Dan exclaimed holding Jim back. "You've changed. You're a man now, Jimmy. You went and grew up on me. Smokes, look at that wound, Jimmy. A beaut," Viejo grinned, unzipping Jim's shell jacket further, holding Jim back and gazing at his blood-gashed chest. Jim was still soaking wet from the river. "Feel all those feelings. And you're in the Light. Isn't He something!? Feel Him. All around you, Jimmy. Close your eyes and feel. Come out. Let it happen, Jimmy. Knew you could do it. Nancy must be praying for you hard right now." Jim closed his eyes and breathed and calmed. He wrapped his arms around Viejo's bony frame and hugged him back, nestling his head onto Dan's chest. "There you go, Pepe," Dan said quietly and held and rocked Jim and patted and rubbed his back. "My son came home to me today," Dan said quietly. "We found each other. He's home, Jimmy. "I'm going to love him … with all of my heart."

Jim lay in Dan's arms and calmed. He closed his eyes and pictured the Jim of the world cast off as burnt ashes and floating down the Wolf River.

"Dan, I didn't want to die."

"You didn't, Jimmy."

"I didn't?"

"On your way to being more alive," Dan said smiling with his eyes.

"I can see myself dying … cah, cah, can," Jim stammered and flooded with feelings again. Dan held Jim tight and rocked him back and forth.

"Easy, Jimmy. Let it happen. You're blessed, man."

Dan held Jim for a long while, and Jim calmed.

"Saw myself die. Who am I now?" Jim asked as he faced his own answer with a hidden thrill.

Dan gently took and lifted Jim's cheek and face and looked into his watery eyes. "You know, Jimmy. I can tell you know. Now I can see you. Who you really are. You're beautiful, man. Nancy knew all along." Jim's face buckled into creases in El Viejo's hand, and tears streamed down his cheeks. "You feel her, Jimmy, don't you? You feel everything here," Viejo whispered. "Go ahead. Go deep. Go all the way. Feel as much as you can feel until you burst with feeling." Jim heaved tears and cried in a staccato moan. He collapsed into Dan's arms. "She must be praying for you, Jimmy. Praying hard, even as we speak," Dan whispered. "You can feel her. Feel that? She's right here. In your heart. In your soul. You have courage now, Jimmy. Courage to feel. You're a man now. Go ahead and feel her. Tell her how you feel. Pray back, Jimmy. She'll know. Nancy will know you're there. Become a prayer, Jimmy. Send yourself." Jim closed his eyes tightly and lay in Dan's arms and let himself bleed tears for Nancy. A long while passed. The sun appeared to be setting and glowed in a textured, early twilight.

"Where are the guys, my buddies, Red Bone and Moon Dog? David was with me on the mountain. Down the river."

"Easy, Jimmy. Feel 'em. Go all the way, man. Send yourself to those guys."

There was a long silence, and Jim squeezed his eyes shut and heaved in-and-out.

"Teach me how to pray, Dan," Jim gasped. "I want. Now I want. Can feel the want. Have I known all along?"

"It's alright," Dan said softly, stroking Jim's head and rocking him gently. "Everything is OK. Everything is good. Calm and receive Him." Jim's breathing slowed, and his chest rose and fell in a calm rhythm. "There you go, Jimmy. I'm with you, man. Right here."

"I am … I still am."

"You were created."

"I feel the guys, my buddies … Moon and David."

"Good guys, Pepe, real good guys. Go ahead and feel them — feel deep … They're good men. Mountain friends. Those are the best friends. Soul mates … forever." Jim released from Dan's arms and sat up. He took a breath and wiped his eyes with the back of his hand. Jim knelt and bowed his head and held out his arms, palms-up. His hands quivered. "There you go, Pepe," Dan said and knelt next to Jim. "You're strong, man. Bow to the Almighty. Weak is strong. Don't run and hide."

"You know."

"I can sense."

"I was scared. I remember being scared. Running and hiding. In my life. Is my life over?"

"You have just begun."

"I'm scared, Dan."

"Understandable. It is scary. It's awesome," Dan said lifting his eyes and gazing around him as the two knelt side by side on the meadow. "Being created. Created and aware of being created. Called by your Creator. You can open and look now, Pepe. With your courage. With your beautiful wound and scar. With everybody sending you off. You did it, man."

"What should I do, Dan? What's happening to me?" Jim asked as he twisted and sat.

"Believe," Dan said as his voice grew quiet. He looked to the horizon, still kneeling. "Receive, Jimmy … and hike!" Dan exclaimed with a big, hopeful grin, turning and finding Jim's eyes. Jim placed his arms on his knees as he sat on the ground. He looked down then up to Dan and met his kindly gaze. "Will you hike The Range with me, Jimmy? The Powder Horns. Spring into early summer out here. Beautiful, man. Been wanting to. Can we be mountain partners? You and me?" Dan asked hopefully and nodded with his eyes beaming. "Will you come with me, Jimmy?"

Jim lifted and put his arm on Dan's shoulder and smiled through his tear-washed face.

"Sure Dan. It'll be great. You and me," Jim said, and his chest shuddered as he breathed in.

"And Him, Jimmy, our Lord Jesus Christ our Sovereign King and Creator of all this, Creator of you and I," Dan proclaimed and spread his arms wide. He breathed in and smiled and twisted in a slow circle. "Be still, Jimmy," Dan whispered with his eyes closed. "Be still and you will feel Him next to us … with us, in us … us in Him … never ending, hallelujah, Jimmy. Rejoice. Jesus lives. Always here, now and forever," Dan said in a whisper.

"I want to know Him, Dan. Nancy knows. Help me, please." A core emotion blurted, and Jim opened to its piercing joy brimming his eyes with tears.

"Feel, Jimmy. Really feel Him. Patience. We've got time. Lot's of it. Let's walk. Take a good, long one. We'll hike the whole range … and find out … together. It's a glorious range. Just look at all these flowers. God's flowers, Jimmy. Bright shadows of The Kingdom. Thy Kingdom come … Thy will be done … on earth as it is in Heaven. Hallelujah, Jimmy. We'll walk and learn. Appreciate having a partner now, really do," Dan said and looked down and worked his jaw. "Mountain partners are forever. We'll check on Danny, my son. Guys call him Butch. He's a skier too. Damn good one. Has it in him, heart and soul. From his old man I guess," Dan said and laughed. The shiny skin of his dark face puckered, and a tear squeezed from the corner of his eye. "We'll see how he's doing in a while. He's workin' through a few things on his own — between him and his Maker. Gotta do what a man's gotta do. We have time. We all have time. There is no time, if there ever was time at all," Dan said and worked his jaw again and lifted his eyes and looked around and up to Jim and to the magnificent pines and alpine meadows shining in the rich, clear light. Jim looked into Dan's eyes and realized that the guy in the yurt who passed him the note was Dan's son. Jim did not know what to say.

"Jimmy, you got your telies somewhere?" Dan asked, sliding on his big mirror shades. "Keep track of your boards. Gonna need 'em when the snow flies again. We'll free the heel together, you and me. Here, throw this on, Pepe," Dan said and pulled the extra pack over for Jim. "Got some hiking boots for you, too. A pack. Boots, gear. A tin cup … a cup of tea. Mountain tea. Comforting … soul comforting, Jimmy. Thank you, Father … for Jim, my mountain partner," El Viejo said, and the corner of his mouth trembled with emotion.

Jim unbuckled and slid off his tele boots and regarded them thoughtfully. The toes were bent. There were scrapes and slashes on the sides, and the liners fit his feet like an old friend. Jim placed the boots side by side. He stripped out of his shells and carefully gathered his gloves and hat. Jim slowly folded and packed everything in the mountain pack as if saying goodbye to a past life. Jim sat down in his thermals, and he was warm. He laced-up Dan's trekking boots. Dan helped Jim to his feet, and Jim slung on the pack and placed his hand on Dan's shoulder. They followed the shoreline until the river narrowed then waded across up to their necks, huffing and puffing in the freezing cold water. The two walked north and east toward the north flank of Peak 21. They spoke easily back and forth, and when Jim came upon his telies and adjustable poles strewn on the granite slab above the roar of Wolf Creek, he carried them all the way back to where his boots waited in the flowers on the meadow. Jim neatly lay his skis and poles next to his boots. Viejo watched as Jim bowed his head in thankfulness for where they had carried him. Jim turned and put his hand back on Dan's shoulder, and the two headed off again for the peaks. El Viejo, The Old One, spoke now and then. Jim listened and felt. He wiped his eyes with his palms and looked around, opening to the wonder of where he was and whom he was becoming.

Jim and Viejo traversed the granite slabs and dried in the sun, until at length they made a lush area at the headwaters of the Wolf. Deep-green sego lilies and bear grass grew abundantly, and huge piles of old snow dripped into the creek. The water was sweet and clear. Jim waded across the ice-cold, rushing stream, and his legs turned blue and numb. He turned and held out his hand to steady Dan.

"Can I help you, Dan?" Jim asked above the rush, nodding and smiling.

"I'll say yes. I'm the old man here," Viejo replied, smiling as he reached for and took Jim's hand.

The crystal water rang over smooth, granite balls — igneous granite — tan and white with black speckles, forged deep in the earth; transformed in molten passion to rise and cool in the crisp and fragrant alpine air. Stone, water and light. Pure. Jim and El Viejo set their packs on the earth against a granite boulder. The smell of mountain herbs — narcissi and alpine sorrel — was rich, and Jim inhaled fully with his mouth closed.

"Good, eh?" Jim said, nodding to Dan and patting him on the back. "Good to be here with you, Dan."

"Oh yeah," groaned Dan, stretching from side to side. "Gettin' old, Pepe."

"You? Naw."

"Feelin' better, Jimmy?" Dan asked as he sat down against his pack and a boulder.

"I'm feelin'," Jim replied and sat next to Dan, leaning against his pack as well. There was a long, comfortable silence. Jim and Dan sat side by side. Jim looked up and around. "So you don't die when you die."

Dan waited to reply.

"Open, Jimmy. Surrender. Wonder," Dan said almost in a whisper as he felt the earth with his fingers and closed his eyes. Another long silence ensued as Jim considered El Viejo, The Old One's, words.

"Didn't amount to much in life," Jim said after a long while.

"There's a bigger picture, Jimmy," Dan replied. Jim listened again. He dropped his head. Dan heard a shudder as Jim breathed. "Miss her?" Dan asked gently, looking over to Jim.

Jim lifted his head to the sky and exhaled.

"A lot," he replied.

Silence settled upon the two. Dan rose and gathered dry spruce sticks. He dug out matches from his worn pack, struck one and cupped the flame in his dark hands. He knelt in his shrunken frame and ragged clothes and placed the flame beneath the smallest twigs. He and Jim watched the flame jump from twig to twig and ignite a warm, snapping fire. Cool air drifted down from Peak 21 and blended with the aura of herbs and pine smoke. Dan pulled two tin cups from his pack and stepped to the creek and filled them with icy water. He placed the cups next to the fire, and the water droplets on the outside of the cups sizzled. The two sat in Silence for a long while and watched the fire and stretched their boots to the flame so as to dry them. The smoke smelled sharp and piney and good. Jim inhaled, and his chest felt heavy.

"Go ahead … feel, Jimmy," Viejo said softly. "A new heart, a soft heart … a new creation," he mused to himself. He reached over and placed his hand on Jim's shoulder and found his eyes. "Don't be afraid. Don't despair. Don't ever be afraid to feel."

"I want her."

"All of her?"

"All of her … yeah, she's somethin', Dan."

"Nancy's beautiful."

"She blew me away. All of her," Jim said dropping his hands.

"Um, um, man. Gotta love that. Good for you, Jimmy. Wantin' her. Manhood. I'm remembering my lady: soft skin with her hair in braids, dusty blonde, sweet smelling, cringing her eyes as if in dire pain. Shuddering, trembling, breathing in my ear; me burying inside her warm, wet tightness. Losing my breath. Her wanting me body and soul. That musty smell. Divine. Children made in all that passion … But Who is it that you really want? And Who wants you?"

There was a long silence as Jim considered Dan's question. Dan rose and collected more wood and placed the brittle sticks over the fire.

"Who was she, Dan?" Jim asked at length. "The girl you just mentioned."

Dan paused. He hung his head, then looked up to sky.

"My wife, Jimmy."

There was another silence.

"Yes? What is your story, Dan? How have you become who you are?

Where have you been? What do you know? How did you come to know?" Jim asked and placed his arm across Dan's shoulder to comfort him.

"I'll tell you my story … in time. My story is my failure. Your failure. My son's failure. Every man's failure. A man has to fail … to feel, Jimmy — to finally feel and see. I'd like to love her again, Jimmy. I really would. To make love to her. To feel who she really is. I'd like to be a better husband. To really see her. To love her again. To love the great Love behind us all."

"Does a man get a second chance?"

"Believe," Dan whispered and looked ahead with watery eyes.

Jim and Dan sat and listened to the creek. They watched the fire and listened to it pop and snap. Coals began to pile and glow with radiance as the fire settled. Jim felt the warmth from the coals, and it was good. He brushed the side of his shell pants, and his hand stopped. Jim reached in and pulled out Butch's note to his wife.

"Dan, might want to know about this," Jim said gently and handed the note to him. "I … was with your son. Back at the yurt. Back at Rattling. In that time. That place. That life." Jim choked on the feelings in his throat. "Can I go back?"

Dan hugged Jim around the shoulder with his arm and looked into his eyes for a long time. He opened and considered the crumpled note. "Um," Dan grunted, cringing his face as if struck by a sudden and acute pain. Tears welled in his eyes. "Did you two get to be bros, you and Danny, Jimmy?"

"He … wasn't in the best shape, Dan. I was … preoccupied. Busy with myself. Always busy with myself. Nothing else but my —" A lump of emotion blocked Jim's voice.

"It's alright, Jimmy."

"Can you see him?"

"I have seen him, Jimmy. Felt Danny. He's … in a tough place. I've been there myself."

"Maybe I've been there too."

"I feel you were headed there, Jimmy."

"How do you know?"

"I am a new creation," Dan said, and his mouth trembled. His eyes filled with tears again.

"Can I understand?" Jim asked, and he placed his hand on Dan's shoulder.

"Yes, Jimmy. I believe you will. I really do."

"You feel responsible for him, don't you, Dan?"

"I am responsible … Partly because of me Danny's there … and now his boy, my grandson … and his son and his son's son and on … and on. You see, Jimmy? I never really knew my own father … or my real Father."

"I want to pray for him, Dan. For Butch your son."

"Pray hard, Jimmy."

"I never prayed before … except this day … that I'm aware of."

"A human being is a prayer."

Jim rose to his knees and bowed his head. Dan took notice and sat forward and bowed his head as well. He placed his hand on Jim's back.

"Father in Heaven," Jim prayed, as the words rose from a source he did not know he possessed. "Father in Heaven right here … wherever Butch is … meet him, Father. Help him. Come to him. Come to me, Father," Jim whispered and turned warm. Tears welled in his eyes. "Help Dan be a good father to Butch, to his son Danny."

There was a long Silence while Jim and Dan listened to the creek and felt the comforting fire. A chill settled onto their backs.

"Thank you, Jimmy," Dan said quietly at length. "It's real." Dan closed his eyes tightly and whispered, still placing his hand on Jim's back, "Father, Lord Jesus, please help my son Danny to become all that You wish. Your original creation. Your beautiful soul You created. Forgive me, my failure as a father … as a husband. Save us all. I humbly ask for Your mercy. Thank You, Father, for Your blessings. For Your love for us. For answering my prayers and easing my loneliness, for coming to me, for bringing Jimmy. Amen."

"Amen."

Both men leaned back against their packs, and the fire blurred through their tears. A long, full Silence fell upon them.

"Whew, man," Viejo exhaled and gazed upward after a long while, "to give up like that. What keeps us away … separate … hopeless and dark? Sin, depravity, ignorance, brokenness. Danny needs me, Jimmy. Really does. Needs us both. Needs our Savior. He is in the shadow of death."

Silence absorbed the two again as they reclined and felt warmth from the fire mingle with the fragrant and cool air.

"What is her name?" Jim asked Dan at length.

"My wife?"

"Your wife, Dan."

"Elizabeth. My wife Elizabeth."

"That's a beautiful name."

"It is a beautiful name. She is beautiful. I pray for her all the time, Pepe. I know she is blessed. Things have been made right. Forgiven. Still, I feel her. I hurt her. I really did. Deeply. I can often feel her wanting me. Loving me. Missing me painfully, Jimmy. Wondering where I am. Wanting to be together again. We're connected, Jimmy. We really are. Chosen for each other."

Dan pushed the tin cups closer to the flames, and they rolled to a boil and hissed droplets onto the scented fire. Dan turned and reached into his pack and pulled out two dirty tea bags from a stuff sack. He placed the tea bags in the cups, and Jim could smell the spicy aroma steaming upward in slow circles. After a while Dan took a spoon and stirred one cup then the other. He pulled them back from the flame, handling each with a faded bandana. Dan carefully passed a cup to Jim, who took it with both his hands and sipped.

"Um, good," Jim said and leaned back again and closed his eyes. Jim felt a calm overcome him. The warmth from the tea filled his insides. The fire felt good. He opened his eyes and gazed up at the darkening clouds through the pine bows.

"Danny's our only son. I can feel Elizabeth grieving," said Dan. "She's a grandmother now. Heck, I'm a grandfather. I can feel them all. The whole family. A family, Jimmy. A family is a man, a husband and a woman, a wife, who love each other — and children … A family is important. Now I know. Now I know, Jimmy," Dan said quietly as Jim listened and absorbed Dan's words and feelings. "Think of me, Jimmy, eh? A grandfather and out here keeping up with you." Jim smiled into Dan's eyes and reached and patted his seasoned hand. "I know Elizabeth's remarried. Not sure what to feel about that. I need help, Jimmy," Dan said. Jim looked up and into Dan's eyes, unable to reply.

The air grew cooler, and the sky dimmed into a deep sunset. Dan stood and pulled a thin, quilted sleeping bag from his pack, sat down and unzipped the bag and wrapped it around their shoulders. The quilted bag felt warm and good and smelled like old fires. The two huddled together under the bag and sipped their tea. The fire began to light their faces.

"Nice," Jim said.

"Um, soft and warm. Found it — this and all the gear. Cast off from other journeyers. Soul gear."

"I can feel them."

"It's good, isn't it, Jimmy? A cup of hot tea. The cool mountain air. Everything. Good for the soul."

Silence resumed. The sun disappeared over the horizon, and slashes of blue, orange and pure-white deepened across the sky in complex layers of evening light.

"What happens to us, Dan?"

"Watch and listen, Jimmy," Viejo whispered and looked upward. A long while passed. The sky turned a translucent and deepening blue, brushed by crimson and purple. Peak 21 rose above while stars pulsed as living jewels in the darkening eastern horizon. The light and air were perfectly still. A harmonic sound started low and gradually built to a loud ringing crescendo from everywhere and anywhere. Joyous cries. Jim sat up with his mouth agape.

"What is it!?" Jim shouted, feeling the earth call with the same excitement inside of him.

"The whole earth rejoices, Jimmy," El Viejo said, lifting his eyes and arms upward. "All of us created."

At length the surroundings grew quiet again. The snapping fire and the constant noise of the rushing creek returned to Jim and Viejo. Jim sat riveted, staring at the night sky and countless stars. After a long while Dan spoke.

"I believe," Dan whispered to the Silence and to the mountain stars, "we are all close to our final journey." He placed his arm around Jim's shoulder and pulled him close. Jim eased onto Dan's shrunken frame and closed his eyes. Weariness, grief and awe mixed into Jim, and he succumbed to sleep.

In the morning Jim awoke to brilliant sunshine. He was cocooned in a down bag and laying on a foam pad. White frost coated his bag and all the grasses, sedges, rocks and earth. The mountain flowers — shooting star and arrowleaf — were closed in their petals. Thin plates of ice lined the edge of the creek. Dan crouched by a small fire and circled his hands around the flame. The secret thrill inside of Jim pulsed and began to glow. Jim lifted his head, still wrapped in his bag. The thrill. The Fire. The pulse … All spoke to his dream, still burning with elation in the center of his being.

"Morning, Jimmy," El Viejo said quietly, noticing Jim watching. "Cold last night. Heck, cold this morning. It's good. A good mountain morning. Good for the soul," Dan added and groaned with deep satisfaction as he stood and rapped ice out of one of the tin cups. "This is the best, isn't it, Jimmy? Well, maybe not thee best. Damn near close. How'd you sleep?"

"Good, Dan. I feel good. Better. Thanks, man. Good to be alive. Can I say that? Am I alive?"

"Holy smokes, Jimmy! Say it. Shout it!" Dan replied with a big smile. "Sing it!"

"Feel it."

"You bet, Jimmy. It is good to be alive."

"Wasn't sure where I'd be when I woke up."

"Right here with me."

"Good to be here with you, Dan," Jim said and sat up, opening his bag to the crisp and fresh mountain air.

"My pleasure, Jimmy. I love you, man," Dan replied and looked up hesitantly at Jim.

"Yeah? Thanks, Dan. I believe it. I really do."

"I'm here for you, Jim."

"It's good," Jim said and inhaled the cold air. Tears welled in his eyes. "My dream, Dan. Last night. Was really good."

"Yeah? Tell me."

"We were hiking, climbing an alpine mountain. Some other people, too … Nancy, David, Moon … others … their river friends, suddenly we were lifted up … It happened … It really happened. I totally felt it. We were all there. It was so real. The sky a soft blue … the clouds … higher and higher. We were on a wing … of cloth. There was someone below … more like a Presence, carrying us higher and higher. Just a thin cloth, a wing … up and up … mountains rising below … lifting above them … easily … the feeling of lifting … so high … flying, not really able to hold onto anything. Having to trust the Guide. Complete trust. We were so high … huge billowing clouds … up to them … dizzying, excited … Whoa it was so real … so beautiful, Dan. Up to the clouds and beyond. Feeling lifting … into another world. We went so high. He was taking us. Just taking us. Leaving the world below. Then dark clouds, soft light and colors. Then rain … too high, scary. He gently circled us back down to the mountains … real, unreal mountains … to the shore of a lake … quiet and beautiful. A rainbow in the soft, misty rain and light. We all stood holding each other … intense quiet … bursting excitement. Quiet. He was with us. This Guide. We could not see Him. But we knew He was there. I woke up, here with you, Dan."

Dan waited to reply, absorbing what Jim said.

"Far out, man," Dan exhaled and exclaimed shaking his head. "That's exciting. Really is exciting; isn't it? Life on eagle's wings. Soaring, Jimmy."

"It is."

"To know Him. To be with Him. To follow. I never realized what life is. What it's suppose to be; what almost no one seems to know," Dan said, laughing and shaking his head.

Dan squinted and looked far off as if peering into his past days.

"What does it mean … the dream?" Jim asked, laughing a little with Dan's reply and feeling the excitement tremble inside of him.

"What does it mean? Shiiii," Dan breathed, "We're on a mighty adventure here, Jimmy."

"What do we do, Dan?"

"Rise, Jimmy … come to understand … to bow … to journey," Dan said quietly, more to himself than to Jim. "What have I learned? … Suffering, sure. Payin' a price, sure. Most importantly, Repent." There was a long silence. "Hey, how about we climb a peak?" Dan asked, reaching over and patting Jim on the shin. "Never done that. The Greater Will is calling me to yonder mountains," Dan said and nodded to the distance. "You can show me. Found some gear. Check out this rope," Dan said, nodding to the rope resting on the top of his pack. "Tell me if it's safe. Wouldn't want to fall off and die," Dan said and paused, realizing what he said. There was a moment of silence, then he and Jim jerked into laughter. Jim felt his feelings erupt as tears flowed with the tonic of laughter. "Ho man," Dan blurted and cried and wiped his eyes. "Don't wanna die. I gotta tell ya, Pepe it's good having you here, bro. Hoo, that's too much." Dan sat back and breathed in and out. His chest rose and fell. "Ho man," Dan exhaled.

"Looks like a fine rope, Dan," Jim said as he wiped his eye and laughed a little.

"Found cigarettes too, and I'm gonna smoke me one because I'm not addicted or anything. Naw, as far as I can tell I'm a near perfect human being. Near perfect as a male specimen gets," Dan laughed, and Jim smiled and laughed with him. Dan pulled a bent cigarette from a crumpled pack of Lucky Strike nonfilters and balanced the blunt cigarette on his lip. He reached to the small fire, lit a twig and touched the flame to the cigarette, which immediately burst into bluish smoke. "Um, um that's good, man. But what's really good about it … right?" Dan asked, spitting tobacco from his tongue. "Same as the dream … The moment. Being here. Being here with you, Jimmy … on this wonderful journey." Dan squinted his eyes as smoke from both the fire and the cigarette circled around his skin-wrapped head and disappeared into the endless blue-gray sky. Dan looked up to Jim and smiled warmly. "What's inside is what is good about it," Dan added. "What you can't see directly but can feel. Can know. Can appreciate. Appreciate so profoundly that you fall to your knees … to your face. Something so large, coming in us, taking us, changing us, lifting us. Thank you, Father. Thank you Lord Jesus for everything. For this cigarette. For Jimmy. For this beautiful morning and for Your mountains and Your creation. For forgiveness. For all the chances You give us. For Your Heaven and Your earth. Even hell. For salvation. For where You are taking us. For Your work in us. Thank You for where you have brought Jimmy … and me. Hallelujah, Father. Please be with us this day. Even more. Lord, we need You." There was a long Silence, and Jim bowed his head.

Silence.

"Amen, Dan. Thanks. I feel a wanting. I want. The same as in the cabin. With the pretty girl … and the man."

"You do," Dan declared thoughtfully.

Jim sat up in his bag and watched the fire and considered his dream and all that Dan said. Dan finished his cigarette with care, closing his eye to the smoke. He tossed the butt into the flame.

"Call it breakfast."

"Um … tea. I'm up for a nice cup of hot tea," Jim said and stood and slid into his shell pants that were now worn and ripped. Jim pulled on his thermal top and jacket, which had also faded and aged. He stepped to the fire on the frosted ground. "What is it you say," Jim added. "Good for the soul … I like that."

"You are soul."

Jim held out his arms and hands to the flame and lifted his face to sky. He closed his eyes and smiled.

"Yes … I am."

"Hey, got shorts and a tee for you."

"Good. Need to wash out the blood from these old clothes. She'll warm up. Good sun. Pure and golden, alpine sun," Jim said and looked up to where he figured the sun would soon burst from behind the east shoulder of Peak 21. Dan handed him a cup of steaming tea. "Thanks, Dan," Jim said, nodding and smiling. Both guys squatted by the fire and warmed. Silence spoke, and each man unfolded as a response.

The two sat and drank tea until the sun spread through the spruce and melted the frost on the bear grass and aster. Jim stripped and dressed in the shorts that Dan gave him. As he pulled on the T-shirt, he stood and looked at the gaping scar across his chest, honoring the changes he most desired. Jim stepped to the creek and washed the blood out of his clothing. He and Viejo then packed, shouldered their modest loads and stepped into the hot sunlight. Jim's wet shells and thermals hung from his pack and dried in the sun. They lunged across the stream and hiked on granite slab and through talus. Dan occasionally placed his hand on Jim's shoulder. The sky was a faultless blue. As Jim walked, he felt His presence by his side. The Presence in the dream. From the dream to waking and walking … the difference was blurring. Jim motioned for Dan to stop. Jim stretched out his arm and closed his eyes, feeling. Dan bowed his head, and the two stood with arms over each other's shoulders and heads bowed. Silence. Presence. Jim's insides jumped with quiet excitement. The two felt arms around their shoulders drawing them all together in peace in the mountain light, and they were never alone.

As the day matured into twilight, Jim and El Viejo made the alpine tundra above treeline. The space was open and expansive. Pure-white granite boulders speckled with black feldspar sculpted among dark-green moss while pink campion mixed with blue forget-me-nots. Pink, blue and green. There were hundreds of tiny blossoms like bells tingling in the breeze. Bristlecone pine spread along the ground on the rock and moss in the lea of boulders, yielding to the incessant wind. Tufts of light-green frost hummock surrounded the granite stones, which were sometimes coated with bright patches of yellow and orange lichen. The colors held Jim, and he fell to his knees. Tears slid down his cheeks. Jim lost his breath as the tundra meadow glowed a rainbow hue into the deepening blue-black sky. A single cluster of profoundly red columbine set against a pure-white boulder. Jim knelt and stared and felt tears run off the end of his chin. El Viejo, The Old One, stood and bowed his head.

"Jimmy," Dan said softly, "I'll find us a nice place to bed down."

Jim nodded hesitantly. Dan slowly stepped through all the flowers with his head bent and his arms out with palms up. Jim knelt and listened to his breathing while the sunset lingered forever. How long had they walked? Jim wondered at length. How much time had passed and where would he eventually end? It did not matter. The moment held him, and the simple joy of walking was all that he needed as the greater Peace held him. Jim gazed to the north and east, and the mountains linked endlessly into the distance until they faded as a white glow … and extended beyond, and Jim knew there was no end. Jim looked down at his darkly weathered hands. He placed his hand on his chest and heart and felt the feeling — the feeling just for him … and for all men … always new … for him alone.

After a long while, Jim stood and walked to where Dan waited by a trickling spring. A rainbow glowed steadily around Jim's body, and he felt light. Dan nodded and smiled as Jim approached and lowered his pack and sat down beside him. Jim could not find words. Dan put his arm around Jim's shoulder and hugged him, letting Jim know there was no need to speak. The Old One then rolled over a granite cobble and set dry sticks in a tepee on the exposed earth. He lit and cupped a match and touched the match to the smallest twigs. A fire jumped to life, joining from stick to stick and circling smoke around its top in perfect completeness. Jim's spirit lifted with the fire, whose warmth and piney scent harmonized with the burning feeling inside of him. Jim sat closer and held out his hands to the glow as a slight chill gathered in the high mountains. The herbs and spring smelled sweetly pungent, while all around the high peaks, brushed with snow, stood motionless in frozen rapture.

Jim and Dan sat in Silence and neither could bring themselves to speak. The twilight lingered forever and deepened into purple and yellow. Vast cumulous clouds born in the day's heat illuminated as pure white. The setting sun lit and gently passed these billows into the fullness of emptiness. Soon all was purple-black, and the sky throbbed with stars — bright and shimmering jewels, which dusted in all directions and curved over the horizon. Jim's throat choked with feeling, and all he wanted was to say, "thank You." Jim rolled over into Dan's arms and drifted off to sleep.

El Viejo tucked Jim into his bag and words came to him that he had never before known: *The heavens tell out the glory of God; the vault of heaven reveals His handiwork. One day speaks to another; night with night shares its knowledge, and this without speech or language or sound of any voice. Their music goes out through all the earth; their words reach to the end of the world. In them a tent is fixed for the sun, who comes out like a bridegroom from his wedding canopy, rejoicing like a strong man to run his race. His rising is at one end of the heavens; His circuit touches their farthest ends, and nothing is hidden from His heart.*

In the morning Jim lay awake in his sleeping bag in the pale dawn. He sensed that Dan was also awake. The two lay inside their bags on the moss and tundra. Frost coated them like fine crystalline hair. Neither could find one sound to distract his attention.

"Dan."

"Mornin', friend."

"Had another dream. I feel things. I can't say. Chest wants to burst. Aches so much."

"Can you tell me?"

"I was climbing a mountain trail. Rugged. Really wild. Made a flat summit. Open. No one around. Not a soul. Then really frightening clouds. Not dark. Lightning inside of them. Off to the distance. Closing all around fast. Exposed. Then in a mountain hut. My father was there. My real father, Dan. He had gotten us the hut … for a trip together. The storm blew in. Still very light out. The clouds were light. The hut became a house. A beautiful house. Really big and sturdy. Modern. Clean. Fireplaces. Tall windows filled with light from the storm. This living

Light. Safe and spacious. Right on top of the mountain. Sitting on a bed with a girl, a woman. At Her feet. Someone I know. The pretty girl. But it was not her."

"Who, Jimmy?"

"The pretty girl in the cabin with the Painted Man. Before I came to you here. Was it Nancy? Was it both and someone else too? I still ache in my chest, Dan. A burning ache. More than I can say. I ache for Her. Fond of Her. So deeply fond. She cared for me so much. I can feel it. Her being fond of me. Showed me a story book. With illustrations. Pleasing. Very pleasing. I was proud of Her. And so fond of Her. She wrote the book and painted the illustrations. Reunited. We knew each other. All along. She knows me. We are deeply fond of each other. Almost unbearable how She feels for me. It was … how can I say; it stunned me, shocked me, held me. Was complete, Dan. Beyond being happy. Everything was answered. Could stay with Her forever. At Her feet. Very, very real. The same feeling out here. But beyond. She is beyond. Return and never leave. Never want to leave Her. Better than anything, ever. Who is She Dan? I ache for Her. I just can't say."

Jim shuddered and wiped a tear from the corner of his eye. His mouth was open. Dan rolled over and looked thoughtfully at Jim.

"Father … and Lover … The Lover of your soul, Jimmy."

Jim found Dan's eyes. The two curled in their bags in the morning chill and considered the dream, and Jim glowed with feeling.

"Why was I taken, Dan?" Jim asked at length, holding onto the dream and to the feelings.

"Um," Dan grunted, shifting and loosening his drawstring.

"There are no accidents, are there?" Jim asked.

"He is mysterious … and deliberate. We are free. But we are loved … ever so intensely. Father and Lover," Dan said quietly, looking hesitantly over to Jim.

"I don't know how I understand … I don't know how to say it … but last night, right over there, I stood outside myself and looked at myself. I saw myself as a disappointment. I knew, Dan. I knew I was going to keep right on being a disappointment … for Nancy … for the Something that was … is … ever near: in me … When in the Something … I felt deep and wide … showing me leaving Nancy. Never really touching her. Never really being loyal … to Nancy's feelings for me … so true and without end … to this deeper, greater Life … her feelings for me in Him … Is it Him, Dan? He took me away before I destroyed myself in my own shallowness. Before losing Nancy in shallowness. Dan, she is in this Greater … cared-for, guided, called … taken from me … protected from me. Nancy is not only Nancy. She is something more. Dan there was nothing to me," Jim said, blurting into tears.

"Easy, Jimmy," Dan said, sitting up and taking Jim into his arms.

"Am I taken, Dan?" Jim asked softly in sudden realization. "From what I was? What I was made by the world? What I made myself? From being nothing?" Jim asked and wiped tears from his eyes with the back of his hand, which quivered with helplessness.

"Come, look here," Dan replied.

The Old One pulled out of his bag and slid on his threadbare clothing. Jim did the same. Dan stepped to the spring and leaned over a pool in the morning chill. Jim came to his side and looked into the pool and gazed upon his reflection. Jim jerked back his head, not recognizing his face. Long, silver hair fell from his shoulders, and his face wobbled in the current. Haggard creases changed as the corners of his eyes and mouth lifted. His eyes closed and gazed upward. He was smiling, and Jim knew he gazed upon himself, returning to the Deeper and to the Greater. In Joy, more himself than ever. Jim felt a new strength and confidence in his core.

"Watch," El Viejo, The Old One, whispered in the quiet, mountain stillness, and he waved his hand across the pool. Jim and Dan were thrown into darkness, but Jim sensed someone with them. Jim's eyes adjusted, and he could see a figure in a light one-piece ski suit unzipped to the navel. The figure sat and pushed sticks around on the forest floor in utter darkness, and Jim knew it was Butch. "Let Danny be with us," Dan said softly. "He needs to hear you. Even though he cannot hear, he will hear. He must choose to hear."

While Dan spoke, Butch lifted his head as something inside of him stirred. He strained to look into the darkness as though the distance faintly dawned.

Jim spoke to Butch. "Who are you, Danny, really? You are not you. The you you think you are," Jim said quietly.

"Um," Dan grunted and nodded. He worked his jaw thoughtfully.

Butch looked up and squinted his eyes, responding to what was inside of him. He had long since given up trying to think his way out of his darkness. Shouting, wailing and beating his chest and the ground only returned to his own hollow ears. But something was happening inside of him now, when he was quiet and listening.

"Your own shallowness, Danny, what did you do?" Jim asked Butch. "My own. Your father's own. Made your own way. Eventually rotting and decaying into the nothing that it was … your own way. I watched myself become nothing. I was saved by the Knower above all time … what had already happened was stopped before it could happen. Danny!" Jim suddenly yelled, bursting into tears of gratitude. "Why me and not you? Can you hear me, Danny? I am saved."

"Um," Dan grunted again thoughtfully, looking down and working his jaw.

"I made myself by the world: satisfied me, pleased me, did all for me … There's nothing to the world, Danny. It's hollow and empty … then I watched me and the world rot and decay and pass away … only to rise again as its own world. Can you see what happened, Danny?" Jim asked earnestly.

Butch shifted on the ground and sat up and put his arms over his knees. An ache came to his heart: a new feeling born of tenderness in secret darkness. He waited and listened to a voice without a voice inside of him.

"Dan?" Jim asked, looking for El Viejo's eyes. "Do you understand?"

"I do, Jimmy."

"There was the girl with Danny, your son."

"The girl with the bells?"

"On her toes."

"The girl is not a girl," replied Dan, El Viejo. "The girl is the world … world as world only, as you say, Jimmy. She led him away."

"He failed."

"I failed."

"We all fail," Jim said. "Is that evil, Dan? Led away by the evil one. There is evil isn't there, Dan?"

"Can be subtle, Jimmy … but devastating."

"Butch!" Jim suddenly yelled and burst into tears as rushes of revelation welled into his heart from the Holy Spirit. "I know you can hear me, man. We're no better than you, OK?" Jim panted and grit his teeth. Dan put his hand on Jim's back and another to reach out for Butch. "She got shrill. Your wife. Got on your nerves. Dried up. Cut you off. Unrecognizable. Lost interest in you. Your hair fell out. She went dull and gray. Your knees blew apart. Couldn't ski anymore. You got tired and sore. Your dick went dead … passing, rotting, decaying, Butch man!" Jim yelled again. "There was nothing to you but you as the world passing away. You hated your wife. Saw your own decay, your own emptiness in her … The young girl with flashing eyes was the world … all you could make for yourself from the world … what you wanted from the world … she would give you forever, " Jim panted. "There was nothing to you, Danny … There is nothing to her. She's a lie. She took you out, Danny!"

El Viejo cocked his head and flexed his jaw, working through the truths that washed into him from Jim and from the Spirit.

"She led him into the mountains," Dan mused, "only to pass like November ferns. You're right, Jimmy. Damn near, learning a lot from you, friend. Wasn't much to me. Easy just to be the world. The world as nothing … nothing led me away to destruction … destroying other lives too … not even caring … no heart. Damn near right, Jimmy, nothing greater … just me, myself and the world," Dan mused and looked up to Jimmy. "It was hollow."

Butch stood and began to pace back and forth. He twitched his head and wrestled with thoughts and feelings as the pictures of his life played as an endless reel — meeting his wife, being young and skiing, their life together, their children, his sons and the whole mixture of emotions, scenes, arguments, disappointments, choices, denials … with his wife … with his body growing older … his skiing buddies dropping off one by one … all flattening into a final despair. Then throwing himself off of Cochran's. Killing himself. Everything that happened afterward and plunging into darkness … Never believed in Heaven, let alone Hell. Butch fell to his face on the ground and in the deepest depths of his guts silently begged for help … to Whom or What he did not know. The Horizon lit further, and a single shaft of Light streamed onto the forest floor and across his tortured face. Butch squeezed his eyes shut and reached out with trembling hands, feeling for the Light.

"Danny, we're here for you," Jim said gently to Butch, urging him to listen. "We're breaking through. Wanna make it. Wanna take you with us. Gonna pull hard … for salvation."

Butch curled onto his side and lay on the ground and sensed the first moments of calm. He blinked and was not sure what he felt. But the Horizon remained illuminated, and Butch marked what he came to see and feel. All the protest, anger, struggle and fear knotted in his guts loosened.

The darkness lifted for Dan and Jim, and they were bathed in warm sunlight on the tundra surrounded by the high peaks. The two sat by the gurgling spring in Silence. Dan rose and sat down by the little fireplace and piled small sticks onto the ashes and buried coals. He bent close and blew hard. The coals ignited into flames, and fine ashes rose then drifted onto the matted earth. Jim stepped over and sat next to Dan and watched the fire. He knelt and touched the ashes on the earth and smoothed them across his fingers. Ashes and smoke. Jim felt all that he confessed burn and vanish into the welcoming, deep-blue sky. He slowly inhaled and exhaled. Jim felt clean and light. Dan lit a cigarette, sat up and rubbed Jim's back, still watching the fire.

"Whew," Dan exhaled, "Damn, Jimmy, you popped my bubble, man. I figured it was all about eternal youth and two girls for every guy."

Both guys laughed. Jim wiped a tear from his eye with the back of his hand.

"Shhi," Jim laughed, and it felt good.

"Heck yeah."

"It's hard."

"It is hard. Doing good, Jimmy. Soul work. Diggin' deep, man. Pace yourself. Get in some good bro-time now. You and me … and Danny."

"Will Danny be OK?"

"Time."

"Changes."

"Choices. Mercy."

"Mercy?" asked Jim.

"Um, Eternal Mercy, Jim." said Dan.

"You're able to bring us to him."

"Not bad for an ex-asshole."

"Ah," Jim laughed.

"OK, ski bum."

Jim laughed again and put his arm around Dan's shoulder. After a time, Dan rose and filled the tin cups with spring water. He set the cups by the fire, and when the water came to a boil, Dan crushed and sprinkled in wild Labrador tea leaves. The steam rose from the steeping tea in soothing spirals of sweet aroma. Jim and Dan sat back and sipped tea, and it was good. The day became bright and sunny. Neither guy moved. The Silence permeated everywhere until Jim and Dan closed their eyes and were lifted erect. The same tingling and rushing that came upon Jim in the cabin returned, and the two strong but gently masculine Hands gripped his chest and lifted him from the ground. Jim gasped for breath and felt himself rise. He closed his eyes tighter and to his surprise clearly saw Nancy. Jim opened his eyes wide and waved his hands in opposite directions across the alpine tundra, and he was with Nancy.

It was early autumn in the Powder Horns and a dry, sage-scented breeze with a trace of coolness brushed open the front door to Nancy's cabin — her new cabin that Scott and Man Called Abe built for her five years ago. Her babies, Michael and Clay, were no longer babies but off at school. Kyle was 8 years old and ski racing. Playing soccer in the fall. One more year and Nancy would be 30. Nancy stood and began her asanas as she had her whole life, first as a warm up and cool down for competing and now before communion with the Risen Lord. Nancy's mind stilled. The Fire that always burned glowed intensely in her chest. Nancy stretched upward in Tadasana, The Mountain, with her arms overhead, breathing fully and rhythmically. It was then that she felt him swept in by the caressing breeze. Nancy gasped for air, and tears brimmed her eyes. Her knees gave way, and she fell to the floor and opened her arms to the doorway and its glare. Jim drifted in, inhaling and exhaling through his nostrils as his chest burst with feeling. He dropped to a knee and hugged Nancy and rocked her back and forth in his arms and lifted her face and gazed into her watery eyes. He gently wiped away her tears. Nancy knelt with her arms out with palms up and knew that Jimmy was with her. She could not see or feel him physically. But she was certain. Absolutely certain that they were together. Nancy rose and stepped to a side bedroom and looked back at the empty living room and doorway for Jim to follow. In the bedroom a little boy sat on his bed on a beautiful hand-stitched quilt, coloring in a coloring book and waiting for Nancy to drive him to preschool. The little boy looked up at his mother with sweet blue and green eyes. Nancy took the boy in her arms, streaming tears and held him up for Jimmy to see.

"This's Jamie, your son. Our son," Nancy whispered to Jim.

"What's ah matter, Mommy?" Jamie asked, looking up and into Nancy's tear-streaked face.

"It's all right, sweetheart," Nancy replied softly, stroking Jamie's head and smiling.

Nancy reached out her hand with trembling fingers for Jim, who took her hand and knelt and hugged his family for a long time with his heart and spirit. Jim closed his eyes tightly and prayed for them. Peace came. Nancy felt calm. Little Jamie placed his head in her lap as she stroked his dark-blonde curls and felt the fresh air and gazed through the framed window at Mad Dog Mountain that was dazzling and golden in the morning sun. Nancy listened to the Silence in the spacious cabin and sensed Jimmy with her. She felt Jim and his secrets and all that he felt for her and her for him … true love. Unspoken. Unbroken. Beyond time. Beyond this hard and fast world to another. Another world. A world waiting. A world coming. A real world. Jim gazed upon his son and caressed his little back and closed his eyes and prayed for a man for Nancy, for a good man and husband for Nancy and a father for his son. Nancy closed her eyes and breathed peacefully and went on feeling Jimmy. She reached up and brushed where she imagined Jim's cheek to be and told him how much she loved him. The phone rang, and Nancy jolted and picked up the receiver by the bed. It was Jamie's work associate, Mike Thornburgh, a good looking guy a few years out of graduate school, an MBA, skier and climber whom Nancy adored and who was on assignment for Jamie, helping David and Margaret at Big Pine. Mike spoke, and Nancy listened to his voice and held out her hand to Jim as her heart ached. Jim stepped back, placed his hands in prayer and bowed. Jim sensed his long silver hair fall forward across his shoulders. His arms and chest felt strong and broad. Nancy felt herself tingle, and the room grew lighter with Jimmy's presence.

"Tonight, yes, I want to. I really do. You'll pick me up?" Nancy asked Mike, and it was at that moment she realized what was happening with

Michael and how she felt about him and what was unfolding — that a life together was being called. Nancy balanced a blend of feelings: longing, excitement and thankfulness. She held out her hand again to Jim. Nancy watched her fingers shake through watery eyes, unable to suppress the rich complexity of the moment.

"Jimmy," Nancy said to Jim within herself, with her heart and mind and soul, closing her eyes tightly. "I've had to get on with my life. I can feel you, Baby. A lot. I know how you feel about me. About us. You're always there. I love you, Jimmy. You're always with me. I have my life now. You understand."

"That would be fun, yeah great. I can't wait. Oh that's sweet," Nancy said to Mike and hid her feelings for Jim as she opened her eyes and sensed that Jim was leaving. "You did? Michael, you shouldn't have. Can't wait to see what you got me from New York. OK, bye-bye now. Let me get little Jamie off to school."

Nancy spoke, and her heart ached. She looked up to feel for Jim.

Jim stood with his eyes kindly set upon Nancy's. He held up his arms. Jim's long silver hair flowed in the gentle breeze, and he was awake in El Viejo's lap in the bright, mountain sunlight in the pristine spring air.

"Jimmy?" Dan asked gently, placing his arm on Jim's shoulder. "Everything OK, buddy?"

Jim lay silently in Dan's care.

"I was with her," Jim replied after a long while.

"Um," Dan grunted and hugged Jim and patted his back.

"I have a son, Dan. He's a beautiful little boy. My son."

"Yes? Tell me."

"I want her to have a husband. A life. A father for my boy … a father on earth. I prayed for them. For that. She knows how I feel about her. How I truly feel. I saw her. I touched her with my heart," Jim said in a whisper. "She touched me back with hers. I felt her. She knows how I feel. I know how she feels."

"Darn, Jimmy," Viejo suddenly gasped, gushing tears. "That's so touching. You're doin' so well … everything you said for Danny and all that you're receiving."

Jim sat up with concern and placed a hand on Viejo's shoulder.

"Dan?"

"Oh jeepers, it's coming on. Happened before, Jimmy. I'm just so darn happy."

"What, Dan?"

"It's so good. So satisfying. I'm so happy. Seeing you growing up and all. Oh Lord, oh man. Here it comes. Too much. Risen Lord taking me. I can fuh … feel … hih … him."

Dan gasped for air and held out his shaking arms.

"Talk to me, Dan."

"Jimmy, I'm happy, that's all — just so happy," Dan gasped and shut and opened his eyes. Jim heard a tearing sound, and Dan's body and old clothes fell away like a shed skin, and Dan began to glow and rise above the ground.

"Holy smokes, Dan, you OK?" Jim asked.

"Jimmy, think maybe I'm going now. Being taken. Maybe try holding my legs. I'm gonna miss you, man. Thinking I don't want to leave you. Maybe not yet. Even though leaving is never leaving. Oh jeepers, I'm so happy. Can hardly say … how happy … I am. Hold me, Jimmy."

Dan's head lifted backwards, and he reached his arms wide and Heavenward. Jim grabbed onto his legs. Dan settled back down to the earth, panting and smiling.

"Hoo … Ho man. That's too much," Dan breathed and smiled and radiated in his new clothes that were his old tatters and body burst into light. Jim looked at Dan with his eyes wide and his mouth in a big "O."

"Um, it's so good. I'm so happy, Jimmy. An unbelievable happiness. Almost unbearable. I don't think I'm long for this world, Jimmy. I really don't. Want you to be OK without me. I love you, man," Viejo said and leaned back against his pack and closed his eyes. Dan's weather-polished features glowed a hue of rainbow colors. Jim placed his arm around Dan's shoulders and watched his face. "Hard to say how I feel. What's happening," Dan said quietly. "A desire. I'm goin' home, Jimmy." Dan sat up and reached around and into his pack. He heaved out the faded climbing rope. "Jimmy, let's climb that mountain … while we still can. The one over yonder. Let's journey to the frontier of the morning." Dan nodded, and Jim followed his eyes to the head of the plateau. He traced a white, shimmering ridge that lifted into the rich blue and met the sky at a perfect conclusion. "Been yearning to climb a mountain and have a mountain partner, a good friend," Dan added softly and stood and shouldered the rope. He took a step and floated. "Steady on the old feet, Jimmy. I feel good. Everything feels like … Jimmy, I just can't say," Dan said and smiled and inhaled and closed his eyes and looked up to the sky. Dan started walking, and Jim stayed at his side. Jim looked with wonder into Dan's face.

"It's good, Dan," Jim declared. "I know from my dream."

"More than good, Pepe," Dan said and nodded reassuringly to Jim as he stepped across the tundra. Dan pulled out his big mirror shades from his worn pocket and shoved them onto the bridge of his nose. "I'm gettin' on in years — good years. Years of good work. Can feel it all. So good. Come on, Jimmy. Let's climb that mountain." Dan nodded to the peak ahead.

"Shouldn't we take our packs, Dan? Are we coming back?"

"Take no bag for the journey," Dan replied quietly, looking off into the distance. "There is no returning." The two hiked and wove between granite boulders that rose to their shoulders. Bristlecone pines grew as gnarled dwarfs between the granite in sculpted beauty. El Viejo stopped at one such tree and regarded its intricate shape for a long while. At last Dan, El Viejo, The Old One, spoke, "What we know is what we discover … in what we are given … in how we choose … and the effort we make … always submitting to the Greater will," Dan said and nodded to the bristlecone. "A tree gives air and shade and needles for soil, precious soil. A tree receives minerals from the good earth. Giving. Taking. Learning. The great lesson. How long before we learn? To hold our branches high and to give … and take with our feet as roots … Living Water … joyfully," Dan added, smiling to Jim.

Dan continued walking. Jim stepped behind Dan and held out his arm and bent his head with his eyes closed tightly, whispering prayers of salvation. Jim opened his eyes and looked with reverence upon Dan's wiry frame and sun-dark hands, lined and creased with a thousand stories. A reverence overcame Jim for Dan and for all that he had come through … a reverence for the great journey for which Jim knew he himself had just begun.

The two hiked for a long time absorbed in His silence. The approach on the plateau funneled to the base of the mountain ridge, and there was no choice but to ascend the granite layers which plunged magnificently into the earth from above. The rock was clean and featured with crystalline knobs of black quartz and feldspar that sparkled in the sun. Dan sat down and lifted his head to the sky and smiled. Jim looked up the ridge line that thrust to vertical and beyond as flakes overhung and extended without end. White met blue. Jim smiled and breathed deeply and felt himself surge with spasms.

"Whew, beautiful. Looks like quite a climb, Dan," Jim said and stood in his threadbare shells and surveyed the one rope slung around Dan's bony shoulder.

"Heck yes, Jimmy," Dan replied, with his eyes now permanently lit in smiles. "We're strong. Really strong. Huge."

"I'm strong. You're strong. It's a big mountain. This looks long … multiday," Jim replied, squinting and smiling up at the granite tiers, rising beyond the first horizon. "We have one rope. No gear. No clothing except what's on our backs. Nothing."

"Perfect," Dan replied, and Jim laughed. He stood above Dan and placed his hand on Dan's shoulder. "Bring her on, Pepe," Dan exclaimed. Jim looked up again, trying to judge the first section of rock. Dan sat down to rest.

"Who is the bride, Jimmy?" Dan mused to himself.

"Sorry, Dan?" Jim asked and sat against a boulder next to him.

"A bride, a marriage, a wife … if the world draws us, holds us in emptiness, decays and passes us, then what is a marriage? Who is our bride, Jimmy? Who is she really? We are the bride."

Jim looked down and worked his jaw because he could feel Nancy in his heart as Dan spoke.

"Go to Nancy again, as a prayer," El Viejo, The Old One, whispered. "Do not leave your bride."

Jim glanced up and around at the peaks and funnels of snow on the high alpine. His throat swelled with feelings, and the view blurred with tears, and he was with Nancy again. She stood by her husband, Michael, in the semidark of their bedroom, and Jim could see snow piled up to the windows in the ghostly-light. "Jimmy," Nancy inhaled and whispered with her heart and soul, as Mike slipped off her flannel shirt and lifted her full breasts, "I can feel you. I love him."

Jim closed his eyes and reached out his arm and spoke to Michael's heart, "Take her in your arms. Be strong and true." Nancy closed her eyes, and her throat arched with deep pleasure as she lay back onto their bed and took Michael into her. Nancy opened her eyes. Michael was gazing into them and stroking her hair as they rocked together, and Nancy ran her fingers up and down the middle of his spine.

Jim peered into the glare of the sun and mountains. He was sweating and shaking and breathing hard. His chest rose and fell. A tear worked its way down his cheek. Jim looked straight ahead and squeezed his fists and pumped his flared chest.

"Whew, that's a little hard, Dan."

"Give, Jimmy. Who you are. Really are, the bridegroom," Dan said quietly but earnestly. Dan slung off the rope, untied the coil and held the end up to Jim. "Lead on, Pepe. I'll follow."

Jim listened to Dan and strained to understand. He worked his feelings down and took the end of the rope and handed it back to Dan with some slack and started throwing off coils so the rope would run free. Jim's hands were trembling, and he cocked his head to the side with a mix of feelings. When he reached the end, and when the old goldline was stacked, Jim peeled out of his shells and tied them around his torso. He wrapped coils of rope around his waist and tied off in a bowline. Jim reached around Dan's shrunken waist and did the same. Without hesitating Jim gripped the rock, and it felt good. He was home. Jim lunged upward and edged from knob to knob. He gently side-pulled on fissures in fluid, commanding motion. The rope paid out, and Jim realized that he had not taught Dan how to belay. Jim reached the end of the rope with a tug at Dan's waist.

"Jimmy, she's all run out," Dan yelled up.

"Climb," Jim yelled, smiling at Dan.

"I'm there. Surfin'!"

Jim knotted a length of rope leading from his waist and wedged the knot into a vertical crack and pulled down so that the knot jammed into the opening. He tossed the rope over his shoulder and slid the coil down to his waist for a body-belay. Dan lunged. Jim felt his gossamer weight on the other end.

"Dan, not much to you, bro!"

"I'm lean, baby. Whew, this is far out!" Dan exclaimed and pushed back into the airy exposure. His tatters flew about in the warm, gentle breeze, and a huge grin held up his mirror shades. He reached an arm high and pointed his index finger. "Rock 'n' roll, Jimmy! We're Glory bound!"

When Dan reached Jim, he was panting and quivering.

"Alright, here's how you belay," Jim said, and he showed Dan how to pass the rope around his waist and how to brake a fall. "Your job is to catch me."

"Save your life, Jimmy?"

"Yeah," Jim laughed, "save my life."

Jim's spirit rose to his chest as his eyes followed the endless rock skyward. He smiled. The pitch rolled-over vertical, and Jim lunged for a protruding flake as he sprinted upward. His feet swung free when he landed the hold.

"Gonna love this, Dan. Pull hard. Stand on your feet as long as you can."

"Sail on, Pepe."

When Jim pulled into the flake and stuffed his way to the top, the ridge gave back to a classic alpine ascent. Jim stood on the top, panting as exposure opened on either side of his faded, hand-me-down boots. He tied the rope from his waist around a rooster head and slung it over his head and back for another body-belay. Jim yelled down to Dan.

"You're on belay, Dan."

"Back at you, Jimmy."

"You say climbing."

"OK, climbing."

"Climb on, brother."

Jim worked the rope and stood with his front leg ready to catch Dan. He felt a tug, and Dan began to move and tugged again as he fell.

"Jimmy?"

"Yeah, Dan?"

"What's the technique here, hombre?"

"Send yourself as a prayer."

Dan laughed, and Jim could feel him inch upward again. "Scared out of my brains, man."

"Don't look down."

"Shhi."

"That's it. Get on those feet. Work up high, then throw her."

Jim felt a tug that pulled him forward slightly, and he knew that Dan had come off the rock below the overhang and was swinging free in space. He heard grunting and scuffling. The rope paid forward again. A dark, weathered hand with bleeding knuckles finally groped over the edge, feeling for the top. Then Dan's big, bony grin.

"Whew hee … far out," Dan exhaled and stood on the knife edge and steadied himself with his arms out. He crouched down and studied his bleeding knuckles. Dan's body glowed, and he floated off of the rock by a touch. "Still a red-blooded male," Dan said looking up to Jim. His polka dot wind shirt flapped in the breeze that buffeted on a comfortable thermal rising from the plateau. "Holiness, Jimmy, we're gettin' high."

Jim leaned back against the rock spine and gazed into the profound blue, which turned luminous black the further he stared, and Jim was with his son, Jamie. He could feel him. Jim took his son's hand. He sensed a big hand, a solid, 10 year-old's-hand. Jim looked down and into his son's sweet face and blue-green eyes. They were hiking together up the talus on the northeast side of Mad Dog Mountain. A short rock spire rose above and out of the scree like a gendarme. Jim could feel Jamie's stepfather, Michael, just in front, carrying a mountain pack with gear and a rope. It was their first mountain climb together.

"That's ah boy. My boy," Jim whispered to Jamie's soul. 'Feel that? Feel me inside of you. No sweat, right? Can climb this with Dad. This and more. Strong and true." Jim's insides felt warm with feelings for his boy. "You'll have good mountain sense. I'll make sure of that."

Jamie felt himself thrill and rise to the alpine vista as he kicked past his father, who said, "Pretty soon Jamie'll be burying his sorry butt."

Jim blinked, and Dan was talking to him as he straddled the ridge.

"Jimmy? You with me, friend? Don't check out now. Wouldn't know what in the heck to do up here," Dan laughed.

"Um, sure, Dan," Jim said and turned and viewed the ridge. "Alpine style now. We move together, Dan. Grab some coils and don't fall off!"

Jim stood to a crouch and took the spine with both hands and a coil and ambled upward with agile reaches. His muscles felt fresh and true. Jim's chest flared with power, while inside he swung his long silver hair from side to side as he moved with ease. Dan pushed up his shades and followed, draping a handful of coils over the edge. Silence overcame the two, and Jim could hear only his breathing and his heart pounding against his chest. Once more the Holy Spirit wrapped Jim with Presence as if wings lifted his back and shoulders as he rose upward on the mountain. Jim climbed with happy motion from move-to-move, looking back to make sure Dan was alright. The two joined in movement on the light and airy ridge. The line of granite reached ever upward, and Jim knew this was the longest route he had ever engaged. Already there was no turning back.

As his movement became rhythmical, Jim was with Nancy. He blinked, and he was floating on a wild slope of downy crystals on his phantom telies, and it felt good — remarkably good — to be skiing again. Jim blinked once more, and he was flowing up the ridge, feeling the wind rock him from side to side. He blinked again and snow. Back and forth until he felt Nancy next to him. She felt good, and he missed her. He looked into Nancy's face as she looked into the fresh snow-covered pines and watched a thread of crystals fall and twinkle a rainbow in the mountain sun. Jim looked again, because he could not match the face and the body with the feeling inside of him … the feeling he knew so well. Nancy's hair was coarse and her skin gently furrowed. Nancy's fullness set against the pure white snow and was easily mistaken for a man's. Jim closed his eyes and felt. He traced the feelings dancing inside of Nancy — their night together in the yurt so long ago … "You are blessed," Jim whispered to Nancy's soul, "You and your family, your husband, your children, our son," Jim whispered again and brushed Nancy's cheek with the back of his hand.

Michael descended the slope in the hush, making long tele-turns in the thigh-deep snow. Michael reached Nancy and touched her shoulder with his gloved hand. Nancy looked up to him and smiled. Michael's hair was white on the sides, and his figure was large. He panted, and there were creases emerging from his sun glasses at the corners of his eyes. Nancy felt their happy years together as a comfortable blanket, worn and faded, but none the less true. A tinge of sadness swept across her insides as Nancy remembered her grown sons as boys … touring with her here in the Southwest Kingdom — especially Jamie's beaming smile, so much of his father in him, the father he never knew. The husband Nancy never physically touched, yet always had. Her big boys were all gone now … as young men striding through the world with handsome power. Her other sons and daughters with Michael were teens and younger. Eight children altogether. Nancy wore the Lord's fertility as a fullness like a bowl filled to the brim and overflowing with joy.

Jim felt Nancy, her life, all of her children and her husband, and it was all good. Nancy was just shy of 45 years. She turned as a gust of wind interrupted the Silence pressing around in the blue and white like a passionate cry … as if someone stood and sang to her love. Nancy reached out her hand to touch Michael's cheek, knowing there was more — much more than her moment could ever speak. Michael dropped into the untouched blanket of white and disappeared between Douglas firs and into Wild Creek Ravine.

Jim looked after him, and a figure stood on tele skis in a dirty-tan, one-piece ski suit, sensing Michael and looking up to Nancy, then dropping to a knee and bowing his head.

"Danny, we are with you," Jim whispered to Butch's soul. Butch lifted his eyes and looked from side to side through his darkness. Nancy followed Michael, and her rainbow aura glided past Butch and vanished into his nether world. The Horizon glowed without ceasing.

Jim blinked again, and the rope tugged easily at his waist. Jim looked down and behind for Dan but did not see him. He gripped with apprehension, squinted and followed the rope off of the ridge and into the sky.

"Jimmy!"

"Dan?"

Dan floated in the breeze above the ridge and held out his arms with his face up to the sun. He could not remove his smile.

"I can't see, Jimmy. But I can see everything. I can't describe it," Dan called down. Jim twisted and secured himself in a notch on the ridge and pulled in the golden rope hand over hand. Jim was not sure what to think as he smiled up to Dan. Coils fell at Jim's feet, and Dan slowly descended like a kite. When Dan touched down, he felt for the rock like a blind man with his hands. He reached for Jim's face. "I can see you, Jimmy … inside," Dan said and turned his wide open eyes this way and that. "I cannot tell what all I see. It's so beautiful, Jimmy. I don't think I'm long for this world. Really don't. Can you make it without me, Jimmy?" As Jim regarded Dan, Peace fell upon him, absorbing into every pore of his skin. Jim took Dan in his arms and hugged him, and the two rocked together, teetering above thousands of feet of exposure, streaming tears of silent joy.

"I'm gonna miss you," Jim said, managing to choke through all of his feelings. An unspoken understanding came upon the two.

"I'll never leave you, Jimmy. You and Danny both. Will you look after Danny?"

"I will, Dan."

"Finish, Jimmy. We will all be in the Lord … I love you, man. Thank you for being my friend … And Jimmy?"

"Yes, Dan?"

"Find Nancy again, Jimmy … who she really is and who you both really are," Dan whispered with effort. "The bride and the bridegroom."

Jim tethered Dan to his waist and turned and continued edging and pulling up the ridge with Dan floating above like a colorful prayer flapping in the wind. The sun became rich and golden as it neared the horizon. When the sun finally set, Jim reached a small alcove cut in the granite blocks. A slight chill settled onto the mountain. Jim pulled on his old shells. Dan glowed and rose above, and when Jim pulled Dan, El Viejo, The Old One, down and held him in his arms, Dan became fine ashes cupped in Jim's weathered hands. Jim knelt and gazed upon Dan's remains reverently for so long that a billion or more stars circled Jim, and he felt dizzy, as if flying beyond time and place. Finally, Jim placed Dan's ashes as a careful pyramid on the pure white stone and watched as the predawn breeze blew him from the mountain, this way and that, until there was nothing … and Jim felt the Lord come to him in this emptiness. Jim calmly lifted his face to the rising sun. Happy tears followed a course down his cheeks and fell onto the mountain. "I love you too, Dan. Thank you, friend. Be with me. Lord Jesus, guide us both," Jim whispered. The Light opened, and the ridge beckoned with all of His Holiness.

CHAPTER 13
RETURN TO FOREVER

Jim ascended again following the surge of Peace that lifted him from movement to movement. His legs and arms trembled with wonder. He felt the goodness of every chip and crack and pull on the ageless rock. Clouds passed below, gathered and perched Jim high in a removed world of reverence. Rock. Sun. Silence. Jim climbed and climbed with joyful reaches. Alone with the Alone. Day became night and became day: over and over again so many times that Jim watched his hands wrinkle with age. After an untold time his movement slowed as the angle eased. Soon Jim scrambled on all fours. Finally he stood, and there was no longer a mountain. Jim stepped over crumbling granite blocks rising from coarse sand, which once composed the airy mountain. Jim stopped and viewed a flat plane where new mountains rose with fresh swaths of snow descending to their foundation. Jim stood and blinked. He fell to the ground and placed his face to the earth, unable to comprehend these awesome miracles.

Jim regained his feet and stripped from his alpine shells in the rich sun and tied them around his bony waist. He stood and bent slightly in his threadbare shorts and T-shirt. Jim surveyed his legs and arms, which were shrunken and creased. He felt with his fingers the slash-scar across his chest. Jim knelt with effort and bowed his head. He then rose in wonder. Nothing entered his mind, which had become the grand vista pulsing with elation. Jim took one step at a time across the wide plane, awash with smooth glacial polish, toward the mountains with his dirty shorts and shriveled legs. His bare chest hung with loose flaps of skin, suggesting an unspeakable age. Jim smiled and clenched his hands together and continued to carefully step. He opened his arms and palms Heavenward in witness to his changes. Jim closed his eyes and lifted his arms high to the sun — a brilliant light burning in holiness — Whose delight in him had no ending.

"Jimmy!?" A voice spoke to him intimately. "Who are you!?" The voice asked, and the voice was Dan gently laughing. "God's own."

Jim stopped walking and closed his eyes in awe. A long while passed as he answered Dan without words and with his heart.

"Go to your parents, Jimmy," Dan whispered. "Love and honor your mother and father. Go back to Nancy. Find her. Your chosen bride. Go back to calling, to service, to courage … unto God, Lord Jesus."

Jim answered Dan again without words, affirming with all of his heart his choice and his inmost desire compelling him onward. Jim stood with his mouth agape.

"And Jimmy?"

"Yes, Dan?"

"It is two girls for every guy!"

Jim erupted into laughter, closing his eyes and cringing with pleasure. Dan laughed too, and their mirth rang without limit.

Jim grew quiet and stood for a long time in solitude. He then felt for his mother and found her. His mother's dress and time and place made no sense, but this was of no regard. Jim felt the wound in her soul from his absence, left ages ago or perhaps ages ahead. Jim took his mother in his arms, and they streamed tears of reunion in deep recognition of mother and son.

"My mother … Peace. We will be together always," Jim told her gently without words. And the mother who had carried her son into the earth calmed and was proud of the man the boy had become.

Then Jim closed his eyes again and found his father … in darkness. Jim lifted the shadows, and his father felt him. "I love you, dad," Jim whispered to his father's soul and hugged him with both arms and held his head in his hands. "I can feel that you love me. You have never left me. Know that we will be together."

And Jim went to his stepfather and held his hand and thanked him for being his stepdad and told him how much he loved him and asked that the Light within, the Spirit, burst into flame. All this was completed without words or sound … by an ancient man, standing alone on an alluvial plane before the majesty of a new mountain range.

Finally, Jim was released to seek Nancy. When he felt Nancy, the image was unclear, but the feeling was sharp and true and could not be escaped. A calling. A riveting calling was coursing through Nancy and into Jim. The calling and Nancy could not be divided. Both responded to a rush of Light and Power that poured into them and into the vessel — the Nation — the free and lawful country in which Jim had dwelt so long ago, and for which in that time and in his shallowness he had no regard — America — poured into Jim's soul with her truth and her beauty. God's vessel. Clarity came upon Jim, and he could see Nancy dressed in black, surrounded and held by a large group of her children and friends. They swayed and lifted Nancy as she nearly collapsed. Catherine held Nancy's arm. Nancy's face was washed in tears. David and Moon Dog held on as well, and Margaret and Jessica and their children, and other souls, whom Jim did not know … Nancy's faithful River friends. Military taps sounded starkly as the bodies of her sons, Michael and Clay, were lowered into the ground in flag-draped caskets. Bold stars and stripes — red, white and blue. Fallen soldiers. American soldiers, who had died for their country. A vast calamity had overtaken the great land. Jim sensed fear and anguish. He stood behind the group, spread his arms and bowed his head in prayer. Nancy's grief was unbearable, and Jim felt every ounce of her pain.

Jim stepped to Nancy and held her in his arms. As he did, both he and Nancy entered the center of a hub. A Figure stood behind in shimmering white. His strong hands with open, bleeding wounds rested upon their shoulders. The events of Nancy's life spun around this center. Nancy closed her eyes and smiled inside, filled with the Lord Jesus and His peace. Jim and Nancy turned and knelt before each other with bowed heads, stripped of all but mutual reverence … while the events of their lives revolved slowly in opposite directions … Nancy's mother and father and her childhood in the mountains; pummeling through racing gates on skis. The River and meeting Charlie, Ace Man, her first husband; her babies being born; Charlie's death; meeting Jim and their moments together, moments she knew were fated; the ride in the helicopter with his body; and all the questions and disappointment; the birth of Jamie, Jim's child; her wedding day with Michael, and their pink and healthy babies, one after another; growing older with Michael; children maturing and leaving one by one; illness and health; children's tears, smiles and laughter … happy days on the mountains. Jim and his childhood turned as well … nannies and day care; his mother and father and childhood scenes; coming to the Powder Horns and dropping into Chute Six; David and their moments together; meeting Nancy for the first time on The Pass in the snow storm; the Rattling Brook yurt and their intimacy; his death on Peak 21 and his feelings for Nancy … And for Nancy more scenes leading up to the present: Michael and Clay in Special Forces uniform, smiling and proud. America at war and Nancy bleeding her heart into her country's soil. An American girl. Around and around the figures and images and feelings moved. Finally, each danced with the other and turned together until they merged, and Nancy and Jim knelt face to face in the center of the hub and smiled into each other's closed eyes and placed their hands palm-to-palm in naked Truth … children in Lord.

"Return," a voice said to Jim from behind. "You can rise and return now, friend."

Jim blinked and turned hesitantly as an old man turns with care. He was standing on the open plane. The Painted Man nodded and smiled. There were furrows on his mountain-polished face and gray streaks along the sides of his ponytail. Jim witnessed the tattoos rising in peaks around his neck. His muscles pumped as he grunted and heaved over both his pack and a mountain pack with Jim's old telies and boots strapped to the sides. The Painted Man nodded to the mountains beyond with a big, beaming smile — the smile of a joyful servant. Jim bent over with effort. Wayne, The Painted Man, untied Jim's shells and stuffed them into the pack. He helped Jim lift the load onto his back. When the pack settled onto Jim's shoulders, he rocked and bent forward and reached for Wayne's arm, steadying himself. Together they took one deliberate step at time, and Jim continued on his way to the peaks. At great length they reached the foothills, where mahogany bush with twisted and red-orange branches grew sparsely. Wayne stayed at Jim's side, and Jim held his arm. Jim stopped and felt the first rise in topography with his big toe. It felt good … to ascend again. He nodded to Wayne and smiled with his old eyes. Wayne smiled back and looked up to the mountains. Jim looked up as well, then down upon his hands, which were glowing a white and rosette hue. The shale at his feet also glowed. When Jim moved, each step felt lighter and lighter. Jim could not speak but only receive that which unfolded in him and as him … and sovereign to him.

Jim closed his eyes and found himself standing before himself long ago below Mad Dog Mountain. Jim watched as he, a young man, slowed and stopped his touring ascent and looked into his own eyes … and as Jim looked back at himself, he saw the passing and the already passed. The already passed felt love and compassion for the boy, who nodded and turned and resumed touring until he disappeared over a rise.

Jim opened his eyes, and he was held by The Painted Man. Jim nodded, "thank you," and placed one foot in front of the other. Soon the two were climbing on rainbow shimmering stones, weaving between waist-high wild grasses of electric yellow and purple bloom. At length there was just the occasional cedar tree — burnt-orange and standing alone — wide and short and splendidly reposed in blissful timelessness. Finally, only snow. Jim fell to his knees and placed his face to the pure crystals in thankfulness. He fell over onto his side and was motionless, breathing in long, raspy breaths … portending death. The Painted Man knelt by Jim's side and closed his eyes and prayed. He pulled Jim's shells from his pack and dressed him. After a long while there was a tearing sound. Jim's body glowed. His creases and wrinkles toned and disappeared one at a time. Wayne bowed his head and covered his eyes with his arm. Jim stood and breathed deeply and opened his eyes wide, feeling the unbearable goodness of the moment.

Jim pulled out his telies from the sides of the pack and slid into his boots, his old friends. He smoothed on a pair of climbing skins and pressed into his three pin bindings, and it all felt good. Jim regarded the mountain pack and realized it was no longer needed. He nodded to Wayne, who shouldered his pack and slid into his gear. Wayne turned, and together they ascended the slope. Soon they were surrounded by radiantly pure white. Jim smiled and breathed and closed his eyes as more and more vitality entered into his being. The two kicked upward on a broad ridge for a long time. The terrain became open and expansive. At length Jim stood in repose. He was young again.

As Jim poised, feeling his strength and energy, he looked deep into the crystals, and he was with Nancy. He glided next to her bulky figure as she stomped down the old road at Aspen Crest and walked straight to a dark, dilapidated A-frame. Nancy pushed open the front door without knocking. Jim barely recognized Nancy's outward features. Only a trace of resemblance suggested the young girl whom he touched so long ago. Jim swelled with feelings for her, and in her heart Nancy felt the same for him. Jim watched Nancy stop and brush away a tear of emotion as it rose from an inner chamber. He jolted as Nancy cried to him … "Stop it! Stop haunting my soul. Do something," she shouted into the hollow chasm of the rotting A-frame. "We can't leave each other. I love you," Nancy pleaded inwardly and dropped to her knees with her face in her hands, embarrassed to be yelling at a dead lover in an empty ski house … yet aware of the Greater reality coming upon her. Jim came to Nancy's side and wrapped his arm around her shoulders and held her hands in his. He looked at the dim room with its yellowing ski posters and dusty champagne glasses. "Help me, Lord," Nancy cried and prayed. "Please help him. He's run off with her … a girl. David told me Michael's left me," Nancy sobbed again, and Jim could feel her every ache as if he was her. Nancy asked herself, *how did I become such a heartless bitch? How did I drive this man away?*

Jim closed his eyes and spread his arms and rose. He could see Aspen Crest and behind and beyond, all the Powder Horns. He soared like a giant bird, like an eagle. Through the lodgepole pines he saw Michael on telies, touring behind a shapely young figure, who laughed and called to him as Michael headed to the Blue Hotel and into despair.

"Rise, sweetheart Nancy," Jim spoke to Nancy's heart from high above. "I love you so much. Is there a choice? For how long have we been together? Is there a beginning or an end? Follow your heart north and west. Find his tracks in the snow before they disappear. Go to Michael. Find happiness with him again. Be a good wife, Nancy. Love Michael with all of your heart. Serve him."

Nancy knelt on the floor of the A-frame and looked at the scanty undies and bra flung over a nicked chair and the piles of gear on the greasy shag carpet, extending back in time to antique Hart and Head Skis with Marker bindings and leather buckle boots. A pair of large red alpine boots sat side by side on the thick pine table with the name Butcher Man written up their spine in black marker. They were cracked and dusty. The top buckles had partially fallen off. Time and decay, sin and corruption, birth and death, Heaven and hell. Nancy felt this insight in her bones. Nancy realized that she and Michael were no better — that they had, without notice, slipped into the shadows — the world as only the world, decaying and passing into darkness. Nancy placed her hands together and closed her eyes tightly. A minute or perhaps an hour passed.

"Lord Jesus," Nancy prayed at length, "have mercy on me a sinner." There was a long, inner Silence. "Lord, You made me. You are in me, and I am of You. Please, Lord Jesus, save my marriage. Save me. Restore us to Holiness … Help me, Lord," Nancy breathed, "to know Your heart, to be Your heart … to know Your eternal life." Nancy calmed and waited without question for an answer. When the Voice without sound came upon her, Nancy flushed with Peace. After a long while, she whispered, "Thank you, Lord," and rose and dug out an old pair of telies and leather boots from a pile of mildewed gear, strapped into everything and headed up the valley through the pines. From above, Jim descended upon a graying Michael, who was pushing behind the youthful figure.

Jim called to him, "Michael, who are you, brother? Why do you live? Where are you headed? … Stay with Nancy. Love her. Be true. Serve her. Your wife … Turn and grow old together … in happiness. Die together."

Michael stopped and creased his eyebrows, struck by an emotion he could not place … nor would the pressure leave his chest. Jim departed as Nancy came upon Michael and the flashing girl with shining dark hair … The evil Snow Princess in her latest incarnation, who held no power over the Lord's children. She turned and stuck out her tongue at Nancy and kept touring. Michael looked at Nancy and back to the girl. He worked his jaw in churning decision. Then he made the choice.

Upon his last vision, Jim saw Michael sitting next to Nancy with his chin up as he drove over The Pass and back to Powder Horn. Nancy held his hand with her eyes closed and with her heart whispering prayers of salvation. Later that night a crescent moon curved next to the ragged peak of Mad Dog Mountain. Jim felt Nancy's quiet breathing as she held Michael in her arms in their bedroom and home, nestled within the soft mountain folds rising to the distant and snowy peaks.

The Painted Man had turned to wait for Jim. When Jim looked up and nodded, Wayne smiled and dropped his pack. Wayne stripped from his climbing skins by lifting one ski then the other. He motioned for Jim to do the same. The Painted Man stuffed the skins into his worn parka. A beautiful snowbowl spread below their feet, and Jim could not see where the space ended. Wayne made a few probes with his pole and slid onto the pristine blanket. He kicked around and swayed gentle turns in perfect rhythm as dust billowed behind and obscured his sturdy frame. Jim's muscles twitched with youth, and his chest thrilled. He stripped off his climbing skins, stuffed them into his ragged parka, cinched the drawcord and dropped in. At first Jim was so taken by emotion that he could not turn. He held his poles at mid-length and felt himself rise and fall. There was a thick ball of feeling in his throat. Gravity pulled him downward, and Jim flowed into a relaxed discipline — surfing one ski then another across the fall line in perfect balance, following a lead that rose from deep within. The snow was like cotton that puffed and smoked across his shoulders and lifted behind in soft, cloudy bliss. The two skied side by side for what seemed forever until each nicked rock and finally met the glowing stone and bare earth. Jim dropped to his knees on his telies and placed his hands in prayer. He fell over and kissed the earth: God's Holy creation. Jim's heart pounded with thankfulness. Wayne reached down and patted Jim on the back and smiled. There was no sound … just an all-pervading Love pulsing from everywhere and everything. "Lord Jesus Christ, guide me," Jim chanted over and over as he knelt before his Maker's presence, breathing hard and pouring tears from his heart.

After a long while Jim rose and wiped his eyes and cheeks with the palms of his hands. Wayne held Jim who collapsed again in silent tears, journeying beyond mere happiness. At length Jim exhaled and smiled to Wayne and patted him on the back. Jim pulled out his skins from his parka with trembling hands. The Painted Man nodded to the remote heights and back to where his pack was no longer visible. Each smoothed on his climbing skins, and Jim followed Wayne's long switch-backs. As Jim ascended, he realized even more strength and energy until he felt he could climb 10 mountains. The skin on his hands grew tight, and there was a sheen about his body. Jim's mind and eyes became sharp and quick. His shell pants and jacket began to hang loosely. Jim patted himself and realized he had become the body of his once 18 years. He kicked past Wayne, who stopped and smiled. Jim cut through the deep powder, sometimes following their snaking descent tracks, which plummeted from the impossible expanse. He had to turn and wait for Wayne, who could not stop smiling for him.

Soon Wayne had fallen well behind and become a dark blotch. Jim stood and waited, inhaling and exhaling with his eyes closed, smiling from the inside. The fullness of Silence filled Jim until he was overpouring. As he balanced on the mountain, Jim found himself with Moon Dog and David. Jim's heart leapt. David and Moon were in a steep couloir, sliding a rope ascender along its tether, tied from their waist. Each was bent over with short skis stuffed in the sides of an impossibly large mountain pack. They were two old guys with hardly any hair left. Jim looked again, and his insides jumped as he felt Kyle with them too. Kyle was a strapping man. He lapped David and Moon up and down the couloir as they supplied a high camp of dug-in tents. They were all together on a first ski descent in a far off mountain range. The guys laughed and wheezed as they climbed. Both David and Moon peered from under wrinkles and deep creases. Each occasionally took a draw from an oxygen mask. Jim yearned to be with them. He stood close by David's side, and listened to David's feelings think back on their time together.

David asked Moon Dog if he thought what happened with Pepe way back when would ever leave them. Moon said no; it was real. David stopped climbing, and Moon reached his side. Each guy leaned over his ice axe. Moon Dog said neither of them could forget Pepe and what happened. It was a defining moment of grace — for him, for them all — that Jimmy lives. Moon went on to say that he thought about Jim from time to time … prayed for him. There was a long silence as each guy listened to his labored breathing at 18,000 feet and stared into the blue-black alpine sky. David said that he missed Pepe and wished he had the chance to get to know him better in this life, to help him along. That what happened out at Rattling and Peak 21 was a profound sign and wonder. He would never forget what happened or look at the world the same, and it was significant that he thinks of Jim too. Moon looked over and locked onto David's eyes through his glacier shades, which were bigger than David's face. Moon looked for a long time … as if each old guy understood that their time on earth was nearing completion … and the end was a beginning — an endless beginning. Moon looked up again into the faultless high altitude sky and mentioned kind words about Jim — about how he was and still is a good bro, even better now that he's probably been on quite a journey, a soul journey — that it will be good to meet up again with him and tell stories, good mountain stories. Moon laughed and said that at the moment they could use Pepe with the same body he had back then.

Jim crouched beside the two and put his arm out and touched David and Moon, saying, "Thank you" in his heart.

Moon spoke again and said that it was easy to forget the deceased — all the bros who have passed on: Scott the Hammer, Man Called Abe, The Colonel, Ace Man. How it was easy to think they were dead and gone, never to be seen again; how it was easy to believe we get lowered into a pine box in the ground and that was it. Time begins. Time ends. Finished. "The world as only the world," Moon said. Moon Dog went on to say that one has to believe and to ask after those who have passed, and you can feel them — that he could sense Pepe getting along, and they would all meet again, sometime, in the mountains … God's mountains … "New mountains," Moon Dog said looking up and around at the breath-taking vista. "I know it," Moon said and held David in his eyes for a long time. "We both know it."

Moon spoke about how grateful he was for the war to have ended and to be in the Hindu Kush. He spoke of their mission work on the continent with the orphans of war. Jim did not understand this, but he felt warmly for Moon Dog and David and bowed to them. When the two resumed climbing, Jim followed their progress and watched the couloir from above for rock and ice fall. When a block from a protalus rampart loosened in the alpine sun, Jim whispered a warning to David's soul. David hit the deck and arrested with his ice ax. Moon Dog instinctively followed as a shower of rock whizzed like cannon balls over their heads. Some of the stone hit the compacted neve and exploded against the walls. David yelled into his radio. Kyle and the others below dove to the sides and to safety. When silence resumed, Moon Dog said something about how maybe they were getting too old for all this. David said, "Naw," and each guy laughed and bowed his head to the protecting Spirit, who compelled them upward. Always upward. At length Moon Dog spoke to David.

"You remember Jimmy's funeral?"

"Like yesterday," David replied.

"Put my arms around his mother and father," Moon said. "They dissolved into tears. They said that Jimmy's death was tragic."

"I remember what you told them, prophecy."

"That his life had just begun."

"They didn't understand."

"They did not believe."

Jim opened his eyes, and Wayne was approaching him. He blinked again, and there was Nancy, sitting side by side with Michael on a porch, holding his hand with a plaid wool blanket spread across their laps. Sweet and cool mountain air caressed their moment. Nancy was reading the Holy Bible. Michael smoked his pipe. Both had lots of gray and wrinkles and a happy glow in their hearts for each other, and for all of their years together and for their children and grandchildren. An aura of unspoken fullness surrounded the couple.

"Hallelujah," rose to Jim's lips, and Wayne looked up and smiled as he reached Jim's side. Jim was startled to hear his own voice. "You knew them all didn't you? David and Moon Dog … and Nancy," Jim asked Wayne.

The Painted Man nodded and looked far away as if peering into a remote time and place that was just as easily right now and forever. Wayne leaned over his poles and looked down and back up and into Jim's eyes. "They saved my life," he replied quietly, "on The River. They led me to God. For this I am eternally grateful."

"I know," Jim said. "Where is the pretty girl? Please. I feel badly about your beautiful mountain cabin … Seems so long ago. Thank you so much for helping me, for healing me. I never thanked you both. Will you forgive me?"

Wayne nodded "yes" to Jim and said, "Your remembrances are like unto ashes, your bodies to bodies of clay." Jim closed his eyes and listened from deep within. He became aware of his clothes hanging loosely from him. Jim held up his arms, which had disappeared inside of his sleeves. He was a boy again. Jim flopped his legs and arms and stepped ahead but could barely do so because his boots were so large.

Jim opened his eyes wide, and he was with Nancy once more. There was church music and singing and clapping, blending tears and pain with peace and celebration into a heartfelt gathering of community, of reflection and reminiscence, of burial. Everyone took the trowel and tossed dirt upon Michael's ashes in a box in a hole in the earth. A long life well lived. Eighty healthy years. Gently passing in his sleep in Nancy's arms, his beloved wife of nearly 50 years. A good part of his life spent helping Big Pine reach rock-solid prosperity. Jim held back and opened his arms and palms in prayer for Nancy and for all of their children and grandchildren and for Michael. Nancy was wind-tanned and thin and handsomely wrapped in a black shawl. Her hair was white. Jim's heart throbbed, but he did not release his feelings. Then he saw Jamie, his son, in military uniform. Jim filled with pride. He stood by his son and placed an arm around his shoulders and beamed and finally could not contain himself as he reached out for Nancy, now 77 years of age. Somewhere deep inside Nancy's heart a spark ignited once again, and she let herself feel for Jim. She knew that he was close by his family, their family.

Jim blinked, and he was held in The Painted Man's arms, who labored with him up the mountain. Jim had nearly fallen inside of this clothing. He looked down and around and up into Wayne's kindly face. Soon Jim felt himself disappear altogether into Wayne's embrace. The two climbed upward for an unnamed time, and Jim closed his eyes, feeling himself gently sway.

***

As Jim rocked in The Painted Man's arms, Nancy clicked the door shut on her forest-green Range Rover on The Pass. She opened the back hatch and slowly, with shaking and jerking motions slid out her mother's old Tuas. She closed her eyes with the effort and felt the cold air clamp her mortal frame. It was a spectacular day of full mountain sunshine. Mt. Mitchell rose behind her, and the Southwest Kingdom spread before Nancy into chutes and bowls, ski peaks and pines. Nancy moved deliberately. She was alone. Since her accident of two years ago, Nancy had been dismissing everyone — her children and grandchildren — to let them get on with their lives of goals and plans. Nancy was departing, and the place of arrival was becoming more real than the frozen crystals squeaking below her tele boots. This realization settled upon Nancy as a comfortable excitement.

Nancy climbed the snowbank thoughtfully, grateful for each step and praying that she would not slip and fall. "Lord Jesus, we've made it this far; please help me up this snow bank one more time." In the past Nancy waited to take a young person's arm, maybe a cute boy, who would watch her with embarrassed attention. Nancy wasn't supposed to be driving up The Pass, and she wasn't suppose to be alone on the mountain. Nancy knew everyone meant well. As she stood and soaked in the first warmth of an early February sun, the accident came back to her. Nancy realized that she was not, deep down, surprised by what happened, as she had been able to foretell all of the major events of her life but had kept this ability a secret even to herself. The feeling of dread, then helpless Peace was unmistakable prior to her boys' death, Michael and Clay. So too, the feeling of elation just before meeting her future husband, Michael. Then there was Jimmy, so long ago, and the feeling of love asking to be found again. Nancy paused and lifted her face to the sun and let herself remember and feel Jim. *Such a sweet lover,* she mused. *I wonder if he'd like this old lady now. I wonder what it all meant. Why it was so unavoidable,* Nancy thought again. Like her other prophesies, Nancy already knew the answer. She quickened inside for a reason she could not construe — but of which she was sure. Always sure. Nancy felt the sun and recalled Charlie, the guys on The River, Michael and her boys. Husbands, sons and lovers. All of her men. She understood she would see them all again. *Matthew 22:30,* Nancy thought to herself. *They will be like the angels in heaven.* And somehow Nancy always came back to Jim. She always felt certain about Jim … but of what she did not exactly know, just a certainty. He occupied a secret place deep inside — a place that Nancy long ago gave up trying to understand by herself — a place that feels him without beginning or ending. *Born to me,* Nancy thought.

A minute passed or perhaps an hour. Nancy's thoughts drifted back to the day before her accident. She had passed a mirror in her hallway and froze. She stepped back to stare at herself and at the mark on her forehead. The seal. Nancy fell to her knees in prayer, shaking and knowing … that her name was written in the Lord's book. She rolled onto her back and could not describe or explain to anyone what she felt or saw or experienced, other than to love them all even more with happy tears … and to tremble with fear and joy.

Her daughter and little grandson, Robert, found her two days later still laying on the floor. They took her to the hospital and everyone wanted to place her in a nursing home. Instead, Nancy went touring up The Pass Ridge alone at age 79 … to meet what she knew the moment had foretold. Nancy slid down a powdery dip and collapsed. It was as if her bones had turned to powder. Nancy lay folded over herself in a ball, racked in so much pain that she could not move or even breathe. Both hips, an arm and a shoulder had shattered. Nancy closed her eyes, knowing that the end had arrived. She cried out for her Savior — a passionate cry for help from the depths of her inmost heart. He came. Nancy witnessed His will as he lifted her beyond her crumpled and pain-racked body. Nancy floated back into the body and all the pain, then rose again. She was faintly aware of someone standing by her side: a man in a ripped one-piece ski suit, wringing his hands and wiping tears away in concern for her. Another man, an old guy with large mirror shades and a polka dot wind shirt, dropped to one knee on his skis further behind. Odd visions. But soothing. Nancy knew she was dying. All she remembered next was David's furrowed and wrinkled face close to hers and Catherine, her long-time friend, next to David. Then rescue litters and helicopter rotors, noise and wash. "No, not yet," Nancy said inside herself, affirming David as he pulled her back to earth by a silver thread attached from his heart to hers. Nancy awoke in the hospital with her sons and daughters and grandchildren by her side, whispering, "Grandma Nancy, wake up, please." No one could understand that she had not wanted to be rescued, nor be in a hospital nor in her home with everyone taking turns watching her.

Today, however, Nancy had given them all the slip. Her sons thought she was becoming difficult and stubborn and a danger to herself. But Nancy felt increasingly removed, perched higher and higher and ready to rise surely into His loving arms. Now she stood on the ridge trail in grateful solitude, drawing deeply the cold mountain air, knowing fullwell what the accident kept saying … knowing that for her whole life the gentle hands of The Potter had been melding her through: births and deaths, trial and pain, joy and pleasure, sacrifice and reward, choice and avoidance, good and bad years, marriage and solitude … and turning, always turning … to the Lord … all for this culminating moment of heart. A long life brimming with richness … with the wealth of Jesus

Christ the Son of God, the Creator — the only Creator and Redeemer — the only Redeemer. The final Judge. But not yet. After her accident and by the power of the Holy Spirit, Nancy was called to astound the medical world by healing her broken bones and by partially reversing osteoporosis.

Nancy pressed into her three pins and gradually toured to the top of the ridge and surveyed the grand vista. She stepped out of her bindings, made a platform in the snow and spread her legs. It felt good to be alive, balanced between Heaven and earth, bent at the waist in Trikonasana, the Triangle, with her arms spread wide: one hand reaching upward, the other touching earth. Ready — quietly and joyfully ready — to knowingly depart. A group of young people brushed by on their way to the backcountry and nodded with curiosity. They stopped. Nancy straightened and smiled. She placed her hands and feet together, bowed to them and said, "Hosanna, young ones … highest praises. God is already in your future. Choose Him." And the Already Passed watched those who were passing turn and tour away over the ridge crest.

***

Jim felt himself cradled as a baby in The Painted Man's robust arms and soaring above with his long silver hair flowing and his powerful body flared and vital — arms stretched out to the mountain winds. Wayne crested the ridge, and the pretty girl met him. Her coppery-brunette hair was pulled into a single braid, and her face was ruddy and glowing with health. Her hazel eyes opened wide with enthusiasm.

"Oh," she gasped with her hands trembling and reaching for Jim, "he's such a beautiful baby. Please let me hold him, my precious Jim."

Wayne smiled and passed Jim in his arm to the Tele Goddess, who slipped him out from inside of his shell jacket. Jim's heart quivered as he watched from above and felt himself being taken in her arms. The pretty girl opened her parka and wrapped Jim in a soft, pastel blanket. Jim gazed into her sun-freckled face as she kissed him on the cheek and rubbed his nose with hers and cooed to him, rocking Jim in her caring arms. The two resumed touring across the ridge. The pretty girl held Jim close to her chest. She lifted him and smiled into his face and into the center of his little being and kissed him on the forehead. Jim giggled with delight, while also soaring above: at once an infant, an ageless child, a man and a returning soul. Jim grew smaller in the Tele Goddess's arms until she held his scrunched little face close and rubbed his tiny nose with hers. Jim gazed into her hazel eyes and shrieked with enchantment. He curled into a ball as the pretty girl pulled up her thermal top and placed him next to her warm and sensuous skin. Her tapered waist worked as she toured, and held Jim higher to her soft and rising breasts. Soon Jim was cradled in her gentle hands, next to her chest, and he descended from above to fully meet her loving warmth.

The Painted Man reached the crest of the peak and nodded to the pretty girl, this angel, who slid to Wayne and kissed him on the cheek. She cupped Jim in both her hands close to her and the soft blanket. Jim wrapped into a fetal curl as the Tele Goddess, without hesitating, carved over the edge and onto the summit chute, which descended beyond sight. Below, a single shaft of brilliant Light spanned upward and shimmered with drifting crystals. She surfed strong turns with Jim closed in her hands and next to her heart with the pastel blue blanket and her shells flapping in the pure and dusty white. Clouds of golden hue drifted all around the dramatic expanse of alpine slope. The crystalline pack released in soft fractured blocks, above and below in a spasm of birthing energy. The Tele Goddess smiled from her core of Peace and released and tumbled over and over into the air, until her hands bore Jim on the outside of her pregnant abdomen, while Jim curled deeper into her soothing womb. The pretty angel of God flew with the roaring crystals in pitch white and blue and gold. Jim suspended deeper into Peace, feeling her wonderful body returning him into the arms of Forever.

ARCHOMAI

Jim gripped the steering wheel of his black Pathfinder as the passionate flakes of an early winter storm brushed onto the windshield, joined and blew away. Fading light gathered into night. Jim turned his head as he groaned, overcome by a feeling of reoccurrence. The grade up The Pass was steep, and his truck kicked into low gear with a high pitch, startling his attention to the here and now. His headlights gathered snow and dimmed. The wipers worked back and forth. Jim reached a long straightaway, and his insides jumped and tingled, and he did not know why. He flushed hot and felt his palms grow sweaty. An expectation leaned him forward, straining to see through the windshield and to the north side of the road. Jim rounded the wide corner where the old Pass Road met the new. A hooded figure stood with tele skis and poles, hitching a ride back up the mountain. Jim drifted by in the muffled snow. He found himself pulling over and stopping. Jim watched as he reached for the passenger-side door handle, pulled the latch and pushed open the door, letting in a flurry of crystals. His fingers trembled. The hooded figure pulled open the door and momentarily stood unseen below a hood with a black shawl wrapped around, soaking with melting snow. The figure froze in place. Jim watched a feminine-sized ski glove, quivering. She looked up. They both gasped. Tears burst from each. Nancy and Jim lunged into each other's arms, mixing salty tears and unable to speak. Nancy tore off her gloves and held Jim's face in her hands. They kissed everywhere and gasped into each other, squeezing their wet faces together, groping with hands and arms, embracing. Their emotions flamed into spirit, and they were above the mountain night and no longer in the world. Down below, the two young people, walking the earth and passing in time, pulled away and spoke.

"Just toss 'em in back," Jim said, nodding to Nancy's skis.

"Hi."

"Hey."

"Thanks."

"No problem atall."

"Jim. My name's Jim."

"Yeah?"

Above the truck and the earthly scene, the Light grew bright and warm. A new land opened before Jim and Nancy — the Southwest Kingdom now in radiance.

You never said goodbye, Nancy said without words to Jim, pulling back her teary face and searching his eyes.

Jim gazed upon Nancy's fresh beauty: her freckled face and her caring eyes. Jim fell before Nancy, and she gently pulled him up, laughing and crying at once.

Will you marry me, Nancy? Jim asked, as he knelt before her with his palms together, bowing to her. Nancy knelt and held his hands in hers and bowed her head. She fell before Jim and kissed his feet.

We can no longer die, Nancy replied, smiling and rising as Jim pulled her to his chest, lifting her face and smiling into her.

Jim felt his long silver hair flowing, and the already passed held hands enwrapped in the Lord's pulsing love, and He beamed upon the passing with affection. Below and on earth, in the world of time and trial, the two reached Nancy's buried wagon.

"So can I dig out your car?" Jim asked.

"Will you ask me to go to the movies?"

"The movies? Yeah sure, the movies!"

"You don't know who I am."

"I might know who you are."

And in the dance of life, the passing separated with burning hearts and rode down the mountain into the night. Above the storm, stars sofl pulsed over Mad Dog Mountain, while all the peaks of the Powder Horns lifted into His perfect stillness.

Jim turned and gazed upon his sister, and Nancy looked upon her brother with affection … matched only by an even brighter Horizon, which beckoned them all together in the Father, without end … brides and bridegrooms all.

DEUS CARITAS EST

POSTSCRIPT

"Yet if there is an angel on his side
as a mediator, one out of a thousand,
to tell a man what is right for him,
to be gracious to him and say,
'Spare him from going down to the pit;
I have found a ransom for him —
then his flesh is renewed like a child's;
it is restored as in the days of his youth.
He prays to God and finds favor with
him, he sees God's face and shouts for
joy; he is restored by God to his righteous
state. Then he comes to men and says,
'I sinned, and perverted what was right,
but I did not bet what I deserved.
He redeemed my soul from going down to
the pit, and I will live to enjoy the light.'
God does all these things to a man —
twice, even three times — to turn back his
soul from the pit, that the light of life may
shine on him."

— Elihu to Job; Job 33:23-30

He who forms the mountains,
creates the wind and reveals
his thoughts to man; he who
turns dawn to darkness and treads
the high places of the earth —
the Lord God Almighty is his name.

— Amos 4:13-14

As a man is, so is his strength.

— Judges 8:21

Keep me, O God, for in thee have I found refuge.
I have said to the Lord,
'Thou, Lord, art my felicity.'
The gods whom the earth holds sacred are all worthless,
and cursed are all who make them their delight;
those who run after them find trouble without end.
I will not offer them libations of blood
nor take their names upon my lips.
Thou, Lord, my allotted portion, thou my cup,
thou dost enlarge my boundaries:
the lines fall for me in pleasant places,
indeed I am well content with my inheritance.
I will bless the Lord who has given me counsel:
in the night-time wisdom comes to me in my inward parts.
I have set the Lord continually before me:
with him at my right hand I cannot be shaken.
Therefore my heart exults and my spirit rejoices,
my body too rests unafraid;
for thou wilt not abandon me to Sheol
nor suffer thy faithful servant to see the pit.
Thou wilt show me the path of life;
in thy presence is the fullness of joy,
in thy right hand pleasures for evermore.

— Psalm 16

CREDITS

Prelude

New English Bible. Oxford University Press, Cambridge University Press 1970 Proverbs 8:22-31 Ecclesiastes 7:26-27

Chapter 1

The Holy Bible New International Version. Cornerstone Bible Publishers, Nashville, Tennessee 1999 Ruth 1:9-10

New American Bible for Catholics. Catholic Book Club Publishers 1990 Psalm 126

Chapter 6

"Half a World Away" — ©1991 R.E.M.

Chapter 7

"You Should be Dancing" — ©1977 The Bee Gees

Chapter 10

"Refiner's Fire" — ©1990 Doerksen Mercy/Vineyard Publishing

The Book of Common Prayer: According to the use of the Protestant Episcopal Church in the United States of America. The Seabury Press, New York 1977

Chapter 12

The New English Bible. Oxford University Press, Cambridge University Press 1970 Psalm 19:1-6

Chapter 13

"Return to Forever" — Original audio title by Chic Corea

The Holy Bible King James version. National Publishing Company, Philadelpia, Pennsylvania 1978 Job 13:12-13

Achromai

"Achromai," Ancient Greek, translated as: To begin
"Deus Caritas Est," Latin, translated as: He is love.

Postscript

The Holy Bible New International Version. Cornerstone Bible Publishers, Nashville, Tennessee 1999 Job 33:23-30, Judges 8:21-22, Amos 4:13-14

The New English Bible. Oxford University Press, Cambridge University Press 1970 Psalm 16

ABOUT THE AUTHOR

Richard Day is a 30-year veteran of the outdoors. He has been active in the pursuits of backpacking, rock climbing, mountaineering, whitewater kayaking and backcountry telemark skiing. His doctorate in psychology and interest in men's issues and theology have led Richard to deeply penetrate the essence of the wild outdoors — especially the heart and soul of backcountry telemark skiing — and where truth is sought. His previous novel, Two Dog River, is considered a cult classic of whitewater fiction and men's literature. Richard Day's eccentric talent continues to delight and inspire.